The Ayatollah Takedown

Books by Matt Scott

SURVIVING THE LION'S DEN SERIES
Surviving the Lion's Den
The Iranian Deception
The Ayatollah Takedown

The Ayatollah Takedown

Matt Scott

SPEAKING VOLUMES, LLC
NAPLES, FLORIDA
2023

The Ayatollah Takedown

ISBN 978-1-64540-907-6

For Amanda and Clarence

Characters

Americans

Ben Thrasher, a.k.a. Jay Jacoby, code name *Jaybird*.....CIA operative

Beth Jenkins, a.k.a. Katherine Jennings, a.k.a. Lilly Rodgers, code name
Raven...CIA operative

Tom Delang..retired CIA agent

Roger Cannon................................President of the United States

Vivian Walsh...former U.S. Senator

Philip Lee.....................................Walsh's limo driver

Latrina Pearl..............................Walsh's former chief-of-staff

Tony Prashad.....................................CIA Inspector General

Kirk Kurruthers................................American of Iranian heritage

Simin Dehghani.....................................Kirk's Iranian fiancé

Jackson Whang, a.k.a. "Dub"........................former CIA operative

Jessica Shannon.....................................CIA disguise operative

Iranians

Farhad Khorsandi........smuggler, People's Mujahadeen of Iran (PMOI)

Donya Karimi..............hacker, People's Mujahadeen of Iran (PMOI)

Vahid Avesta...President of Iran

Marzban Shir-del.....................................Supreme Leader of Iran

Major General Ramin Lajani.......head of Iranian Revolutionary Guard Corps (IRGC)

Brigadier General Mohammad Nassiri..........commander of the Basij

Lieutenant Colonel Nahid Vaziri...........Basij soldier, Nassiri's cousin

Salim Ghiasi......medical student, People's Mujahadeen of Iran (PMOI)

Babak Abbasi...........................PMOI insider/guard at Evin Prison

Saeed Tikdari...................................Avesta's personal assistant

Internationals

Zhang Xu..General Secretary of China

Ping Zhou.........................China Minister of State Security (MSS)

Fang Xin............................China Ministry State Security operative

Eli Shahar..Prime Minister of Israel

Nazir Agab.......................Sudan Ambassador to the United States

Prologue

TEHRAN, IRAN

The Supreme Leader had a sick sense of humor when it came to discipline. Iranian President Vahid Avesta had been hanging in the basement of the Basij's headquarters for six hours. He was intentionally still alive, but he was exhausted and writhing in pain. Rather than hang him by the neck, Avesta's hands and feet were tied to a horizontal bamboo stick behind him, which was held up by two vertical poles. Even at his healthy 170 pounds, his weight placed tremendous stress on his shoulders, hips, and lower back. Because he was hanging in a 'U' position, he was forced to use the muscles in his triceps and torso to straighten himself out to relieve the pressure. This caused him to waste energy he didn't have and made his muscles cramp, which only intensified the already agonizing experience. The sweat dripping from his body sizzled as it evaporated into the moderate flame that danced in the air below his blistered stomach. The blindfold over his eyes allowed him to see nothing but feel everything. This form of torture was called kebabbing.

He had no idea how long he had been imprisoned. Three months ago, Iran was on the cusp of a major alliance between the Persian country and its Arab neighbors: Syria, Yemen, Libya, Lebanon, and Pakistan. The Persia-Arab Coalition would have acted as the Middle East's version of NATO. The five countries were united against Israel in such a way that an attack by Israel on any of them was an attack on *all* of them.

Thanks to blackmail on the Supreme Leader's part, the coalition legally allowed them access to Pakistan's nuclear weapons despite the strong objections of the U.N. nuclear watchdog. Avesta had been set to make the global announcement live on *Al-Jazeera*. It was the Supreme

Leader's plan, but it was Avesta's moment. The weight of Iran's future was on his shoulders. But the moment was not meant to be. American President Roger Cannon interrupted the conference via a hacked feed and revealed that Iran had conspired to start a war between India and Pakistan. The deal fell apart as quickly as it had been envisioned, and Pakistan backed out. It was a public humiliation for Avesta, Iran, and the Supreme Leader.

On what should have been a triumphant day for Iran, Avesta returned to his office and sat silently in his chair, staring out the window while contemplating what punishment the Supreme Leader had in store for him. With each minute he spent thinking about it, his anxiety increased. His chest tightened. He bit his lip so hard that it started bleeding.

The only choice available to him became clear. Avesta reached into his desk drawer and pulled out a .357 Magnum Colt Python revolver. He knew that this wasn't why his security had given it to him, but there was no other way out of his situation. The Supreme Leader had recently killed former Iranian Revolutionary Guard Corps (IRGC) Major General Rahim Shirazi by stuffing him into a sweatbox heated by high wattage lightbulbs and literally melted the man to death. Avesta had no intention of dying that way. There were only three ways he planned to go out: by natural causes, in a blaze of glory, or by his own hand.

At least there is some honor in the latter.

He jammed a bullet into the cylinder before snapping it into place with a jerk of his wrist, and stared at the gun, repeatedly gripping it with his increasingly sweaty palms as he gathered the gumption to do what had to be done. When the time came, Avesta walked to the window of his office and stared west toward Mecca. The gun hung by his side as he collected the necessary strength.

Suddenly, his locked office door was kicked open by Major General Ramin Lajani, the newly tapped commander of the IRGC. Lajani's gun was pointed right at him. Startled, Avesta accidentally dropped his revolver on the floor.

Lajani had been ordered by the Supreme Leader to only arrest the president, but Avesta didn't know that. Seeing what Avesta was about to do to himself gave Lajani pause. He holstered his gun and pulled out a taser, which sent a surge of twenty-five-thousand volts through the fifty-eight-year-old president's body. Lajani hoisted Avesta over his shoulder and carried him out of the Presidential Administration Building in front of the staff.

Avesta woke up inside a concrete room with no windows. The next day, Lajani escorted him in front of the Iranian Parliament and publicly embarrassed him for his failures in front of the elected officials that he depended on to pass his proposals.

Afterward, he was returned to his cell. For two weeks, he was not spoken to. He was fed bread and water through a slot in the door. Eventually, he was slapped awake in the middle of the night and taken to his current location. He didn't bother resisting when the soldiers tied him to the pole. For good measure, the soldier who blindfolded him delivered a hefty punch to his jaw before leaving the room.

"The Supreme Leader wants you to know that you should be a man who delivers on his promises," Lieutenant Colonel Vaziri said.

Hanging from the pole, Avesta had nothing but time to ponder how he would restore himself in the eyes of the Supreme Leader.

As another drip of sweat evaporated in the fire, the cell's steel door screeched open. Avesta blinked his eyes, but it didn't matter because all he could see was the backside of the blindfold. He felt the pole shudder and the heat on his torso faded. Being lifted off the two support poles put more weight on his back. He winced at the pain but dared not cry out. The two guards laid him on his side but kept him tied to the pole. When they left, the acting head of the Basij, Second Brigadier General Mohammad Nassiri, entered and placed a phone to Avesta's ear.

"He wants to speak with you," Nassiri said in his gravelly voice.

"Hello?" Avesta said.

"Have you learned your lesson?"

Avesta recognized the voice immediately.

"Yes, Supreme Leader."

"Iran has been disgraced because of your carelessness."

"I know, Supreme Leader. I humbly ask your forgiveness."

"Will you ever disappoint me again?"

"No, Supreme Leader."

"Make sure you don't. You have one order of business when you leave the facility."

"Yes, Supreme Leader. Anything."

"I want you to hunt down every single member of the PMOI and kill them all but save the one they call Farhad for me."

"Absolutely, Supreme Leader."

"Make sure that you consider one last thing, Mr. President."

"Yes, Supreme Leader?"

"Next time, I won't be so lenient."

Avesta knew he had dodged a bullet and had been given a second chance that few in the Supreme Leader's circle ever received. But he also knew that there would *not* be a third chance.

Chapter One

BEIJING, CHINA

The Supreme Leader of Iran rarely travels beyond his country's borders. He shouldn't have to. First, it opens him up to a potential assassination attempt by one of his enemies, namely Israel. But even more, his primary responsibility is to ensure that Iran is governed in accordance with Sharia law, and that it stays on the course set forth by Ayatollah Khomeini. His authority is absolute and can only be overruled by either word from Allah or the return of the Twelfth Imam, who would emerge from the heavens to fulfill Islam's mission of peace and Divine justice to the world. The day-to-day duties of running the country belong to Iran's elected president, who ensures that the laws are followed under the Supreme Leader's command, who only steps in when necessary.

Today, it was necessary.

Supreme Leader Marzban Shir-Del had recently devised a plan to create a war between India and Pakistan. This allowed Iran to pretend to be a neutral party by supplying oil for the war to both countries, thereby breaking the shackles of global economic sanctions pushed by the United States. The money flow injected the local economy with millions of needed dollars and provided Shir-Del with options. This plan required blackmail to secure Pakistan's cooperation, including its nuclear arsenal, but it was genius. It almost worked.

Shir-Del's lifelong plans of making his country *the* major force in the Middle East were reduced to rubble when Iran was publicly exposed and humiliated on the international stage during a live broadcast the entire world could witness. The Basij later determined that resistance members of the People's Mujahadeen of Iran (PMOI) were the source of the hack by the United States, which brought his dream to a crashing halt.

Shir-Del personally blamed Avesta. Had he exercised his authority in crushing the PMOI, as he had promised, the incident would have never occurred, and Iran would be reigning supreme in the region. Shir-Del couldn't afford the optics of killing Avesta, so he had him punished for his lazy behavior. As a byproduct of this decision, Shir-Del had to take drastic steps to protect Iran from the giant bullseye that was now on its back.

This protection came by way of the Chinese. The two nations had a solid relationship based on mutually beneficial economics. The deal was simple. Iran supplied China with oil, and in return China invested in Iranian industry. The Supreme Leader intended to keep this relationship in place, but Iran's recent transgressions on the world stage made this complicated. China had the benefit of being the world's unofficial banker. This was especially true for the United States, who owed the Far East juggernaut more than a trillion dollars. By cozying up to the Chinese with oil, Iran was intentionally putting its western enemies in a precarious position. They would no doubt try to strangle Iran with additional, stricter economic sanctions, but they would have to tread carefully as Shir-Del was certain that no one from the West would jeopardize their relations with China. Any military action by the United States or their allies was off the table because no one wanted to risk going to war with a billion Chinese, but Shir-Del knew that this protection from China came at a price.

Adding insult to injury, General Secretary Zhang Xu was deliberately keeping Shir-Del waiting inside the Hall of Purple Light. Though the oversized club chair he was sitting in was comfortable, especially given his current medical condition, Shir-Del took this as a sign of disrespect. His Chromosome Six Deficiency kept him from feeling any physical pain, even with a tumor growing in his leg, but it made it extremely difficult for him to keep his emotions in check and he was prone to angry outbursts when perturbed. In order to keep these symptoms at bay, he injected himself with vials of Carbamazepine. Thankfully, he was stocked up.

At Shir-Del's insistence, General Lajani was ordered to stay by his side for protection. Shir-Del had originally kept him at a safe distance as he watched his career with interest. His attacks against the West were creative and his latest coordination with Hamas to attack Israel's Iron Dome was bold and impressive. He had never met Lajani prior to becoming Supreme Leader, but quickly found the General's line of thinking in sync with his own. During discussions of Iran's future, the two men often finished each other's sentences, which made him trust Lajani quicker than he would normally trust most people.

Lajani was the most analytical, calculating, and articulate soldier that Shir-Del had ever met. He also had the Iranian Constitution practically memorized, which made him useful when Shir-Del needed him to help Avesta maneuver around the bureaucracy of Parliament. The fact that both men liked to paint in their spare time was a shared interest Shir-Del could not ignore. Considering the current situation, it was a bonus that Lajani spoke fluent Chinese. Though Shir-Del intentionally kept his relationships at arm's length, Lajani was the only person he now trusted.

Lajani noticed Shir-Del drumming his fingers on a table.

"You want me to find out what's keeping him, Supreme Leader?"

Shir-Del nodded.

"This is insulting."

Before Lajani took a step, the heavy doors to the conference room opened and General Secretary Xu strolled in with his skinny, spectacled female interpreter following two steps behind. Though Shir-Del had seen him on television many times, Xu didn't strike him as an imposing figure in person. He was only five-foot-five. His pointy nose didn't seem to match his chubby cheeks and perfectly combed hair. The only feature Shir-Del admired was the bright, communist red tie that matched the room's walls. Shir-Del made a mental note to have one of the meeting rooms in the House of Leadership repainted so that he could do the same with his golden thobe, the traditional ankle-length robe worn by men in the Middle East.

Xu extended his hand to Shir-Del.

"My apologies for keeping you waiting, Supreme Leader," Xu said by way of his interpreter.

Shir-Del returned the gesture with his bony hand and looked to Lajani to translate.

"I'd like to get straight to business, General Secretary. We have much to discuss."

"Of course. Please sit."

Xu crossed his legs and sat with his fingers interlocked in front of his face. Shir-Del kept both hands propped on his cane.

"Our two countries have enjoyed a reciprocal relationship over the last generation, wouldn't you say, General Secretary?"

"Of course."

"It does me good to hear you say that because I think we can do more for each other."

"How so?"

Baiting the Secretary into questions was part of Shir-Del's political savvy. By making his proposals in this fashion, it always made the person on the other end of the conversation feel like they were present to hear what he had to say when in fact the reverse was true.

"I'm glad you asked. As you know, my country has recently had some entanglements with the United States and some of our Arab allies. Since you hold much of America's financial fate in your hands, I believe that we can come to an agreement that will ensure Iran is protected from any aggression while also benefitting China."

"I'm listening."

The two countries already had a twenty-five-year agreement in place that predated Shir-Del's ascension to the throne of Supreme Leader. It called for China to invest more than $500 million into Iran's economy toward developing its oil and gas sectors as part of the Belt and Road Initiative, which was the cornerstone of the General Secretary's foreign policy and included seventy other countries. In exchange, Iran supplied China with three hundred million tons of oil per year, which would be heavily discounted based on a tiered schedule. The original deal called for China to receive a twenty percent discount for the first five years of the deal, which would decrease by five percent for each of the following five-year increments.

There were now ten years left on the deal, but in order to secure more stability for Iran, Shir-Del wanted to renegotiate. He abhorred his current position. The Chinese General Secretary had him by the balls and he knew it. Shir-Del had already agreed to allow more Chinese visitors to enter Iran. There had previously been five thousand Chinese nationals living in Iran. Now, the number bordered on fifteen thousand and these migrants were setting up businesses in eastern Tehran. He had no doubt that some of them were spies. This was another double-edged-sword for Shir-Del. The establishment of laundromats and Chinese restaurants helped the local Iranian economy, but it saturated the area with Chinese culture. Shir-Del was a proud Persian. He didn't enjoy seeing his city's civilization being chipped away and he didn't under-stand how western countries could stand seeing it happen under the political umbrella of diversity. But given his current predicament, he had no choice but to tolerate it. For the moment, his hands were tied.

"If the Americans have their way, the international community will continue to smother Iran with its economic sanctions. This puts me in a troublesome position, as it could lead to an uprising against me as Supreme Leader. As you recall, the same thing happened to Ghaddafi in Libya. General Lajani will do everything in his power to prevent that from happening, but I'm a realist not an optimist, and therefore have to concede the possibility, no matter how small. Given your own country's history at Tiananmen Square, I'm sure your leadership can understand."

Xu nodded. Because the Chinese government has actively repressed all attempts to tally the death and injury totals on that fateful day in 1989, the true total is unknown. However, it is estimated that government agents killed as many as ten thousand unarmed, pro-democracy protestors, many of whom were run over with tanks. For this reason, the demonstration at Tiananmen Square was never far from the memory of anyone in the Communist Party. Shir-Del knew this.

"Should this happen, our twenty-five-year agreement will abruptly come to an end and you will be forced to negotiate with whatever filthy rebel replaces me. I want to protect myself and our agreement. There are ten years left on our deal, and the agreed terms specify that China will get a five percent discount for the first of those five years and none for the final five. However, I want to offer China a discount of fifteen percent for the first five of those years and ten on the remaining five. In exchange, Iran asks for China to invest another $200 million per year into our economy over the same ten-year span."

Xu sat for a prolonged pause long after his interpreter finished conveying the Supreme Leader's words before he finally shook his head.

"I'm afraid not. China wants a fifty percent discount for each of the last two years."

Shir-Del gripped his cane tighter.

"General Secretary, that's outrageous. Iran cannot agree to that. This deal must be mutually beneficial. With the sanctions against us, our oil ensures our survival. We're not going to give it away."

"I know," Xu said.

A slight grin curled at the corner of his mouth.

Shir-Del leaned further forward on his cane.

"Make me a real offer. I'm not in the mood to haggle back and forth."

"As I said, fifty percent for every year on the remaining contract."

"That's not possible."

Xu frowned and hiked his eyebrows.

"Thank you for making the trip. Perhaps we can work better together some other time."

Xu buttoned his coat and started to leave.

"Wait," Shir-Del said.

Xu winked at his interpreter as he stopped. He knew he had leverage.

"Fifty percent is out of the question, but I can offer you twenty-five percent for every year left on the deal, plus something else."

"Such as?"

"What if I gave exclusive drilling rights to China's National Petroleum Corporation for eight oil wells in the Ahvaz oil fields?"

Xu nodded and sat back down.

"But I want your guarantee that any attack by a foreign power on those wells will be viewed as an attack on China. You will not need permission from our government to militarily intervene. Plus, I want another $100 million in surface to air missiles to protect ourselves from any acts of aggression by America in the Strait of Hormuz."

Xu tapped his fingers for a moment before leaning forward.

"I want one more thing."

Shir-Del put his hand, out as if to say, "go ahead." He had made the Chinese leader a more than generous offer. Now, he was pushing his luck because he knew he could.

"The Americans have been quite good lately at keeping an eye on our military exercises. I want you to give us a two-year lease on Larak Island off your southern shores. This should allow us to avoid any prying eyes."

Lajani stopped translating as soon as Xu mentioned Larak Island. He knew the Iranian Constitution backward and forward. That location was reserved for Iranian military and Revolutionary Guard exercises only. Xu knew this and deliberately looked at Lajani when he made the request. The Secretary was making a point to not only push Shir-Del as far as he was willing to go but to purposely step on Lajani's turf.

Shir-Del looked at Lajani to finish translating. Lajani did, and then switched from Chinese to Farsi to remind the Supreme Leader of an article in the Iranian Constitution that specifically forbids the presence of foreign military bases on Iranian soil.

Shir-Del clenched his jaw. Xu was poking a rabid dog. Like a spectator in a tennis arena, Xu watched the Supreme Leader and his General quietly converse back and forth. He knew that he had them cornered. Shir-Del waived away Lajani's concerns.

"We will allow you to conduct your drills," Shir-Del said, "but they will need to be joint exercises with the Iranian military. This will prevent any issues with the Iranian Parliament. And we insist that your soldiers not wear anything that identifies them as Chinese."

Lajani hesitated before translating. He hated what he was hearing. Shir-Del widened his eyes at him, which was as much of a quiet threat as he was going to receive in front of a foreign dignitary. He had no choice but to succumb to the order.

Xu rubbed his chin to make the Iranians think that he was deliberating, but he knew that he had hit the jackpot. He stood to shake the Supreme Leader's hand.

"Iran can consider itself under China's protection," he said.

The two leaders shook hands and agreed to let their staffs sort out the details. When Xu left the room, Shir-Del grinned at Lajani, a rare show of emotion for him. Lajani nodded in return. When the Supreme Leader excused himself to go to the restroom to take his next shot of Carbamazepine, Lajani snatched his phone and called the general of the Quds Force, Javad Abendini, who answered on the first ring.

"Yes, sir?"

"I need you to do me a favor."

Chapter Two

ARDABIL, IRAN
NEAR AZBERBAIJAN BORDER

"Move!"

Thrasher was yelling at Farhad. Three months ago, Thrasher managed to get a Pakistani soldier in Iran over the Pakistan border so that he could testify that Iran had used him to set up the war between India and Pakistan. In doing so, he got his treasured Iranian source, Farhad Khorsandi, shot. After getting the soldier to a CIA chopper waiting across the border, instead of boarding the chopper with his team, Thrasher ran back across the border *into* Iran to save Farhad. The brass at the CIA ripped him a new one over the incident but Thrasher knew that he had done the right thing. Farhad had done everything in his power to help him in his mission. He owed the Iranian. Besides, CIA sources on the ground in Iran were hard to find, and Farhad had more than proven his worth. Thrasher wasn't about to let him die.

In the months that followed, Thrasher became the only CIA agent permanently on the ground inside Iran, which was illegal according to the Algiers Accords the U.S. signed with Iran after the 1981 hostage crisis. And as Farhad's legend grew for hanging up the phone on the Supreme Leader, Thrasher had become his unofficial bodyguard. It wasn't a role that he wanted or enjoyed. He had joined the CIA to be a tool for the government to utilize when there were no other options, not to be a guardian for a leader of the Iranian resistance. But for now, that's what he was. If keeping Farhad alive meant keeping America safe by inflicting harm to the Ayatollah's government, then so be it: that was his mission.

"I said move it, dammit!"

"I'm moving as fast as I can!"

Thrasher grunted in frustration. Two Revolutionary Guard soldiers were actively hunting them like wild boar, and if Farhad didn't move his ass then both of them would soon be hung by their necks. The problem was the residual pain in Farhad's shoulder from being shot. He could move his arms but running caused the wound to send an electric jolt of pain from one nerve ending to the other. This hindered his ability to evade the IRGC or anyone else.

As Farhad slowly climbed the muddy hill above Abbasabad Village, Thrasher couldn't contain his impatience. He tucked his Sig Sauer P226 into his waistband and grabbed Farhad by the back of his t-shirt to help him up the hill. A bullet whizzed over his shoulder and hit a boulder to his right. He didn't know if the midnight sky helped conceal their movement or if the shooter was just a bad shot, but Thrasher looked up to thank the heavens.

That was a little too close.

Thrasher shoved Farhad behind the closest boulder and heard him hit the ground with a thud. The Iranian grabbed his shoulder.

"Take it easy, will ya!"

"Quiet."

Thrasher could hear footsteps coming up the hill. He pulled his gun out.

"Stay here and don't move!"

"Wait, what? Jay, I'm too exposed!"

Farhad was referencing Thrasher's alias in the field, Jay Jacoby. Thrasher had not yet revealed his bona fide name. Tom Delang got kidnapped and tortured because he trusted the wrong people with the same information, and he would be damned if he was going to end up in the same situation.

"That's the idea. Now, stay there and shut up."

Thrasher disappeared into the darkness.

Sweat formed on Farhad's brow as he braced himself against the rock. The IRGC soldier's squishy steps were getting closer. When he was only fifteen feet to his left, Farhad sat wide-eyed, and tried to control his breathing. The soldier grinned when he saw Farhad. The president had offered a sizable reward for anyone who brought him "the pirate of Iran."

"I got you now, you stupid shit."

Just as the young soldier raised his gun, he heard a low whistle. When he turned, he saw Thrasher standing twenty feet above him. The whistle was the last sound he heard before Thrasher shot him in the head. Thankfully, the silencer he had screwed into the gun muffled the blow of the shot.

Farhad sighed with relief as Thrasher made his way back to him.

"Did you have to cut it so close?"

Thrasher gave him a condescending look.

"Keep your voice down. There's one more coming."

He peeked past the boulder to see how close the other soldier was. With the clouds blocking the crescent moon, it was hard to tell, but Thrasher could hear his spongy steps on the red mud. He estimated that the second bogey was no more than fifty feet down the hill.

Perfect.

Thrasher grabbed the soldier's dead body and hurled it over the hill toward the second soldier. Within seconds, the body of the first soldier hit the second one and sent both tumbling down the hill.

Thrasher smiled.

Direct hit.

Thrasher didn't know it then, but the second soldier cracked his skull on the way down. Though there was a pool of blood on the rock,

Thrasher performed his due diligence and double-checked for a pulse. Standard protocol would normally dictate that he put two more slugs into the man's chest but he needed to avoid this looking like the work of a professional. Seeing that the body of the first soldier was nearby, Thrasher got an idea. He dragged the first body over to the second, and positioned them together.

"Let me see your phone. Stand next to them," Thrasher said.

"Huh?"

"Just do it. And cross your arms so that you look like a badass."

Farhad gave Thrasher a curious look, but did as he was told. Thrasher snapped a few photos.

"Send this to Donya so she can post it on all the PMOI's social media platforms."

"No way! If the Revolutionary Guard sees me standing next to the dead bodies of two of their own, I may as well walk around with the big red arrow pointing down at me that says, 'Shoot here!'"

"You've already got a target on your back, Farhad. Trust me. I've got your back."

"Then let's grab the stuff my friend hid in the hut down below and get the hell out of here before anyone sees us. What's the point of sending out the photo?"

"Because we need to spread the legend of Farhad."

Chapter Three

WASHINGTON, D.C.
THE WHITE HOUSE

Low-level CIA agents are hardly ever called to meet the president in person, but Beth Jenkins had information that President Roger Cannon needed to hear straight from the horse's mouth.

Jenkins had taken some personal time to come back to the States and finish some business with fellow agent Tom Delang before heading back to Pakistan to resume her duties as head of the Iranian Affairs desk. With the U.S. Embassy in Islamabad still recovering from an RPG attack in which she had been personally injured, Jenkins took shelter at a CIA compound in Karachi. Two weeks later, she was set to turn in for the night when she received a call that she was initially inclined to let go straight to voice mail until she saw the name on the caller ID.

Jaybird.

This was Thrasher's code name in the field. He never called to chat or check in. His calls had purpose and he rarely even said "hello." Normally, she would chastise him about his lack of social skills, but this time was different.

"You're not gonna believe what I'm about to tell you," he said.

His statement got her attention, but what he said next shocked her so deeply that she nearly dropped her phone.

Holy shit!

After hanging up with Thrasher, Jenkins nervously dialed Delang, who was sitting on the shore of Honolua Bay in Maui with his wife. His reaction was similar.

"You've gotta be fucking kidding me!"

She knew that the leadership on the seventh floor of CIA headquarters needed to know immediately, but Jenkins decided to wait. She knew that the Director's office and the White House were going to have a mountain of follow-up questions, and she had no intention of walking into such a pop quiz session unprepared.

It was the break that everyone in the international community, not only the CIA, had been waiting for. There was a high-ranking Judas in the Iranian government, and it wasn't just anyone. It was Major General Ramin Lajani, chief commander of the Revolutionary Guard.

Lajani had snatched Farhad off the street during one of his usual bootlegging runs. Based on his account, Lajani had figured out that Farhad had helped the CIA get a Pakistani soldier across the border. Knowing that he was on the IRGC's hit list, Farhad thought he was going to be sent to the gallows of the infamous Evin Prison never to be heard from again. To his surprise, Lajani wanted to stage a coup to overthrow the Supreme Leader, but he needed the CIA's help to do it. Farhad had been selected as his go between.

Overthrowing the Supreme Leader of Iran was a sticky proposal for the CIA. Ever since the agency led the coup to depose Prime Minister Mohammad Mossadegh in 1953, the CIA was numero uno on the Iranian shit list. After all, Mossadegh had been democratically elected as Prime Minister and had nationalized the country's oil by kicking out all investing parties. The British, and their British Petroleum conglomerate, took offense because they had previously signed a multi-decade deal with the Iranian government. Seeing that the British were paying the Iranian workers dirt wages and essentially plundering the country's oil supply, leaving little for the local government, Mossadegh threw out the deal.

After failing to reach negotiable terms with Mossadegh, the British looked to America for help to remove him. President Truman turned them down multiple times. But the Brits were able to convince the newly elected Eisenhower that Mossadegh had warm feelings toward the Soviet Union. This was substantiated when he announced an oil deal with the Soviets. From that decision alone, *Operation AJAX* was born. The CIA's top operative at the time, Kermit Roosevelt, was dispatched to Iran to handle the dirty work. The rest is history.

The overthrow of Mossadegh was originally seen as a great success for the agency. It had prevented the spread of Communism in the Middle East, created a blueprint for overthrowing a government, their British allies regained their stake in Iranian oil, and the U.S. had a new secure Middle East partner in the Shah.

In hindsight, though, the coup did far more harm than good. After returning to power, the Shah used the SAVAK to torture his in-country dissenters, and lived in opulence while many Iranian citizens starved. When Ayatollah Khomeini returned to Iran in 1979, the CIA's coup was one of the top reasons that U.S. Embassy gates were stormed, which ultimately led to the 444-day crisis that held fifty-two U.S. diplomats captive. The hostages were only returned when the American government signed the Algiers Accords, which specified that the United States would never again interfere in Iranian affairs.

Jenkins was keenly aware of this, as was everyone at the agency. She also knew that Iranians had memories like elephants, and still complained about the coup to this day. Getting the CIA involved in another Iranian coup would be a tough sell. But the Iran of today was much different than it was in 1953. There was no Red Scare. Over the last four decades, the Ayatollah regime had blatantly demonstrated how far it was willing to go in its opposition of the West. The newest Supreme Leader had recently proven that with his stunt that put India and Pakistan at war just to remove the country's economic sanctions. Iran's relentless pursuit of nuclear weapons couldn't be ignored either. However, considering the golden egg that had landed in her lap, Jenkins was convinced that now was time for America to act against the Ayatollah regime.

When the president walked in, Jenkins was seated next to CIA Director Henry Wallace at the imposing conference table inside the dimly lit Situation Room in the basement of the White House. At Wallace's insistence, this meeting was totally off-book. No aides. No note takers. Officially, the president, who suffered from migraines, was sleeping one off in the Residence.

After shaking the Director's hand, the president pulled out his wallet and handed him a $20 bill.

"Here. This is from Gloria," the president said referencing the First Lady, "For the pool."

"Okay, who's her horse?"

The president whispered a name into Wallace's ear.

Jenkins raised an eyebrow at the exchange. Any situation that garnered the First Lady's interests was bound to have some juicy Capitol Hill gossip attached to it.

Upon hearing the name, the Director gave the president a confused look.

"Really?" he said.

Cannon rolled his eyes and shrugged. He had agreed to be his wife's messenger regarding the situation so he wouldn't have to listen to her ramble on about the subject.

"Who have we here, Henry?" Cannon asked.

"Mr. President, this is Katherine Jennings. She's the head of our Iranian Affairs desk in Pakistan."

President Cannon was impressed by her confident look and dynamite suit, a black J. Crew blazer and lime green blouse. Other than red, white, and blue, Cannon's favorite color combo was green and black. Jennings scored a point for doing her homework.

"That's not your real name, is it?"

"No, sir. Of course not."

The president smiled.

"Good. It's better for both of us that it stays that way."

The president sat at the head of the table. While Jenkins could have sat next to him and across from Director Wallace, he noted that she sat next to her boss instead. This told him that she was not there to suck up to him. Another point in her favor.

"Okay, let's hear it."

"Sir, we have an unprecedented opportunity in Iran."

"Henry, I don't think it's a good idea to stir that pot right now. Their recent deal with the Chinese has got us between a rock and a hard place. We owe China over a trillion dollars. It's one thing to challenge the bully on the playground. But when that bully has a gang of one billion standing behind him, it's best to back off and reassess."

"Sir, the chief commander of the IRGC, Major General Rahim Lajani, has approached one of our sources in Iran and offered to overthrow the Supreme Leader. He wants the CIA's assistance."

Cannon stopped twirling the gold wedding band on his finger.

"You're kidding. Is this legit?"

"The source is credible and serious, sir."

"How so?"

Wallace turned his chair toward Jenkins as if to say, "you're on."

"Sir, our source in Iran is one of the people that helped Tom Delang escape Iranian custody. He also recently assisted one of our operatives with getting Lieutenant Hasan Wasim out of Iran."

Cannon's ears perked up. He had met with Delang and liked him immediately. Anything attached to his name felt authentic. Getting Wasim back to Pakistan also chalked up a major victory for him against Iran.

"Go on."

"Code named *Buckaroo*, he and I have kept in touch. He's a smuggler by trade, getting mostly alcohol and low-level drugs, like marijuana, into the country. Through him, Lajani reached out and asked for our help."

"Tell me more about Lajani."

"Well, sir, we may have labeled him *Golden Boy*, but on paper, he's no choir boy. Through his career at the IRGC, his name has been attached to car bombings against associations throughout the world aligned with Israel. Remember the bombing a decade ago in Argentina outside a gymnasium frequented by local Jews? That was his. He's active in the hardcore drug trade, selling contraband to Hezbollah, who then uses the profits to purchase weapons on the black market. When the Israeli ship *INS Yaffo* was attacked off the coast of Haifa six years ago, we believe that the weapons purchases were made by way of the drugs he supplied. Most recently, he supplied Hamas with the rockets that attacked the Iron Dome last year."

"He sounds lovely. Why should I entertain anything this man has to say?"

"Like I said, sir, he looks bad *on paper*. But when you peel back the curtain on each of these individual incidents, he looks better. The attack in Argentina killed a dozen people and injured another twenty. But why attack the place in the late evening when it's known to have the lowest level of traffic? The strike against the *Yaffo* heavily damaged the ship but suffered zero casualties. And the Iron Dome attack? Some believe that Iran wanted to see if it could withstand a major assault and tested it for weaknesses. This may be true, but I think he knew that it would protect the Israelis. He did it for show."

"In other words, he's making enough of an effort to impress the Supreme Leader, but he's trying to keep the damage to a minimum."

"Yes, sir. I believe so."

"Let's say that I believe that. What's his motivation? Tell me about the man. Not the General. The man."

Jenkins looked to Wallace. She needed her boss's help on this one.

Wallace adjusted his clear framed glasses.

"Sir, that information has been a little harder to come by, but I reached out to my counterpart in Mossad. Without tipping our hand, we traded some info."

"In exchange for what?"

Surprised by the question, Wallace raised one of his thin eyebrows.

"Never mind. I don't want to know. Continue."

"Long story short, as far as IRGC leaders go, Lajani is the least bad nightmare for them. Israeli analysts seem to have the same instincts as Miss Jennings. Their take is that Lajani is a man who has quietly moved up the ladder by doing just enough to impress and survive. The Iranian leadership hasn't looked below the surface."

"How does Lajani plan to stay below the new Supreme Leader's radar?"

"We're still working on how he can spring the trap by surprise, but as far as him being able to keep his head down, we think it's less about him personally than it is about the IRGC structure. Since Khomeini died, the Revolutionary Guard has steadily acquired more power to become a military, political, cultural, and social complex all rolled into one. In that way, it has become much like the SS was in Nazi Germany. With no personal connection between him and the Ayatollah, Lajani has been savvy enough to let the Supreme Leader only see the successful parts of his attacks and he has impressed him with his willingness to carry them out. He's smart enough to know where the land mines are, and how to sidestep them. This combination makes for a trustworthy man to head up the arm of government that the Ayatollah depends on most."

"So, this is going to be like the Valkyrie plan against Hitler?"
Wallace tipped his hand back and forth.

"Yes and no."

"What else?"

"There's not much else to go on. He was born in Shiraz, joined the IRGC on his seventeenth birthday, and has steadily risen though the ranks. He speaks five languages and has a proven track record as a soldier during the 2006 Lebanon War, which put him on Mossad's radar. We can see that he has good relations with four of the five heads of Revolutionary Guard branches."

"Those being?"

"The Army, Navy, Aerospace Force, and Quds. He personally trained two of them."

"All that means is that he's the lead gangster. If we help them and they turn against us, we will have aided terrorism."

"That's certainly possible, sir, but it's our belief that his relations with those men will enable him accomplish his goal."

"You said that he had good relations with the heads of four out of the five branches. What about the fifth?"

"That's the new leader of the Basij, sir. Mohammad Nassiri. We don't know much about him at the moment, but we're working on it. He looks to be a true fanatic and strict follower of the Supreme Leader. They even come from the same hometown of Khorramabad. We'll have to come up with a plan to deal with him."

Cannon scrunched his lips.

"I don't know, Henry. This seems awfully thin."

Wallace turned back to Jenkins.

"Sir," Jenkins said, "we do have two things going for us."

"Such as?"

"We have CIA eyes on the ground with Buckaroo."

"Good to know. And the second?"

"Lajani has offered us a guarantee."

"You might have led with that. What is it?"

"His family."

"Pardon me?"

"His two wives, daughter, and son have been moved out of Iran at his request. We have agents looking after them in Karachi. If he helps us succeed, they return."

"*Two* wives?"

"Yes, sir," Jenkins said, reluctantly.

Cannon rolled his yes.

This just keeps getting better.

"How did he get his family out of the country without the Supreme Leader noticing?"

"We've verified that his father lives in Pakistan and is bed ridden with leukemia. Lajani used the circumstance to his advantage and made it look like it was a family visit."

"What if he fails?"

"We can decide their fate. As insurance, he'll give us the secret bank accounts that Hamas and Hezbollah use to move their money around on the condition that we don't do anything with them until the coup has been attempted."

Cannon's eyes widened.

"Okay, I'm impressed. What's his end goal?"

"He says he'll take charge of the country for no more than three years after which free elections will take place without American interference," said Wallace. "Gut instinct here, sir, but I think the guy just wants to have a country where people can have a normal life, one that won't be strangled to death with sanctions and can choose its own destiny."

"So, he's a businessman who's willing to negotiate with the western world?"

"I don't know if I would call him a businessman, but he's certainly someone that is willing to legitimately negotiate with us."

"What about Iran's pursuit of nuclear technology?"

"He made it a point to say that all facilities will be shut down, and allow U.N. inspectors, though he'll keep an eye on them to ensure that he's not letting Israeli spies into the country."

"Speaking of Israel, what's his take on them?"

"He's not interested in attacks, sir. I believe this man to be a nationalist. Though Sharia Law will remain in place, he wants Iran to know what it feels like to thrive. But we need you to keep the Israeli Prime Minister at bay. They will no doubt get wind that something is going down in Iran. For this to work successfully, no one can touch this."

Easier said than done.

"I'm not exactly thrilled about Sharia Law staying in place," said Cannon. "What about issues like women's rights?"

"Since Iran is already governed by Sharia Law, all we're talking about is not making changes to any governing process that would upset the locals. With Lajani in place, we can work on the other liberties later. This isn't going to be a short-term fix, but over time, perhaps they will become more like Egypt or Jordan."

"In what sense?"

"They will continue to be governed by religious law, albeit with political influence. Our goal is to make Iran a country that we can work with and ease tensions with both us and Israel."

Cannon narrowed his eyes and exhaled a judgmental breath.

"Make your request."

Wallace cleared his throat.

"Sir, this would be totally off the books. No CIA money would be attached to the operation. Miss Jennings and my operative on the ground will hand in their resignation so there will be no affiliation with the agency or the American government. Everything that will be done will be to help the PMOI and General Lajani return Iran to its people."

"Your man on the ground. Is he trustworthy?"

Wallace hesitated. Thrasher was difficult to describe.

"He's not exactly a dinner date, sir, but he's one of my best."

"Henry, if this goes wrong, or if Tony gets wind of this, you'll have no choice but to resign. Then, you'll have to contend with Congress. I won't be able to protect you."

The president was referring to Tony Prasad, Inspector General of the CIA, who oversees the management of the agency in order to prevent fraud, abuse, or mismanagement. The office is commonly referred to as "The Watchers' Watcher." For Cannon, Prashad was a bit of an ace up his sleeve because the Fijian man was known to have several secretive, but friendly relations with numerous Congressional staff members on the Hill. What impressed Cannon the most, though, was his ability to easily charm even the most ardent of his opponents on the Senate confirmation committee, even during a time when CIA oversight was receiving more scrutiny with each passing day.

Wallace nodded. He knew the game. Not only would the president not be able to protect him; he would also make him out to be a scapegoat. Wallace would become the poster child for a rogue director using the agency to wage his personal wars without Congressional or presidential approval. The entire U.S. intelligence structure would come under fire. It would make the Church Commission meetings from the 1970's look like an after school special.

"I understand, sir," said Wallace.

Cannon turned his attention to Jenkins.

"Miss Jennings, do I need to remind you of your fate and the fate of your man on the ground?"

Jenkins swallowed a stiff lump in her throat. The President of the United States had just threatened her.

"I do, sir."

"And, Henry, I expect you to keep me unofficially informed, but otherwise, I have your guarantee that the CIA or any member of this government will have no footprints on this?"

"Sir, I may have to assist Miss Jennings and her team, but in emergency situations only."

"The two of you understand the ramifications of what will happen if you fail, right? This isn't a 'you break it, you buy it' situation. If the Supreme Leader survives a coup, he could become more powerful and popular in his people's eyes, and more dangerous than ever to the rest of the world. And that doesn't include the social and political blowback for us."

"I do, sir," Wallace said.

The president looked to Jenkins.

"I'm aware, sir, but. . ."

"But?"

"Are we ever going to get a better chance?"

Cannon resumed twirling his wedding ring. Jenkins could see the gears turning in his well-known analytical brain. The president nodded. This was intentional. For the sake of self-preservation, he wasn't about to give a verbal approval. He pulled his phone from his jacket pocket, began typing on the Notepad app, and he showed it to his two conspirators.

Delang acts as your intermediary. Not negotiable!

"Understood, sir," Jenkins said.

Cannon proceeded with deleting the sentence from his phone.

Inside, Jenkins was smiling. Though he had only met the president once, Delang's charms never ceased to amaze her.

"Where are you going to get the money?"

"Well, sir, that's the part you are going to like the least."

Chapter Four

PHILADELPHIA, PENNSYLVANIA

Though she continued to lean on her cane, which she hated to be seen using, former Senator Vivian Walsh was in a jovial mood as she walked outside the steps of City Hall.

After being exposed by Tom Delang and thrown out of Washington for conspiring with the Iranians to have the naval base in Bahrain closed, Walsh went straight into revenge mode. Since Iran had been the root of her demise in the Senate, she used a family connection to set up a CIA operative for the embassy attack in Pakistan, for which she intended to make Iran look responsible. Separately, she brokered a deal with the CEO of Columbia Pictures to have Delang killed. With a five percent stake in the studio, she stood to make millions when Delang's death promoted the movie about his escape from Iran. Though the attack on the embassy succeeded, the attempt on Delang's life failed. With the help of others at the CIA, he was able to make the connection between calls from her burner cell phone and the Pakistani terrorist responsible for the bombings. When the CIA operative that she set up learned about her plan, he returned to the States, and at Delang's insistence, shot her in the leg.

But that was behind her now. The clouds on her career as a disgraced former Senator were beginning to lift.

Walsh and her family were no strangers to money. Her father had gone into business with a college friend at Purdue and, together, they patented machine designs still used by janitorial staffs to scrub and wax office floors across the world. While that money was enough to grant them a higher status in society and rent a politician from time to time, the money she had now gave her what she rightly missed—true power.

While she had financially profited from her time in Washington, her years as a Congresswoman and Senator were cemented by being on the receiving end of power grabs from her donors. They made requests and she followed through. She didn't ask any questions, but there was always an IOU attached. The power she acquired was a ripe cherry on top of any deal.

Despite her lack of hesitation to participate in shady deals, Walsh had a natural ability to foresee technology's future impact on society. Her time in Congress gave her a front row seat to the nation's economy, and a bird's eye view as to what was up and coming from the private sector. The combination resulted in Walsh's financial portfolio flying high. Very high. Higher than she expected. Though the use of any of that information was a gray area with Congressional oversight committees, the best part was that all of it was legal.

One of her perks in Congress was being on the Senate Commerce, Science, and Transportation Committee where she got to see how the incoming president's economic policies trended. She kept her eyes on publicly available information, had the vision to see what was on the technological horizon, and connected the dots to figure out how she could benefit, which made her investments legal. Now, she was reaping the rewards.

Along with her personal stakes in the film business, Walsh was one of the first to prophesize the popularity and accessibility of video streaming as Smart TVs came on the market. In 2013, she bought 25,000 shares of Netflix when it traded at $32 per share. By the end of the year, she'd purchased a total of 75,000 shares, another 100,000 the following year, and 50,000 shares per year through 2018, when she made friends with filmmakers in Hollywood and backed studios there on the condition that their film releases were exclusive to Netflix.

Not long after, she kept her eyes glued to how cable companies were struggling to compete with video streaming companies. With Amazon Prime streaming services ramping up original content in early 2015, she invested 200,000 shares in Amazon, which traded at $534 per share at the time of purchase. During each subsequent year, she bought more.

While others in her party were quick to criticize President Cannon's policies as favoring big business, Walsh witnessed their positive effects. She studied the increased volumes of cargo being imported and exported into the country. With this data in her back pocket, she knew that the value of delivery companies, like FedEx and UPS, would see gigantic increases. She was right. Both companies hovered at $100 per share when she bought shares. Within six months, she'd more than doubled her investments. Even though the stocks remained stagnant for eight years, she stuck with her hunch and kept buying until she saw the expected spike in stock prices.

Though she maintained some of her shares in these companies, when the dust settled and she sold the majority of them at their peak, combined with the wealth she'd inherited from her parents' estate, Walsh had become a proud resident of "Billionaire City." Now, her position reversed. She was the one pulling the puppet strings attached to the limbs of her former colleagues in Washington.

Relying on her knowledge of the shipping business, her latest deal involved buying a stake in the Port of Philadelphia. Unfortunately, its current size limited it from allowing companies with large cargo ships running from the Far East to the east coast to dock there. After placing calls to the North American CEO's of five of the world's largest shipping companies, she baited the hook with the fact that Philadelphia's terminal costs were lower than those of their rival terminals in Newark.

Her union connections didn't hurt either. From those calls, she was able to secure a commitment to have their Transpacific vessel services call port in Philadelphia on a more consistent basis. All she had to do was grease the palms of city officials to secure the land necessary for expanding the terminal. The project would take at least a year to finish, but it would ultimately become a long-term staple in Walsh's portfolio, giving her leverage with the national economy. After all, national crises come and go, but cargo must always keep moving.

As she approached her waiting limo, Walsh's usual driver held the door open but lowered his head to hide the smirk on his face. Without so much as looking at him or thanking him for the gesture, Walsh awkwardly climbed in on her good leg. As she reached to make herself a celebratory drink from her loyal decanter of Maker's Mark, a highball glass filled with three fingers of bourbon was handed to her by someone she didn't recognize.

"Who the hell are you?"

"I'm insulted. Don't you remember the faces of the people you've tried to kill?"

Walsh studied the dark-haired woman with scratches and scars on both sides of her face.

"That's a fairly long list. You'll have to be more specific."

"I should have figured as much."

Walsh glanced past her mystery guest and yelled to her driver.

"Philip, you'd better have a good answer for this!"

When the driver rolled down the cabin window, she didn't see the face of her regular driver. Instead, she saw someone she'd hoped to never see again, and he was quick to point a gun at her.

"Hello, Senator," Tom Delang said.

Walsh's bug-eyed response spoke for itself. She turned back to her mystery guest.

"I guess that would make you Jennings."

Jenkins nodded. Walsh was not aware of her bona fide name, but certainly knew her alias in the field. After all, she'd tried to have her killed by an RPG attack at an embassy in Pakistan.

"If you don't take this, I'm going to drink it myself."

Walsh accepted the glass of bourbon.

"What do you want?"

"We have an opportunity for you, Senator."

"For what?"

"Redemption."

"How so?"

"First, you sign this."

Jenkins snapped her fingers and reached back to Delang. He handed her an "Eyes Only" security agreement, which she handed to the former Senator.

Walsh was familiar with the legally binding document that required her to keep her mouth shut about what she was about to hear. She momentarily debated her situation, but it was pointless. They had too much dirt on her. Pulling a pen from her Gucci handbag, she signed it and threw it back at Jenkins.

"Let's hear it."

"Your riches haven't gone unnoticed. We need some of it."

Walsh raised an eyebrow, confused.

"You want *my* help?"

"We need you to supply us with fifty million to personally finance an operation."

"I take it that Cannon and Wallace don't want to touch this?"

Jenkins didn't answer, which was an answer for Walsh.

"What's the op?"

Jenkins turned back to look at Delang and gave him an "are you sure?" look. She was running the op, but it was his idea to leverage Walsh to do it. He nodded, but she had no intention of giving Walsh any more information that she had to.

"The PMOI is making a run at deposing the Supreme Leader of Iran. It's their show, but they need some heavy pockets to pull it off."

"And if I refuse, you'll release the information connecting me to the Pakistani Embassy attack?" Walsh said.

"Life has its perks from time to time," Delang said.

"What guarantee do I have if the coup fails?"

"None," Delang said.

Walsh's face turned red as she leaned forward.

"I don't think I heard you correctly."

"You heard me just fine. There are no guarantees here. Consider it motivation for you to help the operation succeed."

"So, this is a heist. Not an investment request."

"Call it what you want, but let's just say it will pay your debt in full to me and Miss Jennings."

Walsh sat back. A malevolent burn for revenge bubbled in her gut. The "debt in full" remark was a sweet stab at her. She had used the same phrase when Delang discovered her murderous plot against him.

Fuck you, Delang.

"There's something else in it for you," Jenkins said. "When the coup succeeds, the Iranian economy will open back up and the Office of Foreign Assets Control will eventually remove the trade restrictions between the U.S. and Iran. I'm sure you can use your contacts in the shipping business to secure a vessel service that will have an exclusive route between the Iranian ports and your newly expanded port here in Philly. You'd make up your investment in a matter of months. If the terminal can keep its costs as low as you say, then your profit shouldn't be a problem."

"How did you . . ."

Jenkins gave her a sideways look.

"Right. How exactly do you plan to pull this off?"

"We'll set up a front business in Isfahan and run the operation from there. You don't need to know any more details than that," Jenkins said.

Walsh continued to evaluate Jenkins while she returned an assertive glare of her own. Delang seemed to be a wild dog on a leash, but Jennings appeared reasonable. Though she despised Delang, the idea of helping them take down the same Iranians that got her booted out of Congress was too tempting to pass up.

"Send me the account information. You'll have it by tomorrow."

Delang drove back to Walsh's residence in Chestnut Hill where Jenkins had parked her car. She checked her phone when it dinged with a new text message.

DUB: He's fine. Leaving now.

Dub was a nickname for an agent who had worked under her during her time in Pakistan. His real name was Jackson Whang but given the initials of his first and last name, his fellow agents called him "J-Dub." Thrasher would later shorten the name even further. Dub was also the agent responsible for giving Walsh the limp in her leg after he shot her for using him in her Pakistani Embassy scheme, which resulted in Jenkins's injuries. Jenkins found out later that Dub was blind to Walsh's actions. The director threw him out of the agency, but at Jenkins's request, didn't have him arrested. Suffice to say, he owed her a few favors.

"Don't worry about your driver, Philip. One of my colleagues slipped him a mickey and watched over him. He'll wake up with what feels like a monster hangover, but he'll be fine. Thanks for your time, Senator," said Jenkins.

As she exited, Delang stayed put and pointed his Glock-19 at Walsh. The silencer was already screwed in and ready to go.

"Let's be clear. I don't care about the legalities of your security agreement. If you fuck us on this, the gloves come off. There's nothing that will stop me from coming back here to finish you off."

"You can cut the Robert DeNiro act, Delang. Piss off."

Walsh went to leave the vehicle but jumped back when she felt a bullet fly past her neck and clip her dangling diamond earring. Astonished, her skin immediately turned ashen. Delang wasn't fucking around.

"That was to remind you that I don't aim for the leg."

Chapter Five

CAMP DAVID

President Cannon knew that he had to tread carefully with his up-coming conversation with the Prime Minister of Israel, Eli Sahar, but it was necessary. Thankfully, the recent meeting he'd had with his CIA personnel was well-timed. Sahar was scheduled to speak with him in person about a variety of issues, including recent instability in the West Bank, potential Palestinian statehood, and increasing the trade between their two countries. This meeting had been on the books for months, but Cannon had no doubt that the CIA knew.

Given that they worked together on a weekly basis, sometimes daily, Cannon and Sahar had an on-again-off-again relationship. They respect-ed one another, but some days were better than others. It wasn't unusual for them to be totally on the same page on one issue on Tuesday and then have a prickly meeting where they only felt like friends after five o'clock on Wednesday. It was a never-ending, vicious cycle. For Can-non, each meeting with Sahar felt like he was spinning the barrel in a game of Russian roulette.

The best part about the relationship was that each man knew that the other desired peace in the Middle East, and that this could not be possi-ble without Israel's surrounding Arab neighbors recognizing it as a state.

To a certain extent, they had succeeded. The problem was that the U.S. had to make a conscious effort to continually tiptoe around any negotiations. In terms of diversity and financial investment, they had a big stake in the game with its Arab allies and had to evaluate all pro-posals on multiple levels. Sahar knew this all too well, but from his perspective, the U.S. never understood that Israel had no choice but to take a hardline on every issue. There were two billion Muslims in the world. Even though most of them are peaceful, roughly ten percent were known radicals, which meant two hundred million people wanted to wipe Israel off the map. The Jews had already endured one Holocaust. Sahar would be damned if it would happen again.

Fortunately for Cannon, Sahar had been bitten by the golf bug and was limited by the fact that Israel only had two courses. Upon hearing this, Cannon wasted no time inviting him to Camp David. Since Eisenhower had been a board member at Augusta National, he saw to it that a driving range and one par three hole were installed at the presidential retreat. When Cannon showed it to Sahar during his first year in office, the Israeli fell instantly in love with this perk. The driving range had become their unofficial meeting room and a way for them to speak without their respective staff. The only bad part for Cannon was that Sahar had a track record of being more flexible when he was flushing his irons, and less so when he was hooking or slicing. Today, Cannon prayed to the golfing Gods for good hits.

The sun was starting to peek its head over the Maryland pine trees when Cannon grabbed his clubs and headed out to the range so he could stretch. The Secret Service agent at his side insisted on carrying the president's golf bag, but Cannon let him off the hook. Feeling the weight of the bag on his shoulder, and hearing the clubs click together as he walked, was one of the few things in life that made Cannon still feel like the regular Joe he grew up being in Corpus Christi, Texas.

When he arrived, Cannon was surprised to see that Sahar had beaten him to the punch. The Israeli had once served in the Sayeret Matkal special forces during the 1982 Lebanon War, but he'd been discharged early when a brick wall fell on him during a mission. The injury resulted in several back surgeries with lingering effects. Sahar would never turn down the opportunity to practice his swing but loosening up beforehand was essential.

Cannon's lips tightened as he tried to contain his laughter. Sahar's blue plaid shorts reminded him of a geriatric mall walker.

"Eli, how are you feeling today?"

"A little stiff, but ready to out-hit you, Roger."

Sahar winked. Cannon smiled as he shook his hand. He took the good-natured ribbing as a sign that Sahar was in a cheery mood.

"So, what's the topic for today?"

"Let's hit a few first."

For the next twenty minutes, the two leaders said little to one another as they went about their routine of hitting three or four balls before changing clubs, and then doing the same. Sahar was always sure to watch Cannon hit first, who appeared to pay no mind to this fact but was aware of it. As a single digit handicap, Cannon could pretty much make the ball do whatever he wanted but he made sure to hit an errant shot from time to time in order to rock Sahar into a false sense of security. Sahar made a point to whistle as he watched his good shots sail past those that he thought Cannon mishit. When both men hit their wedges close to the 100-yard marker, Sahar broke the ice.

"Are you going to tell me what the movie is about or are you going to make me guess?"

Sahar restrained himself from rolling his eyes at his own question. As a movie buff, Cannon habitually spoke in code about sensitive political topics using movie speak. This immature move annoyed the hell out of Sahar, especially with no staff around, but it was a quirk he had come to accept.

Cannon smiled as he hit a ball within three feet of the flag.

Let the games begin.

In his head, he heard the theme music to *The Price Is Right* as he chose his next words carefully.

"Someone made a pitch to me earlier today."

"About what?"

Cannon turned to watch Sahar take his shot.

"The plot is still unfolding, but it would involve you ignoring what you hear about Iran over the next few weeks."

Cannon winced as Sahar topped his ball, and watched it bounce three feet before rolling down the hill. Sahar slowly turned to Cannon and gave him a condescending, sideways look.

"Excuse me?"

"Wouldn't you want to see a movie where the Iranians take back their country from the inside without outside help from you or me?"

Sahar's eyebrows raised with interest.

"Impossible. A major studio would have to fund the project."

"That's being taken care of by a private citizen."

"And what part would I be cast to play?"

"None. You would be a spectator. No hands on the reins, period. It's got to be a total inside job."

Sahar leaned on his Callaway club and tapped the top of the grip.

"We've seen this movie before. Sounds like a remake of the 1953 version," he said.

"Not this time. My producers have resigned and are helping the cast members rewrite the script. They'll live or die by their own pen."

"There is no yellow brick road in this picture. You should have learned that in Iraq."

"We know."

Sahar squinted at Cannon. He knew the president was holding back.

"You've got a wizard behind the curtain, don't you?"

Cannon smirked.

"More like a golden goose."

"It must be a big one. We tried this before about a decade ago. Couldn't get the movie made. Not enough players to make it sell."

"This one will be a blockbuster."

"Sounds like everyone is going all-in."

"And then some."

"Here's the problem. If the project bombs, the blowback will leave me dealing with the ramifications."

"Hence this conversation. I didn't have to tell you about this."

"And what are you going to do about your Chinese investors? Their recent deal with the Iranians should put your film in jeopardy."

"If everything goes to plan, that situation will handle itself."

If.

Sahar swayed his head from side to side before he resumed swinging. Cannon watched and waited for a rebuttal.

"You realize that I can't put on the earmuffs. My team will be hearing what's happening on the ground."

"I know. And I'm asking you to instruct them not to intervene."

Sahar stepped forward to meet Cannon eye to eye.

"No bullshitting me on this one, Roger. How confident are you that the picture will get made?"

"You know as well as I do there are no guarantees. We're never going to get a better shot than this. Our director is a big-name player. This is as good as it's ever going to get."

"Are you absolutely sure I can't help?"

"You can help by keeping an eye on Hezbollah and Hamas. With the new player in place, we think that we can cut them off at the knees, but there's no telling how they will respond. If I need to break the emergency glass, I'll ask. Otherwise, we *must* let this play out on its own."

"I don't know if I can do this, Roger. You're putting millions of Israeli heads on the chopping block if this goes wrong. We've experienced genocide before. I'm sure as hell not going let it happen again."

Sahar gave Cannon a stern look. Cannon took a step forward.

"Eli, I know about the Speed Agiles that you bought off the books."

Designed by military contractor Lockheed Martin, the Speed Agile Contact Demonstrator (SACD) was a four-engine, multi-mission aircraft that can carry larger and heavier cargo payloads than conventional aerial vehicles with power lift systems. What made it special was that it was equipped with stealth technology, a simplified mechanical design and a low-drag integration system that created greater efficiency and versatility in the air. More important, Department of Defense tests had proven that they could go undetected by Iranian radar technology. Cannon wasn't sure how, but he knew that Sahar was aware of this.

While the plane would be a Godsend for any country's air force in times of war, the United States and its European allies intentionally restricted stealth technology sales to Israel because they feared that they would use them proactively against Iran. It was a fine line for the international community to walk. Israel had a right to defend itself, but their version of that was to prevent an attack before it happened. The international community wasn't about them to let them start a war that would put them in the compromising position of choosing between helping Israel and its Arab allies.

From Israel's perspective, if they wanted the stealth technology, they had no choice but to buy it on the black market. But if anyone from the U.N. found out, the Jewish state would face massive sanctions. In Sahar's estimation, they would likely be short-term, but it would create a weakness that Iran and its Muslim enemies would take the opportunity to exploit.

Sahar diverted his eyes.

"How long have you known?"

"Long enough."

"I have the right to protect my people."

"I know, which is why I didn't order CIA special ops to interrupt the sale. You needed an ace up your sleeve. But that doesn't mean I'm going to let you use it."

"Meaning?"

"Meaning the Lockheed Martin CEO and I are friends. I'm sure you know that."

"So?"

Cannon raised his eyebrows. Sahar squinted his eyes at the American president.

"You had them install a back door in the computer system, didn't you? So, you could shut it down if we ever put it in the air."

Cannon shrugged and grinned. Sahar let out a frustrated breath. The president had him cornered. While he had no current plans to use the stealth plane, if he didn't use it when his generals called on him to do so, they would think of him as weak. If he did use it, the Americans would either cause it to malfunction or they would alert the U.N. about the purchase. That is, unless Sahar agreed to step back from the American plot in Iran.

"This is a big ask, Roger."

"The biggest."

Sahar studied the red haired American. It was clear that Cannon understood not only how big of a risk he was taking but how much he was asking of Sahar to tell his people to stand down. The problem was there were too many ways the plan could go wrong. Too much shit could roll down hill and land directly on Israel's doorstep.

"I expect a good seat in the theater if this works out."

"Eli, if this works out, there won't be a bad seat in the house, but you'll surely have the best one."

"Fine. But, Roger, don't make me regret this decision."

Chapter Six

PHILADELPHIA, PENNSYLVANIA

Walsh was downstairs in her home gym, exercising her injured leg by walking her usual two miles on a treadmill while watching CNN. She turned when she heard a knock at the door.

"Come in, Philip."

Philip Lee was her regular limo driver, the same one who Jenkins took out of commission so that she and Delang could corner Walsh in the limo. Philip had once been a standout forward on the Temple University basketball team, which was in Walsh's district when she served in the House of Representatives. Consistently scoring twenty points and grabbing twenty rebounds per game, he caught the admiring eye of Hall of Famer and beloved former Philadelphia 76er Julius Erving, which then garnered the attention of NBA scouts in his sophomore year. This captured local headlines and a few national outlets such as *The Sporting News*.

Walsh watched Philip play against in-state rival Penn State. After Philip hit the game-winning shot, Walsh wasted no time speaking to him about his future endeavors in front of the media cameras. During her first House re-election campaign, Walsh was in a tight race with her opponent and hoped that photos of her with the popular local player who local fans were hoping would become the next "Dr. J" could boost her numbers. While the photo op may not have been the deciding factor in her campaign, her numbers never fell after the photos were published, and she was easily re-elected.

Philip wasn't so fortunate. The following spring, a motorcycle accident ended his playing career, and he eventually lost his scholarship.

With no money to pay for tuition to finish his finance degree, Philip had to start over. After spending three years feeling sorry for himself, and working as a financial planner for Charles Schwab, Philip moved to the Washington, D.C. area, hoping to start a new life and meet someone with influence who could assist his parents with the legal troubles they were having with Homeland Security. Since members of Congress are known to take long road trips, he chose a job with a limousine company they were known to hire.

Within a year, he was fortunate enough to give a ride to Vivian Walsh, who had just been elected to the Senate. He recognized her immediately. Though she was always impeccably dressed, he quickly noted that the contagious smile and charming personality she had displayed in front of the cameras after his winning game were now gone. He found her cold and intimidating. She glanced at him only once, didn't recognize him, and paid him no attention other than to tell him that he needed to "speed the fuck up" because she needed to get to her meeting. Philip didn't say anything, but he overheard her complaining about a certain Senator from Florida, Raymond Giles, who she wanted to oust as Chairman of the Senate Armed Services Committee. This name immediately rang a bell with Philip. Giles had a quiet reputation as a philanderer with young lobbyists on Capitol Hill.

Two weeks earlier, Philip picked up a lobbyist for the pharmaceutical industry from Quill, a bar in downtown Washington. As Philip held the door for his passenger to enter the limo, he could tell that the man had a major buzz, which loosened his lips. He revealed what most didn't know about Giles, that he had a special condo in Alexandria, Virginia occasionally used for romantic rendezvous with members of the same sex. After hearing about the Senator's sexual preferences, he dropped off the young man for what he assumed was such another tryst.

Philip made note of the address. The next day, he boldly walked into Walsh's office in the Capitol Building. All it took was the mention of dirt on Senator Giles to her chief of staff to get him in to see Walsh. Once Walsh remembered meeting Philip back at Temple, he gave her the information about Giles. Walsh was highly suspicious. It was hard to believe that a kid from her home district would walk into her office with information she needed to oust one of her political rivals. It was too much of a coincidence and set off instinctual alarm bells for Walsh.

Seeing that she was skeptical, Philip provided her with the address of Giles's secret condo and asked her to call him if the information panned out. When Walsh asked Philip what he wanted in return, he said he needed her help with his parents' visa troubles with Homeland Security. Walsh thanked him for the information but made no promises. Fortunately for Walsh, Philip's story was spot-on. Walsh would later have Giles's apartment bugged with audio and video surveillance that she used to get him kicked out of Congress, which allowed her to nab his spot as Chairman of the Senate Armed Services Committee.

While she was under no obligation to do so, Walsh rewarded Philip by accommodating his request. She discovered that his parents had tried to bring medicine into the country without a proper medicinal license. When they protested, the agent on duty personally saw to it that they were placed on a watchlist, which delayed their immigration status. Walsh resolved the issue with a couple of phone calls.

Philip, the mysterious ex-basketball player turned limo driver, had proven to be an asset, but Walsh couldn't be sure that he wasn't part of a larger ploy. For the next three years, she kept him at arm's distance, but time after time the young man came through with information about her political rivals. He was paid for his services and slowly gained her trust until he finally refused ad-hoc payments and asked Walsh if he could be her full-time driver and private investigator. To ensure his loyalty, she had her chief of staff, Latrina Pearl, conduct several deep background checks on him, and it took nearly a year before she accepted his proposal.

Philip had now served her full-time for seventeen years, and after getting kicked out of Congress, thanks to Tom Delang's testimony that fateful day on Capitol Hill, Walsh no longer had a chief of staff. Philip became her confidant, her rock to lean on, and a reliable hatchet man. Until yesterday, there had never been a blemish on his record.

"Good morning, ma'am."

Philip was dressed in his usual black suit and tie, but Walsh could tell by the look on his face that he was in an irritable mood. She grabbed the remote and muted the TV.

"How are you feeling?"

"I've got a splitting headache, and I'm highly pissed off."

"Good. You should be."

"Senator, I'm sorry. One minute, I'm in my neighborhood bar, drinking my usual Crown and cranberry juice, watching the Phillies game. The next thing I knew, I was back in my apartment with no knowledge of how I got there."

"It's not your fault. These people are good at what they do. But next time, be more aware of your surroundings. *Never* let your guard down."

She sternly pointed her finger at him.

"It won't happen again, ma'am."

Walsh stepped off the treadmill. Philip handed her a towel.

"Thanks. Do you have what I need?"

She wiped the sweat from her brow.

"Yes, ma'am. Right here."

He held up a thumb drive. Walsh grinned and snatched it out of his hand.

"Thanks. You can go now. Be ready to go to the conference in an hour. And shut the door on your way out."

"Of course, ma'am."

After the door was shut, Walsh rushed to a laptop and inserted the thumb drive, opened the file, and clicked Play.

Bingo.

Walsh heard everything she'd hoped to hear. What Delang and Jennings didn't know was that Philip had installed a recording system in her limo to use for future blackmail in her business dealings. The two CIA agents didn't perform their diligence to check the limo when they'd stolen the car. Walsh smiled as she listed to the recording of her conversation with Jennings and Delang. The voices were crystal clear.

The question now for Walsh was what to do with it. Jennings was right. If their plan in Iran worked out, Walsh could call the CEOs of the shipping companies and arrange for their vessel services to start calling Iran and have the cargo discharge exclusively in Philly. She stood to make millions of dollars from the deal. As much as she wanted to eliminate Delang and Jennings, she couldn't. Not yet.

Walsh tapped her fingernails on the table. Her next move would require some thought. She shut the laptop and got back on the treadmill. She had one more mile left to run.

Chapter Seven

IRANIAN AIRSPACE
TWO WEEKS LATER

An eerie feeling came over Jenkins as she stared out the window from her aisle seat at the rolling dunes of the Dasht-e Kavir Desert. On the surface, at least, the operation was going well. She should have felt ecstatic. But her operational experience told her that it was only a matter of time before karma or whatever other forces of nature there were in the spy world came crashing down to kick her and her team in the ass.

Typing out her resignation letter to the CIA management brought back memories of the day she decided to join the agency. She grinned as she thought about the young person she was then, and how far she'd come. After graduating from Florida State, Jenkins was convinced that the only way to change the world was through better communication by way of diplomacy. Her parents had been diplomats in the Nixon era and were fascinated by his acknowledgement of Red China, so they enrolled her in a language school at an early age. With aspirations of becoming a U.S. ambassador to a Far East country, she became fluent in Chinese, Vietnamese, and Korean by the time she started college. After graduating, she went to her State Department interview on September 11, 2001, but was nearly struck by a falling lamppost on the highway when American Airlines Flight 77 knocked several of them down as it screamed overhead. Like many Americans on that day, she was shocked when she witnessed the plane crash into the Pentagon.

For Jenkins, it was the moment where the rubber met the road. Diplomacy alone wouldn't do what was needed to keep her country safe. To hell with her competencies in Far East languages. Her defenses kicked into high gear and she joined the CIA to fight the battle against terrorists in the Middle East.

She was acutely aware of what her resignation now meant. She was on her own. Technically, a lifeline existed, but it was razor thin. To boot, if the op went south, it was all but confirmed that *all* ties with her would be cut. She would go on the run, and survive below the radar for a while, but would likely end up dead by the hand of an assassin sent by her own government. This realization gave her pause, but she was reminded of what Thrasher told her after he sent in his papers without a thought.

"Are you fucking kidding me? Sign the damn papers! This is what you signed up for. Don't wuss out now."

It was a classic Thrasher reply, and while he wasn't wrong, his comments concerned her. This was an operation that could depend heavily on whether Lajani liked the people he was working with. To say that Thrasher had sharp elbows was an understatement. She needed to find a way to have him dial down his rhetoric.

She hit SEND and started packing.

Walsh followed through on her promise to post the $50 million into the Swiss bank account. Jenkins had wanted to avoid meeting with Walsh altogether and instead use one of her dark web hacker contacts to take the money out of her account as severance pay for almost getting her killed, but Delang talked her out of it. Taking the money was easy but ensuring that they followed Swiss privacy rules and using an account that couldn't be traced was not guaranteed. Her hacker contacts were good, but there was no such thing as leaving no trail at all. Someone in the intelligence field with the right set of skills and a modest amount of curiosity could poke around and identify the funny business going on behind the scenes. Besides, Walsh would tear the world apart to find her missing cash. It wouldn't take long for her to put two and two together once she saw Iran making the news again. Eliminating Walsh and stealing her entire fortune afterward was tempting, but Jenkins snapped herself out of such thoughts of retribution. That wasn't who she was. Delang was right. For this op to succeed, they couldn't afford to have their fingerprints on anything that could end up tying them back to it.

Her trip to Iran would be laborious and exhausting, but if she wanted to keep the agency clear of any allegations, it was necessary. After a layover in Los Angeles, she flew to Shanghai and took a cab to a Sheraton hotel along the Huangpu River, which was well-used by American tourists and had a picturesque view of Shanghai Tower.

Since the Chinese government kept close track of all visitors in and out of their country, especially Americans, Jenkins couldn't stay for a day and then hop on a plane to Iran. Because she was undercover, she needed to make it appear that she never left Shanghai for the duration of her mission. When she arrived at the hotel, after sweeping the room for bugs and closing the curtains, she was met that evening by friend, fellow agent, and master of disguise, Jessica Shannon, who had been selected to serve as Jenkins' body double in China for several reasons. Both ladies had a love of riding horses, were short in stature at just over five feet, and had jet black, straight hair. Shannon also had facial scars from a botched operation in Myanmar that were similar to Jenkins's. For Shannon, the assignment was like a vacation. She would stay in her fellow agent's hotel room and go about her touristy business. It would be like Jenkins, traveling as Angela Stapley, never left.

But before Jenkins could leave, Shannon needed to make her look like a Chinese national who was leaving to start a business in Iran. Restructuring her face, hiding the scars, and turning her from a busty forty-one-year-old white woman into a bearded Chinese man in his mid-thirties with a limp in his left leg took several hours, but Jenkins was more than pleased with the result.

"Here. Bottoms up," Shannon said.

She handed Jenkins a water glass filled with a disgusting purple liquid with white foam at the top. Jenkins cringed at the sight of it, but she knew what she had to do. She pinched her nose and tossed back the foul-tasting, syrupy fluid in two large gulps. Her shoulders shuddered as it went down her throat.

"Yuck!"

Female vocal cords are thinner and shorter than those of men. While there was nothing the CIA's Directorate of Science & Technology could do to about lengthening her vocal cords, they could certainly alter their thickness. The thinness of female vocal cords was one reason why female voices were generally higher pitched than men. The concoction she had swallowed coated her vocal cords with a temporary mucus that would dissolve within twenty-four hours. Jenkins and other operatives in the agency called it "liquid Lysol." It was nauseating as hell but always seemed to get the job done.

"You're not done yet."

Shannon tossed her a nasal spray bottle, which contained a liquid that would thicken her nasal cavities within seconds. It would feel like her nose was congested, but the combination of the spray and the drink would lower her voice enough octaves to make her sound more like the man she was pretending to be.

"Last thing. The team wanted me to give you this."

Shannon held up a small object between her thumb and forefinger.

"Finally," she said.

Two months ago, Jenkins went to the dentist with a toothache in one of her front teeth. Following a root canal on her lateral incisor, she needed a crown, which triggered an idea. The crown could be used as a bug. She came up with the idea of equipping it with Bluetooth technology and a microphone. Place it over a worn-down tooth, sync it up with a phone app, and no one would ever know that someone was listening on the other end.

The Science & Technology team got a kick out of the idea.

"So, it's a Bluetooth tooth?" one of them said, laughing.

Shannon tossed it to Jenkins. She examined it under the light of a nearby table lamp.

"It's even color matched to the rest of your teeth. But you have to take an antihistamine to dry your mouth out beforehand because the saliva can distort the clarity of the audio feed. R&D is working on perfecting it, but in the meantime it's probably best to keep the conversations short," Shannon said.

"How short?" Jenkins asked.

"Ten minutes. Fifteen tops."

"What's the range on the signal?"

"A mile and a half, max."

"Will it set off a metal detector?"

"When someone pats you down or waves a wand over you, do they ever check your mouth?"

"Not unless I'm going to prison."

"Yeah, don't go to prison. With some help, you can take it out if you need to. As long as the device isn't turned on, you'll be fine getting through airport security. We tested it in Yantian a few weeks ago, and it didn't raise any flags. Now, sit down and tilt your head back so I can remove your old crown and glue this sucker in."

After Shannon removed the original crown and inserted the new one, she gave her friend a goodbye hug, and Jenkins headed out. Thanks to Shannon's disguise efforts that now made her look like a Chinese man, the manager of the hotel chatted her up in the elevator in close proximity without noticing that she was actually the same woman he had personally served at the check-in desk. He even inquired about how he could get her in bed. It was an awkward conversation for Jenkins to talk about having sex with herself as a separate person, one that was not tested at The Farm, but she managed.

Confident in her newfound look and carrying a real passport that Shannon had altered from a Chinese source, the guard at the airport passed Jenkins through without a second look. This was also why she chose to enter Iran via China. Thanks to recent agreements between the two governments, Iran no longer required visas for Chinese entering their country.

After a long flight and another layover in Qatar, Jenkins finally landed at Isfahan International Airport. When she stepped outside, she saw a familiar, scowling face wearing the Arnette sunglasses he was never seen without, but this time he was sporting an unfamiliar, lengthy beard, and a Team Iran soccer cap as he leaned against a white van, waiting for her. Still disguised as a Chinese man, she extended her hand.

"Salam," Jenkins said.

Thrasher returned the handshake.

"Salam," he said.

When he slid open the backdoor, Jenkins saw someone hiding under a blanket. Thrasher took his normal surveillance precautions before driving and honked the horn like the other crazed Iranian drivers.

"Your flight was late. I was standing out in the fucking heat in this damned flannel shirt forever," Thrasher said.

Thrasher was referring to the fact that he had to wear long sleeves to hide the tattoos that covered both of his arms. Tattoos weren't illegal in Iran, but they were frowned upon as they were considered a sign of western influence, so he wanted to avoid any attention.

"Kurt Cobain called. He wants his shirt back," Jenkins said.

Thrasher glanced at her in the rearview mirror as she removed her wig and prosthetics.

"Jackie Chan's agent wants you to stop stalking his client."

"Charlton Heston wants you to trim your beard, Moses."

A giggle came from the rear of the van as Farhad appeared from under the blanket.

"Are you two always like this?" he asked.

"You know how he is. The only way to survive Thrasher's lovely personality is to give it back to him," said Jenkins.

Thrasher gave her the bird from the front seat.

"Hi, Farhad."

She leaned over the seat to give him a hug. Farhad was her most closely guarded and trusted source. Though she had corresponded with Farhad several times, either by phone or text, Jenkins hadn't seen him in person since he'd entered the U.S. Embassy in Ashgabat, Turkmenistan after helping rescue Tom Delang. Thrasher had filled her in on Farhad's efforts to locate the Pakistani soldier who was blamed for starting the India-Pakistani war and how he'd helped to sneak him over the border into U.S. custody. Jenkins didn't know if Farhad was a hugger or if such an expression was common for a woman to make to a man in Iran, but after learning that he'd taken a bullet on a mission to help one of her operatives, she felt that she owed him the heartfelt gesture.

"Hi, *Raven*," he said. "Why does your voice sound different?"

Raven was Jenkins's code name in the field. She thought about correcting him and asking him to call her Katherine, but she decided against it. On this operation, making the local assets feel comfortable was a priority.

After explaining that her voice would return to normal in a few hours, Jenkins noticed that Farhad was wearing his favorite Han Solo t-shirt, and that it was developing holes from repeated, excessive wear. She reached into her backpack and handed him a gift.

"Here, I brought something for you."

"What's this?"

"See for yourself."

Farhad unfolded a brand-new, black *Star Wars* t-shirt with the vintage franchise logo. His face lit up.

"Wow, thank you!"

"You're welcome. I couldn't let you wear your shirts into rags."

"Good God, man. How many of those things do you have?" Thrasher said.

"There's no such thing as too many, my friend."

Thrasher rolled his eyes. Jenkins wiped the sweat from her brow and turned to Thrasher.

"When's the last time it rained around here?"

"Hell, I can't remember. Too long. Maybe one day this damned country will figure out a way to generate rain using cloud seeding the way the UAE did a couple weeks ago."

"Using *what*?"

"Nothing. Something I saw on the news. I'll tell you later. Did you ever get the toy you asked for?"

Thrasher was intrigued by Jenkins's request for a specially made tooth. After removing her fake beard, Jenkins tapped the tooth with her fingernail.

"I'm wearing it now. We can test it when we have some downtime. Were you able to get the local business front up and running?"

"Yeah. It's a coffee and tea house in the Central District, not far from the Isfahan City Center. Donya calls it the Jupiter Café. It blends right in."

"Everyone that works there knows what they're doing? We don't need anyone from the Revolutionary Guard stopping in and getting curious."

"We'll be fine. Several of the PMOI family members have experience working the machines, and they will let us know if anyone odd comes in."

"And Donya? Where is she?"

"The space we rented has a large apartment above it," said Thrasher. "I finished sound proofing it the other day, but I still sweep it for bugs daily. She should be by later."

"Are we set for the meeting?"

Farhad paused.

"He said he'd be there tonight."

Jenkins noted his nervous reaction.

"Are you up for this, Farhad? Once we have this meeting, there's no going back."

"Iran has been ready for this for a long time."

"I'm not asking about Iran. I'm asking about you."

"Truthfully, I'm scared shitless."

"Good. You should be."

"Aren't you?"

Jenkins didn't answer.

Chapter Eight

Shir-Del was in a chipper mood but he dared not show it. Optimism wasn't a luxury he could afford. That was his mistake when he ascended to the throne of Supreme Leader only three months ago. He'd been too optimistic about his rule instead of motivating his subordinates to propel Iran into the future by intimidating them as his predecessors had done. It was a mistake he would be sure to never make again.

Inside the House of Leadership, Lajani, Avesta, and Nassiri waited patiently for him to arrive. Avesta had the look of a wilted flower and appeared heavier around his mid-section. This was not because of a gluttonous appetite after he emerged from being tortured. His torso was heavily bandaged due to the blisters that had not yet fully healed.

Nassiri sat across from Lajani but said nothing. He avoided eye contact with his superior, but his mind was filled with contempt. As far as he was concerned, Lajani had faked his way into his current position. The recent attack on Israel's Iron Dome was nothing more than a fireworks display. Any real leader who wanted to annihilate the Jews would've coordinated an attack from the inside and killed anyone that stood in his way.

Lajani was aware of Nassiri's feelings and only promoted him to be the head of the Basij at Avesta's insistence. Since the Supreme Leader tortured him, it was important to Avesta that every effort was made to eradicate the PMOI, and he needed a piranha to head the Basij and get it done. This wasn't an easy decision for Lajani. He needed another officer who was sympathetic to his coup plans and would not arrest Donya or any member of her team. But he also needed to keep Avesta in place so it would appear that he was working with him to do the Supreme Leader's bidding *and* because Avesta was a weakling who was key to his plans to overthrow the Ayatollah. Reluctantly, he promoted Nassiri to First Brigadier General. However, the fact that Nassiri's hometown of Khorramabad was the same city where the Supreme Leader earned his bones as a religious leader gave Lajani credibility as someone who was sympathetic to the Supreme Leader's agenda.

All three men stood as Shir-Del entered the room. As he sat at the head of the glass table, he kept his cane situated on his lap, and said nothing as his two aides served tea.

"Leave us," he told them.

When the door shut, Shir-Del jumped straight into business.

"Give me a status report."

Nassiri went to speak first, but Lajani cut him off.

"Supreme Leader, I have a gift for you."

"I'm in no mood to have my rear kissed, General."

Lajani reached into his pocket and pulled out a jar.

"Think of it as more of a spoil of war, Supreme Leader."

Lajani set the present in front of the Supreme Leader. Shir-Del held the jar up to the light and studied it. It appeared to be a piece of withered bark and grapes, floating in formaldehyde.

"Explain."

"Supreme Leader, those are what remains of the testicles of the mighty Farhad or "The Pirate of Iran," as he's been called. At President Avesta's insistence, one of our surveillance teams kept an eye on a building in eastern Tehran that was rumored to be used by the PMOI for drug distribution. Last night, the suspect was spotted entering the building. Less than an hour later, we breached it to apprehend him per your orders. Unfortunately, the coward was playing with methamphetamines and an explosion occurred before we could take him into custody.

He died on the scene, but I felt that you would want a reminder of your victory. So, I personally cut his balls off and preserved them as a trophy for you."

The expression on Shir-Del's face immediately brightened.

"Is this true, Vahid?"

Avesta was frozen stiff but couldn't show it. He hadn't given any such tip to Lajani, and he had no idea what he was talking about. Lajani was covering for him and trying to help him find redemption with the Supreme Leader.

"Yes, Supreme Leader."

Shir-Del looked back and forth at Avesta and Lajani. The slight smirk on his face indicated that he was pleased. Avesta had clearly understood his assignment. Though he had wanted Farhad alive, Lajani had the wherewithal to act and the viciousness to bring him a keepsake that he could place next to the skull of former General Rahim Shirazi in his personal library in Qom.

"Well done. Both of you."

Nassiri was less impressed. He hadn't heard of any explosions in eastern Tehran. And if there were, why didn't the Basij respond? And who was this surveillance team? Something didn't sound right, but he kept his mouth shut and made a mental note to check on it later.

"What about the rest of the PMOI?" Shir-Del asked.

Lajani sat back and deferred the answer to Nassiri. If he were lucky, Nassiri would hang himself by not having an answer that the Supreme Leader wanted to hear.

"We've rounded up more than a hundred members, Supreme Leader, and the search continues. However, the public is going to great lengths to conceal them," Nassiri said.

Lajani tried not to grin as he watched Shir-Del sip his tea. He knew that the Supreme Leader wasn't happy with the answer.

"I expected more," Shir-del said.

"Supreme Leader, our hunt continues. My men are working around the clock to squeeze every source they have for information."

Shir-Del put down his tea and stood with the assistance of his cane. "Come over here, General."

Nassiri did as he was instructed and stood at attention, five feet from Shir-Del, who flipped up his cane, grabbed it by the bottom, and wheeled it around like a baseball bat so the handle struck Nassiri across the side of his face. The General timbered over immediately, and held his hand against his jaw. As he waited for the stars to clear, he felt the brass, fritz handle from Shir-Del's cane lift his chin.

"I don't want excuses. I want results. The next time we speak, you'd better have some."

"Yes, Supreme Leader."

As Nassiri recovered, Shir-Del sat back down.

"Vahid, what measures are you taking?"

"Supreme Leader, I've signed an order that has been passed by the National Congress stating that anyone found hiding members of the PMOI will immediately be brought up on espionage charges and subject to a sentence of death. No lashings or prison time. There will still be a trial, but it essentially creates an express lane that guarantees an outcome in our favor. I've also ordered a reward of five thousand Euros to anyone who submits a tip that leads to the successful capture of a PMOI member."

"There are still hundreds of members out there and our country isn't exactly swimming in such funds at the moment. Where are you getting the money?"

"We've had to step up our human trafficking activity along the Iraqi border," Lajani said. "The funds will come from there."

"Is the initiative successful?"

"So far. It's resulted in a twenty percent increase in arrests," Avesta said.

Shir-Del nodded.

"General Lajani, what about our joint exercise with the Chinese?"

Avesta squinted, unsure what the Supreme Leader meant. Shir-Del was referring to the Chinese landing on Lark Island per their agreement. He had informed Avesta about the oil deal but intentionally wanted to keep him in the dark about the arrangement on the island.

Lajani nodded and tugged at the collar of his uniform twice. It was his way of saying that the Chinese soldiers had arrived and been given the Quds Force uniforms.

"The situation is developing nicely, Supreme Leader," Lajani said.

Shir-Del nodded.

"And there is no disruption to the oil flowing to the Chinese, President Avesta?"

"No, Supreme Leader. Basij soldiers are patrolling the oil fields to protect their interests."

"Very well. All of you continue your efforts. Now leave me. I need to pray."

Lajani held the door for Avesta and Nassiri, who he didn't bother to help off the floor.

As Avesta cringed at the bruise forming across Nassiri's face, it occurred to him that he and Nassiri had both endured the Supreme Leader's wrath.

This shared experience could be useful.

Chapter Nine

ISFAHAN, IRAN

The café was busy when Thrasher, Jenkins, and Farhad arrived. They used a side entrance that led to a stairwell hidden by a closet door marked "Electrical Room" that was only accessible via deadbolt lock. Thrasher handed Jenkins a spare key. Only he, Farhad, and Donya had copies.

When they reached the apartment upstairs, Jenkins wasn't impressed with their quarters. The apartment was less than a thousand square feet, had only one small bedroom that barely accommodated a twin-size bed, a bathroom that thankfully had a shower, and what could barely be called a kitchen with a range that had two working burners. There were two sagging couches that had seen better days and a twenty-seven-inch TV in the corner that was at least ten years old. The largest area was the dining room, with an oak table large enough to seat eight, which would serve as their operations center.

Jenkins gave Thrasher an uninspired look.

"*This* is the PMOI's base of operations?"

Thrasher rolled his eyes.

"The room at the Ritz was booked, okay? This is the best we could do on short notice. Besides, these guys have been a traveling circus ever since the Iraqis raided Camp Ashraf in 2011."

Camp Ashraf used to serve as PMOI headquarters in eastern Iraq. Despite their dogged history with the Iran-Iraq War, after Saddam Hussein was put to death, the Iranians and Iraqis made honest attempts to try and play nicer together. One agreement they signed was an extradition accord in which the Iranians leaned on the new Iraqi leadership to declare the PMOI to be a terrorist organization, which allowed Iraqi forces to blitz the camp. Hundreds of PMOI members were captured, tried, and sentenced to death by firing squad. Their bodies were hung outside the city's gates to warn the remaining PMOI leadership that thankfully escaped. Donya and her team had been on the run ever since.

When he inquired as to Donya's whereabouts, Farhad was told by Babak Abbasi, another PMOI team member and one of Donya's trusted lieutenants, that she'd left to assist some of the others to set up some VPN's in Shiraz but would be back later that night.

Internet usage in Iran was a tricky road to navigate for the government that wanted to prevent the spread of information as well as those fighting for it. It was controlled by the Supreme Council of Cyberspace. The Iranian president served as its head and the board included the director of the Ministry of Intelligence and chiefs of the Revolutionary Guard. Each year, the council spends between five and ten billion dollars on its National Information Network (NIN), which acts as the domestic information gatekeeper. It requires the use of Iranian email systems, blocks popular website services, inhibits encryption use by disabling VPNs, and bans any non-government official from using security software developed outside the country.

As the internet age was born in the mid-nineties, Shir-Del's predecessor had the vision to see its potential threat to the grip he had on Iranian culture. He recalled his personal friend, People's Republic of China (PRC) leader Deng Xiaoping, once telling him, "If you open a window, both fresh air and flies will blow in." That statement stayed with him. Concerned that the internet would destroy Ayatollah Khomeini's vision for Iran, he wasted no time reaching out to his Chinese friends for assistance. In exchange for an oil deal, China provided them technology derived from its Great Firewall, allowing the Ayatollah regime to regulate internet usage in Iran the same way China does inside its borders.

While Iranian citizens struggle to access information, the government has no issues acquiring outside help to prevent them from doing so. Three years ago, an Iranian intelligence agent working inside America bribed an executive from a San Jose technology firm into providing them with a copy of its content control software, SmartFilter. It has now become the primary engine for Iran's content control. When the firm was made aware of the breach, its teams began working tirelessly to update the software so it would render the stolen version obsolete, but the Iranians proved to be more skilled in program design than anticipated. Iranian Intelligence allegedly still has a viable spy network inside Silicon Valley that keeps Tehran informed of developments that allow them to keep up to speed.

Due to Shir-Del's increased relationship with China, Iran has gone a step further in its censorship. The Supreme Council of Cyberspace used speed throttling to frustrate internet users. It mandated that all internet providers restrict download and upload speeds for all residences and internet cafes.

This is where Donya and the PMOI came in. Thanks to Thrasher and Farhad, she was able to smuggle in Wi-Fi boosters from Europe. Coupled with her hacking skills and their recent inside man at the Revolutionary Guard, she was able to rewrite the programs to bypass the download speed laws, allowing Iran's citizens better access to outside information. The bad part was that increased speeds were becoming more temporary. The new head of the Basij had teams developing software that allowed them to pinpoint with better accuracy where download speeds were spiking, which made it easier to arrest Iranian freedom fighters. Lajani was working with Donya to find a way to sabotage the program, but in the meantime, Donya and her team spent their days and nights traveling all over the country, trying to install the boosters. This allowed them to create allies within Iran's borders that they could use to their advantage, but demand was more than they could handle, and they were having to get creative to avoid the Basij.

Given President Avesta's recent reward system for turning in PMOI members, it slowed down the process because now Donya had to better screen those requesting their assistance. Eleven of her most valued members had already been turned in because of this decree, so there was no doubt that the Basij was on to their operation. Donya's impatience was now in high gear and she was pushing Lajani to move up the coup's timetable.

Jenkins and Thrasher were hammering out some preliminary plans with Farhad when Donya returned at midnight. Though she was exhausted, Farhad proceeded with introductions.

"It's nice to finally meet you, Donya. I've heard nothing but good things from Farhad and Jay," Jenkins said.

The two women shook hands.

"Thank you. I'm very excited about your being here. What do I call you?"

"Lilly Rodgers."

It was strange for Jenkins to utter that name. For years, her main alias in the field had been Katherine Jennings, but since she was now officially divorced from the CIA, she couldn't use it because there was a chance it could be traced to the agency. Technically, Thrasher was in the same boat, but he'd been in country working with the PMOI for months. There was no sense in him altering his identity.

Donya smiled.

"At least your alias is better than his."

She looked to Thrasher.

"Jay Jacoby."

She used air quotes when reciting his cover name. Thrasher gave her a thumbs up, which meant something other than what it meant in most other countries. In Iran, it meant "up yours."

"So, how'd it go out there?" Farhad asked.

"Not bad. I made a half dozen more installations, but the roadblocks are getting worse."

"How'd you manage to get past them?"

"I started making the latest people we did installations for give me a ride to the next house. The old lady disguise that Jay helped me with worked perfectly, but I had to buy my way past the last checkpoint. Thanks for the last-minute loan."

Donya gave Farhad a flirty wink.

"Speaking of money, what's the situation there?"

"We can talk more about it later, but it's been secured," Jenkins said.

"Okay, good. I'm going to get some sleep. Will you wake me up when he arrives?"

"Sure thing," Farhad said.

Donya gave Farhad a cryptic smile as she closed the door to the next room. As Farhad pondered what brought on the look, Jenkins approached Thrasher.

"That was brief. I'm not exactly getting a warm and fuzzy feeling," she said.

"Cut her some slack. She's been working eighteen-hour days and only catnapping in between. Trust me, she's one of the good guys."

Jenkins nodded and turned to Farhad.

"What's next?"

"The only thing we can do. Wait."

Chapter Ten

"He's here."

Jenkins eyes popped open as Thrasher nudged her awake. It was just after 3 a.m. local time. She'd been asleep for less than two hours. After flattening out her clothes, she pulled her hair into a ponytail and looked in the mirror. She stared at her image and rolled her shoulders backward as she tried to put herself into the right frame of mind.

Game face on. First impressions are everything.

She grabbed her phone and activated the app that synched with her new Bluetooth tooth. Though she was no longer technically with the CIA, she wanted her first conversation with Lajani on the record. Plus, it was a good chance to take her new toy for a spin.

Tucking the Glock 9mm that Thrasher had gotten for her into her waistband, Jenkins emerged from the spare bedroom and saw Donya, Farhad, and Thrasher on their feet, looking toward the door. Thrasher held his gun at his side. It was obvious that he wasn't taking any chances with their invited guest. Farhad was at the doorway, holding the door open as heavy footsteps echoed up the stairwell. Just before Lajani entered, Jenkins leaned over to whisper in Thrasher's ear.

"Try and be nice, okay?"

Thrasher responded with a disapproving look but didn't say anything.

Jenkins was surprised by Lajani's height. She'd seen numerous photos of him and estimated that he was at least six-foot-three, but when he walked through the door dressed in his standard IRGC uniform, he was six foot even at best. His hooded eyes surveilled the room under his standard issue IRGC hat. He only looked at Jenkins briefly before he saw Thrasher approach.

Lajani's first meeting with Thrasher was a sullen one. Thrasher didn't shake his hand and never took his eyes off him. He couldn't even remember Thrasher blinking. Thrasher let Farhad do most of the talking, but when he did speak, it was in a harsh tone. Although Lajani had brought no weapon to the meeting, it was clear that Thrasher didn't trust his intentions. Not that he blamed him. On the surface, a CIA operative and the chief commander of the Iranian Revolutionary Guard had as much reason to meet as oil and water. All non-direct communication from Lajani went through Farhad.

The mood of the subsequent handful of meetings with Thrasher went marginally better each time, but Lajani remained as unsure about Thrasher as Thrasher was about him. He had no doubts about the operative's lethal capabilities, but his moodiness and consistently brash responses made him uncertain as to whether this was a man who could be trusted to keep his cool when needed, and to organize such a large-scale operation to help him rid Iran of the Grand Ayatollah.

"Mr. Jacoby," Lajani said, citing Thrasher's alias in the field.

Lajani politely extended his hand, but Thrasher did not reciprocate.

"You know the deal. Arms up," Thrasher said.

Lajani thought about criticizing Thrasher for his lack of manners but decided against it. It was no time to ruin the mood. For the mission to be successful, the CIA's help was paramount. He was hoping that Thrasher's female counterpart was more level-headed.

This guy has about as much personality as a cardboard box.

Lajani nodded and did as he was instructed. Thrasher removed the Browning HP 9mm from the man's belt as well as a Walther PPK .380 ACP from his ankle. To Jenkins's surprise, Thrasher only removed the chamber bullets and magazines before handing the weapons back to Lajani. Doing so was highly irregular, but Jenkins knew that it was Thrasher's way of showing good faith. He glanced at Jenkins.

Nice enough?

Lajani hiked his eyebrows. He was surprised to be given his guns back. Once finished patting him down, Thrasher turned to Jenkins and nodded.

Showtime.

Jenkins stepped forward and extended her hand.

"General Lajani, my name is Lilly Rodgers."

She noted that his greying beard was thicker up close than it was from a distance, and he had many small skin tags scattered around his neck. Lajani loomed over her but was captivated by her confident brown eyes as he returned the firm handshake.

"You're CIA?"

"No, sir. The CIA isn't in Iran, but I am here to assist you with your request. We have much to discuss. Please have a seat."

Confused by the "CIA isn't in Iran" comment, Lajani gave Farhad a sideways look. Farhad made a "simmer down" motion with his hand. Once everyone was seated, Lajani kept his palms flat on the table and waited until Jenkins decided to break the ice.

"General, would you like to start with an update?"

Lajani nodded, then looked directly at Farhad.

"You're dead," he said.

Thrasher, who was sitting directly across from the general, pulled his weapon out from beneath the table, and pointed it at him.

"Wait, Jay, that's not what he meant," Farhad said.

Thrasher lowered his weapon.

"My apologies. Poor choice of words. Farhad has been gaining quite a bit of attention from the Supreme Leader and President Avesta. I needed a victory to put them at ease, so I faked his death."

Thrasher looked at Farhad.

"You knew?"

"Yes."

"You might have mentioned this to us. It could complicate things."

"Not at all," Lajani said, "Farhad told me about your clever idea of making him a legend. I told Farhad to make a series of videos of motivational speeches supporting rebellion against the Grand Ayatollah and evidence of government suppression, but he did it with dated newspapers and old news broadcasts in the background. We can continue to release them as we please, but the government will think they were made weeks ago."

Thrasher looked to Jenkins who gave him an approving look.

Smart.

"What can we do to help you?" Jenkins said.

"First, tell me what you mean by the CIA not being in Iran."

Jenkins leaned forward. She knew this was going to be a sticking point.

"General, I don't think I need to remind you of the affect that the CIA-led coup in 1953 had on your country. There is no desire in Washington to have any American ties to your plans. Jay and I have officially quit the CIA. That said, we have access to every resource we need to help you accomplish your goal."

Lajani leaned back in his chair and looked at Farhad.

"This is not what we discussed," he said.

Before Farhad could speak, Jenkins responded.

"It's the way it has to be, General. For this to work, Iranian freedom must break through the Supreme Leader's walls from the inside, not the outside. Otherwise, it will never be recognized as legitimate."

Lajani tapped his fingers on the table before finally nodding.

"How much money were you able to secure?"

"Fifty million," said Jenkins.

"That should work nicely," he said.

"I hope so," Donya said.

"Tell me about your plan, General," Jenkins said.

Over the next hour, Lajani went over the details of his master plan. While he assured Jenkins that his commanders of the Ground Forces, Navy, Aerospace Force, and Quds Force were loyal to him, they would have to be paid sizably for their treasonous efforts plus additional funds to buy the loyalties of the lower-level soldiers in each of the Revolutionary Guard's five branches.

"The key to Iran's future is its past. There are five main areas of Iran that are essential to control if the coup is to be successful: Isfahan, Mashhad, Shiraz, Tehran, and Qom," he said.

Isfahan's history dates back to the Bronze Age and still retains artifacts connected to much of the country's glory during the Persian Empire. Once the internet is freed up, images of revolutionary freedom and a celebration at Naqsh-e Jahan Square and the Fire Temple will do wonders amongst the locals. Mashhad's history is equally important. It is home to the shrine of the eighth Shi'a Imam as well as Harun al-Rashid, who was the fifth caliph to succeed the Prophet Muhammad. Many have dubbed it the spiritual center of Iran. The problem is that Mashhad literally meant 'place of 'martyrdom'."

"What if the coup results in widespread bloodshed due to martyrdom?" Jenkins asked.

"Hopefully, a military presence there will assure them that we're still in control and that won't occur," he said.

Jenkins's eyes met Thrasher's. She didn't like hearing that hope was a strategy.

Shiraz was special because it is the country's artistic center and home to many of Iran's poets and literary writers. Their creativity and diversity would be key in implementing long-term change, so it was essential to have the community on their side. Lajani went on to say that he had been able to smuggle two hundred PMOI members into the country from Turkey, and had them establish residence in Shiraz, which energized the locals who oppose the Supreme Leader.

"As a bonus, the city is also home to large Jewish and Christian communities. I don't know what role this will play, if any, but I believe it will help the cause more than hurt it."

"What about Tehran and Qom?" Thrasher asked.

Farhad chimed in.

"Tehran is obvious. It's the country's most populated and its capital city. Once the news that the Supreme Leader is gone has spread, the new government under the General's rule will reopen trade with other countries that previously backed economic sanctions against Iran. This will allow us to live the freer lifestyle we've long desired. But with the Revolutionary Guard Ground Forces controlling the city, the trick is going to be ensuring that they are in place to help and not there to suppress our newfound freedoms."

"Qom is going to be the biggest problem," said Donya. "While Mashhad is the spiritual center of Iran, Qom is unquestionably its religious capital. It's home to most members of the Guardian Council, its most fanatical clerics, and the university that spreads the altered versions of Islam like a virus. General, I'm sure that you know this, but heavy military presence is going be required in order to keep that city stable."

"My men will arrest as many of the city's known radical clerics to keep them from inciting violence, but I'm afraid looting, riots, and martyrdom will be unavoidable."

"What will you do with them?" said Jenkins. "The radical clerics, I mean. You're not going to start your new rule with executions, are you? We can't condone that."

"I've kept files on many of them. They will come before a military tribunal."

"But they're not military soldiers."

"They are in a religious war," Lajani snapped.

"What about the Basij and Nassiri?"

"I'm working on that. I've got an idea, but I can't tell anyone about it yet."

Thrasher and Jenkins looked at each other again.

"What about the responses from Hezbollah and Hamas? Once word of the coup reaches them, they're not going to be happy," Jenkins said.

Lajani nodded.

"I know, but I can't control everything. What I can tell you is that we will cut off their funding and supply chains. Crushing them will require assistance from other governments."

"And the internet?" Donya asked.

"Once Avesta and the Supreme Leader are out of the way, I'll remove all restrictions that the Supreme Council of Cyberspace put into place so you can do everything you need."

Thrasher tried to hide a smirk. The Supreme Council of Cyberspace may be real in Iran, but to him, it sounded like a group from *Spaceballs*. He looked at Jenkins.

"What do you think?"

"It's one hell of an uphill battle," she said. "It's got maybe a thirty percent chance of working. General, how confident are you that the people of Iran will respond favorably to this? We can't have a situation like we had in Iraq fifteen years ago where we expect people to be dancing in the streets only to find that we've kicked the hornet's nest."

"Iraq was a failure because westerners made assumptions about an Islamic culture that they didn't understand and tried to put into place hand-selected leaders that hadn't been part of the country in decades. With Iran, these people know me. Our own Revolutionary Guard will be in control, and we will continue to covet Sharia Law. I *will not* overhaul the country. I want it to operate the way that it wants to without trade restrictions and without starting wars with Israel or anyone else in the west. It's time for the Iranian people to get behind the wheel of their own destiny, a peaceful destiny."

His words were exactly what Jenkins wanted to hear, but there was still one hurdle to jump, the one President Cannon specifically warned her about.

"If this fails, the Supreme Leader will only become stronger. Are you prepared to do *whatever* needs to be done to help it succeed? I hate to sound cliché, but failure isn't an option."

"Iran deserves nothing but my best efforts. You have my assurances that I will do everything in my power to reach the end goal."

Jenkins glanced over at Thrasher, as if to say, "it's your call." After he nodded, she stood up and approached Lajani. He rose from his chair, too, and they stood in front of one another.

"It looks like we are in this together, General."

Jenkins extended her hand once again. The two stared each other down as they shook hands. It was a defining moment, one that they both knew had to succeed.

"Give Farhad the account details," Jenkins said. "I'll send you ten million today."

Chapter Eleven

BETHESDA, MARYLAND

Tom Delang found himself in uncomfortable, new territory. He'd joined the agency in his early thirties after working in the Middle East as a salesman for a prestigious communications company. Thanks to that experience and his extensive contacts, CIA leadership saw to it that Delang was put into the field right away. Until his kidnapping, he had served his country and the agency loyally for twenty years and had become the most reliable operative in the region, a position that seemed to fit him like an old pair of shoes.

During this time, he always had to deal with cables and updated intelligence reports from headquarters. There was no getting around it. Any field operative would be stupid to blatantly ignore the intel that he or she was being sent, but the cables from the home office always came with several thick layers of bullshit that no one in the field wanted to deal with. These daily cables were often referred to as "The 10,000 Mile Screwdriver" because they were headquarters' way of putting the crank to operatives in the field or second guessing their decisions from behind the comfort of an armchair on the other side of the globe.

Delang had a natural ability to determine what intel was real and what was an attempt to micromanage his operations. He also had the luxury of having the local station chief act as a buffer between him and headquarters, so that he didn't have to deal with any unsolicited opinions from those on the outside that weren't helpful.

His new, unofficial role turned his old one inside out. Rather than being the operative on the inside looking out, he was now an outsider looking in. Serving as the conduit between his friends in Iran and the

Director of the CIA, and by extension the president, Delang had to confront bureaucratic oversight that he tried so actively to previously avoid. Not only did he now feel the weight that went into "The 10,000 Mile Screwdriver" cables, but now he was the one holding the tool.

Having been on the opposite side, Delang made a conscious effort to keep his cables as lean as possible. Thankfully, Jenkins and Thrasher always welcomed his feedback. They trusted him implicitly, but Delang knew that this wasn't his operation. It was theirs, and he had to trust them to make the right decisions in the field. On the other hand, this operation was too important for any type of trial and error. *Every* decision had to be correct, and because of the overwhelming political effects, oversight was essential. Delang technically had veto power over Jenkins and Thrasher's decisions, granted to him by Wallace, but from six thousand miles away, he knew that it ultimately carried little weight. It was a tight line for him to walk, and he loathed not being on the ground with them.

When Jenkins initially contacted him about being the unofficial conduit between her team and Wallace at the personal request of the president, Delang was ecstatic about the opportunity. It gave him a chance to get back in the spy game, and potentially be a part of a successful regime change in Iran. That could mean a better peace in the Middle East without making the same mistakes that the agency made during its original coup of Mohammed Mossadegh in 1953.

Delang never had second thoughts about helping, but he felt a hidden storm brewing if the mission failed. Though he never specifically asked Jenkins, Delang was aware that if that happened, Director Wallace would be barbecued in public, ridiculed in private, forced to resign, and could potentially face charges in international court for his attempts at another coup, for which he would be forced to take sole responsibility. Jenkins and Thrasher would be targeted for assassination by colleagues who would pull the trigger on them as if they'd never met them. It would all be for the sake of the directive they were given, but Delang knew the other agency personnel would have their work cut out for them.

Jenkins and Thrasher wouldn't be taken out easily. While Jenkins was a more than capable agent, Delang knew that she didn't have the natural brutal and predatory instincts required to shoot first and ask questions later when the full power of the agency came after her. Thrasher's rabid instincts would instantly kick into high gear. Delang could practically visualize him going on offense and starting his own private war against the agency before he would allow them to put him down like Old Yeller.

Delang knew his fate would be similar, and since he lived in the States, his death would be easier to pull off. Since being kidnapped, for fear of the Iranians coming for him to finish the job they started, Delang routinely checked his cars for bombs or any other tampering. He had his house regularly swept for bugs and remained on high alert when he was out in public. Once the agency placed a target on his back, it was just a matter of time before they got to him. All it would take is a car running a stop sign at the right angle, a crash on I-95 that would be made to look like an accident, or a shooting that would appear like a mugging.

There were a thousand scenarios in the CIA's arsenal that could be used to kill him. Delang had no choice but to make peace with that. The most difficult part would be keeping the operation from his wife, Abby. After he had returned home from his kidnapping, he had sworn to her that there would be no more secrets. But his op was totally off the books, and he had no choice. In that moment, Delang knew how Michael Corleone felt in *The Godfather Part III.*

Just when I thought I was out, they pull me back in.

If the mission failed, his fate would be sealed. Delang took solace in the fact that Abby would be financially taken care of after his death.

Before he signed the publishing contract for his memoir, detailing his captivity in Iran, Delang had a clause added that if he died under mysterious circumstances, the publisher and his agent would claim that the Iranians came back for him and finished the job. This would undoubtedly cause sales to skyrocket, allowing Abby to live comfortably for the rest of her life. In order to prevent that from happening, Delang was left with only one choice: ensure that the mission succeeded.

He hadn't yet sold their home in Bethesda, Maryland. Abby was an impressive bookkeeper and nagged him about it because keeping up the mortgage on a house they weren't using was wasteful, but he couldn't bring himself to do it. It was the only material possession he still had that was attached to his time as the CIA's most valued operative in the Middle East. Thankfully, the sentimentality he felt for his old home came in handy once he received the call from Jenkins.

He had initially told Abby that some of his retired agency friends who had gone to work for the Atlantic Council, a think tank on international affairs in Washington, D.C., needed his insight for a project. When Abby asked how long it would take, Delang said he didn't know, but he suggested she make the drive to Bethesda in a few weeks so they could be together. His plan was to then tell her about his new position as a conduit for the Iranian operation, which the director dubbed *Operation Exodus*. Telling his wife would violate explicit instructions from the president and Director Wallace. Although Abby knew where he had worked and what he did, she was smart enough to never inquire about his "time away," as she called it, but this time was different. Though she would undoubtedly freak out after being told, it was a reality Delang would have to accept. He made her a promise, and he intended to keep it.

After the seven-hour drive from their new home in Murrell's Inlet, South Carolina, Delang was delighted to see his fortress. After entering a pass code on the keypad, the reinforced steel gate would not release without a palm print and retinal scan, which he had installed after he returned from Iran. Abby had been concerned about their safety and made him reinstall all the doors so that they swung outward instead of inward to prevent them from being kicked open. After locking all the double deadbolts, he went upstairs to his private office, which Abby called "The Delang Dungeon." It was sound proofed and had bulletproof windows that could be frosted for privacy by remote. He promptly checked the monitors to ensure that all six of the external security cameras were still working. Once he had successfully locked himself in, Delang wasted no time getting to work.

One problem he immediately encountered was managing the eight-and-a-half hour time difference between Washington and Tehran. It was essential that he work the same hours as Jenkins and Thrasher because he couldn't afford to miss any intel. He also had to balance the needs of Director Wallace, who was on east coast time. All he could do was catnap in between. Keeping information flowing between both sides was tough enough but keeping it straight in his head on minimal sleep was exhausting.

Since Wallace lived less than ten miles away, he and Delang agreed that he would stop by daily on his way home for updates. The time difference meant that Jenkins and Thrasher were probably still asleep and information that needed to be passed on to them would be available during their morning coffee. Thankfully, Wallace always brought fast food with him when he visited. He knew it was Delang's guilty pleasure, and it gave the director a chance to hide his unhealthy diet from his wife, who was pushing him to eat better. After making small talk over their McDonald's feast, Wallace noted that it was time for the veteran agent to give him the latest updates on the Iran operation.

"I think you and I would've loved to have been a fly on the wall last night," Delang said.

"Do tell."

Delang gave Wallace the rundown about the meeting that transpired the night before between Lajani and the team. Wallace couldn't help but grin and shake his head. In his position, he was rarely provided with good news, and he could barely believe his luck at having Lajani be the inside man to overthrow the Supreme Leader.

Wallace's excitement became evident to Delang when he gave him what he thought was a lengthy list of responses that he wanted from Jenkins, which he would later wean down, including pushing Lajani on his plans to control the cities once the Supreme Leader was ousted. He didn't want post-Ayatollah Iran to look like post-Saddam Iraq.

Afterward, the two headed downstairs for a drink. Delang poured three fingers of Clover bourbon whiskey on the rocks into two high ball glasses. Wallace didn't hesitate to down his first drink in a single gulp. It was obvious to Delang that Wallace was facing pressure on this mission. He quickly slid his glass back over the counter to Delang for a refill. When Delang poured the second drink, Wallace took a small sip.

"Totally off the record, do you trust him?" he said.

"Lajani? It's hard to say. Personally, I think we have one chance in three of being able to pull this off. That said, the fact that he came to us is encouraging. My gut feeling is that he's legit. He's the ultimate insider, and without the Revolutionary Guard, we can't pull off this operation. But, with the Iranians, you never really know."

"You think Thrasher can do this?"

"Of course. Don't you?"

"It's less about effectiveness than him being able to nurture the relationships to get this done. He's an excellent field operative, my best in fact, and his brain continues to impress me. His ability to come up with quick, creative solutions in short order is mind-boggling."

"So, what's the problem?"

"He makes it hard to defend him because his brain and his mouth are rarely in the same place at the same time. This mission requires a finesse that he wasn't born with. His knee jerk reactions often make him a loose cannon, and I usually end up doing damage control. You've spent time with him. You know what I'm talking about. But there will be no opportunities for second chances or damage control on this op. It's all or nothing, and I feel like I've given the responsibility to a man that routinely carries matches into a situation that can only be compared to parting a Red Sea full of gasoline."

"I see your point. Just keep in mind that Beth is at his side. She has the diplomatic personality you need, and she'll keep him in line. This won't work if we can't trust them to do their jobs. Plus, it's always good to have a wild card in the mix. It keeps everyone on their toes."

"Hmm. I guess that depends on if the wild card and the joker are one and the same."

Delang narrowed his eyes at the remark.

"Are you talking about Thrasher or Lajani?"

"Both, actually. What if there are two wild cards in this deck?"

"Then, I guess jokers are wild."

"That's what I'm afraid of."

"But there's one thing to remember."

"What's that?"

"In this case, we have the cards marked."

Chapter Twelve

TEHRAN, IRAN
PRESIDENTIAL ADMINISTRATION BUILDING

Avesta was sitting at his desk, trying to work out his thoughts on paper while he waited for Nassiri to arrive. Using Nassiri to help him get back into the Supreme Leader's good graces would be tricky, but he needed an ally outside of Lajani. It was apparent that Lajani had too much influence with the Supreme Leader. After the way Lajani helped him in the latest meeting, it seemed he would continue to help him, but leaning on him for further assistance would make him appear weaker than he already was. Avesta couldn't risk Lajani whispering to the Ayatollah that he needed to be replaced.

He needed a partner to work hand in hand in a mutually beneficial relationship. Since Nassiri had also experienced the Supreme Leader's wrath, Avesta believed they could successfully join forces on an issue that would keep the Ayatollah's enemies at bay. By accomplishing this without any orders, they could both regain the Supreme Leader's respect.

Win-win.

Overnight, Avesta brainstormed on what the potential impact would be and how he would produce it. Lajani had already scored a major political victory by ensuring that the "legendary" Farhad was dead, so he needed to come up with an idea that would also help Nassiri shine. Despite his pondering, he came up with nothing. All he could do was pray for assistance.

His longtime assistant, Saeed, knocked on the door and entered.

"Mr. President, General Nassiri is here to see you."

"Please show him in, Saeed."

The right side of Nassiri's face was swollen and badly bruised from the Supreme Leader's cane strike, but at six-foot-two and stocky, he was still an imposing man. He barely offered a greeting and was clearly in a foul mood as he sat in the captain's chair across from the presidential desk.

"How's your face feeling?" Avesta asked.

"Sore. A tooth got knocked out, but thankfully, my jaw isn't broken."

"Good to hear."

"What did you want to see me about?"

"We're both in the doghouse with the Supreme Leader, but I think we can help each other. With the Farhad person dead. . ."

"I don't think he's dead," Nassiri interrupted.

"Wait, what?"

"I'm not buying Lajani's story about the incident at the drug house in eastern Tehran."

Avesta paused. As far as Nassiri knew, Avesta and Lajani had been working together. If Nassiri was right, and Farhad was still alive, it put Avesta in a precarious spot. On one hand, he could actually capture Farhad or someone like him, and score points with the Supreme Leader. On the other hand, Farhad being among the living meant that he had failed Shir-Del once again. He had been wondering why Lajani had covered for him in the meeting by telling the Supreme Leader that he was part of the drug house raid. He wasn't covering for him at all. He was backing Avesta into a corner by pointing to faulty intelligence that Lajani said he had provided, but didn't. However, he couldn't admit to Nassiri that he had been outmaneuvered.

Lajani's savvier than I thought.

"What makes you say that?"

"His reporting matches, but something doesn't add up. I can smell it. I have my cousin, Lieutenant Colonel Vaziri, checking a few things for me."

Rather than dig deeper into the story, Avesta decided to deflect by tapping into Nassiri's emotions.

"What is it between you and Lajani? Why do you hate him so much?"

Avesta noticed Nassiri's demeanor immediately change.

"That's none of your business, Mr. President."

"Please, General, call me Vahid. You can share with me. What you say to me here stays in this office."

"Sorry, rule number one in my book is to never trust a politician."

Avesta nodded.

Smart man.

"What about trusting a friend?"

"When did we become friends?"

"As of right now. I need to lean on you for your help and you need to lean on me for mine. That's what friends do for each other."

After a moment of squinting his eyes at him as he chewed his lip, Nassiri nodded. Avesta tried to contain his smile by rubbing his forefinger back and forth on his lips.

Checkmate.

"I'm not going into too much detail, but I think Lajani is a paper tiger. This country needs to be led with ruthless aggression by the Revolutionary Guard. He may have promoted me through the years, but he did it with bullshit assignments, and has always kept me under his thumb. I've grown tired of the glass ceiling he's placed above me."

Interesting.

"I can understand that. I think I have an idea to break that glass ceiling."

"Tell me."

"Have you received any recent information from the Ministry of Intelligence regarding the PMOI members? I'm specifically interested in their leader, Donya Karimi."

"You're in luck. Last night, the Minister of Intelligence called me with some credible information, and I asked him to keep it between us for twenty-four hours."

A quiet relief washed over Avesta. Allah *was* listening to his prayers.

"This miserable whore has been going around the country for months, helping people with their internet speeds, and she keeps slipping through our fingers. I don't know how, but she's well-funded, and she's getting help. Our analysts were able to intercept multiple phone calls from a handful of clients that wanted her help. I have my team running their addresses now."

"Can I see the list?"

Nassiri pulled his phone from his belt, flipped to the message, and handed it to Avesta. The sight of one name made the president's eyes pop.

"This one. Hadi Zare. I know him. He's friends with my son. I'll tell him that I know what he's up to and threaten him with a sentence at Evin Prison. He'll set up a time to meet this girl. How soon can you mobilize your men?"

"I have some waiting on standby."

"Good. Get going."

"Just so you know, this isn't a capture mission. I'm going to behead this bitch myself."

"I'm counting on it."

Across town in his office at Revolutionary Guard headquarters, Lajani ripped off his headset and dialed Donya's burner cell phone. He listened to the continuous ring, begging her to pick up, but there was no answer. Left with no other choice, he knew who to call next.

"What is it?" Thrasher said.

"You need to find Donya. Now."

Chapter Thirteen

SHANGHAI, CHINA

Fang Xin had been in China's Ministry of State Security (MSS) for just a year when he came to the Minister's attention after he stumbled onto an American spy network operating in Shanghai. Six months after coming onboard, he was assigned to the United States desk, and had the remedial job of keeping track of Americans entering the country. The MSS wanted to ensure that any American visiting was not associated with a U.S. intelligence agency. It was a thankless job for minimal pay that involved reviewing spreadsheets for days at a time, but it kept him employed and fed.

Last fall, the MSS scored a major cyber espionage victory over the U.S. when its hackers breached the security servers of several credit card companies. In order to protect their clients, the companies initiated a patch that closed the digital back door to the Chinese servers within a day, but the damage was done. Xin had all the information he needed. He cross-checked the credit card data with the rewards points used by Americans who registered as passengers with the three major state-owned airlines: Air China, China Southern Airlines, and China Eastern Airlines. Unfortunately, he found nothing. If CIA agents were sneaking into the country, they were smart enough not to use their real names to rack up rewards points.

Playing a hunch, he asked the cyber analysts to see if they could hack into the servers for the companies that distributed the rewards. Within a week, they had enough raw data to keep them occupied until the next Chinese New Year. Fortunately, Xin knew which rocks to look under. He compared the rewards data with the shipping addresses used to send the rewards and found dozens of discrepancies. The names on the shipping labels didn't match those on the credit cards used to book the flights, which garnered the rewards points. When he reached out to his agents in America, they tracked down the addresses, stole the mail from their mailboxes, and reported back to Xin with the names listed on their utilities bills. As expected, they matched the shipping labels. The American agents had found a way to access the rewards points they had racked up via their government positions after all and were using them to treat themselves.

Noting that four of the Americans listed were still in-country, Xin got permission from his bosses to set up a surveillance team. If they were spies, three of the Americans were exceptional at their tradecraft, and were able to either evade their surveillance or conduct their operations in a way that was unknown to the MSS.

One American, however, was much looser with his skillset. Xin and his team tracked the American to the home of a State Council official, Jie Tang. Upon bugging Tang's home, they found that he was accepting bribes from the Americans in exchange for the names of MSS agents operating in Hong Kong. The Americans had flipped the Hong Kong agents and were using them to fly into North Korea to perform surveillance on specific officials they thought they could flip. Due to the close relationship between China and the North Koreans, MSS agents moved in and out of the country with relative ease.

Xin reported back to his superiors who acted swiftly and with considerable force. Tang was arrested, tried, and executed for his treason. The American spy was captured and shot within the hour. The other Americans on Xin's list were arrested and incarcerated in the notorious Tilanqiao Prison in Shanghai, which had earned the nickname "The Alcatraz of the Orient." The U.S. State Department was still working on their return. For his hard work, Xin was promoted to the lead analyst monitoring the United States, but he maintained the responsibility of checking on Americans in the country who he deemed suspicious.

One American had come to his attention three days ago. Since all Chinese citizens are soldiers of the state, this enabled the MSS to have ears everywhere. A manager at the Sheraton Hotel along the Huangpu River in Shanghai was particularly enamored with the breast size of one of the American guests. Since his English was excellent, he intended to ask her out on a date, but when he walked down the hallway of her floor the next morning, he noticed a local man with a limp emerging from her room. Disappointed, but not deterred, the manager got on the elevator with the man and engaged him in conversation, attempting to get details about what he assumed was a night of passion with the busty American woman. The man was pleasant but said that nothing happened because the woman was a workaholic whose legs couldn't be loosened by a crowbar, let alone a few drinks. Discouraged, the manager accepted the information, and didn't bother to knock on the woman's door.

When he saw her two days later, the manager noticed that one of the scars on her face looked less curvy than it did two days earlier. It seemed like nothing but having witnessed his own employees being arrested by state officials for not reporting suspicious activity, he reported the guest to the MSS and the case was assigned to Xin.

In the morning, he met the manager as he was leaving to go home. He told Xin that the American woman had left an hour ago. Unsure of when she would return, Xin could either wait for her to return and begin his surveillance or he could search her hotel room and risk getting caught. Mulling over his choices, he went with option B, and the manager gave him the key.

The room was a mess. Xin tripped over dirty clothes and towels scattered on the floor. The bathroom was full of so many bottles of perfume, canisters of hair spray, skin cream containers, and make-up utensils that it looked like an Avon hurricane had hit it. But something seemed odd about the French perfume. The bottles were on their side. Surely a woman with such fine taste would take better care of such expensive products. Xin thought the bottles had been placed that way on purpose, so that the American could check if they were in the same position when she returned. This was a classic tradecraft move, which aroused Xin's suspicions.

He turned his head when he heard the door open. The American had come back earlier than he expected. He slowly drew his pistol from his waistband, screwed in the silencer, and lowered himself against the wall to avoid being seen in the mirror. As he listened to her footsteps, Xin worried when she stopped moving.

Did she notice the clothes on the floor were disturbed?

His thought was interrupted by a bullet piercing the drywall above his head. Xin instinctively fired two blind shots from behind the bathroom door to buy himself some time. The American fired twice more. Luckily for Xin, the bullets hit the vanity cabinet. He stood up and fired three more shots that sprayed across the wall as Jessica Shannon dove over the bed.

The third bullet hit her in the torso. Xin heard her scream in pain. With his enemy wounded, Xin grabbed one of the bottles of perfume and emerged from the bathroom and slowly approached his target. He could hear her breathing heavily as she assessed her wound. When she reached over the side of the bed to fire her next shot, Xin tossed the bottle of perfume at her and fired a shot of his own. The bullet shattered the bottle, sending glass fragments and jasmine liquid hurtling toward the woman. Shielding herself with her other arm, she stumbled to the door. Shannon got off another errant shot, but Xin's next shot hit her in the back. She instantly dropped to the floor, face first.

Xin approached with caution. He kicked her gun away and flipped her over with his foot. Blood was dripping from her mouth as she attempted to speak. Xin noticed a prosthetic scar hanging off her face that extended from a real scar. He ripped it off and showed it to her.

"Who do you work for?"

"Post office," Shannon whispered in Chinese, smiling.

Xin threw the fake scar at her. He started to question her further, but more blood began gushing from her mouth. The bullet had hit her in the left side of her back. He knew it had punctured her lung, but it might have gone through the rib cage and hit her heart. Knowing that she wasn't going to make it, Xin stomped on her throat with the heel of his boot until her larynx was crushed and she couldn't breathe.

Before phoning in the incident to his bosses, who would call in a crew to collect the body and clean the scene, Xin continued searching the room. Inside her suitcase, he found a hidden compartment with a magnifying glass, art pens, and clear plastic stickers that he knew were used to create fake passports.

CIA.

Since he knew that the woman he had just killed was not the same one who had entered the country, he assumed that the one on the floor was her disguise expert. He also found a picture of a bearded Chinese man in his mid-thirties, which had to have been used on a real Chinese passport to exit the country. He didn't know why the woman on the floor hadn't yet destroyed the photo, but he was thankful she hadn't.

He snapped a picture of the photo and sent it to his contact at the General Administration of Customs and asked him to run it through their database for a match. By the time the cleanup crew finished, his friend texted him back. A passport with a picture that matched the one that Xin sent him had recently been used to board a plane out of the country. Xin compared the new picture with the old one and saw that it was a close match, but the eyes on the new photo looked feminine to him whereas the eyes on the original were definitely male. When he asked the passenger's destination, he received an unexpected reply.

Isfahan, Iran.

Chapter Fourteen

YASUJ, IRAN

Riding through the Susian Gate in Yasuj, one can feel the history of Alexander the Great and his armies doing the same on their way to pillaging Persia more than twenty centuries ago. Known for its markets of textiles, carpets, and pottery, Yasuj had recently become popular among locals and tourists for its Museum of Archaeology. In a country where it was unwise to even utter the name of Alexander the Great, the city's museum managed to sidestep this issue by placing coins, pottery, and statues from the Bronze Age on display. It even contained evidence from the first human inhabitants in Iran.

Donya loved traveling there because she always made time to stop and sit next to the numerous streams running through the stone valleys where she could enjoy the beauty of the waterfalls that many wouldn't expect to see in Iran.

When she got a call from a friend of a friend who said that they worked at the museum and needed assistance to boost its internet download speeds so that the archaeologists could better perform their duties, she jumped at the chance. She took the normal precautions of screening her new customer by having some of the other PMOI members travel to Yasuj a day ahead to ask around about him. With no red flags, Donya jumped in her van and made the five-hour ride south of Isfahan on the carefully planned route that Farhad had given her. Thankfully, there were no IRGC roadblocks along the way.

The museum sat in the center of what would be called "downtown" by westerners, but was surrounded by locally owned grocery stores, basket and carpet vendors, and spice merchants. Sitting in her van, she patiently scoped out the area. It was a busy day on the street, which was a good sign for her. She should be able to walk about without drawing attention. For the sake of her own safety, Donya slumped down in her van and observed the square for a half hour. Unfortunately, the area surrounding Yasuj was also filled with several military bases. Revolutionary Guardsmen were known to patrol the street, looking for excuses to make trouble for women who weren't covering enough skin.

Satisfied that the coast was clear, Donya put the necessary gear in her rugged backpack and walked toward the museum, sure to keep her head down. As she passed the shops, the hypnotic aromas of mint and cilantro from the restaurants filled the air. She smiled, knowing that she would have to stop at one of them for some lamb kabobs after she was finished with her duties at the museum so that she could enjoy them at the waterfalls on her ride back to Isfahan.

Without warning, one of the passersby grabbed her by the arm and yanked her into one of the spice shops. As she stumbled into the store and was dragged to the back, she heard a collage of screams behind her. Glancing back, she saw that the person she had been walking behind was now laying on the sidewalk with a pool of blood forming on his back.

***

"Dammit, you missed!" Nassiri yelled into his radio.

He was sitting in his car across the street, watching Donya.

"Sorry, sir, but she moved at the last second. It looked like someone grabbed her," said Sgt. Taftian, his sniper on top of the adjacent roof.

"Did you say someone grabbed her?"

"Affirmative, sir. I'm waiting for her to come out of the shop, but I don't see her."

"Someone knows we're here," Nassiri mumbled.

Nassiri grabbed his gun and ran from his wife's Subaru toward the spice shop. Seeing an infuriated Revolutionary Guardsman running in full uniform and carrying a gun, the frantic crowd parted. Once inside the shop, Nassiri's head swiveled left and right, desperately searching for Donya. But all he found was her backpack halfway between the entrance and the back door. In between was a gun that had apparently fallen out.

She ran out the back!

He ran toward the back and kicked open the door. Making sure there was no one with a gun on the opposite side, Nassiri paused and moved to the side. When he peeked around the corner, he saw a woman in the same blue colored burka that Donya was wearing, running down the alley. Extending his arm through the doorway to take a shot, a fist slammed down on his gun. He dropped it before he could pull the trigger. A man seized his wrist, pulled him forward and struck his nose with an elbow, cracking it on impact.

Nassiri covered his face and bellowed in pain as his assailant grabbed him by the back of the neck and repeatedly rammed his head into the side of the steel door until he collapsed to the ground and blacked out.

"Nighty night, fucker," Thrasher said.

***

Fifteen minutes later, Donya parked her van in the lot of the observation station below the Margoon Waterfall and hid in the back with a revolver in her trembling hand, ready to shoot anyone that approached. Her shoulders jumped when she felt a knock against the side door, but she relaxed when she heard a familiar voice.

"Hey, it's me, don't shoot!" Thrasher said.

Donya slid open the door and let him in.

"You okay?"

"Yes, but what the hell was that?"

"Lajani called. The Basij knew that you would be here. They set up a sniper to take you out."

Donya's hands were trembling. The reality of the situation was setting in.

"What happened to the guy who was chasing us? Is he dead?"

"Unfortunately, no. I dropped my damn gun in the store when I was racing you out the back. But that fucker's nose will never sit right, and he'll wake up with one hell of a concussion!"

"Jay, will you calm down! I was almost killed. I don't need you yelling at me!"

Thrasher took a deep breath. What little sensitivity he had went out the window when his adrenaline got the best of him.

"Sorry."

Thrasher reached over to hug Donya, who began crying on his shoulder.

"What do we do now?"

"You need to get the hell out of here and hide out for a few days. No more techy visits. I don't give a damn who calls you. And get rid of all your burner phones. Have Farhad help you get some clean ones."

"Okay. What's next for the plan?"

"I don't know. I need to talk to Lajani. But considering what just went down, I think our timetable just got moved up."

Chapter Fifteen

HAMEDAN, IRAN

When Donya returned to Isfahan, Farhad could tell that she was visibly shaken. Her eyes were glassy from crying, her face was flushed, and her lip was bleeding from biting it too hard. After filling him in on her near assassination, Farhad wasted no time putting together a go-bag of new burner phones, clothes, and extra cash from the floor safe he'd just installed. Donya was clingy and followed him from room to room. It was early afternoon when she arrived and there was lots for him to do that night, so he jumped in his car and followed her as far as Hamedan. When he saw the signs for Ali-Sadr Cave, he called his friend, Noshad, who owed him a favor.

The Ali-Sadr Cave is the world's largest underwater cave complex. Its exact date of origin is unknown, but some archaeologists believe it dates back to the Jurassic period. It is only accessible by boat, which snakes its visitors through the elaborate network of rock formations. Thanks to glittery cauliflower stone and a colorful kaleidoscope of stalactite covered ceilings, the cave is one of Iran's most sought-after tourist destinations.

Knowing that he needed to settle Donya's nerves, Farhad called and asked her to pull over. Thankfully, she agreed. It was near sunset, and the caves had just closed, but Noshad had a rowboat waiting, which Farhad would lock up with the others once he was finished.

As Farhad rowed through the dark entrance of the intricate web of caves, Donya sat in silence, reliving her moment of near death and evaluating the fragility of her own mortality. When they reached the largest room in the cave network, he pulled up the oars and handed

Donya a beer. The can was warm, but it helped calm her nerves. For at least five minutes, she said nothing. There was only the sound of bubbles fizzing from their cans as the boat slowly floated them under an array of coral, mahogany, and fuchsia stalactites.

"You okay?"

Donya nodded.

"It's been a long time since I've been in here. What's this room called?"

"Freedom Hall."

Donya grinned.

"Cute."

Farhad grinned back.

"I thought it was appropriate."

"The realism of our plan really slammed me today."

"We both knew this wasn't going to be easy. We're risking our lives for this. You're not alone."

"I know, but nearly getting my head blown off gives me a lot to reflect on."

"Like what?"

"What if we succeed? Then what?"

"Then we'll have what we've been fighting for. A country without a Supreme Leader."

"What if Lajani's not trustable? Many men change once they ascend to power. Are we trading one dictator for another?"

"I hope not, but I don't think so. He strikes me as being committed to bringing Iran back to a fully functional, non-terrorist state."

"But he'll have the entire Revolutionary Guard at his fingertips."

"He already does. If he wanted to start a war, he would've done it by now."

"You really believe we can be free?"

"My friend Kirk once told me that freedom isn't easy. I guess we'll find out what our version of that means. But I believe we can become freer than we are now. That's why we joined the PMOI, right? Besides, we've come this far. We have to see it through."

Donya cracked a smile.

"Come sit with me."

Farhad carefully moved from his seat at the bow of the boat to a seat in front of her at the stern.

"You really believe our country can change, don't you?"

"Honestly, I don't know. I know we'll never be like America. Iran has always clung to its past. But if we can get rid of the Supreme Leader, I'm hoping people will get a sense of what the future can be if we embrace the types of experiences in the world that our Supreme Leader has kept hidden from us. The trick will be weaving our faith into it."

"You've thought about this a lot."

"Haven't you?"

Donya gazed warmly into Farhad's eyes. His optimism reassured her that she had done the right thing by bringing him into the group and it reminded her of why she joined eight years ago.

"Did you see all the stickers on the way here?"

She was referencing the pirate stickers that Farhad's followers on Instagram had begun placing on their car bumpers. It was not a trend that Farhad had started. In fact, he didn't like the idea because if the Revolutionary Guard caught on it would be a way to identify his supporters, which could mean killing them. But once people start a trend, it's difficult to stop it.

"It's kind of embarrassing, actually."

"Why? You're their hero. The legendary Farhad who boldly takes on the Revolutionary Guard," she said in a playfully deep voice.

Farhad paused.

"Well, Iran has killed more than its fair share of so-called heroes. I just want to survive."

Having confronted the possibility of her own death, Donya nodded. For the first time, she understood what Farhad was constantly facing.

"What will be the first thing you do once the Ayatollah is gone?" she asked.

"Get really drunk in public."

Donya laughed so hard that she spit up her beer. She was practically convulsing in laughter when she realized it was dripping down Farhad's face.

"Thanks. Thanks a lot."

He smiled.

"I'm so sorry."

She laughed.

"Just for that, you'll have to buy me a round when I go out."

"I can do that. It will go well with my plans once we oust the Supreme Leader."

"What do you mean? What's the first thing you're going to do?"

"Go on a date and hold hands with the man I'm with."

Donya put down her beer and reached forward to place Farhad's hands between hers. Noticing the beer remnants still dripping from his face, Donya removed her blue hijab, shook out her long brown hair, and used it to delicately wipe away the warm liquid.

Farhad froze, unsure what to do. He had been so busy running errands for the PMOI and being their designated beer smuggler that he had failed to take notice of Donya's flirtations. She was a few years older than him, and because she was the leader of the PMOI, he wasn't aware that she thought of him this way.

Have I been blind?

Even though he had seen her without her hijab on many occasions, there was something about the way her hair fell on her face as she stared at him and dabbed the cloth against his cheek. He nervously lifted her chin with his forefinger and kissed her thin lips.

Thankful that he had made the move, Donya wrapped her arms around Farhad and kissed him deeply as the water effortlessly guided them through the cave under the collage of sparkling stalactites.

Chapter Sixteen

TEHRAN, IRAN

Nassiri shoved Avesta's assistant aside and kicked open the door to the president's office, where he was meeting with his senior staff.

"Out!" Nassiri shouted.

Startled, the staff looked to the president, unsure what to do.

When no one moved, Nassiri pulled the Browning 9mm from his holster and put it to the side of the Minister of Foreign Affairs' head.

"I said get out!"

The staff, including the Minister of Foreign Affairs, wasted no time shuffling out of the office. After they left, Nassiri holstered his weapon and gave Avesta an evil sneer.

"You wretched son of a dog. . ."

Three members of Avesta's personal security burst into the office with their weapons aimed at Nassiri. The commander of the Basij glanced at them over his shoulder before giving an ice pick glare back at Avesta.

"It's okay," Avesta said to the security team. "Leave us."

"Sir. . ." said the lead member of his security team.

"Go," Avesta said.

When the security team closed the damaged door, Avesta had some choice words for Nassiri.

"How dare you storm into my office like that! Don't ever disrespect me again, especially in front of my most senior officials!"

Nassiri backslapped Avesta across the face so hard that his bottom lip split open. It bled immediately. He kicked the back of Avesta's legs, brought the president to his knees, and grabbed him by the back of the neck.

"You fucking set me up," he said.

"What? I have no idea what you're talking about."

"I found that miserable bitch, Donya. My sniper had her dead to rights, but she got snatched away at the last minute. When I gave chase, someone did *this* to me."

Nassiri grabbed Avesta by the hair and turned his head so that he could see what Thrasher had done. There was dried blood in his mustache and beard. His eyes were beginning to blacken. His large, hook nose was offset to the left. A large purple bruise had formed at the top of his temple.

Alarmed, Avesta's eyes bulged.

"What happened?"

"The whore had help, and whoever it was, he was good."

Nassiri let go of Avesta and allowed him to climb to his feet.

"One of yours?"

Nassiri gave Avesta a stern look and met the president face to face.

"None, repeat, none of my men would *ever* turn against me."

"Then, who was it?"

"I hardly got a look at him. The bastard nailed me before I could see him. Who did you tell about this operation?"

"No one, I swear!"

Nassiri was sick and tired of politicians like Avesta trying to cover their asses. He seized him by the lapels of his expensive black suit and pushed him against the wall so hard the picture frames fell to the floor. Avesta gritted his teeth, still sore from the kebabbing incident.

Pulling the Böker Magnum knife from the back of his belt, the Basij commander held the tip of the blade to Avesta's balls.

"You tell me now or I swear to you your wife will have to start playing with another man's dick for pleasure."

"Wait, wait. I have no fucking clue what you're talking about!"

"No, you told someone. I bet it was that weasel assistant of yours. Either way, you and I are done. You're on your own with Lajani *and* the Supreme Leader. Don't call me again until you figure it out."

Nassiri released Avesta and stared at him as he backed out of the presidential office.

Avesta adjusted his suit and tie and wiped the sweat from his brow. *How could this be possible?*

A variety of scenarios ran through the president's head. He knew he hadn't told Saeed about the operation, but an idea popped into his mind.

"My computer. . ."

That was the only explanation. He rushed to his desk and buzzed for Saeed.

"Yes, Mr. President?"

"Call the Ministry of the Interior and have them send their best computer services technician immediately. I think I've been hacked."

***

In his office across town, Lajani was smiling as he listened to the scene between Nassiri and Avesta. His plan was working perfectly. Avesta had been backed into a corner with no one he could depend on. That is, except for himself. He patiently rolled his fingers on his desk, knowing that the call would come any minute. Like clockwork, ten minutes later, his cell phone buzzed.

"Lajani."

"General, I have a serious issue and I desperately need your help."

"Absolutely, Mr. President. How can I help?"

"I think my personal computer has been hacked. Someone from the Ministry of the Interior is on their way to look at it, but I think we should discuss how to handle this."

"What do you need me for?"

"I'd like your help dealing with the situation. And I'd like it if the Supreme Leader didn't know about this."

Lajani grinned.

"You're putting me in a tough position, Mr. President. The favor I did you in the meeting was one thing, but now you're asking me to keep secrets from the Supreme Leader about an issue that could affect our state security."

"Please, General, you're the only one who can help me. Otherwise, I'm a dead man."

Score.

Lajani paused. He wanted the tension to build on the other end.

"I'm not in my office right now," he lied, "but I'll be there before the end of the day. In the meantime, keep your mouth shut."

Lajani hung up the phone and banged his fist on the desk in celebration. It was time to pounce. First, he buzzed for his assistant.

"Yes, sir?"

"If anyone asks, you haven't seen me since early this morning and I went out to observe a training exercise, understood?"

"Of course, sir."

On his way out the door, Lajani grabbed the burner phone from his armoire and dialed a number he knew by heart.

"What is it?" Thrasher answered.

Lajani pursed his lips.

Will this guy ever be happy to hear from me?

"I've got Avesta right where I want him. It's time to initiate."

"Are you sure? Are the other pieces in place? All your men are set to move?"

"My men are ready. They'll follow my orders. Just be ready to wire more money. We're going to need it."

"What about what's his name from the Basij?"

"Let me worry about that."

Lajani paused. Thrasher was covering the mic to the phone, but he was obviously talking to the woman who called herself Lilly Rodgers.

"What do you need from me?"

"How soon can you be here?"

"Probably four hours. I'm still in Isfahan."

"Meet me outside the bank near the Presidential Administration in Tehran and call me when you get there. You'll get more details then."

"I'll be there."

Lajani hung up with Thrasher and made more calls. There was no going back now.

Chapter Seventeen

ISFAHAN, IRAN

Above the café, Thrasher filled in Jenkins on what happened with Donya. After assuring her that she was okay, the two of them made notes on butcher paper taped to the wall. Jenkins had Iran mapped out with the names of Lajani's men next to the cities of Isfahan, Mashhad, Shiraz, Tehran and Qom, as discussed with Lajani. While Thrasher rolled his eyes at the questions Delang passed along from Director Wallace in the morning cable, Jenkins shared the Director's deep concerns about Qom. If people of the world thought that the news coverage of Fallujah during the second Iraq War was bad, Qom had the potential to be ten times worse unless Lajani was able to control the city the way he claimed he could.

During their discussions, Thrasher's phone rang, which he answered with his usual lack of cheer. It was Lajani, and he was ready to pull the trigger.

"Now?" she said.

Thrasher nodded.

"Does he have all the pieces in place?"

Thrasher continued talking with Lajani and then hung up.

"Well?"

"He says he's got Avesta politically boxed in and wants to move."

Jenkins eyes darted back and forth, looking at the web of scribbles she had made on the butcher paper.

"I don't know. I don't think we're ready."

"What can I tell you? It's his show and he says it's 'go' time."

Jenkins made the sign of the cross on her chest. Only prayers would help them now.

"How much time do we have?"

"He wants me to meet him in Tehran. It will take four hours to get there, plus at least two to do whatever he needs. So, call it six hours minimum."

Jenkins quickly sent an encrypted message about what was transpiring to Delang via a third-party messaging system.

"Okay, let's go."

"No, you stay here and man the fort. I can handle this."

"Not this time, Ben. I'm going."

Thrasher nodded and began putting on his public disguise of a hat and sunglasses. Thanks to his half Native American heritage, his skin color helped him blend in among the Iranian population. His Moses-like beard was an added bonus. While Thrasher fixed himself, Jenkins noticed that he had become even more chiseled and had added considerable muscle mass.

"Where'd you get your gym membership?" she asked.

"What?"

"You've bulked up. Where's your weight room?"

Thrasher looked at his arms. For all his personality flaws, Thrasher was not a vain person, and wasn't overly obsessed with his physique.

"One of Donya's hideouts has drums of chemicals. I moved them around to clean the place up. It ended up being a good workout, so I kept going until I could pick them up. I ended up using them to put a barricade around the old chemical plant."

Jenkins nodded as she donned her black chador that stretched to her ankles. On their way down the stairs, she was still carrying the matching hijab in her hand.

***

Inside the coffee house, Fang Xin's caffeine high was in full bloom. His knee was bouncing up and down as he finished his sixth espresso.

After landing in Isfahan, he'd received a tip from his boss that American agents were using new businesses in Isfahan as a cover. Xin rolled with the information and began riding around the downtown area. Aware that the American woman exited the country on a Chinese passport, he made his way to the Central District, where his analysts had told him Chinese nationals were living. Roaming around the district, he questioned people on the street about new businesses in the area. All of them pointed him to several new shops near the City Center.

Finding the American woman wouldn't be easy. The CIA was one of the best at disguising its agents to blend into public situations, but hiding facial scars was a lengthy process for any make-up artist. He was hoping she might be lazy enough to take a stroll without having to take the time to go through it. Coupled with the fact that her busty physique was tough to hide, even under a chador, he might get lucky. It wasn't much to go on, but the analysts at the Ministry of State Security hadn't got back to him on several issues, so that was all he had for the moment. He decided to take a seat at the newest coffee and tea house to review some of the latest intel he'd been sent.

After three hours, he decided he'd been sitting long enough. There was no sign of the woman among the workers or the patrons, and he had other locations to check out. Knowing he would visit the location again, he dropped money on the table and left.

As he turned the corner to the next location, an ice cream house, he saw a man and a woman exiting a side door. Though he only got a brief glance before she put on her hijab, he noticed that the woman had facial scars. Playing a hunch, he decided to follow them.

***

Thrasher opened the side door and performed his standard surveillance while Jenkins put the hijab over her head. He saw one man at least fifty yards away.

"Where are you parked?" Jenkins said.

"Down there."

He pointed to a white Khondo Samand down the street. As they walked, Thrasher replayed the image of the man behind them. He wasn't Iranian. He was Chinese. The hairs on his neck and forearms began to tingle.

"We've got company," he said in Farsi.

Jenkins made sure not to turn around.

"Who?"

"The Chinese guy. About fifty yards back."

"That can only mean one thing."

"Uh huh. You've got your sidearm with you, right?"

"Yeah, tucked in my waistband underneath this awful thing. You?"

Thrasher gave a "are you kidding?" look.

"What's your plan?" she asked.

"Car. He's on foot. We've got wheels."

Thrasher and Jenkins continued walking to the car without acknowledging that anything was wrong. When they got in the car, despite repeatedly turning the key and pumping the gas pedal, the engine wouldn't turn over.

"Come on, dammit!"

"He's getting closer, Ben."

Jenkins kept an eye on the man in the mirror and soon developed a sick feeling in the pit of her stomach. With the man only twenty yards away, there was only one play to make. Jenkins drew her Sig Sauer P226 from under her chador. She unbuckled her seat belt, turned around, and fired three rapid shots out the window.

Because she was in the passenger seat, she had to fire with her left hand. When the Chinese man saw her turn around, he knew what was happening and dove out of the way. Sparks flew as her shots hit the street instead of its target. With the car unable to start, there was only one option.

"Run!"

Thrasher and Jenkins rushed out of the car and kept their heads down as they weaved around the cars parked on the street. A bullet zipped by Jenkins' head and shattered the rear windshield of the car next to her.

As they neared the end of the street, Thrasher pulled his weapon and fired two shots that bought them enough time to make a run for it around the corner.

"There!"

He pointed to an abandoned building that unbeknownst to them had been slated for demolition to build a new mall. As they entered the building, two more bullets nailed the brick at the side of the door's entrance, inches from Jenkins. She ducked and returned fire with three more shots of her own that hit nothing.

Thrasher didn't know the building layout, but it looked like an old textile factory. Fortunately, the abandoned machines provided plenty of cover, which gave them an advantage.

"Go upstairs and take the high ground," he said.

"Tacoma two-step?"

Thrasher nodded. She was referring to a play in the field taught at the Farm by a training officer who was from Tacoma, Washington. But as soon as she took her first steps, the wooden stairs gave way. The wood cut her leg and she screeched in pain. Thrasher came to her aide and pulled her leg out of the hole, but he had to hurry. The Chinese operative wasn't far behind.

"There, now hurry up!"

Thrasher took shelter behind one of the remaining industrial sewing machines as he watched Jenkins make her way to the catwalk upstairs.

***

Xin peeked through the entrance of the building. Seeing and hearing nothing, he stepped inside. His eyes and ears were on high alert. All he needed to see was a slight shadow or hear a foot moving along the dusty ground. He looked at the decrepit stairway. At first, he thought there was no way he would use it to go upstairs, but then he noticed fresh blood droppings.

Like trailing a wounded animal in the woods.

Following the evidence, he gingerly ascended. After thankfully not falling and reaching the top of the stairs, he saw footprints in the settled dust and more drops of blood. He grinned. It was only a matter of time before he had his target. He stayed on the left side of the rusty catwalk. If one of the two tangos was still downstairs, he didn't want to be seen close to the railing that overlooked the factory floor, which would enable them to take a shot at him. As he continued to follow the blood trail, he stealthily searched behind the thick metal pillars and bails of abandoned wool. He found nothing.

A shot rang out from behind and hit a bail of wool. He returned fire, but saw no one. Before he could turn around, a second shot rang out. This one hit him square in the back, dropping him to his knees. A third shot rang out. Xin never even saw the shooter. The left side of his skull blasted out, and he fell to the ground with what was left of his face.

Chapter Eighteen

"Clear!"

Thrasher came around the corner and saw Jenkins standing over the Chinese corpse. He sidestepped the gray brain matter and pool of blood flowing toward him.

"You wanna tell me what that was about?"

"He's gotta be Ministry of State Security. Someone in China must have alerted him about me."

"Great."

"Oh my God…"

"What?"

"Jessica."

Jenkins and Thrasher exchanged depressing looks. They both knew that if a Chinese operative was in Iran looking for her it could only mean that they had a fallen colleague, someone they both knew well and relied on. Plus, if the Chinese were now on to them, it put their mission in jeopardy.

They turned to hear sirens screaming their way.

"Now what?"

"Now we get the hell out of here!"

"What about the body?"

"What about it? It's a condemned building. Fuck 'em!"

Thrasher and Jenkins sprinted back to the café. Fortunately, since they hadn't been there long, there wasn't much to clean out, and Lajani assured them that no one from the IRGC had any intel about it. Jenkins grabbed her computer and rolled up the butcher paper from the wall. Thrasher stashed the cash and burner phones that Farhad put in the floor safe as well as their IRGC uniforms. They were downstairs, evacuating the café with the rest of the crowd just as the Isfahan police arrived.

When they got back to the car, Thrasher rolled his eyes when the damn thing started on the first key turn.

"Figures."

"I'll text Farhad and let him know that the café is burned," Jenkins said.

When she was done texting, she turned to Thrasher.

"When do we tell Lajani?"

"Let's wait until we're closer to Tehran. I don't want him playing cowboy and doing anything rash."

For two hours, they sat in silence. Thrasher's adrenaline was running throttle as they drove on Route 7 back to Tehran, and it showed on the speedometer. As they weaved in and out of traffic, Jenkins looked over and saw that they were going over ninety miles per hour.

"Slow down, Speed Racer. It's fine to drive like an Iranian, but we can't afford to attract any attention."

Thrasher eased off the gas. It was time to call Lajani.

"We hit a snag."

He turned to Jenkins as he listened to Lajani.

"What?" she mouthed.

"No, wait for us. We're almost…"

The line went dead.

"Dammit!"

Thrasher pounded the dashboard with his fist.

"That son-of-a-bitch! I'm gonna fucking kill him myself!"

"Ben, will you calm down, and tell me what's going on?!"

"We've gotta hightail it to Tehran. He's initiating his plan."

"Shit."

Two hours later, they pulled into downtown Tehran. Ironically, the route to the Presidential Administration building took them past the old U.S. Embassy, which now served as the U.S. Den of Espionage Museum. They also saw a mural painted on the side of an apartment building that depicted the U.S. flag with skulls where the stars should be, missiles streaking downward that served as the red stripes, with the words "Down with the U.S.A." plastered across it.

Among a racket of horns honking on the congested streets, they made their way through a maze of high-rise buildings. Both agents remained on maximum alert. Their disguises were good, but downtown Tehran had Basij soldiers stationed everywhere, and CIA agents operating inside Iran could never be too careful.

When Thrasher parked around the corner from the Presidential Administration Building, in front of Melli Bank, just as instructed, Lajani was nowhere to be found.

Chapter Nineteen

TEHRAN, IRAN

For years, Lajani had been secretly keeping files on every IRGC soldier he had ever met, ranking each soldier on a scale of one to five. When he made it to the rank of Major, he decided to roll the dice with his superiors and alert them to what he had been doing, and he tried to make it sensible from an administrative standpoint. Rather than ranking the soldiers according to how fanatical they were, which was the actual point of his exercise, he explained that the system could be used to determine a soldier's future in the IRGC, based on their lethal effectiveness and commitment to Shi'a Islam.

His superior at the time loved the idea. When he passed it along to the commander of the Revolutionary Guard, the process was implemented immediately across all branches of the military. Now that Lajani occupied the head job, he could use the system he invented against the IRGC.

Sitting in front of him at a military hanger at Mehrabad Air Base were eight hundred of the Revolutionary Guard's deadliest soldiers. All of them were dogmatic Shiites of the highest caliber who sat at the top of his list. They wanted to wipe Israel and its American puppet off the map for good in order to hasten the return of the Twelfth Imam.

The hangar door was open and a C-17 plane sat outside on the tarmac.

"Atten-tion!" a soldier yelled.

All soldiers stood as Lajani came into the room.

"Sit down."

Lajani slowly walked by with his hands behind his back, staring intently at all of them.

"Men, I have just spoken with the Supreme Leader, and he's given us permission to work on a mission that will finally take a major offensive against the pig Zionists."

Every soldier in the room clapped and cheered. His words had kicked a nest of hatred within each soldier, and he could feel it swarming.

"This is not a mission to take lightly. It is highly dangerous, and some of you may not make it back. But I can see in your eyes the dedication and courage required that will allow Iran to conquer the region in the name of Allah. Do you accept this mission?"

"Yes, sir!"

Every soldier shouted in unison.

"Do you accept this responsibility?"

"Yes, sir!"

"Are you prepared to make the ultimate sacrifice in the name of the Prophet?"

"Yes, sir!"

"Excellent! Unfortunately, you cannot deploy immediately. It will take at least one month of training, possibly two, at a facility specially built outside our base in Mashhad. Is that clear?"

"Yes, sir!"

"After completing your training, I will meet you there and provide further instructions. When I arrive, I expect you to demonstrate your drills for me with nothing less than elite precision! Will you do this for me, men?"

"Yes, sir!"

Lajani nodded.

"May Allah be with you in the great crusade that stands before you. And we will not disappoint Him in the execution of our duties, will we?"

"No, sir!"

"I have full confidence in all of you and every aspect of your skills. Load up!"

Some soldiers grabbed their gear and ran immediately toward the plane. Others wanted to shake Lajani's hand. They finally had a commander with the balls to take on the Israelis. Lajani shook every hand extended to him, smiling, and patting each one on their back. He watched them board the plane and watched it lift off into the blazing afternoon sun.

Then, he heard footsteps behind him. As he turned around, he saw Omar Saeedi, the lead engineer for all Revolutionary Guard aerial vessels. He was wearing purple overalls and was wiping grease from his fingers. Eight years ago, Lajani had saved his life by transferring him to another post when he had heard there was an impending attack coming from Mossad.

"Everything was recalibrated correctly?"

"Of course, General."

Lajani nodded.

"You'll have your money within the hour."

"Thank you, General."

"No, Omar. Thank *you*."

When Lajani got back to his state issued IRCG Jeep, his phone rang. It was Thrasher.

"Hello?"

"We hit a snag," Thrasher said.

"What kind of snag?"

"The kind that I can't talk about on the phone."

"Anything I need to be concerned about?"

"Not sure yet. Possibly. I'll tell you more about it when I see you, but we can't use the café anymore."

Lajani's palms started to sweat. It was time to commence, and the wheels were already falling off the wagon.

"If that's the case, I'm not waiting for you to get here. I'll arrest Avesta and lock him up at headquarters. Get back to Tehran. Park near Melli Bank outside the Presidential Administration Building. I'll meet you there. We can talk next steps."

"No, wait for us! We're almost. . ."

Lajani cut him off and sped toward the Presidential Administration Building. During the forty-minute drive, a plan began to formulate in his head.

Chapter Twenty

Lajani waited in front of the bank for over an hour. Concerned that something had happened to Thrasher and Jenkins, he texted Farhad. When he received a response, Lajani powered down the phone, and kept it on his person. He couldn't wait any longer. It was now or never. He drove his Jeep to the front gate of the Presidential Administration Building. Having visited the president on multiple occasions, he recognized the guard on duty, Sgt. Sohrab Moradi.

"Sergeant, how are you today? I heard that your wife just had a new baby boy."

"Yes, General. Eight pounds, eight ounces. We named him Komeil."

"Congratulations. Strong name for a boy. You'll be sure to stop by my office so I can see him, won't you?"

Moradi was taken aback that the chief commander of the Revolutionary Guard was making such a request.

"I'd be honored, General!"

"Excellent. Unfortunately, right now, I have to escort the president to an urgent meeting. Don't hold us up when we come back through, okay?"

"Understood, General."

Once inside, Lajani walked with steadfast purpose toward the president's office. Seeing the intense look on his face, the staff walking the halls put their backs to the wall and let him pass. He walked into the president's private office without acknowledging his assistant.

When he entered, he saw Hamid Mousavi finishing his duty of checking the president's computer. Mousavi was a senior member of the Ministry of Intelligence's Cyber Division. Having worked with him in the past, Lajani knew him well.

"You're all set, Mr. President," Mousavi said.

"Thank you. Close the door on your way out. I need to speak with the General."

"Yes, sir."

Lajani nodded to Mousavi on his way out.

"What did he say? Has your computer been hacked?"

"No, my computer hasn't, but there is another matter we need to discuss. Let's sit."

Avesta motioned toward the olive covered couch. Lajani gave the president a curious look. The president went to his desk and retrieved an object from one of the drawers. Lajani felt his blood pressure rise when he dropped it on the coffee table in front of him.

"It wasn't my computer that was hacked. It was *this*."

Lajani saw a framed picture of the Supreme Leader, Avesta, and himself, standing together with their hands raised on the balcony of the Edifice of the Sun at Golestan Palace on the day Shir-Del was named the new Supreme Leader. A staff member took the picture and got it developed right away. When he gave it to Lajani, an idea sparked in his head. He had it framed immediately and outfitted it with a listening device he could use to keep an eye on Avesta. At the time, Lajani didn't know what he would need it for, but he thought it was a good idea to ensure that he wasn't being cut out of any plans that were pertinent to him or the Revolutionary Guard.

Once the bug had been installed, he paid Avesta a surprise visit, which ended up being the same visit where Avesta gave the go-ahead to create a war between India and Pakistan that eventually led him being in the Supreme Leader's doghouse.

Avesta turned the picture frame over and exposed the bugging device.

"And you're the one that gave it to me, you fucking traitor!"

Lajani jumped up and pulled his gun.

"Mr. President, by the power given to me by the Iranian Constitution and the Supreme Leader himself, you're under arrest for failure to execute the demands of your office. Stand up!"

"Oh, I don't think so."

Suddenly, a dozen Basij soldiers stormed through both doors to Avesta's office. All of them were holding M-16 rifles. Lajani's head spun left and right. The last person through the door was Nassiri, but he wasn't holding a weapon. In this situation, he didn't have to.

"Drop it," Nassiri instructed.

Lajani relented and tossed his Browning 9mm on the couch.

Nassiri nodded to his cousin, Lt. Col. Nahid Vaziri. He and another soldier approached the General and put handcuffs on him. Lajani didn't resist. Once they were secure behind his back, Nassiri stepped forward and sent a ferocious punch to the General's gut, dropping him to his knees.

"I always knew you were a coward! Now, everyone will see the yellow streak running down your back."

When Lajani looked up, Nassiri punched him in the jaw.

"And that is for holding my career back!"

Nassiri went to kick him, but Avesta pulled him back.

"That's enough."

Avesta squatted down to speak to Lajani.

"I never thought it would be you. You had all the power the country could give you. Only the Supreme Leader had more authority than you. To think the chief commander of the Revolutionary Guard was spying on me. We're going to search through every aspect of your life, General. What will we find?"

Lajani said nothing as he spit blood on the president's highly polished shoes.

"My, how you have fallen from grace, General. We're going to take you before the Supreme Leader. Nassiri and I will sit at his right hand while we observe the punishment he has in store for you."

Vaziri turned the General on his stomach, looking for anything that would aid him. He found the General's IRGC issued phone and the burner phone he'd used to call Thrasher. He handed both to Nassiri, who held up the two phones for Avesta to see.

Avesta nodded and stood. Nassiri glanced over at Vaziri.

"Get him out of here. I've got another stop to make."

"Bring them back alive," Avesta said.

"Yes, sir."

Before leaving, Nassiri looked at a trail of text messages on the burner phone. One of them caught his eye instantly.

LAJANI: Where will you be if I need you?

UNNAMED CONTACT: Hamedan, but I'll be back in Isfahan later tonight.

***

Thrasher and Jenkins were parked down the street from the bank, keeping an eye on the front of the Presidential Administration Building. Jenkins chewed her fingernails. The monotonous clicking bite annoyed the hell out of Thrasher, but he was too consumed by his instincts tickling the hairs on the back of his neck to tell her to knock it off. Thrasher tried to carefully balance his thoughts of wanting to strangle Lajani for hanging up on him and reminding himself that Lajani was the key to Iran's future.

For the moment, there was no denying it: Thrasher's emotions were in high gear and logic was shoved out the door. He gripped the steering wheel so tightly the veins in his forearms protruded. As his pulse quickened, a heavy but familiar scowl solidified on his face.

If the wide-mouthed bastard had just waited, we could've regrouped and done this fucking thing right!

"Oh shit," said Jenkins.

They spotted Lajani. But instead of the cuffs being on Avesta, Lajani was the one wearing them, and he was bleeding from the mouth.

"Dammit, they know!" Thrasher shouted.

Jenkins searched her mind for their abort scenarios.

Thrasher's burner phone rang. It was Lajani's number, but since they could see him being escorted out of the building, it had to be someone else.

"Dump it. Someone's testing the numbers he dialed from his phone."

Their eyes popped open as they looked at each other.

"Oh no," she said.

"Farhad and Donya."

Chapter Twenty-One

HAMEDAN, IRAN

It was late afternoon, but Farhad and Donya were still in bed together. Donya was asleep, but Farhad was awake, using the tips of his fingers to gently stroke her back as she curled up next to him. Wanting to be undisturbed for their sexual escapades, they had turned their phones off.

Donya moaned and kissed Farhad on the neck.

"Again? Well, if you insist," Farhad said.

Donya smacked him on the torso and gave him a flirtatious look.

"Easy, Mister Pirate. What time is it?"

Farhad looked at his watch.

"A little after four. Why?"

Donya leaned over and kissed him once more.

"Time for us to get back to work."

Farhad groaned.

"I guess duty calls."

Donya stood up and let the sheet fall away, exposing her ample breasts.

"You better rest up. You'll need your energy later."

She winked.

"As you wish, Boss."

He smiled.

While Donya searched for her phone, Farhad found his and several high-pitched pings echoed when he turned it on. Before he checked his multiple voice mails, he decided to answer the most recent text message first.

"Lajani texted me. He says we may have a problem, and wants to know where we are," Farhad said.

"Do we tell him we're together?"

"Why not? It won't affect our plan. Years down the road, we'll be able to tell people that Iran's first official act toward freedom was us sleeping together."

Donya rolled her eyes and smiled. Farhad returned the text to Lajani, identifying the motel's location. Donya finally found her phone, which had slid under a desk when she'd flung her clothes off earlier. She checked her first voice mail.

"Oh my God. Did you already text Lajani back?"

"Yeah, why?"

"Break the phones and get dressed fast. We need to get out of here!"

Donya threw Farhad his pants as she rushed to get her clothes back on.

"Why? What the hell's going on?"

"Do you have any voice mails?"

"Yeah, I was just about to listen to them."

"Do it fast."

Both were from Jenkins, letting him know that the Basij had arrested Lajani.

"Oh, shit. Whoever I just texted must've had Lajani's phone, and I just told them where we are."

"Exactly. Now, grab your keys!"

"Hang on. I need to call Jay and Raven."

"If you use the phone, they can pinpoint our location. Break it, and let's go. We can call later!"

Farhad threw on his t-shirt, hopped into his jeans, and was shuffling into his shoes as he and Donya hustled out the motel room door and down the stairs. Once outside, they could hear sirens howling toward them.

"They're close. You drive," Donya said.

Donya tossed the keys to Farhad. They jumped into her van and tore out of the motel parking lot. They barely made it a block before they saw a pair of Basij vehicles headed toward them. Farhad turned his head away as they sped past, but quickly checked his rearview mirror to see if they were turning around. The tires from the Basij armored SUV's smoked on the road as one of them popped a U-turn. The other turned onto a side road.

"They saw us."

"Floor it!"

Donya's van was no match for the speed of the Basij's armored SUV. Despite speeding through an intersection with traffic coming from all directions, the armored truck reached them in less than twenty seconds and slammed into their bumper. The first smash gave Farhad and Donya a wicked sensation of whiplash, but they didn't veer off course. The second time, though, the hit caused the van to lurch forward, swerving left and right. Farhad spun the steering wheel in both directions, struggling to regain control. Donya looked behind them.

"Here they come!"

The armored truck slammed into the back of the van again, jolting them forward, then oddly backed off. But instead of swerving or rolling over, Farhad and Donya felt a massive pop of tires beneath them. The Basij had set a trap. The other Basij vehicle had gotten ahead of them and laid a spike strip in the road. The van slid on its rims another thirty feet with sparks flying along the asphalt before the van crashed into a parked car. The airbags deployed on impact, breaking Farhad and Donya's noses. Concussed from the impact, they were unable to move.

Moments later, the Basij launched tear gas canisters, which overwhelmed Donya and Farhad. Their eyes filled with water and snotty fluid gushed from their sinuses. They had extreme coughing fits as the peppered vapor burned their throats. Combined with the whiplash of the collision, both of them quickly passed out.

Two minutes passed. The Basij saw no movement in the van.

"Approach with caution," Nassiri said.

Two men approached both sides of the vehicle, wearing respirators and holding M-16 assault rifles.

"Clear!" the first soldier said.

"Clear," said the second man.

Nassiri lowered his weapon and slapped the hood of the armored truck in celebration.

Got 'em!

As the tear gas dissipated, Nassiri and two soldiers from the second vehicle approached the van. He looked inside to confirm the identities of the two individuals. Nassiri couldn't believe his luck when he saw who it was.

I knew Lajani was hiding him!

"We got them both, men! Farhad and Donya!"

All five men exchanged high-fives. People living in the neighboring apartment buildings curiously watched from their windows.

"Great job, men! Put them in the back of my truck. You've got three minutes," Nassiri said.

Just as he gave the order, gunshots rang out. Two of his men were hit in the neck, killing them instantly. Nassiri ducked behind the van. He peered out from the side, searching for the spark of the enemy's gun through the clearing smoke. When the next shots rang out, the bullets pieced the van's side panel, barely missing his head. His two remaining men were crouched next to him. To the soldier on his right, he pointed to his ear.

"Get back to the truck. We'll cover you!"

The soldier nodded. As he ran back toward the second truck, Nassiri and his partner provided cover fire. Nassiri quickly noticed that his shots were the only ones he was hearing. He looked to his right and noticed that his man had been shot in the head.

Nassiri continued to search the area and was startled when he heard rocks crunching behind him. He turned to fire, but someone grabbed his gun and forced the weapon up against his throat to try and choke him out. Through the hovering tear gas and fluids pouring out of the man's eyes and nose, Nassiri saw the familiar face of his enemy, the same man who had knocked him unconscious outside the museum in Yasuj just a day ago.

Chapter Twenty-Two

As it all unfolded, Thrasher and Jenkins had been carefully following the Basij vehicles from a safe distance.

"Dammit, why doesn't this kid answer his damn phone?!" Thrasher yelled.

Jenkins spotted Donya's van headed toward them in the opposite lane, a quarter of a mile away.

"Wait, is that them?"

"Looks like her van."

"Pull over, I'll wave them down and they can jump in."

The Basij vehicles promptly popped a U-ey, leaving a trail of smoke. The smell of sulfurous burnt rubber hung in the air.

"Wait. Something's not right. Only one of the Basij cars is giving chase."

"Where's the other one going?"

Thrasher looked in his rearview mirror and saw that the street was deserted.

"I've got a pretty good idea."

He slammed their car into reverse and floored it. After rushing through the intersection and nearly causing an accident, when he was two blocks clear, he saw what he expected. The other Basij vehicle a hundred yards in front of them. One of the soldiers was running a spike strip across the road. Both he and Jenkins winced when they saw Donya's van hit the spikes and slide on its rims along the asphalt before hitting a parked car head on.

"You think they're okay?" Jenkins asked.

"I saw the airbags extend, but they might be knocked out. You take the left side. I'll take the right. We'll have to cap these sons of bitches off one by one. If we're lucky, we can grab Farhad and Donya from the van."

From their respective vantage points behind the pillars of two nearby buildings, Thrasher and Jenkins witnessed the Basij launch tear gas canisters toward the van. They watched as Donya and Farhad both succumbed to the fumes.

When the Basij soldiers gathered to congratulate themselves on their catch, Thrasher and Jenkins took aim from their offensive positions. Despite their training in being exposed to tear gas, no one was immune to it. After eliminating two soldiers in a row, Jenkins took cover as a hail of bullets clustered her way. Thankfully, they only pecked away at the cement pillar.

Thrasher ran out of bullets after eliminating his last man. He approached one of the remaining two men on foot. As he crept up behind the one crouching in front of the van, the sound of gravel grinding beneath his feet gave away his position. The soldier turned to fire his rifle, but Thrasher caught it and forced it up against the man's neck. The soldier was as strong as Thrasher and he had a hard time pushing it into his throat. To gain an advantage, Thrasher sacrificed his grip against the rifle with one hand and flipped the respirator off the man's face. He recognized him right away.

Nassiri.

With the haze of tear gas still hanging in the air, Nassiri's face began spewing the same fluids as his own. Thrasher groaned when Nassiri kneed him in the lower abdomen but managed to snatch the rifle away. Hunched over in pain, he saw Nassiri reach for a sidearm on his belt. With no time to turn around and fire, Thrasher hit Nassiri in his face with the butt of the rifle. Nassiri fell over on his side and the gun flew out of his hand.

Rifle in hand, Thrasher approached Nassiri's body with the intent of double tapping him in the chest. Nassiri was on his stomach with his head turned to the side. That's when Thrasher noticed that the Iranian was wearing orange ear plugs. His eyes popped open.

Where's the other man?

"Behind you!"

Jenkins's warning came too late. Thrasher abruptly covered his ears. Through the tears leaking from his eyes, he saw the other soldier holding an ultrasonic rifle that emitted a blaring, high decibel pitch, coupled with flashing lights. Without earplugs of his own, Thrasher fell prey to the weapon's deafening sound. Helpless, he sank to his knees.

Though the ultrasonic rifle roared across the ground, Jenkins darted from behind the concrete pillar, nearly stumbling on the concrete fragments on the ground. She knew that if she didn't get into position to take the soldier out, Thrasher would be dead in seconds. The blaring noise began to disorient her with each passing step. Her head began to throb. Finally, she flanked the soldier from behind a Toyota pickup truck. Dazed from the effects of the gun's pulsating racket, and with her eyes watering from the tear gas, her hands shook, and her vision blurred as she took aim. The first and second shot went wild.

Dammit!

Her headache was getting worse. At any moment, she could pass out from the pain. She only had one more shot. Jenkins squinted her eyes, gritted her teeth, tightened the muscles in her arms and squeezed off one more round that hit the soldier directly in the head. A pink mist filled the air, and the ungodly noise from the ultrasonic rifle finally ceased. Jenkins collapsed to the ground.

Thrasher's senses remained disoriented. As he tried to get up, he felt a crushing blow to the side of his head. Looking up from the ground, he saw Nassiri retrieving his lost sidearm twenty feet away. With his equilibrium still out of whack from the ultrasonic weapon and the punch to his head, Thrasher labored to his feet but was kicked back down by Nassiri, gun now in hand.

Look him in the eye with no fear. Don't let that bastard think you're afraid.

Nassiri stood over him. The gun was pointed right at Thrasher's head.

"I don't know who you are, and I don't care, but this is as far as you go, asshole."

Before Nassiri could pull the trigger, Jenkins, still unstable, fired additional shots that missed him. He returned fire with three shots of his own. One of them shattered a car window. Jenkins's shriek caused Thrasher's adrenaline to kick back into gear, and he punched Nassiri in the balls. The Iranian doubled over and dropped to the ground. Thrasher scrambled to his feet and ran off.

Nassiri managed to fire off a few shots, but with his hands shaking from the blow, the bullets sprayed everywhere and missed their intended target. When he finally got back to his feet, he searched around for Thrasher but saw nothing. There was only a crowd of people gathering on the street to find out what had happened. His enemy had vanished.

Nassiri surveyed the carnage and the bodies of his deceased men. The rage he felt inside distracted him from the throbbing pain in his groin that was steadily surging to his kidney. As the sound of sirens got closer, he limped to the van. Farhad and Donya were still knocked out and thankfully unharmed by the barrage of gunfire.

A malicious grin crept across Nassiri's face.

"I have just the place for the two of you."

Chapter Twenty-Three

IRANIAN AIRSPACE

Captain Saber Kazemi's knee bounced up and down as he sat in the front row of the Revolutionary Guard's C-17. Excitement surged through his veins. Elated thoughts of murdering Israelis danced in his head. When he turned around and looked at the hundreds of men under his command, he could tell that all of them shared in his delight. They finally had a mission to confront the Jews once and for all, and a commander like Lajani with the guts to carry it out.

Kazemi looked at his watch. They would be landing soon and when they touched down, he wanted every soldier on the plane to hit the ground running, ecstatic about the mission. He unbuckled his seat belt and stood to address his men.

"Marg bar Israel! [Death to Israel!]"

All eight hundred men cheered and repeated the chant.

"Marg bar Israel! Mar bar Israel! Marg bar Israel!"

As the chanting continued, Kazemi turned his head when he heard a strange noise. The soldiers heard the same thing and the chanting stopped. The plane's engine was sputtering. Then, they couldn't hear the engines at all. Kazemi hauled ass to the cockpit.

"What the hell is happening?"

"I don't know, sir!" the pilot said. "The fuel gauge says we have half a tank left but the alarms say we're out of gas!"

"We're dropping altitude, fast!" said the co-pilot.

The pilot spoke into his headset.

"Mayday, mayday, mayday!"

"You and your men should brace for impact," the co-pilot said.

Brace for impact, my ass.

Kazemi ran back to his men.

"We've got a major situation and the plane may crash. Everyone get to the back and grab your parachutes. We'll have to make a jump for it!"

Everyone clambered over the seats to reach the back of the plane, but many were knocked over when the plane began to nosedive. Kazemi used all his strength to climb to the back and retrieve as many parachutes as possible, but when he finally reached the storage cache, his stomach dropped. There were no parachutes inside.

***

A half hour later, Saeed received an alert on his phone. The message made him rush into the president's office. Avesta had just finished a call when he burst in.

"Mr. President, I'm sorry for my interruption, but there's something you must see."

"What is it?"

"A friend of mine was leaving Khar Turan National Park when he looked up and saw a plane diving in the sky! Here's the video."

Saeed handed Avesta the phone. As he described, a plane was flying over his friend in a nosedive, headed toward the ground. But the plane wasn't a civilian airliner. Avesta grabbed the remote on the table and turned on the state-run station, which showed the breaking news of a plane crashing into an uninhabited area between Abbasabad and Sabzevar.

No civilian casualties. At least that's good.

"Get the Minister of Defense on the phone."

After several minutes, Saeed finally got Minister Javad Ghafour on the phone.

"Please hold for the President, sir."

Avesta snatched the phone from Saeed.

"Javad, the TV is reporting a plane crash. It looks like a military transport plane. Do you know anything about this?"

"Yes, Mr. President, General Lajani booked a flight for an elite group of Revolutionary Guard soldiers to fly to Mashhad Air Force Base. He said that. . ."

Avesta stopped listening as soon as he heard the man's name.

Lajani.

Chapter Twenty-Four

TEHRAN, IRAN
SA'ADAT ABAD DISTRICT

Farhad woke up on the sticky floor of a jail cell. One look around and he knew where he was.

Evin.

It doesn't look like much from the outside. If it weren't for the sign above the front gate that reads "Evin House of Detention," it would appear to be a storage garage or a worn-down warehouse, but Evin Prison is one of the world's most notorious incarceration facilities. Built during the last years of the Shah's reign, it was originally intended to be used as a holding facility for prisoners awaiting trial. Technically, with many prisoners eventually transferred to the Central Prison of Tehran after their conviction, this remains true. However, it is not unheard of for prisoners to serve their entire sentences at Evin, regardless of the status of their cases. Female prisoners occupy one ward, but there are nine holding male prisoners, each with multiple levels. One is rumored to be a dungeon.

When the Shah was overthrown and the Islamic Republic under Ayatollah Khomeini took control, the size of Evin Prison was expanded to house fifteen thousand inmates. It was also outfitted with its own courtrooms and execution yards. Khomeini's henchman made it their priority to hunt down and arrest PMOI members during the years of his reign.

Most executions are done by way of hanging, but death by firing squad is also a familiar practice because the guards want to keep the inmates on edge with the sounds of the gunshots. For those who are hanged in the sentencing yard, their bodies are brought into the exercise yards and hung on display as a reminder to the rest of the prisoners of what may, and likely will, happen to them if convicted or if they display any disobedience during their stay.

Unlike the secretive Revolutionary Guard black sites where staff is kept to a minimum, Evin is widely known to have a surplus of well-armed guards and sophisticated, western technology to keep its prisoners secured. The only way to get a non-Iranian inmate out of the facility is through legal channels. But considering Iran's difficult relations with the West, its government often turns away U.S. State Department pleas for releasing its people of interest. Most are eventually let go, but not until the intended damage, psychological or otherwise, has been done. For foreign civilians looking to get their loved ones freed, their only hope is the flexibility of the Iranian justice system, which can be considered stringent, at best.

What makes Evin Prison more renowned than the country's larger prisons is that it mainly houses high profile political prisoners who have spoken out against the Ayatollah regime, been charged with espionage, or committed what the Iranian legal system terms "anti-government activities."

This has a broad spectrum of meaning, including distributing Christian materials, taking pictures of government facilities without official press credentials, and spreading propaganda deemed threatening to the government. Unlike other prisons in Iran, though, political prisoners at Evin have a higher release rate. What little is known about Evin today comes from those who were held there and have been bold enough to speak out about their experiences.

After hours of interrogation, prisoners are blindfolded as they are walked to their cells. If one is "lucky" enough to receive a so-called standard cell, it will seem more like a janitor's closet than a room. Most are no more than eight feet wide with only a blanket for a bed. The cells are lit by a single bulb that is never turned off.

Some of the older cells made for multiple prisoners are mostly reserved for women in Ward 4. They contain numerous bunkbeds with a grimy, unsanitary carpet that is rarely cleaned. Since they are not equipped with toilets, some of the rooms have had the carpet removed because inmates had accidents after being forced to "hold it" while they waited for guards to come and escort them blindfolded to the bathroom. All discussions between the inmates in these rooms must be done in a hushed tone.

In the windowless solitary cells, the tile floors are only cleaned on request by the prisoners, and even then they are responsible for cleaning them. What little food is provided to the prisoners is usually riddled with flies and dead gnats.

Farhad pulled his body up from the sticky floor in Ward 1, which was caked in dirt, blood, body oil and human waste. Thankfully, the small metal sink had running water, so he rinsed himself off. There was no soap, but it was better than nothing. Satisfied that he was as clean as he was going to get, Farhad grabbed the thin military blanket, laid it on the slate-colored tile, and sat back down.

Lost in his thoughts, his hands began to tremble as reality set in.

Where's Donya? Is she okay?

Do Jay and Raven know what happened?

The prospect of being tortured began to race in Farhad's mind. If he were lucky, his death would be quick, but given his reputation on social media, he knew that the Revolutionary Guard had been hunting him and would have a special discipline waiting. Nothing was off the table. Caning or whipping would be too mild at this point. Stoning or having molecular acid thrown at him was more likely.

Farhad shook his head. The thought of his apartment located on the northeast side of the prison's outer walls popped into his head. He remembered having many beers out on his balcony, staring at the stone walls that lined the prison's exercise yard. Perhaps it was destiny that he would end up there.

He jumped to his feet when the door opened. An imposing, muscular guard stood at the door with a baton in one hand. The name patch on the trademark stone-blue uniform said ABBASI. Farhad stared at the man but said nothing.

"Turn around. Put your hands behind you back."

The guard put handcuffs on Farhad and blindfolded him before yanking him away from the wall to escort him down the hall. Another guard, Yali, joined Abbasi in taking hold of Farhad's arms.

"Watch your step."

Farhad didn't know where he was being taken. When they arrived in a chilly room downstairs, Abbasi removed the blindfold. The room was lit by a single bulb on a chain that highlighted a metal table, bolted to the floor. Farhad could see a man in an IRGC uniform standing behind the table with his hands behind his back, but the darkness concealed his face.

"Take off your clothes!" Yali said.

Farhad's shoulders jumped at the command, and he stripped until he was stark naked. After he tossed his clothes aside, the man standing behind the table spoke.

"Bring him over here."

Before Farhad could see who it was, Abbasi and Yali punched him repeatedly in the gut, head, and kidneys. Once he was on all fours, they dragged him to the lit area, where his arms were extended to the side and strapped down by chains tied to metal bars at each end of the table. At first, he thought he was about to get whipped, which he had endured before, but if so, why was he naked? When the two guards chained his ankles to anchors in the floor, panic set in. Farhad tried squirming his body in every direction but he could barely move. When he settled down from his wiggling fit, the mysterious man squatted down to meet him eye to eye.

"Well, well, well. If it isn't the infamous Pirate of Iran," Nassiri said. "I knew all along that Lajani faked your death. When I grabbed his phone and started texting his contacts, I had no idea any of them was you. He was at least smart enough not to attach a name to your contact number. Imagine my surprise when we finished our little game of chase, and I saw you and that bitch Donya in the car."

Farhad said nothing. When he didn't respond, Nassiri slapped him across the face.

"Maybe this will elicit a response."

Nassiri pulled out his phone and placed it in front of Farhad. The blood immediately drained from his face. The video showed Donya strapped down on a table. Nassiri forced him to watch multiple soldiers violate her. He could see blood trickling down her leg as the soldiers forcibly pumped her from behind. As Nassiri turned up the volume on the phone, her screams echoed throughout the room and inside Farhad's head. The last image on the video was a closeup of tears rolling down Donya's face.

"Farhad. . ." she whimpered.

When Nassiri stopped the video, Farhad screamed a litany of profanities at him as tears welled up in his eyes. Nassiri slapped him again.

"You can stop, little girl. Nothing can help you now. Your whore is now our toy, Lajani is locked up and you belong to us. We're going to publicly lynch you in front of Azadi Tower, where we will demonstrate to the people that you are nothing more than a cowardly little weakling and *no one* can stop the power of the Supreme Leader."

"Someone will come along and take my place," Farhad replied.

"And we will crush them, too."

Nassiri turned to the two guards.

"Aren't pirates known to wear shark teeth as a necklace?"

"I think so, sir," Abbasi said.

"Well, for once, I think the shark should be the one to wear the teeth of a pirate."

Nassiri pulled out a pair of rusty pliers from his back pocket. He gripped Farhad's face by the sides of his jaw, trying to get him to open his mouth, but Farhad's mouth stood firm. Yali stepped forward and pinched Farhad's nose, so he had to open his mouth to breath. That's when Nassiri gripped one of his front teeth with the pliers. The tooth was harder to pull than Nassiri realized, and he pulled it at the wrong angle. Instead of pulling the tooth cleanly, he broke it off near the top. Farhad screamed in agony as Yali laughed.

"No matter. That was just an attempt for a keepsake. I have more concerning personal business to address with you."

Nassiri showed Farhad a picture of him standing next to the dead Basij soldiers that Thrasher had killed only days before. Donya had posted it online to help ignite the PMOI movement, but it was inevitable that someone at the IRGC would find it.

"These men were under my command. You've fucked our country for years, smuggling your booze and drugs across our borders. And you fucked me when you killed two of my men. They were good soldiers with a bright future. Now, it's time for me to return the favor!"

Nassiri held up his hand, and Abbasi tossed him Farhad's clothes. Nassiri placed his finger underneath Farhad's chin and lifted it so he could watch. Farhad cringed at the sound of his beloved *Star Wars* shirt being ripped in half. When he was through, Nassiri nodded at Abbasi.

"Mind if I let the new guy do it? It's time we indoctrinated him into this process."

Nassiri shrugged as he stood in front of Farhad to record his reaction with his phone.

Farhad heard the guard pull out his baton and braced for impact, but Yali didn't strike. He thought it was a delayed reaction intended to serve as another form of torture as he anticipated the beating, but he heard a strange clawing sound instead. What Farhad couldn't see from his position was that Yali had also pulled out his pocketknife and was digging the blade into various spots on the wooden baton to create jagged edges.

Evin is one of the world's harshest prisons because of its reputation for torture, murder and especially rape. Female prisoners are the primary victims. Their vaginas become so ravaged by the guards that they are rendered incapable of having children and their anuses are often so bruised they become confined to a wheelchair for months, unable to walk.

But the vicious rapes are not limited to female captives. There have been reports of men being bent over tables with their arms strapped down while being penetrated from behind with raw shafts of timber, and having their penises stretched by weights strapped to them. These reports are limited because the male victims who were fortunate enough to survive have been reluctant to share their stories.

Yali laughed as he continued to violently plunge the craggy baton up Farhad's ass. He cried and screamed, in a way that could only be known by rape victims. When Yali finally withdrew his baton, he noticed excrement leaking out.

"Look at that," he laughed, "the Pirate of Iran shit himself!"

Nassiri moved around to video it all, including Farhad's face.

"So much for the mighty Pirate of Iran."

"Now what?" Yali said.

Nassiri laughed.

"Again!"

Chapter Twenty-Five

On the other side of the compound in the highest security Ward, 2-A, Lajani groggily awoke to find himself in white prison garb inside a white padded room.

The white room.

One of the favorite forms of torture at Evin is psychological. Termed "white torture," the prisoners are dressed in pure white prison attire and thrown into a bleach-white, padded, sound-proofed room, equipped with a white sink. The lights do not generate any shadows and are illuminated 24/7. Prisoners are only fed tasteless, white rice served on white paper plates with white plastic silverware. The guards even handpick dead, black flies from the rice to maintain the all-white effect. Any requests to use the restroom are communicated by slipping a piece of white toilet paper under the door.

A prisoner's term in a white room is determined by the warden and can be for months or years. By the end of their stay, prisoners who do not experience hallucinations or psychotic breaks are robbed of even the most rudimentary social skills.

Lajani felt around the padded room for any cracks in the structure that would allow him to communicate with anyone on the other side, but he knew it was no use. The Iranian government pinched pennies in all government operations but spared no expense when it came to incarceration. Lajani had also been part of the consultant team when the white rooms were built back in the late 2000's. Had he known he would end up in one, he would have found a way to build them with a means of escape known only to him.

Time was its own weapon. The lights and blinding whiteness of the padded rooms was so intense it caused Lajani's eyes to water. When they became too strained to take it anymore, his only option was to close his eyes and try to sleep. But even then, he could sense the room's brightness. When he opened his eyes, the light felt ferocious. His only choice was to continue to endure it or move around blindly. He chose the latter, which brought its own challenges, so he decided to use his time wisely by counting his paces from one side of the room to the other. Nine to the door and four to the sink. With those specs complete, he began doing push-ups and sit-ups. Self-imposed exercise was the only way to make time pass without wallowing in the depression of his situation. He was on his fortieth sit-up when Nassiri opened the door.

"Get up and turn around. Face the wall!"

Lajani didn't protest. While his back was turned, two guards stormed in and beat him with their batons. All Lajani could do was fall to the floor in a fetal position.

"Don't you dare puke on the floor!" Nassiri said.

Once the beating was finished, one of the guards rolled Lajani onto his stomach, put a knee in his back, and cuffed him. When they pulled him to his feet, Lajani had a blindfold placed over his eyes, which was also white.

It was removed when Lajani was seated in the middle of the warden's office. Despite the summer heat, a flame burned in the fireplace with a poker sticking out. Above the fireplace, a boar's head was mounted on the wall. To his left was a pair of crossed, antique axes that the warden was never shy to brag about how they dated back to the Persian Empire.

But the balding, plump warden was nowhere to be seen. Instead, standing directly in front of him, leaning on his cane, was the Supreme Leader. Avesta stood next to him. Lajani went to stand but was pushed down. When he looked back, he saw Nassiri behind him.

"I trusted you," Shir-Del said.

When Lajani said nothing in return, Shir-Del glanced at Nassiri, who promptly smacked Lajani in the back of the head.

"Answer your Supreme Leader when he speaks to you!"

"He's not my Supreme Leader. Only Allah stands above us all," Lajani said.

Enraged, Shir-Del reached forward and squeezed Lajani's cheeks with his bony hands.

"I sit at Allah's side along with the Prophet to do his bidding, so you will honor me!"

Shir-Del looked to Nassiri.

"Stand him up."

Shir-Del wielded his cane and struck Lajani as he had done to Nassiri days earlier. Nassiri couldn't help but smile as he pulled Lajani to his feet and seated him back in the chair.

Karma is a bitch, isn't it?

"I don't trust easily. The fact that you operated with such reckless disregard under my nose to undermine my authority burns me to my core," Shir-Del said.

"Oops," Lajani said through his swelling lips.

Shir-Del lifted Lajani's chin with the brass handle of his cane.

"I assure you that you will be much sorrier than that."

Shir-Del glanced up at Nassiri again. This time, he struck Lajani in the back of the head with the butt of his gun.

"The chief commander of the Revolutionary Guard is bestowed with the great honor of using all the powers of his rank to exert the Supreme Leader's authority. I trusted you above all others. You *were* my right hand, Ramin."

"And now?"

"And now you find out what it means to be without one."

147

Shir-Del looked up and Nassiri whistled for the two guards waiting outside. They entered and removed their belts to strap Lajani's forearms down to the arms of the chair. Nassiri went to the wall and removed one of the antique axes. It was then that Lajani noticed that the blade was sharpened to perfection.

"I'm going to enjoy this," Nassiri said as he took back the axe.

"No," Shir-Del said.

Nassiri stopped and looked at the Supreme Leader awkwardly.

"*I'm* going to enjoy this."

He traded Nassiri his cane for the axe. Avesta took his place behind Lajani and pushed down on his shoulders to minimize any squirming. Shir-Del stared at the General as Lajani braced for what was coming. The Supreme Leader reared back the axe, then came down on Lajani's wrist just above the joint that connected to his right hand. Lajani wailed in pain. Unfortunately for the General, Shir-Del's weakened state meant that he didn't have the strength to cut through the bone and cartilage in one strike. As Lajani's severed hand hung off the end of the chair, Shir-Del pulled back the axe once more and cut it off on the second blow.

Lajani's wrist squirted blood on the warden's carpet. On the verge of passing out, the general's body shook involuntarily.

"Oh no you don't," Avesta said.

The president grabbed the poker sticking out of the fire and passed the red-hot tip in front of Lajani's face. For a second, Lajani thought they were going to brand him or burn out his eyes, but instead they rolled the scorching metal over the wound to cauterize it.

"This is for the soldiers you had blown up in the plane!"

The stench of scalding, burning flesh filled the room as Lajani screamed with all the might his lungs could muster before he passed out from the pain.

"Dress the wound, put him in a solitary cell with no light, and wait for my instructions," Shir-Del said.

"Yes, Supreme Leader," Nassiri said.

Shir-Del turned to Avesta.

"I will address my people. First thing tomorrow, we take care of *all* the conspirators. They will learn once and for all that the Supreme Leader of Iran cannot and will not be overthrown."

Chapter Twenty-Six

TEHRAN, IRAN

Jenkins awoke to see a skinny Iranian man in bifocals standing over her. Startled, she cried out.

"Jay!" said the man.

"It's okay. It's okay!"

Thrasher ran to her aid.

"This is Salim Ghiasi. He's PMOI. He's a doctor."

"And in a pinch, a little bit of a dentist."

Salim smiled.

Jenkins laid back down, but she panicked when she felt the bandage on her face and realized she could only see out of one eye.

"What happened? Why can't I see out of my left eye?"

"When a bullet pierced the window of the car you were ducking behind, you took some glass to the eye and neck," Thrasher said.

"There was considerable bleeding," Salim said.

Jenkins let out an exasperated sigh.

How many scars am I going to get in this job?

"Will I be able to see out of my eye again?"

"The damage was mostly to the sclera, so it should recover fully. The eye is one of the fastest healing organs in the body. But you need to rest."

Jenkins nodded. With her limited vision, she evaluated her surroundings. It looked like someone's bedroom.

"Where are we?"

"My apartment," Salim said.

"Where's that?"

"Eastern Tehran. Not far from the airport."

"What kind of doctor are you?"

"Medical student, actually, but I'm studying to be an oncologist."

Jenkins's good eye popped open and she sat up.

"What happened to Farhad and Donya?"

As he popped some Excedrin to help with his crushing headache from the ultrasonic rifle noise, Thrasher motioned for Salim to leave the room.

"I'll be back in a little while," Salim said.

Jenkins looked at Thrasher as soon as Salim closed the door.

"Well?"

"The Basij has them. Once you got shot, I had a choice to make. I could save you or them, but not both."

"That was a shit choice. You should've killed that last Basij guy and gotten us all out of there."

Thrasher's eyebrows clenched together.

"Listen, lady, easier said than done. I had tears and snot running down my face from the tear gas, most of my senses were knocked out of whack by the acoustic gun, and whatever I had left had just been nailed in the head by that psycho. So, why don't you cut me a little slack and show me some God damned appreciation!"

Thrasher was incensed. Jenkins watched the vein in his forehead bulge. She reached up and grabbed his hand, which helped to lower his blood pressure.

"Is that how you feel when I fly off the handle at you?" Thrasher asked.

"Yeah, pretty much," she said.

They laughed.

"What about Lajani?"

"No word."

"What *do* we do now?"

"I don't know."

A depressing silence loomed in the room. Thrasher opened his mouth to speak but was interrupted by a knock at the door.

"Come in," he said.

Salim had his phone in his hand and an alarmed look on his face.

"I'm sorry, but I just got a text message from my sister."

"Okay. And?"

"Her husband, Babak, who is one of our members, is a guard at Evin Prison. He personally saw Farhad. The Basij is going to hang him and Donya tomorrow at Azadi Square. They're going to make an example of them for everyone to see."

Jenkins gave Thrasher a desperate look.

"We're never going to get them out of Evin," she said.

"I know."

Thrasher bit his lip as he searched for a solution.

The only way to get them is at the Square.

Jenkins noticed he had dark circles under his eyes. The man could be an ass, but he was always committed to his mission, which often compromised his personal health.

"When's the last time you slept?"

"Hell if I know. I've been getting a few hours here and there."

"Why don't you go into the next room and take a nap? It's going to take a miracle to go along with that Moses-like beard you're sporting, so I need that unconventional brain of yours working on all cylinders."

Thrasher huffed out a laugh and wiped his eyes.

"Yeah, okay."

His eyes wandered around the room. A Holy Bible sitting next to a Koran on Salim's bookshelf caught his eye.

"You're a Christian?"

"In hiding, but yes," Salim said.

Thrasher's eyes widened.

Moses.

Without warning, he darted past Salim. Thrasher opened the door to the balcony and stared up at the sky. It was full of white, puffy clouds. Remembering what Lajani told him about the key to Iran's future being its past, he smiled, and ran back inside. Jenkins noticed a familiar, clever look on his face when he returned to the bedroom.

"I've got an idea. It's *way* outside the box, but without an army, it may be our only shot."

"Tell me," Jenkins said.

"You need to make some phone calls."

Chapter Twenty-Seven

RIYADH, SAUDI ARABIA

Tariq Al-Masari was resting comfortably, reading a book on the patio of his home next to the pool. It had been a tough year for the former Saudi ambassador to the United States. After years of working long hours and nearly losing his dear friend, Tom Delang, he began developing a toothache. When he couldn't ignore the pain any longer, he went to the dentist and was told that the problem wasn't his tooth; it was the muscles underneath his trapezoids that ran up his neck. A day later, his personal physician told him his neck muscles were the tightest he'd ever seen. After prescribing some muscle relaxers, the doctor cautioned him to reduce his working hours.

"I'll try, doctor, but this is the Middle East. Relations with the West are tense, at best."

"Nonetheless, you need to slow down. At this pace, you're going to work yourself into a heart attack or a stroke."

Truer words were never spoken. Despite using the muscle relaxers, Al-Masari had a heart attack three weeks later. Feeling pressure in his chest and numbness down his arm, he fell over, and shattered a glass table in his office. His secretary found him bleeding on the floor, clutching his chest and barely able to breathe, so she called an ambulance. When Al-Masari arrived at the hospital, the doctors determined that two heart valves were ninety percent blocked and a third was sixty percent. He was immediately sent into surgery for a triple bypass.

After his surgery, Al-Masari's wife begged him to quit his job. Seeing the tears in her eyes, he agreed, and he didn't have to wait long to give his notice. Word of the ambassador's heart attack reached the

Crown Prince within the hour. Upon hearing that Al-Masari's surgery was successful, the Crown Prince paid him a visit in person.

"Tariq, you've brought great honor to our country and to the position you hold, but this is too much."

"Your Royal Highness, I will recover. I can still be of great use."

The Crown Prince held up his hand.

"I won't hear of it, Tariq. You are one of my most loyal subjects. I will always rely on you, but you've given everything to your country. I won't let you give your life. Understood?"

"Yes, Your Royal Highness."

After a lengthy recovery, Al-Masari grew tired of moping around the house. He needed something to do, a sense of purpose. Finally, the Crown Prince appointed him to chair the kingdom's Green Project for the Ministry of Environment, Water, and Agriculture so he could address the country's growing pollution problem. At first, Al-Masari was lukewarm to the idea. He was happy to serve his kingdom, but the environment wasn't exactly a thrilling assignment, and he had no experience in the field of science.

A month into the new assignment, a deputy brought him a study from one of their scientists regarding his study of frogs. Since frog skin is the first line of a frog's defense against environmental or microbial pathogens, the scientist theorized that a deep study of a frog's innate immune functions could lead to better protection for the kingdom's soldiers and agents from the General Intelligence Directorate, the Saudi version of the CIA, against chemical attacks overseas. This interested Al-Masari, as the study put him back in the arena of defending the kingdom against foreign agents. He funded the project immediately. After depleting the kingdom's frog levels to a bare minimum, he reached out to an old colleague from Sudan, Nazir Agab, for an additional supply.

The study had only been operational for six weeks, but Al-Masari was feeling optimistic. The results were minuscule but promising. However, when the United States' animal rights activists got wind of the study, they protested and called his office incessantly. Despite everything he'd done to nurture the relationship between Saudi Arabia and the U.S., his calls for assistance from his political contacts in the States fell on deaf ears. No one in the political world gave a damn about frogs. No one, that is, except the animal rights groups. It became such a headache that he decided to take a few days off before one of them gave him another heart attack. In the meantime, he had tens of thousands of frogs locked up in a scientific lab waiting to be used in the experiment.

Al-Masari looked up from his book to see his tidy butler standing next to him, handing him his cell phone. He had purposely left it inside to ensure himself some quiet time.

"I'm sorry, sir, but your phone has been ringing non-stop for the last half hour."

Al-Masari begrudgingly accepted the phone.

"Thank you, Ekram. This may be important. I'm not to be disturbed under any circumstances until I am through."

"Yes, sir."

Al-Masari watched Ekram close the door before answering the call. "Hello?"

"Hello, my friend."

The former ambassador's mood improved immediately.

"Tom, Tom, how are you, my friend? How's Abby?"

"We're both well, Tariq. How's your health?"

Delang and Al-Masari had met each other years before Delang joined the CIA. It was right after the Khobar Towers attacks and Al-Masari had just joined the country's diplomatic service. He was at a technology conference, looking for ways to upgrade the technological infrastructure for the kingdom's defense systems when he met Delang, who was a salesman for the Avnet Corporation. Their introduction led to what is now the Saudi Telecom Company, which led to necessary updates in the country's security measures, but more important, it became the start of a wonderful and heartfelt relationship between Delang and Al-Masari. The two men made a conscious effort to stay in touch. Delang even left in the middle of his Bahamas vacation to attend the funeral of Al-Masari's mother.

After 9/11, while Delang was making his bones at the CIA, Al-Masari's star was also on the rise, and he eventually became Saudi Arabia's Ambassador to the United States. When CIA management realized that Delang and Al-Masari were close friends, they never hesitated to dispatch Delang to work with the ambassador to help resolve petty political differences or convince him to assist on joint counter-terrorism operations.

During one of these meetings, Al-Masari's chief of security betrayed him and arranged for the Iranians to kidnap Delang. While he was eventually returned home, the stress of the incident weighed heavily on Al-Masari. He never forgave himself for being responsible for his friend's kidnapping.

"The doctors tell me I'm fully recovered, but if the people from PETA keep calling my office about the lives of frogs, I'm bound to end up in the hospital sooner than later."

Delang laughed.

"I can only imagine."

"Are you and Abby still planning to visit this year?"

"Of course. We're thinking October, but I was wondering if you could help me out with something first. It's not a small request, so I'll owe you big-time."

"Anything for you, my friend. How can I help?"

"I'm going to need to switch to your secure line."

"I'll call you right back."

Al-Masari went inside to his private office and dialed Delang's number from his secure cell phone. When he answered, Delang filled him in on the operation in Iran.

"Oh, my goodness, Tom. Didn't the CIA learn their lesson the first time?"

"It's different this time, Tariq. Lajani came to us. Our people are there to lend a helping hand, but it's privately funded and it's his op to win or lose."

"That's a big gamble, Tom."

"Tell me about it."

"What do you need from me?"

"Aren't you guys experimenting with cloud seeding?"

"You know we are. How does that factor in?"

Using cloud seeding technology to combat drought was not a new concept. Once dry ice entered commercial production in the 1920's, desperate farmers began firing it into the atmosphere via cannon to create condensation that would water the farmers' crops. As technology advanced, scientists switched from using dry ice to using non-harmful chemicals, such as potassium chloride or magnesium hydroxide, to interact with the clouds to make it rain. In either case, the rainfall created was short-term and only generated water based on a percentage of the volume of dry ice or chemicals launched into the sky. The technique got to be too expensive for rural farmers.

The United Arab Emirates (UAE) recently decided to try a different tactic that recently showed tremendous success. Rather than dispelling chemicals into the air, UAE scientists launched drones into the sky, equipped with small-scale emissions units that determined the precise voltage required to make them disperse an electrical charge to the clouds' air molecules that would make them release water droplets. The first results produced a colossal thunderstorm and a third of an inch of rain. Once Al-Masari heard about it, he informed the Crown Prince, who gave him the necessary funds to start the project in the kingdom.

In theory, if enough electric emissions units were dropped into the sky, it could result in a massive downpour with the potential to include hail. While the purpose of the cloud seeding was to prevent widespread drought, Thrasher had come up with another way to use it that could rescue his team from their current predicament.

When Jenkins told Delang what happened to Farhad and Lajani, at first, he was irate, not only at what had transpired, but that he only found out so much later after the fact. The president and Wallace would surely chew his ass out. Then she told him about Thrasher's radical plan, which he thought was one of the most preposterous ideas he had ever heard. But, given the circumstances, it had merit and was worth trying.

Al-Masari listened to Delang's pitch, but his old school political instincts and his business sense kicked in.

"I don't know, Tom. If it ever got out that the kingdom had a hand in this operation, the blowback could be tremendous."

"That may be true, Tariq, but the United States is in the same boat. The potential downside can't be ignored, but the upside can't be either. We may be on Iran's shit list, but you know as well as I do that Saudi Arabia and Iran aren't exactly best friends. If there is a chance to change the world and the Middle East forever, shouldn't we take it? I don't think our shot at that is going to get any better than this."

Al-Masari bobbed his head back and forth as he considered the thought.

"This isn't going to be cheap, Tom. The kingdom would expect to be paid for this."

"We've got the money. How many drones do you have?"

"Fifteen. How many do you want?"

"All of them. Do you have enough emissions units to fill them all?"

"I don't think it will be a problem. When do you want to launch?"

"I'm still working on the details of the exact time, but it will be tomorrow morning. Can you swing that?"

"I can. Anything else?"

"Yes. How many of those frogs can you spare?"

"Thousands, but I can't give you all of them."

"Where can I get more?"

"You'll need to call a mutual friend of ours."

Chapter Twenty-Eight

TEHRAN, IRAN

Shir-Del emerged from his private prayer room in the House of Leadership with a stoic look on his face. Nassiri joined him as he walked to the podium.

"Did you shut down all of the country's internet access as I asked?"

"Yes, Supreme Leader. Your address will be televised, but not posted online. But I can't promise that it doesn't get out by some other means."

"Such as?"

"Someone could record the televised address with their phone then repost it using another VPN. The PMOI has been vigorous about bypassing our restrictions. It's usually short-term, but it's possible nonetheless."

"It's worth the risk. I'm confident that after what transpires, we will have total control."

"Did Allah speak to you, Supreme Leader?"

"He did. By Allah's grace, we are pressing forward."

Nassiri hesitated before responding.

"It would be easier to simply eliminate them and avoid the pageantry."

Shir-Del turned and gave Nassiri a sinister glare.

"*Never* doubt the word of Allah who speaks through me. Understood?"

"Yes, Supreme Leader."

Shir-Del swatted him away.

"One minute, Supreme Leader," said a camera man from the state-run television station.

Standing at the podium, Shir-Del appeared to calmly study his notes, but he was furious. Of all the things that could happen during his reign, the chief commander of his own Revolutionary Guard planning a coup against him was *not* on his radar.

In the days of Ayatollah Khomeini, the dissenters would be dealt with privately and the gossip of their demise would spread across the country. In those days, word of mouth was all that was needed to instill fear in those that dared oppose them. That was as true then as it was today, but Shir-Del was short on time. Given what happened three months ago, when his plot to start a war between India and Pakistan was uncovered, the resentment toward him, locally and internationally, was at an all-time high. Word of mouth alone wouldn't do the trick.

The difficult part would be admitting there had been an attempted coup against him. This was not an incident the Supreme Leader would normally disclose. After all, if it was attempted once, admitting to it would encourage the possibility of it happening again. But Shir-Del intended to slam the door shut on that prospect. Nothing could be left to chance. He would make a spectacle of the rebel deaths so that no one would even dream of summoning the courage to revolt ever again.

During his prayer session, he sought guidance from Allah. When he emerged from the room, he had made up his mind.

Shir-Del looked up from his notes and nodded at the camera man, who held up his fingers while he counted down from three.

"My brothers and sisters of Iran. I come to you today with news that is glorious and unfortunate. Today, I received news of an internal coup to overthrow my rule by the former chief commander of the Revolutionary Guard, Major General Ramin Lajani. Praise be to Allah that this feeble attempt was not successful. As you can plainly see, I am alive, untouched, and still in control of our great nation. Despite any rumors to the contrary, President Avesta continues to function in the full powers of his elected office. In the name of the great Allah and the Twelfth Imam, whose return we await, our country is thriving.

"Unfortunately, not all efforts during the pathetic takeover were quashed. At former General Lajani's order, hundreds of our most loyal and dedicated soldiers from the Revolutionary Guard were ordered to board a plane under the ruse of performing an exercise drill. As you may have seen on the news, that plane crashed. There are no survivors.

"As a result, I have made General of the Basij, Mohammad Nassiri, the new chief commander of the Revolutionary Guard, effective immediately. Under his direction, Revolutionary Guard soldiers have arrested other known conspirators within Lajani's inner circle and are in custody. One of these individuals is the so-called "Pirate of Iran," who has desecrated our magnificent faith by smuggling alcohol and drugs within our borders. Another accomplice is responsible for polluting our children's minds with horrific online access to pornographic websites from the West. These putrid conspirators will be dealt with harshly.

"While the Basij continues to make all attempts to arrest other collaborators, Lajani and his band of misfit conspirators will be executed swiftly. I invite all my loyal subjects to come to Azadi Square tomorrow morning at 8 a.m. to face their betrayers so that you may participate and witness their deaths.

"As ordained by Allah, your Supreme Leader stands above all in our country, and by his mighty hand I cannot be defeated or harmed. Those who oppose me are destined to fail. Once the conspirators have been eliminated, we will turn our focus to the enemies outside our borders, where they, too, will learn the severest of lessons.

"Praise be to Allah."

Shir-Del peered into the camera and closed his statement with a long look of commanding authority.

"And we're out, Supreme Leader," the cameraman said.

"On the contrary, we've never been more in."

Chapter Twenty-Nine

TEL-AVIV, ISRAEL

Israeli Prime Minister Eli Sahar was eating dinner with his wife when he was interrupted by one of his senior aides.

"Sorry to interrupt, sir, but the Director of Mossad is on the phone. He says it's urgent."

The prime minister's wife, Dina, gave him an annoyed look.

"I'm sorry, dear. Please excuse me."

Sahar pointed to the phone in the dining room, but Samuel shook his head.

"It's a video call, sir. You should take it in your private office."

Sahar nodded and walked down the hall. After closing the door, he hit the JOIN NOW button. Director of the Mossad, Yonas Lavi, looked concerned.

"Yonas, what's the problem?"

"Prime Minister, we have some growing concerns about Iran. The following message just aired on their state network."

Lavi played the broadcast from the Supreme Leader. Sahar placed his hand over his mouth. He had kept his conversation with President Cannon a secret from the one person in his government that he should not keep secrets from, and now it was coming back to bite him, just as he had feared.

Fuck.

When the video was done, Lavi appeared back on screen.

"Yonas, did we see this coming?"

"No, sir. There was no intelligence to indicate a coup, least of all from the leader of the Revolutionary Guard. But, there's one other thing."

"What is it?"

"One of our regular drones picked up some military activity on Larak Island in Iran."

"What kind of activity?"

"It's hard to say at this point, sir. It looks like an exercise of some kind, but the way their soldiers are moving doesn't look right."

"I'm not following you, Yonas."

"Sir, we've studied the Iranian military for years. This isn't something that gets taught in a guidebook, but you and I are familiar with the way an Iranian soldier marches and carries himself in the field. The soldiers we're looking at march differently, and most of them appear much shorter in stature than we're used to seeing. I'm not saying there aren't short Iranian soldiers, but this doesn't pass the smell test."

Lavi shared his screen with Sahar and showed him some of the drone footage. Even at high definition, the images couldn't determine the soldiers' height, but compared to some equipment they were standing next to, on average, they looked shorter.

"I'm not sure what the Iranians are up to, but I recommend we raise our military's defense readiness. Whatever the Supreme Leader has planned, we can't put our citizens at risk."

"I agree. I'll make a call to the Defense Minister as soon as we log off. Keep me informed of any unusual activity or chatter in Iran."

"Yes, sir."

Sahar ended the video call, but before he called the Defense Minister, he needed to make a more important call.

Chapter Thirty

WASHINGTON, D.C.
THE WHITE HOUSE

President Cannon was gently shaken awake from his slumber by his new chief of staff, David Bernstein. Seeing Bernstein's six-foot-five frame leaning over him in the middle of the night was never a good sign. Cannon sat up immediately.

"Sir, Prime Minister Sahar is insisting that he speak with you. He doesn't sound happy."

Cannon looked at the glowing red lights on his bedside table: 3:13 a.m. He wiped the sleep from his eyes and put on the navy-blue robe embroidered with the presidential seal that Bernstein handed him.

"Thanks. I'll take it in the next room."

"He's on line two. Would you like me in the room with you?"

Cannon hesitated. If the call was about Iran, he hadn't even told his chief of staff about what was going on there.

"In the room, yes, but don't join us on the call."

"Yes, sir."

After running his fingers through his greying red hair, Cannon looked at the First Lady, who groaned and rolled over to go back to sleep.

He picked up the phone in the next room.

"Eli?"

"Didn't I warn you what could happen if your mission failed?!"

"Whoa. What are you talking about?"

"Your movie is shut down. The supporting cast has been caught and will be executed tomorrow."

Sahar had Cannon's full attention. His sleepy eyes popped open and a sickly feeling crept into his stomach.

"Where are you getting this?"

"Roger, at some point, your country is going to have to learn not to get intelligence second-hand. The Supreme Leader admitted that there was a coup against him but he caught everyone involved."

"Everyone?"

"He didn't provide any names but he said he knew it was Lajani who was responsible for the attempt, and that at least two more individuals are facing execution in Azadi Square. Then, he said he would turn his focus to all his other enemies. That puts my country directly in their crosshairs, Roger!"

Cannon was stunned at the revelation. The last update he had received from Director Wallace said the set-up for the coup was progressing nicely.

"One other thing, Roger. What the hell is happening on Larak Island? We're seeing military activity out there. When we spoke before, you didn't say anything about that."

"Larak Island? It wasn't even part of any plans. Whatever's going on there doesn't have anything to do with us."

"Well, you better get your defenses ready because we sure as hell are! If that Iranian bastard so much as spits in our direction, we're going to have one hell of a response waiting for him, using our new stealth planes. I don't give a shit about any potential sanctions!"

The president rubbed his forehead and pounded his fist against the table. He had rolled the dice on the coup in Iran, and it'd come up snake eyes.

Bernstein approached, holding out his cell phone for the president.

"Director Wallace for you, sir."

Cannon gave Bernstein a confused look. He was glad that his CIA Director was calling, but the timing was too convenient. He turned back to his call with Sahar.

"Eli, hold on for one moment. Please."

Cannon took Bernstein's phone.

"Henry, I'm getting news from the Israelis that I should have been getting from you. This better be good."

Cannon listened to developments in Iran he already knew about, thanks to Sahar, but Wallace also told him about an idea Thrasher had that was being facilitated by Delang. His face scrunched up as he listened to the ludicrous idea, but it was his only card to play, and it could ease tensions with his Israeli friend. Cannon tossed the phone back to Bernstein, and quickly switched back to his call with Sahar.

"Eli? Are you still there?"

"Against my better judgement, yes."

Cannon closed his eyes, relieved that Sahar hadn't hung up.

"Good news. We need you to use those planes you've been hiding from us after all."

Chapter Thirty-One

Walsh woke up feeling a little stained, but optimistic, nonetheless. Her meetings with the Philadelphia City Council a day earlier continued to progress. Mayor Jim Davis was especially excited about the prospect of more vessel traffic coming through the port because it meant additional revenue for the city that was not part of his original budget.

Walsh's idea for expanding the city's shipping terminal had been tried by others before her but failed. The gateway to the Delaware River would be dredged to accommodate larger, heavier vessels. The area to the west of the docks would be cleared out to accommodate an on-dock rail in Philadelphia. This was similar to the city's competitor in Newark, which allowed the containers to load westbound trains without the added expense of trucking them from the terminal to the rail ramp.

For Walsh, this killed two birds with one stone. It would make the local union happy because their workers would be responsible for trucking boxes from the dock to the rail staging area. It would make customers and shipping lines happy because it would cut costs in half from the usual movement over public road, and there wouldn't be separate fuel surcharges or any chassis utilization fees.

Likewise, it would make rail vendors happy because it enabled them to charge the shipping lines more per container for the use of the on-dock rail. As a bonus, the new operation would increase the value of the rail vendor's stock, which would elate their stockholders.

Considering that Walsh owned more than 100,000 shares in the rail vendors' stocks, she hit the trifecta with her idea. Not only was she milking the cow; she was responsible for generating the milk.

Councilwoman Nancy Stewart had initially been one of Walsh's biggest critics for expanding the size of the port because of the cost to taxpayers to dredge the Delaware River, and the endless noise that would generate in her southeastern district. She also claimed that clearing the area to the west of the terminal would cause local truckers to wait in excessively long lines while the area was under construction, which would result in delivery delays. This point hit a nerve with the businesses in her district, which included distribution centers for business, such as Walmart, Target, Costco, and the all-important *Live!* Casino. Since it was an election year, Stewart hadn't been shy about voicing her concerns to the media.

But Walsh was too seasoned in the political game to see Stewart's threats for anything more than they were. Stewart's polling numbers were down, and she was receiving stiff competition from a challenger in her district. Stewart needed Walsh to contribute to her campaign. Now that she was a rich, private citizen and not an elected U.S. Senator, Walsh was more than happy to oblige the irritable request, and the issue disappeared.

The meeting with North American CEOs of the top-five shipping companies in the world, Maersk Line, CMA-CGM, Hapag Lloyd, Med Shipping, and China's state-owned China Ocean Shipping, were also progressing well. All of them had doubts about Walsh's aggressive timeline to get the port expanded. But since her brother-in-law's construction company, which Walsh owned a fifteen percent stake in, would get the contract, she knew it would get done.

Getting the shipping companies to use the Philadelphia port also meant taking vessel calls away from the port of Newark. Even though Newark's terminal costs were higher than Philadelphia's, which was the worm on Walsh's hook, this didn't mean that the board at the Newark terminal was simply going to let the largest capacity vessels from the top-five shipping lines leave their facilities without a fight. They were becoming combative in their negotiations to lock the shipping lines into long-term deals.

Since she had gone to graduate school at Penn State with the Newark Terminals' CEO, Vincent Rizzo, Walsh thought she could simply fix the problem by throwing some money his way. Rizzo, however, wanted more. He wanted to sleep with Walsh, and he wasn't sheepish about asking. In most situations, Walsh would have done one of two things to any man who attempted to use her as his whore in a business deal. She would either tell him to go fuck himself and then wreck his career after she pulverized him in the negotiations, or she would blackmail him with any dirt she could find. If enough dirt wasn't available, she would manufacture it. This wasn't to say that Walsh was immune from using her sexual prowess to close a business deal or to gain political leverage. She had done so on more than a dozen occasions, but those encounters were on her terms. Being leveraged into doing anything was something she wasn't in the habit of tolerating.

This time, though, was different. Rizzo had been her boyfriend during their college years and their relationship was serious enough that they had talked about marriage from time to time. But as Walsh's political aspirations grew, the relationship suffered. Feeling neglected, Rizzo did what many men in his position do but all women hate: he became clingy and desperate, which drove Walsh further away. After graduation, she worked for her mother who was the acting U.S. ambassador to Ukraine. For Walsh, the summer in Kyiv was a breath of fresh air and a much-needed break from her boyfriend. Considering that the relationship had been on the rocks for months, Rizzo was confident that the time away would add an element of perspective upon Walsh's return to the States. He could not have been more wrong. After two-and-a-half years together, Walsh ended the relationship over the phone. She hung up before Rizzo could say anything and never saw him again until three weeks ago.

Walsh couldn't believe her eyes when Rizzo's handsome Italian figure walked into the room, but he greeted her warmly and seemed to have let bygones be bygones. The one-time power couple quickly fell back into their old groove. Rizzo's advances toward her weren't exactly one-sided. As cold as Walsh could be, she still had a small place in her heart for Rizzo. Her issue, though, was that these feelings interfered with her sense of logic. She had trouble figuring out whether their sleeping together was reigniting a real flame or if it was an act of revenge on Rizzo's part that would have no bearing on the terminal deal. If Walsh played her cards right, though, she could potentially win Rizzo back and close the deal. It was a fine line to walk, but if push came to shove, closing the deal was her priority.

Walsh was wearing her rose colored, satin bathrobe and putting on a pot of coffee when Rizzo approached from behind, warmly hugged her waist, and gave her a kiss on the neck. It was a move he knew was sure to turn on Walsh every time.

"Hey, you. Last night was amazing," he said in his heavy Manhattan accent.

"It sure was. Even better than I remembered."

Walsh turned around and put her arms around his neck.

"Oh, so you *did* remember?"

"I never forgot."

As the two embraced in a passionate kiss, Walsh heard someone clear their throat from the door. It was only then she noticed that Rizzo was naked.

"For God's sake, Vinny, put some pants on!"

Walsh tossed him a dishtowel that he quickly hung on his erection. She turned to face her driver.

"Philip, what the hell?!"

"I'm sorry to interrupt, ma'am, but there's something I think you really need to see."

Philip was known for his discretion. It was one reason she hired him. If he was standing in her kitchen at five-thirty in the morning, the information must be important.

"Vinny, go back upstairs. I'll be there in a minute."

Rizzo nodded and left the room. Walsh approached Philip, obviously annoyed.

"This better be good."

Philip handed her his iPad.

"Here, you'll need these."

He handed her earbuds.

"For what? I'm not deaf!"

"No, ma'am, but I don't think you want your present company to overhear this."

The look on Walsh's face changed as she watched the video of Shir-Del's address. If Delang and Jennings had failed, her future plans for Philadelphia's terminal just took a major hit. She could still get the shipping lines to convert the Pacific string vessels from Newark but securing cargo ships from Iran with an exclusive call into Philly was part two of her plan. If the coup wasn't successful, it cut into her potential profits. The fact that she would see no fruit from her $50 million dollar payoff in hush money wasn't lost on her either.

"Where'd you get this?"

"After I listened to the limo conversation between you and the CIA lady, I did some digging on Iran and made sure I received alerts coming from there. This pinged on a blog before the website was shut down."

"Good work. Keep me posted on anything else you hear. I'll meet you in the car in a few minutes."

"Yes, ma'am."

As Philip left, Walsh power-walked to her office down the hall, grabbed her cell phone, and dialed a familiar number. She would be damned if Jennings and Delang were going to screw her out of millions.

"Hello, Senator," Latrina Pearl said.

Pearl had been Walsh's chief of staff in Washington, and the two had a sisterly bond. After Walsh was unceremoniously kicked out of Congress, Pearl managed to snag the chief of staff job for the Chairman of the House Permanent Select Committee on Intelligence, Peter McCoy (R-SC).

"Hey, Trina. Sorry to call you so early."

"It's okay. I'm awake. What's up?"

"I need a pretty big favor."

"Name it."

"Is that cabana boy of yours still mad at you?"

"Not for a good reason, but I've been stringing him along for the last few weeks. Why?"

"There's a CIA agent who goes by the name of Katherine Jennings. Do you think you can charm him into looking at her personnel file and briefing you on it?"

"It depends on what you're planning to do with it. Assuming her activities are still classified, he could get into a lot of trouble if they find out. And if that happens, the dominos will eventually fall on me, and no lucky charm in the world will save my career from that kind of blow-back."

"I'll make sure your ass is covered."

Pearl let out an audible breath over the phone. She loved Walsh and knew what kind of power she had, but this request could mean trouble with the Justice Department that could land her in jail.

"It might take me a couple hours."

"That's fine. I can meet you at the apartment tonight."

"Okay. I'll be in touch."

Walsh grinned as she hung up the phone. The security clearance she had signed was limited to the operation in Iran, but Jennings was fair game. It was time for Walsh to see what kind of skeletons the agent had in her closet.

***

Outside, Philip leaned against the limousine and lit a cigarette while he waited for Walsh. Driving for the ex-Senator was exhausting. He had to know when to listen, when to give her sensitive information, and when to keep his mouth shut. His brain was constantly generating thoughts. He knew that his mother would chastise him for smoking, but the relief he felt when he exhaled the smoke gave his mind a much-needed break.

Before he finished his second drag, his phone pinged with a text. He looked to see who was bothering him during his coveted moment of grace. The sender was unknown, but he knew who it was.

UNKNOWN: Did you give her info from the website yet?

PHILIP: Yes. A few minutes ago.

UNKNOWN: And?

PHILIP: She didn't look happy.

UNKNOWN: This deal is important to the shipping line. It's worth hundreds of millions. Does she have a plan to deal with what has happened?

PHILIP: She's making calls now, but I don't know to who. I'll keep an eye on her.

UNKNOWN: Make sure you do.

Chapter Thirty-Two

TEHRAN, IRAN
ISLAMIC PARLIAMENT BUILDING

Lajani's left hand was cuffed to a chain around his waist. Since his right hand was gone, the guards had to place a second set of handcuffs around his bicep and connect it to the waist chain. He had been held inside a private office on the opposite side of the main Assembly Room inside the pyramid shaped building for more than an hour but was not sure why. He thought he would be dead by now, but apparently Avesta had other plans before they killed him. All he could do was sit in his chair and wait to see what happened next, but even sitting presented challenges. His body was still in shock. He was sweating profusely. His breathing was short and labored. He had been given no anesthetics, so the pain cascaded up his arm. The blisters from the cauterization were filled with fluid. The skin around the edges of the wound was crispy, and a stench lingered from his burned flesh. All he could do was lose himself in thoughts of how he would die.

He remembered how Shir-Del had killed his predecessor, Rahim Shirazi. After Shirazi failed to keep Shir-Del's longtime friend, Rasoul Haddadi, safe, he also failed to deliver a CIA agent to the Russians in exchange for a new weapons system. For Shir-Del, letting his friend die was bad enough, but Shirazi's mission failure was the last straw. Shir-Del had Shirazi taken to an uninhabited area outside Isfahan, where he was chained inside a steel container he had specially equipped with a hundred 1500-watt UV lightbulbs. The gossip around Tehran was that Shir-Del flipped the switch himself. Lajani had no reason to doubt it.

Overnight, the heat from the lamps increased and Shirazi was slowly and excruciatingly cooked to death.

Lajani didn't know what type of death the Supreme Leader had in store for him, but whatever it was, he knew it would be brutal and unhurried. Due to the Supreme Leader's taste for the dramatic, it wouldn't surprise him if tickets to his execution were sold to the public.

The General shook his head. There was no use succumbing to such thoughts. However it would happen, his death was inevitable. He needed to make peace with that. What he couldn't make reconcile was the fact that he had used his family's life as collateral to the CIA. It was the best way to convince the Americans he was serious about overthrowing the Supreme Leader, but now that he had failed, their fate was in the agency's hands.

What would become of them? Would the CIA trade them to the Supreme Leader in order to prevent an attack on American soil? Or would they be part of some other bargain?

Regardless, his failure meant that he had signed their death warrant.

He had been married to his beloved first wife, Yasmin, for twenty-three years. It hadn't always been perfect, but he loved her. Her stubbornness and insistence on testing his patience inside the home is what made him bring in a second bride, Ziba, who he had married only six years ago. He loved her, too, but mostly because she kept Yasmin on her toes. If the CIA sent them back to Iran, Lajani knew that Nassiri would personally see to it that both women were raped and given to other Revolutionary Guardsmen as servants.

His boys, both by way of Yasmin, were fifteen and nineteen. He had been grooming both of them to join the Revolutionary Guard, albeit in a government under his rule instead of the Supreme Leader's. In order to rid Iran of the traitorous blood line, the Supreme Leader would ensure that they be hung on display for all of Tehran to see. His mother, father, brother, and nine cousins would undoubtedly suffer the same fate.

As the faces of his family flashed in his mind, Lajani's left hand began to tremble. A lump formed in his throat. The last time he saw them was at a stash house in Karachi. Considering Lajani's rank in the Revolutionary Guard, they all looked at him in confusion about why they had been taken away from Iran, but they were more concerned about him leaving. When they repeatedly asked what was going on, Lajani could only reply that everything was fine, and that getting them out of Iran was a precautionary measure. Standing at the door before he left, Lajani took one last look at each of them so their faces would be burned into his memory. Whenever he had doubts about his ability to succeed, he would remember who he was fighting for. He could not permit himself to fail. Yet he had. On top of it all, he had abandoned the family he had sworn to protect.

The door to the office opened and Avesta spoke to the guard.

"Get him up. It's time."

The guard yanked Lajani to his feet and escorted him down the hallway. Inside the steel grey Assembly Room were all two-hundred-ninety members of Parliament, plus the Vice President, Nima Balouch, who Avesta had personally requested to be there. With Avesta leading the way, Lajani was paraded down the main walkway as the Parliament Chairman, Ehsan Balsini, banged his gavel and called the assembly to order. Lajani received malevolent stares from each of the elected officials lining the rows.

"At President Avesta's request, the Assembly has been called to this emergency meeting. I would like to thank the assembly members for coming on such short notice," Balsini said.

The assembly members universally banged their fists on the arms of their chairs in recognition of the chairman's comments.

"President Avesta, you have the floor."

"Thank you, Chairman Balsini. I would like to thank the assembly members for convening so quickly on a matter of utmost importance. I've called you here for two purposes. First, I shall clear my good name that has been slandered. As you are all aware, three months ago, I was ushered into this room by Major General Lajani like a lowly dog, and I was publicly embarrassed for the unfortunate failure of the Persian-Arab Coalition that took place on television. This flogging was an insult to me and my family. Ever since, I have had to walk on ice in front of all of you and live with the shame of my failure. I tell you today that the incident I speak of was not of my doing. In fact, it was part of a larger set-up by General Lajani."

Moans and boos from the crowd filled the Assembly Room. Balsini banged the gavel to bring the room back to order.

"Second, as you have no doubt seen the televised message from our great Supreme Leader, General Lajani attempted to lead a coup against him so he could take control of the government for himself and leave all of you twisting in the wind."

Members of Parliament stood and shouted degrading insults toward Lajani, who stood like a statue in front of the chairman with a blank stare on his sweaty face.

"While the Supreme Leader has the authority to name Lajani's replacement as chief commander of the Revolutionary Guard, our Constitution legally requires members of this Parliament to vote on stripping General Lajani of his military rank, his formal removal as head of the Revolutionary Guard, and a legal decree charging him with being the mastermind of the political crimes he has committed so that judges in our legal system may sentence him to death upon receiving his guilty verdict. It is my recommendation. . ."

Balsini's chief aide unexpectedly entered the Assembly Room and whispered something in Avesta's ear.

"Mr. Chairman? I wasn't finished."

"Apologies, Mr. President, but the Supreme Leader is about to speak at Azadi Tower to address General Lajani's conspirators. By law, all Parliamentary business must cease when he speaks publicly."

Balsini's aide grabbed the remote and changed the channel on the eighty-five-inch flat screens affixed to the wall. For the next ten minutes, every member watched as the conspirators were paraded in front of an angry mob. Reactions inside the Assembly Room were no different than those in Azadi Square. Chills came over everyone as they watched the Supreme Leader and they became captivated by a thunderous storm gathering behind him as he spoke. Allah was with him. Allah was with Iran.

Chapter Thirty-Three

TEHRAN, IRAN
AZADI SQUARE

Farhad sat in the back of a Basij armored vehicle with a bag over his head. A musty cotton gag had also been stuffed in his mouth.

Probably a dirty sock.

Because his ass hurt so much, he adjusted his position on the bench seat. A Basij soldier promptly smacked him in the back of the head.

"Sit still!"

Farhad didn't move. All he could do was endure the anal pain and let an avalanche of depressing thoughts swallow him.

Where was Donya? Was she alright?

Have Jay and Raven abandoned me?

His negative thoughts were interrupted when he overheard two Basij soldiers whispering.

"Can you believe this is happening?"

"No, but the Supreme Leader knows what he's doing."

"Is the General going to be out there?"

"I don't know, but I heard he was being brought in front of Parliament."

Three bangs came from outside the truck's doors. It was time. One of the Basij soldiers removed Farhad's hood and gag. He tried to take inventory of his surroundings but the soldier cracked him in the jaw.

"Time for you to face your sins, you traitor."

One soldier opened the rear doors of the truck while the other picked Farhad up by his armpit. When he stepped out, the scene outside was a site to behold. Though it was a sunny day, with large, puffy clouds scattered in the sky, an ocean of his fellow Iranians encompassed Azadi Square. There was no way for him to know exactly how many people had come to witness his demise, but he estimated that it must have been close to a million. He had never seen such a crowd. All their faces were beet red with hatred and rage as they let loose a steady stream of roaring boos when he appeared.

Moments later, another round of heckling echoed across the Square. For the first time in days, Farhad saw Donya standing ten feet away. Her teary eyes met his and a moment of joy washed across their faces as each of them saw each other alive, but that feeling would not last long. They saw the walkway toward the Square. At the end of it was a platform affixed with six posts, and a stage behind it. Their eyes met. They both knew that this ending had always been possible, but now that it had arrived, there was no denying its existence.

The guard yanked Donya by the arm and marched her toward the stage, followed by Farhad. Each did their best to walk, but their legs were weak, and any movement was strenuous, due the injuries they sustained at Evin. As the citizens standing behind the barricade shouted profanities, spit and threw garbage them, Farhad looked down and saw a trail of blood in front of him. Donya's injuries were so severe that blood continued to trickle down her leg. He wondered if she would still be able to have children, but he stopped himself. They were experiencing their final moments in life and any such thoughts were ridiculous.

Farhad and Donya had their backs shoved against the posts. The back of Farhad's head hit it with such force that he saw stars while the soldiers tied his hands and secured his feet with a rope. They did the same to Donya. As the stars from his eyes faded, he saw four individuals being marched toward him with equal hatred from the crowd: generals from the Navy, Ground Forces, Aerospace Force and Quds Force. He didn't think it was possible, but another wave of disappointment swept through him. It was official. The Supreme Leader knew everything. They had failed.

After the generals were tied to their posts, cameras from the state-run TV station panned across each of them. Farhad wasn't sure this mattered because nearly every person in the crowd had their cell phones in hand to record their downfall, but he figured they wanted close-ups so people at home could see the faces of those who had committed the ultimate offense against their Supreme Leader. An unexpected cheer came from the crowd. Farhad and Donya looked at each other, wondering what was happening. When they heard the voice, they knew.

The Supreme Leader took the stage, dressed in his most pure white thobe and turban that glowed in the daylight peeking through the clouds. His thin fingers gripped the sides of the podium as he spoke into the microphone.

"Welcome, my brothers and sisters. You have come today to bear witness and participate in the greatest example of justice our great country can bestow upon its citizens. Standing before you are six traitors who have conspired against me to rob you of your government. The penalty for these despicable crimes is death!"

The crowd cheered. As the Supreme Leader read off the names of each conspirator, hissing and boos rose up toward each of them. But when he read Farhad and Donya's names, the hairs on their skin stood erect as the screaming reached to the heavens. When the noise died down, Farhad felt an odd drop in temperature as the wind picked up.

Then, the Supreme Leader continued.

"The deaths of these cowards will not be merciful. We will ensure that they are agonizing as we slowly extract the life from their bodies before hearing their desperate pleas to die. Make no mistake, they will be alive when their bodies are carried on this stage to have their necks stretched to the point where their souls are suffocated and ripped into Hell by the devil himself!"

As the sky darkened, tentacles of lightning began to streak above Azadi Tower. For those in the monstrous crowd, it was as if nature was in sync with the Supreme Leader. The rumbling thunder shook the ground beneath their feet. In that moment, they all knew without question that Shir-Del had been handpicked by Allah to lead their country against all who opposed Iran.

Shir-Del grinned to Nassiri. He knew he was right to air the executions on live television. The cameras rolled as the sky turned more crimson with each word that rolled off Shir-Del's tongue. The image of the heavens responding to him spread across the world like a virus. He wanted everyone to know, once and for all, that the Islamic faith was the true and righteous faith of the world and that he stood next to the Prophet at the right hand of Allah.

"As a reward to my loyal subjects, you may step forward and stone each of the conspirators until they are on the threshold of death!"

The crowd cheered as Shir-del turned to Nassiri who then pointed to a Basij soldier standing below the stage. The soldier motioned to a slender young man with short hair and a wispy beard, who looked to be the same age as Farhad. After climbing over the guardrail, he eagerly stepped forward with his bag of rocks, gave a slight nod of acknowledgement to the Supreme Leader, and tossed a rock up and down in his hand like a tennis ball as he debated who would be his first victim.

Farhad diverted his eyes from his first executioner, looked at Donya, and slowly blinked three times, which was meant to symbolize the words I-LOVE-YOU. He'd never used such a code before and wasn't sure she would understand, but a brief flash of warmth flowed from his heart to his toes when she returned the gesture. As the man reared back to throw the stone at him, Farhad looked up to the sky, hoping to get one last glimpse of the sun as he gathered the strength the endure the excruciating punishment that was about to befall him. There was no sun, only dark clouds in a reddening sky, accompanied by splashes of lightning and massive thunder rumbling in the foreground. He squeezed his eyes shut and tightened every muscle in his body as he braced himself for what was coming. But the impact from what pinged his forehead was far too soft to be a rock. When he opened his eyes and looked down at the ground, he saw a pebble of ice the size of a toman coin. Confused, he looked to the sky again.

What the hell?

Suddenly, a torrential downpour of rain and hail began streaming from the sky. Running for cover, the crowd protected themselves as best they could, but the pellets of hail recklessly beat down on them as the rain intensified. Multiple bolts of barbed lightning stretched across the sky and was promptly matched by erupting thunder that echoed around them.

Because of his Chromosome Six Deficiency, Shir-Del's body would eventually respond with bruises and bumps from the hail pecking away at him, but he could not feel the impact. He stood frozen on stage, unflappable and in disbelief.

As the violent storm continued to drop sheets of rain and buckets of hail on Azadi Square, something else began falling. Farhad couldn't believe it when the first one bounced off his head. Frogs. Thousands of them fell from the sky and slapped the running crowd with their slimy bodies. The frogs that survived the fall hopped around randomly. Some of the crowd stood across the street under a covered walkway. They stared in astonishment and recorded the incident on their phones. Frogs raining from the sky could only be interpreted as an act of Allah, as written in the Koran. Was Allah trying to communicate with them and

186

spare the lives of the conspirators? If so, did this mean the conspirators were right to try and remove the Supreme Leader?

Nassiri crouched down on the stage with his hands covering his head, five feet away from the motionless Supreme Leader. He covered his eyes and saw those who had found shelter gazing at the barrage of frogs. There was no doubt what they were thinking. He looked up at Shir-Del, who remained standing, seemingly unaffected, as he continued to be battered with the elements of the storm. If he was right about the reaction from the crowd, Nassiri needed to whisk the Supreme Leader away as quickly as he could.

"Supreme Leader, we *must* go!"

Nassiri pulled Shir-Del away and escorted him off the stage as fast as the old man's legs would let him. After he shoved the Supreme Leader into his vehicle, he looked back at the Square to see that all the conspirators had vanished.

Chapter Thirty-Four

Still strapped to a post, Farhad slammed his eyes shut and hung his head as he continued to be pummeled by rain, hail, and frogs.

"Hang on, Donya!"

Suddenly, he felt his hands go free, and then his legs.

Is this a miracle from the heavens?

Before Farhad could finish his thought, he was yanked away and dragged through the Square. He couldn't see who was pulling him and didn't care, even when he slipped and fell on the grimy frogs. Farhad looked for Donya, but he could barely see through the elements of the storm. When he reached the opposite side of the Square, a van was waiting. His savior tore open the door and tossed Farhad in the back.

"Hurry up, will ya?!" the man shouted.

Farhad recognized the voice.

Thrasher frantically waved the others into the van. Moments later, Donya, the four Generals, and Jenkins rushed inside. Once he heard Jenkins slam the door shut, Thrasher hit the gas and tore off down Sa'idi Expressway.

Moments later, the storm stopped as unexpectedly as it began.

"Everybody okay?" Jenkins asked.

Farhad, Donya, and the four Generals nodded.

"What the hell was that?!" Farhad said.

He saw Thrasher looking at him in the rearview mirror.

"Divine intervention," he responded.

Thrasher and Jenkins both smirked.

"Don't tell me you prayed for that to happen," Donya said.

"In a way," Jenkins said.

Donya and the others looked at each other, confused.

"Someday you'll have to tell me how you pulled that off," Farhad said.

"Maybe," Thrasher said.

Farhad rolled his eyes.

Thrasher looked at Farhad in the rearview mirror.

"What the hell happened to your tooth?"

"Nassiri tried to yank it out with a pair of pliers but he broke it off instead."

Thrasher cringed. Jenkins noticed blood dripping down Farhad and Donya's legs.

"Are you two okay?"

"No," Donya said. "I can barely walk."

Jenkins reached into her backpack and pulled out a spare set of clothes.

"Here, these are ours. I'm not sure how well they'll fit, but they're clean. We'll stop and get you something in a little while. I was able to grab your new *Star Wars* shirt, though."

Jenkins tossed them the spare garments, and she noticed the male generals staring at Donya.

"Divert your eyes, gentleman," she said.

Farhad's *Star Wars* t-shirt felt like a blanket of security. As Farhad and Donya undressed, Jenkins noticed what they were wearing under their thobes.

"Why are you wearing diapers?"

Farhad and Donya exchanged looks, embarrassed.

"The soldiers didn't want to clean the blood from their trucks."

Thrasher saw blood soaking through their clothes.

"Were you?" said Jenkins.

Farhad and Donya lowered their heads.

Thrasher repeatedly pounded his fist on the steering wheel.

"Mother fuckers! I'm gonna kill every single one of those deranged pieces of shit!"

"Jay, not now!"

Jenkins reached forward and took Farhad and Donya's hands.

"It's not your fault. I'm so sorry."

Neither responded.

"So are we," the General of the Quds Force, Javad Abendini, said.

"Sorry guys. You can open your eyes."

Jenkins looked at the group of Iranians. They looked like they'd been through hell. In a way, they had.

"Jay, head back to the doctor's apartment. We need to get them checked out."

"Roger that."

Each of the Iranians had an understandably defeated look on their face, but Jenkins knew this wasn't true. Despite their conditions, there was still time to turn the coup around, but everyone needed to get back on the clock.

"Where's Lajani?" Jenkins asked.

"I overheard a Basij soldier say that he was being taken before Parliament," Farhad said.

"Parliament? What the hell for?"

Farhad shrugged.

Jenkins pulled out new burner phones from her backpack and tossed them to each of the Iranians.

"Start making some calls."

"To who?"

"Everybody."

Chapter Thirty-Five

TEHRAN, IRAN
ISLAMIC PARLIAMENT BUILDING

As the stoning was about to commence, the mood in the room was resoundingly against Lajani. When the violent downpour of rain and hail descended on Azadi Square, the sea of hatred started to part. Some Parliament members considered it a direct response from Allah while others were frustrated that nature had delayed the conspirators' punishment.

But when frogs started dropping from the sky, every member stood in silence, overwhelmed and bewildered. Lajani also stood in amazement as he observed the spectacle on TV.

Was Allah intervening on the conspirators' behalf as he had with the prophet Musa?

For the next hour, every member of Parliament engaged in heated arguments with their fellow colleagues over the strenuous objections of Chairman Balsini, who desperately tried to restore order. His continuous gavel strikes became nothing more than white noise over the clamoring in the room.

Lajani began to smile, and the pain in his arm subsided a bit. He didn't know how it was possible, but he had just gotten all the leverage he needed for his plan to succeed.

The verbal chaos in the room was suddenly broken by the sound of gunshots outside the chamber doors. Minutes later, they burst open. Loyal soldiers of the PMOI, Ground Forces and the Quds Force marched with unwavering purpose toward General Lajani, shoving aside any official who got in their way.

When Quds Force General Javad Abendini reached Lajani, he began to uncuff him. Avesta lunged to stop him, but it was pointless. The six-foot-six soldier towered over the president, palmed his face, and shoved Avesta to the ground like a bully on the playground.

Balsini banged his gavel.

"What is the meaning of this?!"

Lajani rubbed his arm and spoke.

"Mr. Chairman, it's true that I conspired to overthrow the Supreme Leader. I will not plead innocent to those charges. But as you and the rest of Parliament have now witnessed with your own eyes, Allah has interceded in the execution of my fellow colleagues. Under Chapter 1, Article 2, of our Constitution, the actions of Allah supersede all orders from the Supreme Leader, the President, the Council of Experts, or this Parliament. Allah, himself, has now deemed the Supreme Leader unfit to hold his office."

The room erupted in shouts from members loyal to the Supreme Leader. Balsini banged his gavel so hard on the table that the mallet broke off from the handle.

"That's preposterous! Those frogs could have come from anywhere."

Lajani laughed. Thankfully, he wasn't the only one. Some of the other officials in the room snickered as well.

"From where? It was a bright, sunny day when I was brought to this building. There are no waterspouts in this region that could have carried the frogs here. How else can the chairman explain this?"

Balsini looked around the room, hoping to find someone with a reasonable explanation, but all he saw were blank stares.

"Mr. Chairman?" Lajani pressed.

Avesta rubbed the side of his face and stood to address the room.

"Mr. Chairman, it is your legal right to call the room to a vote to determine whether this was an act of Allah or a freak accident of nature," the president said.

Lajani was annoyed that Avesta was correct. The chairman had that right. All he could do was wait and hope that the votes swung in his favor. He called Abendini over and whispered into his ear.

"Position four armed guards to each side of the room. Ensure that they have their weapons, but do not under any circumstances threaten any member of Parliament. This *must* be a clean vote. Make sure that soldiers stand ready outside the chamber doors. No one comes in. I don't care if it's the Supreme Leader. *No one comes in.*"

"Yes, sir," Abendini said.

Lajani sat calmly in a chair that was brought to him. Avesta sat on the opposite side of the aisle, but he was by no means calm. Lajani could practically feel the hatred in the icy glare directed his way. Though he knew he should keep an eye on Avesta to ensure that he didn't try to assault him, Lajani held his wrist above his missing hand and quietly prayed.

Over the next two hours, Parliament voted on what they'd witnessed on TV. Balsini covertly tried to delay the voting process while his chief aide reached out to a trusted member of the Aerospace Force. Perhaps there had been aviation activity over Azadi Square when the frogs dropped from the sky. As the voting ended, his aide returned and slipped him a piece of paper.

NO ACTIVITY IN THE AREA

The hairs on Balsini's neck stood up. It was true. Allah had intervened.

Twenty minutes later, the voting was concluded. The final tally was 192 to 98. In his commitment to prove the General wrong, Balsini neglected to turn off the TV sets in the room. Had he been paying attention, he would have seen the actions of the crowd in Azadi Square. After the frogs fell, they dropped to their knees and prayed to Allah in acceptance of what had happened. These images were on full display during the voting process, and undoubtedly helped sway the voting.

"The motion has passed. The great and merciful Allah has spoken. Should any member of Parliament come forward with evidence to the contrary, the motion can be recalled with another vote. But for now, the Supreme Leader has been removed from office."

Lajani stood from his chair after Abendini handed him a thumb drive. Two of Abendini's men promptly placed Avesta and Vice President Balouch in handcuffs.

"What are you doing?!" said Avesta.

"Mr. Chairman, under Chapter 9, Article 113, foreign military bases are forbidden in Iran. President Avesta is guilty of conspiring against this government."

"Nonsense! There are no foreign military bases in Iran."

Lajani walked over to a laptop connected to a TV screen and clumsily plugged in the thumb drive with his one good hand. A video showed a Chinese military plane landing at Larak Island.

"As you all know, I recently escorted the Supreme Leader to China, where he successfully negotiated an oil deal with our Chinese friends in exchange for protection from the West. What you do not know is that the Supreme Leader also agreed to allow Chinese soldiers to come to Larak Island and perform military training exercises away from the United States' eyes. You can see the Chinese soldiers coming off their plane."

Lajani pressed the button to go to the next screen.

"In order to hide the Chinese activity from everyone in this room, at the Supreme Leader's request, IRGC uniforms were provided to the Chinese. You can see hidden video of the uniforms being handed out here."

Avesta's jaw dropped as he stood rooted in shock. He knew nothing of this. Lajani had played his cards wonderfully.

"I say to you now, Mr. Chairman, that the Supreme Leader has committed a crime against this country, and since the military chapter and article of our Constitution come under the provision of Executive Power, so, too, has President Avesta."

Balsini chewed his lip. Lajani had done his homework, and he was right.

"Take the president into custody."

"No, wait!"

Avesta pleaded his innocence as he was escorted out of the Assembly Room.

"As ordered by our Constitution, the Council of Experts shall now be convened to begin deliberations on a new Supreme Leader."

"Mr. Chairman, those meetings will not be necessary," Lajani said.

"Not necessary, General? Iran must have a Supreme Leader to rule our country."

"Mr. Chairman, you're fully welcome to call on the Council of Experts if you like, but the officials in this room have already voted that the scene that transpired at Azadi Tower was an act that came directly from Allah. As such, it is not only an act to free my fellow colleagues. My so-called traitorous actions were not just to recall the *current* Supreme Leader. They were to permanently remove the *office* of Supreme Leader. Therefore, if the word of Allah rules over all of us, and this Parliament agrees that Allah intervened in agreement of my actions, then the office of Supreme Leader is no longer required."

Gasps echoed across the room, followed by incessant shouting and screams. Lajani nodded to Abendini, who pulled his sidearm and fired a blank shot into the floor to bring the room back to order.

"What, then, is your suggestion, General Lajani?"

"Mr. Chairman, with no Supreme Leader and no functioning Executive Branch in place, Iran is left with only it's military to protect it. In accordance with our Constitution, as chief commander of the Revolutionary Guard, I shall assume control over this government by way of martial law until such time that new elections can take place. However, I vow to you today that Sharia Law will remain in effect."

All members of Parliament held their breath and stared at the chairman, wondering what his next move would be. Sweat was beading on Balsini's forehead. He was cornered by the law and had no other choice.

"So ordered."

Chapter Thirty-Six

Abendini escorted Lajani out of the Assembly Room to an IRGC issued Humvee. Small crowds were moving toward the Parliament building, but protests had not yet begun.

"I need you to get to Qom with as many men as you can spare," said Lajani. "When the clerics get wind of what happened inside, they are going to turn the city upside down. I'm trusting you to keep everything in order. Make as many arrests as you have to, but only use force when needed."

"That may not be easy. You know what we're up against," Abendini said.

"I know. Do your best and keep in touch. This is our only chance."

Abendini nodded and opened the door for the General. Lajani was pleased to see Thrasher and Donya inside. Farhad was in the driver's seat. He immediately sped away. Thrasher noticed the man's missing hand right away.

"What the hell happened in there?"

Lajani ignored him. He noticed that Donya wouldn't look at him. Farhad barely glanced at him in the rearview mirror. Lajani saw tears welling in Donya's eyes and noticed blood on the floorboard. He soon realized it had dripped down her leg.

"Did they...?"

Donya nodded.

"Me too," said Farhad.

Lajani placed his one good hand over his eyes. Knots began to form in his stomach.

It's all my fault.

"I'm so sorry. I never intended for this to happen."

"We know," Donya whispered.

"I know this won't make up for what happened, but I didn't make it out unscathed either."

Lajani held up his right arm so they could see his missing hand. He saw Farhad's eyes bulge in the rearview mirror. Donya gasped and covered her mouth.

Then it hit home for Thrasher that Lajani was the real deal. The man was a warrior. He didn't know if he would be able to endure the same punishment, but Lajani had proven what he was willing to sacrifice in order to rid Iran of the Supreme Leader's violent rule.

"I've heard about things like that happening here, but I've never seen it with my own eyes," he said.

Lajani gazed at Thrasher. He could tell that he was genuinely concerned for his well-being. It was the first human characteristic he had seen from the man.

"Now, do you understand what the Supreme Leader is capable of?" said Lajani.

Lajani turned to speak to Donya but he stopped and sat upright when he noticed Thrasher extending his left hand.

"Iran is lucky to have you, General," Thrasher said.

Lajani looked at Thrasher before returning the handshake. They nodded at each other. Lajani had finally earned Thrasher's trust and respect. Donya joined in by placing her hand over both of theirs, and finally smiled at Lajani.

"Are you still with me? I can't do this without you."

"We're with you," she said.

"But first, we need you to tell us what happened with the Parliament," Thrasher said.

Lajani gave them the rundown, which astonished each of them.

"Farhad, pull over. You and Jay need to change seats."

"Why?"

"Because our next stop is the Presidential Administration building, and they will expect someone who looks like a soldier to be driving."

"Are you kidding? After what just happened? The guards there will kill us before we get through the gate," said Donya.

"You're going to have to trust me as much as I trust you because once I get through the gate, the next step is yours."

Farhad did as he was told and changed seats with Thrasher. It was a ten-minute ride from Parliament to the Presidential Administration building. As Farhad feared, the guards were on high alert when their Humvee approached the gate. Thankfully, Thrasher was dressed in the IRGC uniform that the PMOI had given him.

"ID, please," Sgt. Moradi said.

"He's my ID," Thrasher said.

He pointed to Lajani in the back seat, who wasted no time getting out of the Humvee. Since Moradi was carrying a submachine gun, Thrasher cunningly let his right-hand drift to the gun on his hip, just in case the guard decided to play hero.

"Hold it, General!" Moradi said. "Hands up!"

Thrasher pulled his Sig Sauer P226. From below the window, it was pointed directly at the guard. His finger was on the trigger and was ready to fire, but he wanted to give Lajani a moment to work his magic.

"I'm afraid that's difficult to do in my case, Sergeant."

When Lajani complied with the guard's request, he saw that the General was missing his right hand. Aghast, Moradi took a step back as he saw his grotesque nub.

"If the Supreme Leader was right about you, then I'm sure you deserved what you got, General."

"Sohrab," Lajani said, addressing the Sergeant by his first name, "it's true. But, if they can do this to me, they can do this to anyone. Do you want your boy growing up under the thumb of a government that would dish out such vile punishment, or do you want him to grow up in a new Iran, where such an act is a thing of the past?"

Moradi paused for a moment and lowered his weapon. Unbeknownst to him, Thrasher lowered his weapon in the Humvee.

"I want my boy to grow up in a country whose leader believes that Iran's destiny is more than jihad with the West."

"I do, too. And I'm trying to put us on that path."

Moradi waived them by. When Thrasher reached the front entrance, Lajani dished out orders.

"Donya, come with me. I need you. Jay, take Farhad to wherever the PMOI is holing up. Tell Lilly I'll call her."

"Wait, what about me?" Farhad asked.

"Start making more videos. People need to know you are alive. Tell them what happened to you in prison. It's time we built Iran's morale. Don't post anything yet, though. Wait for my call."

Donya hustled to keep pace with the General as he made his way down the hallway to the president's office. Surprisingly, all of the presidential staff had abandoned the building. They had gotten word from their fellow Parliamentary colleagues about what had happened, and wanted nothing to do with what was to follow. Only Avesta's personal aide, Saeed, was present. He hung up his phone when he saw Lajani and Donya.

"General, what's going on? Who's that with you?"

With his one good hand, Lajani punched Saeed in the face with such force that the presidential aide instantly dropped to the ground. Lajani grabbed him by his collar, dragged him into the president's office, and propped him up against the wall.

"Listen, Saeed. Avesta is in jail and I'm more than happy to let you join him. Or you can help me."

Petrified, Saeed nodded.

"Good. Do you have access to the president's personal computer?"

"Yes, General."

"Show me."

Saeed walked Lajani and Donya into the same private office where the General had been arrested only hours before and logged into the computer.

"Is that it?"

"Yes, General."

"If you pull any tricks, my associate will find them, and then I'm going to shoot you."

"No, General. You're logged in as requested."

Lajani turned to Donya.

"Time for you to do your thing."

As Donya sat, Lajani hit Saeed in the face with another robust blow. Lajani caught the young aide as he fell, and carried him to an adjacent sofa.

"What was that for? He did what you asked!" Donya said.

"I'll make it up to him. He can't know how or what we're about to do. Find the application on the computer for the National Intelligence Network (NIN)."

Lajani picked up the phone and called Hamid Mousavi, the same senior agent from the Ministry of Intelligence's Cyber Division who had come to inspect Avesta's computer right before Lajani was arrested. What Avesta didn't know was that Mousavi was one of Lajani's other conspirators.

Four years ago, when Lajani was still a Colonel, Mossad had hacked his computer and pulled files regarding a proposed surprise attack on the Israeli Embassy in Greece. When Mousavi discovered the breach during a routine network update, Lajani knew he had to spin the incident or his superiors would have him killed for his negligence. With Mousavi's help, Lajani convinced his bosses that he had laid a trap for the Israelis, and they'd taken the bait. The attack on the Israeli embassy in Greece never happened, but armed with the knowledge that the Israelis had accessed the computer, Lajani fed Mossad with false leads for a couple weeks, which resulted in no loss of life for either side. For his assistance, Lajani made sure that Mousavi was promoted and put on a fast track to move up the Ministry's food chain.

While Lajani hadn't planned for Mousavi to be called to service the president's computer, the senior agent didn't miss the chance to plant a bug on it that would allow him to remotely access the computer.

"Hello?" Mousavi answered.

"Hamid, it's me."

"General! Are you okay?"

"We'll talk about that later. Were you able to crack Avesta's password to the NIN?"

"Yes, sir. This morning."

"Does the Director know anything about it?"

"No, sir."

"Good. Log into Avesta's computer. Donya, give Hamid the remote access he needs when you get the pop-up."

Seconds later, Mousavi logged in and the keys to the online kingdom belonged to Donya and Lajani.

"Thanks, Hamid. You'll have your payment in a few hours. Stay alert."

"Of course, General."

Over the next thirty minutes, Lajani had Donya revoke all government user access to the NIN, except his. The next step was to log into the SmartFilter application and remove restrictions on download speeds while unblocking popular social networking platforms.

"Start with Facebook and Twitter. Unrestricted access for all users."

"What about other websites?"

"We'll have to go through the list one by one after I go on TV. I'm not opening the floodgates."

"That will take forever."

"Do you want this to work or not? Look, I certainly don't want the people to have access to pornography, but we've got to loosen the restrictions. Never give people everything at once. The idea here is spread the word about the atrocities that occurred under the Supreme Leader and show the world what's developing. If everything goes to plan, the people will want more, which gives us all the leverage we need."

Impressed with how much Lajani had thought the situation through, Donya nodded.

"Well, hop to it!" Lajani said.

Excited, Donya ignored the pain she felt when she twisted in the chair. She began pounding away at the keyboard, removing Iran's online restrictions. The moment she'd dreamed about had finally arrived.

"I'm on it."

"Good. I'll be right back."

"Where are you going?"

"I need to make a phone call."

Chapter Thirty-Seven

WASHINGTON, D.C.

While she was in Congress, Walsh kept an apartment at the Watergate complex. Her main residence was in the Kalorama neighborhood, but she used the apartment for her most clandestine meetings, and any time she brought home a gentleman for the occasional romp. Thanks to the scandal that took the same name, there was something about the allure of the Watergate that captivated Walsh. It was as if the complex called to her. Perhaps it was because she lived and thrived in the arena of scandals. However, the difference between her and President Nixon was the fact that she got away with hers. That is, until that fateful day when Tom Delang walked into the hearing at the Capitol and provided the testimony that sent her packing.

Though she would go on to sell her home in Kalorama, Walsh could never bring herself to get rid of her Watergate apartment. She loved it too damned much. The corner view of the Potomac was breathtaking, and she found watching the local Paddle Club row downriver from her balcony to be soothing after a stressful day. Walking next door to the Kennedy Performing Arts Center for a show was an added perk.

When she moved back to Philadelphia, she gave her ex-chief of staff, Latrina Pearl, a spare key. Since Pearl would be staying in Washington, she trusted her to use it whenever she wanted for whatever she desired as long as she kept the place clean, and that the sheets were always changed. Walsh was a classic neat freak, and detested clutter of any kind.

After a nap on the two-hour drive south from Philly, she had Philip stop by Sequoia, her favorite restaurant in the District, for lobster bisque so that she and Pearl could have their discussion over dinner. That was over an hour ago. The food had gotten cold, but Walsh's temper was red hot. She loathed being kept waiting for an appointment. The ashtray in the kitchen was filled with the butts of six Virginia Slims, and she was taking a long drag off her seventh when she finally heard keys rattling at the door. Knowing how impatient Walsh could be, Pearl didn't bother to say hello when she opened the door and entered.

"I'm *so* sorry, Senator," she said.

"Our food is cold."

"I know. I'm really sorry. Traffic. And shit is hitting the fan at the office."

"Save it. I'm hungry. Let's eat first."

On top of her impatience, Walsh was also known for her testy conversations whenever she was hungry.

Because she was the one who was late, Pearl wasted no time grabbing the containers from the plastic bag, pouring the bisque into bowls and heating them in the microwave. She could tell Walsh's happy meter instantly went up once she had her first spoonful.

"I didn't ask earlier, but how've you been? Is McCoy treating you well?" Walsh asked.

"I like him. Quite the straight arrow, though. Unusual for a politician in Washington."

"Give him another term or two. Washington changes everyone."

"I'm betting on it."

"Were you able to get what I needed?"

Pearl hesitated.

"My guy was extremely reluctant because Cannon and Wallace have been so good to him. For obvious reasons, security protocols at the IG's office are tight, even for him. But I played him right, and he pulled the file for me."

"How much did he want?"

"Fifty grand, and a dinner date. I've got him wrapped around my little finger."

Walsh waived away the request. Fifty grand was chump change to her.

"What'd you find out?"

"He says that your agent's real name is Elizabeth Jenkins. And if you think Peter McCoy is a straight arrow, he's never seen a CIA agent with such a squeaky-clean record. I mean, it's not totally perfect, but there's not much there you could get her on."

"So, you got nothing out of him?"

"I didn't say that. He found one thing I think you could use. Four years ago, she was on an operation in the Sudan. She was hunting someone who supposedly had information on Ayman al-Zawahiri."

"The guy who assumed control of al-Qaeda after Bin Laden was killed?"

"Yeah, him. Anyway, she used a local gang banger to set up a meeting. It went bad, and the kid got killed. It turns out the gang banger's father had real pull with the local drug cartels and put a bounty on her head. You're still friends with the Sudanese ambassador, aren't you? What's his name? Nazir something?"

"Nazir Agab. What was the kid's name?"

"Esraa Abass."

Walsh nodded. This info could be useful. She had good relations with Agab. All she would have to do is slip him intel about Jenkins's whereabouts. He would tell Sudanese intelligence, who would pass the info on to the local drug lord. If she was lucky, a few weeks later, the drug lord would fly someone to the States to take care of Jenkins, once and for all.

"But there is a little bit of bad news," Pearl said.

"What's that?"

"Your agent may be dead."

"Excuse me?"

"There are reports of someone with her cover name and description being killed in China."

China? That made no sense. Jenkins was supposed to be in Iran.

"That can't be right. I just saw her a few days ago. I can't tell you how, but I know for a fact she wasn't in China. Did you get a copy of the CIA's report on her supposed death?"

"Not yet, but I'll get it."

"Okay let me know what you find, and if you need any more money."

"No problem. Sorry that I can't stay, but I have to run."

"What? You just got here. At least finish your bisque."

"I'll have to take it with me. McCoy needs me back at the office."

"Hang on. What did you mean earlier when you said shit was hitting the fan?"

Pearl gave her a curious look.

"You haven't heard?"

"Apparently not."

Pearl pulled out her phone and handed it to Walsh.

"See for yourself. I'm not sure how, but it's all over the internet."

Walsh played an Instagram video made by one of the spectators in Azadi Square.

"Things are getting crazy in Iran. We're getting reports that the Supreme Leader's days are numbered."

Walsh tried to hide her reaction. Earlier in the day, she had watched the Supreme Leader's address, saying the coup had failed. Now, just hours later, he could be gone.

Did Jenkins succeed in her mission or was she dead?

Pearl noticed the confused look on Walsh's face.

"What is it?"

"Nothing. Would you mind keeping me up to speed on this?"

"We'll have to talk when I get back. I'm not sure when that will be, but if what McCoy thinks is happening is actually happening, you'll see everything on CNN."

Chapter Thirty-Eight

KHORRAMABAD, IRAN

Nassiri escaped with Shir-Del without anyone noticing. Within minutes, they were clear of the horrendous storm that had descended on Azadi Square. As Nassiri sped down the freeway, leading southwest out of Tehran, he glanced in his rearview mirror at the Supreme Leader, who had a blank, lifeless stare on his freckled face.

"Supreme Leader, are you okay?"

"Allah has opened up the heavens and spoken to me."

"I think He spoke to all of us, Supreme Leader."

"Yes, but I heard His voice over the storm. He spoke to me personally."

Nassiri raised an eyebrow.

"What did he say?"

"He said we must prepare."

"Prepare for what?"

"One final battle."

"A battle?"

"One final battle between Iran and the West."

Nassiri wasn't one to question the Supreme Leader, not even in private, but if Shir-Del could have seen the confused look on his face, it would have spoken volumes. Even if it was true that Allah had spoken to him directly, Nassiri didn't think the Supreme Leader was grasping the severity of what had just happened.

Allah *had* opened up the heavens. That was for certain. Everyone in the Square had witnessed it. What the Supreme Leader didn't realize was the effect such a dramatic scene would have on his reign after it went viral.

Once they were outside Tehran, Shir-Del instructed Nassiri to take him to Qom before going anywhere else. Inside his home were multiple boxes of Carbamazepine and syringes, which were vital to the Supreme Leader's health. Unaware of Shir-Del's closely guarded secret, Nassiri was confused about what he was loading into the Humvee. He grabbed the first ones the Supreme Leader pointed to in a hidden closet. When he finally gathered the gumption to ask, Shir-Del didn't tell him about his Chromosome Six Deficiency or the tumor growing in his leg. He only revealed that he suffered from a condition that reduced his blood cell counts and caused his skin to break out in rashes if he was subjected to stressful situations. Upon hearing this, Nassiri stuffed as many boxes as he could into the vehicle. If he was correct about what was about to happen to his country, it was essential for the Supreme Leader to remain in good health.

Before leaving, Shir-Del asked Nassiri to go back inside and roll up his favorite painting. He took one last look at his beige, two-story home, affixed with authoritative, thick columns, and wondered if he would get to see it again. Nassiri emerged from the house with the painting under his arm and his phone in his hand.

"Supreme Leader, I have bad news. I undoubtedly believe that Allah spoke to you, but many in our country are confused by the incident. They believe Allah interceded in your judgment of the conspirators. Therefore, they were right in what they did. Here, take a look at some of the videos from social media."

Shir-Del snatched the phone from Nassiri and watched in disbelief. As the video came to an end, a text alert popped up from one of Nassiri's staff contacts in the Islamic Assembly.

THE ASSEMBLY VOTED WITH LAJANI. MARTIAL LAW!

Shir-Del shoved the phone into Nassiri's chest.

"Drive. We need to get out of Qom before Lajani's reinforcements arrive to secure the city. It's imperative that we turn the tide in our favor."

"Where to, Supreme Leader?"

"The castle."

During the four-hour drive from Qom, Shir-Del became surprisingly chatty. Nassiri revealed that he was born and raised in Khorramabad. Shir-Del divulged that he didn't like the city when he first entered the local university because it had a high population of Sunni Kurds and Christians. However, over the two years he spent there, he came to fall in love with its atmosphere and the rare, local language of Luri, which he became fluent in.

Shir-Del collected many loyal friends during his time there and tried to visit at least once a year. As his knowledge of the Shi'a faith deepened, his reputation around the city spread. When planning his visits, word quickly spread around town that he was coming. Though he hadn't intended his visits to become speeches and lectures, that's precisely what happened. At first, these gatherings were with friends he had made at the university and their respective families. By the time he made it to the Guardian Council, he found himself surrounded by ten thousand locals. This was where Shir-Del began to master the art of speaking to a crowd and developed a taste for vain theatrics. No one in the crowd expected him to reveal anything about himself. They only needed to know why they should follow him and listen to what he had to say.

Nassiri was one of those who consistently attended Shir-Del's speeches and they inspired him to join the Revolutionary Guard. When he shared this, Shir-Del grinned.

"Thank you for your loyalty, General."

Allah is with us. We shall prevail.

Shir-Del had been in the middle of delivering a speech in Khorrama-bad when the locals received word that his predecessor was close to death. Panicked, they turned to Shir-Del for guidance. At the time, it wasn't official that he would be named the next Supreme Leader, but everyone in the crowd knew it was a sure bet. In front of an audience of two hundred thousand, the future Grand Ayatollah calmed their worries and assured them that he would guide the country into a place of prosperity that the world would respect and fear. The then-Supreme Leader died two days later with Shir-Del at his bedside, watching over him.

Though he didn't subscribe to it, one aspect of the city that Shir-Del came to appreciate were the many locals who were followers of Zoroastrianism. If he was to triumph in his quest to prove Lajani a fraud, those who believed deeply that good will always conquer evil would be necessary witnesses. He just had to show them the way.

During the drive, Nassiri called every Khorramabad man and woman he knew to be loyal to the Supreme Leader and asked them to gather at the Falak-ol-Aflak Castle so they could make plans to return their country to its rightful leader who had been ordained by Allah. He also called as many of his loyal, Lajani-hating Basij soldiers as he could find. He asked them to spread the word and bring as many weapons as possible. By the time they arrived, Nassiri estimated that more than fifty thousand people were waiting for them, lining the walkway, and cheering for the proper ruler of their land. Being a showman, Shir-Del shook the hands of those who wanted to see him as he walked toward the castle.

The Falak-ol-Aflak Castle is an imposing, sixty-thousand square foot structure, dating back to the Sassanid era, eighteen hundred years ago. The seventy-foot high mud-brick walls loom over the now residential area below its position on a large hill. It dominates the city's horizon and is protected by the Khorramabad River on eastern and southwestern sides. Its position was intentional because the builders knew the wind would dry the brick and clay foundation on top of Golestan Spring, which provided water to its inhabitants via a forty-foot well that is still in operation.

While it served as a military installation in ancient times, the last Shah dynasty used it as a political prison until 1968. Today, it is a museum vital to the country's tourist industry. For Shir-Del, it was the perfect place to make his stand against his enemies and would eventually serve as *the* monument to his ultimate victory.

Seeing the Supreme Leader trying to hide his struggle to climb the castle stairs with his cane, Nassiri offered to help, but he was refused and was told to walk two steps behind. Shir-Del knew the importance of never appearing weak. When he reached the castle courtyard, he waved to the crowd and received deafening cheers. Afterward, he motioned Nassiri to follow him into what used to be one of the main military chamber rooms on the north side.

"Close the door," Shir-Del said.

When the heavy oak door slammed shut, Nassiri wondered whether the Supreme Leader was now locked in or if the opposition forces were locked out.

"How can I be of service to you, Supreme Leader?"

"First, when you bring my medicine inside, do so discretely, and don't forget my painting. Then, have your soldiers collect food and supplies. I'm not sure how long we will be here, so we need to stock up. We'll need a few of the town's chefs to work full-time as well."

"Of course, Supreme Leader."

"Does this town still have a construction or excavation company?"

"There's one on the other side of town that uses it for their archaeological digs."

"Good. Have them block off the driveway and stairs leading into the castle from the ground level with whatever barriers they can find. I want to eliminate any chances of an invasion."

"Consider it done, Supreme Leader."

"I want Basij soldiers patrolling the complex around the clock. Rotate them as needed. Be sure to post some of them on the old escape routes. Be sure that you give the townspeople as many weapons as you can spare, but don't shortchange your soldiers. The townspeople need to be our first line of defense."

"Yes, Supreme Leader. I'll see if I can obtain any leftover weapons caches nearby."

"Excellent. Now, how do we handle this social media situation?"

"I have an idea. Many people think that the storm of frogs was a sign from Allah sent to protect the conspirators, but I think we can spin it in our favor."

"Explain."

"Everyone was running for cover while the rain, hail and frogs poured down. But you, Supreme Leader, stood perfectly still and absorbed the torrential downpours. How did you do that?"

Shir-Del debated his response and decided that Nassiri needed to know. At this juncture, he was his only true ally.

"Because of my condition."

"I don't understand."

"General, if my condition is kept in check, I don't feel pain. However, stress can induce skin rashes, eye and muscle cramps, increased blood pressure and reduced blood cell counts. It can be quite dangerous if not monitored."

"You don't feel pain?"

"Hand me your gun. Remove the bullets."

Nassiri did as he was told. Shir-Del set the tip of his pointer finger on the edge of a nearby table.

"Watch this."

Shir-Del used the butt of the gun to strike his finger with severe force. Though the bone made a pronounced snapping sound, Shir-Del never made a peep. He held his crooked finger up for Nassiri to see. The Basij General stood in awe but came back to attention.

"Without disclosing your condition, I think we can use it to our advantage."

"I'm listening."

"I'll find one of the videos from the storm and edit it so that it focuses on you. If you feel no pain, your condition makes you stand above the rest of the population. It makes you superhuman. God-like. Someone so God-like and with such a unique condition could only be blessed by Allah. And, if you have been blessed by Allah with such a gift, then only you can be the rightful Supreme Leader. Many people will get behind this idea."

Shir-Del nodded.

"I like it. The door swings both ways. Do it. Make it spread like a wildfire."

"I'll make it my first priority, Supreme Leader. What about Lajani and the PMOI?"

"We will deal with them, but I have an idea that can change the momentum drastically in our favor, and quickly, too."

"Tell me, Supreme Leader."

"Do you trust me?"

"Always, Supreme Leader."

"Are you prepared to make any sacrifice? Even one that may cost some of your men their lives?"

"Anything for you, Supreme Leader. You are the light to guide Iran back to its rightful place in the world."

"How many men do you have here?"

"About a hundred, but there are more on the way. Probably another hundred."

"Excellent. Do you have any satellite phones in the Humvee?"

"Yes, Supreme Leader. They're not the most modern version, but they work."

"Okay. How much do you know about the oil fields in the southeast?"

Chapter Thirty-Nine

SOUTHEAST IRAN
AHVAZ OIL FIELDS

It was a bold plan and a huge gamble by Shir-Del. Though he told the Supreme Leader otherwise, it didn't sit well with Nassiri. But he needed to have faith in his Supreme Leader, and it was essential that he display that trust.

After their conversation, it took another four hours for Nassiri's loyal reinforcements to arrive. More showed up than he expected. In total, there were now roughly a thousand. Nassiri decided to take a hundred men with him to the oil fields, while the rest stayed to protect the Supreme Leader. It wasn't a large number, but to make his men appear to be militia rather than formalized soldiers, he needed to keep his forces small. Besides, his soldiers were well-trained and could handle themselves in rocky situations. Thankfully, the teams brought plenty of rifles, RPGs, and grenades to make a stand when they came under attack.

Convincing his soldiers to go to the oil fields was not easy. Nassiri insisted that they take their tactical gear, even as he ordered them to wear civilian clothing. His men had been trained not to question authority, but Nassiri could tell that they were confused by the order, so he explained why it was necessary to deceive the enemy.

Nassiri didn't have much of an internal moral compass, but he felt a slight sting in his soul when he gave the next order.

"Men, as you know by now, former General Lajani is leading a coup against our great Supreme Leader. In order to seize control of the country, he has decided to capture the one element essential to our economy—our oil. He has enlisted the help of the rag-tag PMOI to help him. Our intelligence is scarce, but we know the PMOI has positioned its so-called soldiers around the oil rigs in Ahvaz. Be advised that they will likely be wearing IRGC uniforms. We're not sure how they got them, but it's an obvious attempt to demonstrate security on their part. Our mission is to terminate all members of the PMOI and re-secure the fields as covertly as possible. Remember, we're dealing with a location surrounded by oil, so make sure you don't miss."

This was a blatant lie, but Nassiri had been ordered by the Supreme Leader. Although soldiers at the oil fields were dressed in IRGC uniforms, he knew they were not PMOI; they were Chinese. The Supreme Leader's plan was simple. His deal with the General Secretary Xu stipulated that if the oil fields came under attack, the Chinese were authorized to use military force to intervene. Since Lajani had most of the IRGC in his pocket, Chinese assistance was essential to resume control *if* he could convince them that the PMOI was a continuous threat to his regime and to China's, too. It would take additional negotiations on his part, but Shir-Del was confident that he could convince the Chinese to help him retake Tehran. By sacrificing his own soldiers, disguised as PMOI, he knew it would come at a heavy price, but it was a card he had to play. Retaking Tehran was crucial, and he couldn't do it without the Chinese.

This plan meant Nassiri had to send a company of his own Basij soldiers, and even though he had few at his disposal, they were destined to die. This bothered him, but he knew it was for the greater good.

Nassiri and his men, led by his cousin, Lt. Col. Vaziri, left Khorramabad late in the afternoon. With no air force or helicopters to fly them to Ahvaz, they were forced to drive. Nassiri decided that he and the team would stop on the north side of Dezful, which was protected by the Zagros Mountains. This provided them with protection from any lookouts the Chinese or PMOI might have planted along their route.

After a short rest, Nassiri gave the men one last motivational speech.

"Remember, men, you are fighting for the glory of Iran! Never forget that."

"For Iran!"

The men checked their gear and weapons one last time and departed Dezful at 1 a.m. When they arrived near the oil fields two hours later, Nassiri had them stop a mile out. Ten men stayed with the vehicles to aid in their escape, while Nassiri and Vaziri escorted the men to a position seven hundred meters outside the oil fields, where they crouched in the dirt and sand. Prior to departing, Nassiri told Vaziri the truth about their mission. He didn't like it any more than Nassiri, but he understood the reasoning behind the Supreme Leader's decision.

Nassiri pulled out a pair of night vision binoculars and observed the security around each of the eight oil drilling rigs. Then, he handed the binoculars to Vaziri.

"We're exposed out here. The sand and dirt can only do so much to shield us."

"I know."

"What do you think about the security?"

"Looks like standard patrols around the front and back. Our men take out their guards in the watchtowers first, then sneak in from the east and west. If the Chinese are as good as they claim, they should suffer minimal casualties and take out our men. What I worry about is what I can't see."

"Which is?"

"If we were guarding those rigs, wouldn't we have more men positioned around them? There may be more inside that building on the northwest corner."

"Isn't it usually reserved for men working the rigs?"

"Yes, but something doesn't feel right."

"Sir, it's the middle of the night. We've made the trip, we have our orders from the Supreme Leader, and you know what the outcome is supposed to be. Let's get this over with. If the Supreme Leader is right, everything will fall into place once we get back."

Nassiri nodded, reluctantly.

If the only way to regain control of Iran from a spineless traitor like Lajani is to follow the Supreme Leader's plans, so be it.

"Give the men their orders."

Vaziri gave the men Nassiri's orders, convincing them that this was an easy in-and-out operation against a bunch of amateurs with guns. The men ran to their positions, confident of a quick and decisive victory. After crawling to their designated areas, they awaited further instructions. A slight desert wind rolled over the sand. Nassiri and Vaziri waited in silence and tried to accept the fact that they were delivering a death sentence to their men.

"Awaiting your orders, sir," said the team leader on the east side.

The team leader on the west side repeated the same request.

"You have a green light," Nassiri said.

He grabbed a satellite phone from his backpack. Shir-Del picked up on the first ring.

"Yes?"

"The men are engaging as we speak, Supreme Leader."

"Excellent. Do not deviate from your orders. I'll call Secretary Xu now."

Chapter Forty

BEIJING, CHINA

It was going to be a long day for General Secretary Xu. Two days ago, he had been notified by Minister of State Security Ping Zhou that a woman believed to be an American agent was killed in a Shanghai hotel. Based on an inside tip, the Chinese agent who made the kill was dispatched to Iran, but hadn't been heard from since.

After enjoying a sunrise breakfast of jianbing and scallion oil pancakes, Xu strolled to his limousine. Halfway to the Ministry of State Security building, his assistant, Tao, received a call from Minister Zhou. When Tao told him who was calling, Xu squinted his eyes. He didn't understand why the information couldn't wait until he arrived, but his gut instinct told him what the call was about. When Xu took the phone, he was surprised to hear Zhou and the Minister of National Defense, Jing Lin, on the line.

"Are you sure?" Xu asked.

"It's consistent with the report we received yesterday," Zhou said.

"I'll be right over."

Xu turned to Tao.

"Change of plans. Take me to the Ministry of National Defense building."

When they arrived, soldiers were waiting. He was escorted to an elevator at the other end of the building and taken three floors down to the secure command center, where Zhou, two of his analysts, Minister Lin and General Chen, chief commander of the People's Liberation Army, were monitoring the situation. Everyone stood when Xu entered. After taking his seat, he folded his hands in front of him as he observed the night vision images from the multiple high-definition screens.

"How many?"

"They look to have one small company of men, General Secretary," Minister Lin said.

"Our men are ready?"

"They've been in place for twenty-four hours, sir. They're ready," said General Chen.

Xu nodded.

"Attack."

General Chen picked up the phone and passed along his orders to the men on the ground. Within minutes, the Chinese soldiers stationed around the oil rigs in Ahvaz oil fields began covertly picking off the Iranian Basij one by one. Xu counted a dozen dead Iranians, and more continued to be shot with each passing moment when the central phone in the command center chimed in.

"General Secretary, you have an urgent phone call from the Supreme Leader of Iran," an aide said.

"Put him through," Xu said.

He put on his headset to translate the conversation both ways.

"Supreme Leader, this is quite a surprise. To what do I owe the pleasure?"

"Hello, Secretary Xu. I have some urgent news to report."

"By all means."

"As you have no doubt heard, General Lajani attempted a coup that I successfully squashed. Lajani remains in custody and awaits his death sentence, but we are still sorting out which members of the Revolutionary Guard can be trusted. In a last-ditch effort to secure power, Lajani has dispatched vigilantes from the People's Mujahadeen of Iran to seize control of the oil fields in Ahvaz. Per the terms of our agreement, China is authorized to utilize its military power to intervene. As that problem has now become a reality, I call on you now to request China's assistance to protect Iranian and Chinese national interests."

Xu saw Minster Zhou grinning.

"That's quite unfortunate, Supreme Leader. But, I'm unable to offer Chinese assistance."

There was a pause at the other end of the line.

"I'm expecting China to own up to its end of the deal."

"The terms of our deal, Supreme Leader, were that China would intervene should any *foreign* power try to seize control of the oil fields. The PMOI is not a foreign power. They present a problem born and bred within your own borders. It is a *domestic* problem that is yours, and yours alone, to fix."

Xu could tell that the Supreme Leader was tongue-tied. He had just thrown him a big-league curveball and the Iranian whiffed. Xu looked up at the screens. The Iranian body count was adding up. Across the table, he saw General Chen rolling his pointer finger through the air.

Keep him talking.

"Secretary Xu, Iran desperately needs your help. *I* need your help."

Xu smiled.

He's desperate.

"You need help, Supreme Leader, but China has a long-standing policy of not interfering in civil matters. But if the PMOI ends up seizing control of those oil fields, you should know that China will hold Iran responsible for any oil that does not flow to us."

Shir-Del felt himself backed into a corner. It was a clever play by Xu, and he had surely underestimated him. While he was confident that the Chinese would kill the Basij soldiers he had sent, it was still possible for the Iranian soldiers to prevail. If so, as far as Xu was concerned, because the IRGC soldiers had on civilian clothing, it was a PMOI assault that could result in a disruption of oil flow. If he was in control of his country, as he had falsely said, he would be responsible for the repercussions of the PMOI's assault. Shir-Del needed to adjust his tactics. He calmly collected his thoughts before replying.

"Secretary Xu," Shir-Del said, "I cannot guarantee the safety of Chinese interests in Iran without assistance from your military."

In the China command center, Xu received an "okay" sign from Minister Zhou.

Time to drop the net.

"Actually, that's no longer your concern, Supreme Leader," Xu said.

"Excuse me?"

"You didn't stop the coup against you. You're neck deep in it. General Lajani called me yesterday and informed me of his newfound situation. He thought you might have a trick or two up your sleeve and would try to stage an assault on the Ahvaz oil fields by having Revolutionary Guard soldiers pose as PMOI militia. Apparently, he knows you better than you know yourself."

General Chen rolled his hand in the air in an animated fashion. The Iranian body count was reaching a point of no return. The battle was nearly over. Xu just had to keep the Supreme Leader on the phone long enough to delay him issuing an order to abort.

"You have insulted me," Xu said, "and you have insulted China with this elaborate stunt. I have renegotiated our oil deal with General Lajani. He's agreed to give us an additional ten percent discount on the oil on top of the original twenty-five in exchange for pulling our soldiers out of the training facility on Larak Island within six months and keeping our investment in Iranian infrastructure."

"He *what*?"

Xu had to momentarily put the phone on mute to hide his laughter before pressing the button to resume his conversation.

"It seems that China will continue its partnership with Iran after all. Good luck to you, Supreme Leader. Enjoy your title as long as you can."

As soon as Xu hung up, the others in the command center applauded the General Secretary. When they looked back at the TV screens, they counted more than eighty Iranians dead, and those that remained were retreating.

In Khorramabad, Shir-Del stood in shock. As he tried to process what had just happened, his satellite phone rang, and he had no doubt who was calling.

"What?!" Shir-Del said.

Chapter Forty-One

SOUTHEAST IRAN
AHVAZ OIL FIELDS

Nassiri and Vaziri scanned the oil fields through their night vision binoculars. Their hearts pounded as they watched their men advance toward their certain fate. Vaziri saw the muzzled flash of the first gunshots under the dark sky.

"That was fast."

Before Nassiri could nod, five more flashes lit up the field. Vaziri depressed the button on his radio.

"East leader, report."

"Taking fire! Taking fire!"

"Something's not right," Nassiri said.

Flashes of muzzled gunfire lit up the dusty oil fields like fireflies. Nassiri's eyes popped open, and he gave Vaziri a startled look.

"They were waiting for us. It's an ambush!"

"What are we supposed to do? We knew we sent our men to die."

"Not like this."

Nassiri redialed the Supreme Leader, but the line was busy. The version of the satellite phone he and the Supreme Leader were using was outdated and didn't have call waiting.

"Dammit!"

After throwing down the phone, Nassiri picked up his binoculars and scoured the fields. His men were taking heavy fire. Those that weren't hit were dragging their injured comrades to safety while fending off the attack.

Nassiri dialed the Supreme Leader again.

"Come on. Pick up. Pick up."

Again, the line pulsed with an annoying busy signal.

Fuck!

Nassiri hung up and gazed through his binoculars.

"How many have we lost?"

"It's hard to tell, but it's bordering on half."

As Nassiri watched the carnage, his mind searched for answers.

"Well? What do you want to do?" Vaziri said.

Nassiri considered his answer.

"Sir?"

"Let's go."

"Go? What about the men?"

"There's nothing we can do. Anyone who survives will know we set them up, and if they got a good look at any of the shooters, they'll know they were attacked by the Chinese and not the PMOI. The Supreme Leader specifically said no one but us should come back."

Vaziri was hesitant to respond.

"Yes, sir."

Nassiri dialed the Supreme Leader once again. This time, he picked up.

"What?!"

"Supreme Leader, the Chinese were waiting for us."

"I know! Secretary Xu told me Lajani told him yesterday to expect this tactic."

Nassiri closed his eyes and squeezed the phone.

Lajani.

"What now, Supreme Leader?"

"The circumstances are unfortunate, but you know what to do. Get back here immediately."

"Yes, Supreme Leader."

Nassiri turned to Vaziri.

"Come on."

Nassiri and Vaziri crawled back to the main road and double-timed it back to the escape vehicles. To make it appear they had been in battle, they rubbed dirt and sand over their bodies and had their assault rifles in hand as they approached the men who remained.

"General, what happened?"

Nassiri was out of breath from running.

"Gather around."

The ten men gathered in a circle around Nassiri and Vaziri. Nassiri didn't bother to speak further. He nodded to Vaziri, and they sprayed the men with bullets.

Chapter Forty-Two

TEHRAN, IRAN

Lajani sat behind his polished desk on the fifth floor of Revolutionary Guard headquarters, trying to calm his nerves. Despite being dressed in his finest uniform, his right arm was in a sling. The lights brought in by the crew from the state-run TV station shined brightly on him, but his head was bowed as he prayed to Allah for strength and guidance.

"Are you ready, General?"

Lajani opened his eyes and nodded to the cameraman, who counted down from five and pointed. The feed was live.

"My fellow Iranians, this is Major General Lajani of the Revolutionary Guard. I come to you today with great news about the future of Iran. For over forty years, our country has been ruled by a Supreme Leader. Because of the people's suppression under the rule of the Shah, the original intent of having a Supreme Leader was good. However, while the state of the country was by no means good under the Shah, as you have witnessed, Iran has suffered greatly under the rule of the Supreme Leaders that followed him. Over a million Iranians died in the Iran-Iraq War. When it was over, we had nothing to show for it but a war-torn country and severe financial loss that nearly bankrupted us. The covert wars with Israel and our other enemies in the West have gotten us nowhere. The results of our missions have resulted in economic sanctions, which have all but cut us off from the rest of the world. Iran may have survived, but it has not thrived.

"Despite the earlier message from the Supreme Leader, I can confirm to you now that I not only attempted a coup to remove him from power; I have succeeded. His attempts to butcher my colleagues who aided me in this task were thwarted by acts of Allah himself. By now, you have either experienced the scene at Azadi Square or have seen the videos in the media, so you know I speak the truth. It has been determined by our higher power that Iran's rule under a Supreme Leader should not continue.

"Therefore, under the powers given to the chief commander of the Revolutionary Guard by our Constitution, I have assumed control of our country and declared martial law. I know this will not be received favorably by everyone. Be advised that riots and other illegal activities to protest this announcement will not be tolerated. On my order, Revolutionary Guard soldiers have been stationed across the country. They have orders to obstruct and end any violent activity.

"However, the decree of martial law is *temporary*. I do not intend to change the inner workings of Iran. Our country will always be ruled by Sharia Law, and it shall remain under my authority. My intent is to make Iran more accessible to the rest of the world. Our country has suffered long enough. The time has come for Iran to live and enjoy the fruits of the world without altering our culture. In turn, the time has also come for the world to realize that Iran has much more to offer than war.

"Earlier this afternoon, I released nearly all internet restrictions imposed by the previous government. I ask you to spread the word of what Iran is like, the joys it brings to the world, its history, culture, and most important, what it was like to live under the reign of the Supreme Leader. As you can plainly see, I, too, have suffered at the hands of the Supreme Leader and his government."

Lajani removed his arm from the sling and showed the camera the ghastly wound remaining from his missing hand.

"The world needs to be aware of the torments endured by those of us who refused to succumb to his iron fist. I leave you now with words of encouragement. Iran has entered a new stage in history, and we cannot reach our destiny without your participation. Good night, and by the grace of Allah, long live the new Iran."

"And we're out," the cameraman said.

Lajani looked at Donya, who was sitting in the corner with her laptop open.

"Make sure it gets picked up by every global news outlet," he said.

Chapter Forty-Three

ASHEVILLE, NORTH CAROLINA

The August heat in Asheville, North Carolina was sweltering, but the sunset in the Piedmont Region was fetching at any time of year, and the crisp mountain air made summer nights more tolerable. It provided happy times for Kirk Kurruthers and his new fiancé, Simin, as they moved into a new phase of their life together.

A year ago, neither one of them could have imagined that an Iranian woman would be engaged to an American man, especially considering the precarious circumstances under which they met. Kirk had traveled to Iran on a quest to avenge the death of his grandfather. Since he needed the help of a local Iranian, he found Farhad online and the two had chemistry right away. However, the man Kirk wanted to kill was Simin's biological father, a man she hated because he raped her mother.

When Farhad secretly told Simin of Kirk's plans, she didn't hesitate to help. Upon meeting, Kirk and Simin were immediately smitten with one another. But as well-laid plans often do, they fell apart when Kirk and Farhad were imprisoned. During their escape, the two men emerged with a third man, a kidnapped CIA operative she later learned was Tom Delang. Simin tried to assist them in their escape across the border, but she was also captured. Amazingly, the four of them made it into the U.S. Embassy in Turkmenistan. Delang would later help to bring Simin to the States where she and Kirk would fall in love.

With the chaos of the past now well behind them, Kirk and Simin settled into the city where his grandfather had lived so that Kirk could visit his grave. Together, they pursued a new interest in wine and fine cheeses, which they purchased from the local market and enjoyed under their covered patio on weekend afternoons. Because this reminded Simin of a trip they took to Paris, she called their ritual "Frenchy Time." It wasn't the type of scenario that Kirk had ever envisioned himself enjoying, but the combination of a blended cheddar mixed with a whole grain mustard, called Red Dragon, and Simin's newfound love for German Riesling wine, made these indulgences irresistible.

Under normal conditions, Kirk found discussions related to their upcoming wedding to be emotionally exhausting, but Frenchy Time became a neutral setting to discuss such delicate issues. Since neither one of them had any living relatives, the ceremony would be small, with a few local friends they had made since settling in the Asheville area.

The latest subject for debate was whether Simin would convert from Islam to Christianity. Kirk wasn't pushing it on her. She brought up the issue on her own. Kirk didn't care either way, but Simin considered it a tremendous choice because it could mean the official beginning of leaving her Iranian roots behind. She loved America and loved Kirk even more. Though she knew that neither one expected her to change her religion, she wanted to embrace them with both hands, but doing so meant leaving behind one of the only pieces of herself that had been constant during her struggles in Iran. The back-and-forth conversations had become a vicious cycle with no ending in sight, but the smooth wine and savory cheeses helped Kirk get through them.

Simin embraced the connectivity of Instagram while she was in Iran because it was the only major social media platform the government allowed. Once she came to the States, she eagerly signed up for Twitter, Facebook, and YouTube. After receiving certification to become a paramedic, she started her own YouTube channel, where she posted videos on emergency medical situations that educated the public on how to assist a patient until an ambulance arrived. The channel quickly caught on and became a hit among emergency responders because it made their job easier once they arrived on scene and it helped save lives. It took only six weeks for Simin to attract 375,000 subscribers and the numbers were increasing.

When Kirk walked outside with two glasses of wine, he was enamored by the sight of their new twenty-one-week-old puppy, a golden retriever named Gypsy, laying in Simin's lap. Having had a golden retriever earlier in his childhood, Kirk knew they were one of the gentlest and most intelligent breeds that grew up to be loyal and lovable companions. But he had forgotten that in order to reach that state of grace, owners had to endure what felt like two years of hell in terms of vandalism, training, and misbehavior.

While most puppies are prone to sleeping for long parts of the day, Gypsy was not. She fought the fatigue like no other dog he had ever seen. He and Simin termed eight o'clock in the evening to be "the witching hour" because that's when Gypsy was the most tired, and since she fought her weariness, it was also when she displayed her most rambunctious behavior before she finally collapsed. Thankfully, Simin found a way to take advantage of the situation by posting videos of Gypsy's antics on Instagram. Though they'd only had the dog for six weeks, Simin had collected nearly 200,000 additional followers to her personal account and she was toying with the idea of creating a new profile dedicated to her new pup.

Considering how exhausted he was after a long day of digging holes in the yard for new fence posts, Kirk was grateful that Gypsy was asleep.

"How long has she been out?"

Kirk handed Simin a glass of wine and chopped up pieces of carrots for the pup. She immediately took a sip.

"She just conked out."

As Kirk walked past Simin to get to his chair, he didn't see the dog toy at her feet. When he stepped on it, the toy let out a high-pitched squeal that made Simin's eyes widen. Knowing that even the slightest noise could wake up the dog, she gave Kirk the evil eye. Though Gypsy opened her eyes, thankfully, she went right back to sleep.

Kirk shrugged and mouthed the word "sorry."

"When is your next shift on the Boo-Boo Bus?"

The Boo-Boo Bus was the name Simin had assigned for working as a paramedic on the ambulance.

"Tomorrow night. I've got the late shift."

"Got time for dinner? I was thinking about making buffalo chicken pizza."

Simin smiled.

"That'd be nice."

She leaned over and gave her fiancé a kiss. For Kirk, the taste of the semi-sweet wine with a hint of apple on top of Simin's pillowy lips was heavenly.

"Did you want to try that new bier garden downtown this weekend?"

"They serve food, right?"

"Yeah, I think so."

"Would you mind grabbing my phone so I can check the menu? It's charging on the coffee table. I would get it myself, but. . ."

Simin pointed down at Gypsy as she took another sip of wine.

Kirk gave her a sideways look.

"Come on, babe, this is supposed to be our 'us' time. No phones, remember? We can look at the menu later."

"I know, but now that you've brought it up, you've got my stomach doing the talking for me. Please. We'll take a look at the menu and then you can put it back. I promise."

I doubt that.

The convincing smile on her face matched the sun shining through her unmistakable streak of blue hair. It was all she needed to make Kirk weak enough to concede.

When Kirk picked up the phone, he grimaced when he saw hundreds of notification messages. He was scrolling through them when he went back outside.

"Simin, how long have you been charging your phone?"

"I don't know. The battery died earlier. I haven't checked it since. Why?"

"You may want to have a look."

Simin's eyebrows scrunched together as he handed it back to her, and they slowly raised as she scrolled through her social media feeds and private messages.

"Oh my God. We need to turn on the TV."

Simin jumped up so fast that Gypsy nearly fell out of her lap, but she quickly caught her and carried her inside. After putting her down on the doggie bed, she grabbed the remote and turned on Al-Jazeera. The broadcast of Lajani was playing over the headline.

REVOLUTIONARY GUARD CHIEF OUSTS SUPREME LEADER

"What the hell?" Kirk said.

Simin said nothing as she scrolled through her Twitter feed.

"Look at this."

Kirk walked over and they watched multiple testimonial videos on her phone from Iranians who had been tortured under the Supreme Leader's regime. Most of them weren't shy about showing their scars. The last video was the most disheartening because it came from someone they recognized.

"Farhad?"

Simin held one hand over her mouth as she listened to Farhad reveal the details of his rape. Kirk became so enraged his face reddened from

236

his rising blood pressure. Before they could finish the video, an unknown phone number with a +98-country code flashed across the screen, which was the country code for Iran. Simin didn't hesitate to answer.

"Hello?"

"Hey," the voice said.

Simin put the call on speaker so Kirk could hear.

"Farhad! What's happening? We were watching the news and saw your video on Twitter."

"Hey, buddy, it's Kirk. You good?"

"Kirk, this is one time I can honestly say that I'm *not* good even if you *are* good. It's probably going to be a while before I can walk without flinching."

"Farhad, please, tell us what in the world is going on," Simin said.

Over the next ten minutes, Farhad provided them with the coup's detailed plans and what ensued. Had Thrasher been standing next to him, he probably would've slapped him upside the head for revealing so much information, especially on a non-secure line, but Farhad knew that Kirk and Simin were at the top of his trustable list. Still, they struggled with what they were hearing.

"I don't believe this. Did we learn nothing from the coup back in the fifties?"

"Kirk, it's different this time. Lajani's legit. He doesn't want Iran to be the America of the east. He wants us to have our own identity. The first thing he's going to do is start rebuilding relationships with the West to reopen trade."

"What about Israel?"

"Too soon to say, but they aren't on his radar right now, which is a good sign."

"I can't believe I'm actually starting to wish I was there to see all of this for myself. Is there anything we can do to help?"

"I'm glad you asked. Simin, no one's better at social media than you. Donya is personally asking you to build a website and be the host of the PMOI's social media campaign to expose the Ayatollahs for what they've done. This will be crucial in rebuilding Iran into what we want it to be. Will you do it?"

Simin stood in shock at the tremendous opportunity she was being given. When Kirk saw the determined look on her face, he knew the answer.

"Absolutely."

Chapter Forty-Four

KHORRAMABAD, IRAN

Nassiri and Vaziri raced back from the oil fields as fast as possible, but they ran into trouble an hour outside of Khorramabad near the city of Chameskh. PMOI members were setting up roadblocks, hoping to confront Revolutionary Guardsmen and seek retribution, steal their weapons, or both. Vaziri spotted a dozen interlopers three hundred meters away as the sun peeked its head over the horizon.

"Are you seeing this?"

"If these dogs want a fight, let's give them one," said Nassiri.

Vaziri grabbed the loaded Norinco CQ assault rifles from the back seat. When they were within two hundred meters, Nassiri slammed the pedal to the floor. Unsure what was happening, the PMOI members froze in the middle of the road. When the Humvee was inside a hundred meters, Vaziri hung out the window and opened fire. Though the vehicle was approaching at ninety miles an hour, the shots hit with remarkable accuracy. Seven of the twelve PMOI members were killed before they could raise their guns. Four scattered behind their own cars and fired their weapons but they hit nothing. One man, who couldn't have been more than twenty-five-years old, continued to stand his ground in the middle of the highway, firing shots from his AK-47 that hit the windshield but missed Nassiri and Vaziri.

Vaziri pulled himself back inside.

"Is this guy nuts?"

Nassiri didn't respond. He tightened his grip on the wheel and plowed forward.

"What are you doing?"

"Insects deserve to be splattered on the windshield."

Twenty meters. Vaziri didn't know if it was Nassiri's hatred for the PMOI or the fact that he had just murdered his men in cold blood, but it was clear that his fury was driving them forward. Ten meters. Vaziri was sure the man would jump out of the way at the last second. He didn't. Nassiri mercilessly bulldozed over him. Vaziri even heard him chuckle when the Humvee bounced as the tires squashed the man's body.

When they returned to Khorramabad, Nassiri was relieved to see locals and Basij commanders collaborating well with one another. As they approached the Falak-ol-Aflak Castle, it was clear that the city had a military presence.

Inside, Shir-Del was waiting for them in a leather chair in the center of the north chamber. They had barely taken two steps inside the room when he started in on them.

"Tell me what happened."

Though he hated reliving the incident, Nassiri explained how the Chinese were waiting for his men when they arrived. When he finished telling the story, Shir-Del nodded. Lajani's vision was far better than he gave the man credit for. The Supreme Leader glanced at Vaziri and then back at Nassiri.

"Nahid, give us a minute."

"Yes, sir."

After he left, Shir-Del pointed to the boxes of Carbamazepine in the corner that were hidden by a thick blanket. When Nassiri offered him a vial, Shir-Del immediately shot up using a syringe from his pocket. Nassiri watched but said nothing until he heard the Supreme Leader breathe a sigh of relief.

"Give me an order, Supreme Leader."

Shir-Del removed the needle from his vein and put the cap back on the syringe.

"Were you able to post the videos to social media, showing me with-standing the storm in Azadi Square?"

Nassiri retrieved his phone from his pocket and scrolled. With every-thing that had happened, he had forgotten to check the feeds.

"Your supporters are reposting and sharing the video. Looks like it's gaining some traction."

"How much?"

"Not enough that Lajani won't catch wind of it and try to take the posts down, but your believers are out there. Social media may be quick, but news takes time to spread."

Shir-Del shook his head.

"Not fast enough. We need to go on offense. I don't care what you have to do. Track down the PMOI headquarters and kill them all. No torture. I want them dead! I want their friends dead! I want their families dead! If you find anyone with even the smallest connection to them, kill them! But no matter what, you are to bring the one they call Farhad to me without so much as a hair out of place, do you understand?"

"Yes, Supreme Leader. I'll make it my first priority. What about La-jani?"

"He may know the ins and outs of Iran, but he is one man. The PMOI has enough reinforcements to drive a culture change. Take care of them, and then we'll take care of Lajani."

Nassiri left the Supreme Leader alone to pray. Vaziri was waiting in the hallway. He motioned for him to follow.

"What was that all about?"

"We've got a lot of work to do."

"Tell me what you need."

"We need to track down the PMOI. Based on what's going on, they must be holed up somewhere. We need to narrow down our search."

"I figured you would say that. I was working on that before we left."

Nassiri smiled. His cousin had always been ambitious.

"Excellent. What'd you find?"

"It looks like Lajani has removed all internet restrictions. Fortunately for us, we can follow the PMOI members on social media. I've tried to focus on Farhad and that Donya girl, but they've been careful about what they've posted. There is nothing I can go on. However, some of their colleagues haven't been so careful. I saved half a dozen videos that have solid images in the background. What do you think?"

Vaziri handed him his phone. Nassiri watched the videos one by one, repeatedly scrubbing them back and forth, looking for clues. He didn't recognize anything on the first nine but saw something on the tenth. He saw a man walking past the Blue Mosque in Tabriz. The building didn't point to anything specific, but it jogged his memory of something in Donya's IRGC file.

"Here," Nassiri said.

He handed Vaziri back his phone.

"Got something?"

"Maybe."

Nassiri pulled out his own phone. Thankfully, he'd downloaded a copy of Donya's and Farhad's file directly to his phone and didn't have to go through the IRGC's internal network to get it. By now, he was surely shut out. As he scrolled through her file, he saw that her father, Hashem, had been an outspoken critic of the Ayatollah regime. Former IRGC chief Rasoul Haddadi would later have her father killed for his outspoken antics, which prompted her to join the PMOI, but before doing so, she had worked as a secretary in her father's chemical factory on the outskirts of Tabriz. It was a stretch, but Nassiri knew that people usually go back to what they know.

"Let me see your phone again."

In the third video, Nassiri saw one of the female PMOI members in a room he didn't recognize. She walked past a poster on the wall advertising workplace safety. Though the wording was blurry, Nassiri deciphered the words at the bottom: KARIMI CHEMICALS OF TABRIZ. Feeling more confident about his theory, he smiled as he watched the video one last time and took a screenshot of one segment. When he zoomed in on a t-shirt laying on the back of a chair, he recognized the iconic words: *Star Wars*. Nassiri knew one specific PMOI member renowned for wearing that shirt: Farhad. The image sealed Nassiri's decision.

"I think I know where they are."

Chapter Forty-Five

TABRIZ, IRAN

The set-up at the chemical factory was perfect. It was a secluded building that wasn't being used because Donya could never force herself to sell it. In fact, she used the profits from her smuggling operations to pay the taxes on the land, albeit under a disguised name. The red letters of KABIRI CHEMICALS OF TABRIZ were still affixed to the front, but many light bulbs inside didn't work, and the windows were dirty.

Thrasher had surrounded the building with abandoned barrels full of acetone and benzene to keep a degree of separation from any prying eyes. He didn't want any drifters or misfit kids squatting in the parking lot, and if anyone from the Revolutionary Guard got suspicious, the barrels' bright orange hazardous stickers would make them think twice about storming the building.

Except for the occasional rat and clusters of dust bunnies, the inside of the building was practically empty. There was no machinery on the factory floor, which echoed with every noise. The offices contained some leftover desks and chairs, but most of the PMOI members used the space as bedrooms when they needed to hide out.

The main conference room on the third floor had been converted into a party room of sorts for Donya and her friends to relax away from the meddling hands of the Basij. A kegerator sat in the corner, along with other kegs of beer stacked on top of one another, and Jenkins figured the couches had been used for more than just sitting. In the center of the room, a plank of plywood on top of chemical drums served as a make-shift table to play a variety of drinking games, but Thrasher also moved the drums around to work out. Jenkins chuckled at the thought of someone trying to kick Thrasher out of the room so they could party. Anyone who dared to move him would certainly have gotten a response that would make them not try twice.

Prior to Lajani pulling the trigger on his plan, Jenkins and Delang communicated back and forth via a secure drop box and encrypted software. Per the president's orders, under no circumstances was anyone to speak by phone unless it was an absolute emergency that pointed to less than global Armageddon. Ironically, the call Jenkins made to Delang about the seed clouding ultimately made Azadi Square appear like exactly that.

However, with Lajani freeing up communication lines to the outside world, Thrasher and Jenkins felt more at ease about calling Delang, albeit on a secure satellite phone. Events were transpiring too quickly to send encrypted messages digitally and await feedback. Cannon and Wallace needed to be kept up to speed with the best intel available. In order to do that, Jenkins needed to speak to Delang by phone, which he was still leery about. But given the severity of the situation, he understood the need to do so.

Jenkins's vision was slowly coming back, but the bandage annoyed her, so she took it off. However, since her eye wasn't fully healed, the lights in the room irritated her, and she was forced to talk on the phone with her eyes closed.

"I figured you guys were going to kick the hornet's nest on this one, but I never expected *this*," Delang said.

"Oh, ye of little faith," said Jenkins.

"That's not what I meant. Wallace says that every leader in the world has been calling the president non-stop. As soon as he finishes one call, he picks up the next."

"That's a good thing, right?"

"In principle, yes. But he's supposed to be flying blind on this and has to act as surprised as everyone else about what's going on."

"So, in lieu of not having information to spread, what is he telling them?"

"He's playing the optimistic card, trying to set up a global conference to discuss Iran's future. Obviously, this is contingent on Lajani. But the peace plan will be based on the intel you get him."

"This isn't going to be another version of that debacle where we tried to rebuild Iraq with an American model, right?"

"Affirmative. He's taking it one step at a time and letting Lajani's actions pave the road. What's the latest?"

Over the next hour, Jenkins provided Delang with updates according to the major metro area strongholds of the new Revolutionary Guard. Isfahan and Shiraz were going in the right direction. With the social media videos, the people of Isfahan were taking solace in the fact that Allah had intervened and had a new destiny in store for Iran. Considering that Shiraz was one of the most liberal of cities in Iran, opening up the internet gave the people a much-needed platform to express themselves, and the videos being posted were mostly positive.

The results from Tehran were the most surprising. Since the IRGC was no longer there to suppress their freedoms, people had taken to the streets celebrate the Supreme Leader being removed from power. The trick was convincing the newly liberated population that the Revolutionary Guardsmen in the street weren't there to harm them. Some people were throwing glass bottles and trash at the soldiers. Under orders from Lajani, the men were not supposed to fight back, as that would risk riots and confusion. Luckily, the remaining IRGC soldiers devoted to the Supreme Leader didn't know that. When they took to the streets to retake the city by force with guns of their own and began attacking those celebrating their release from oppressive rule, Lajani's loyal Revolutionary Guardsmen stepped in and killed them. Upon witnessing these random scenes, those beating the drum of their newfound freedom were slowly getting the point.

Serving as the unofficial spiritual capital, Mashhad was on the verge of its own civil war. When videos from Azadi Square surfaced, half the population thought they were a Divine sign that regime change was necessary, but edited videos, which focused on the Supreme Leader's resistance to the storm, were also circulating. With half the city's population already faithful to the Supreme Leader, this added fuel to the fire. Jenkins suggested that Cannon pressure the CEOs of the social media companies to remove those videos, but Delang corrected her. Doing so would trigger rumors of U.S. government involvement, which couldn't be allowed to spread. He was right. If Jenkins wanted the opposition videos to go away, she would have to speak to Donya about doing it from the inside.

Lajani's forces were trying to maintain order, but despite their fire-power, in a city of three million people, they couldn't be everywhere at once. Lajani also received word that soldiers in Mashhad were worried about what the opposition was planning.

As expected, Qom was the biggest area of concern. Local clerics and those in training at the local university were shouting from every street corner and rooftop that what was happening was sacrilege and a viola-tion of Iran's Islamic Law. Even though Lajani had plenty of soldiers assigned in Qom, they met extreme resistance. The soldiers were doing their best to keep aggressive clerics at bay, but emotions were running high, and many soldiers were getting itchy trigger fingers. It wouldn't take much for a bloodbath to begin, which Lajani *did not* want.

Convinced that their martyrdom would allow them into heaven, some clerics baited soldiers into shooting them while their colleagues filmed the episodes so they could be uploaded online. Since the clerics had extensive contacts to their followers in the rest of the Muslim world, they could use the videos to throw gasoline on the fire they started. Lajani was especially worried about this, so he doubled the guards at the borders and closed the airports to prevent members of Hezbollah and Hamas from getting in, but he knew this was a band-aid. Cutting off their funding would have positive long-term effects, but both groups were resourceful and could still do considerable damage in the short-term.

"Is Israel doing anything to help?" Jenkins asked.

Delang laughed.

"Oh yeah. If you thought Operation Wrath of God from the 1970's was bad, this one will be way worse when word gets out. When Lajani took over and cut off funding to Hezbollah and Hamas, Prime Minister Shahar didn't wait. He gave Mossad permission to go full Rambo. No arrests or trials. They're cleaning house by eliminating their known targets in both groups across the globe. I'm betting that Lajani saw that coming. It's probably what he hoped for."

"You want me to ask him?"

"No. This is one of those situations where the question is better left unanswered. The good news is that what happened on Larak Island has caused Israel to cool its jets a bit, but Cannon has ordered surveillance drones so the CIA can keep an eye on what the Chinese are up to. What about the Supreme Leader?"

"No word yet. Thrasher's working to track him down. He's been on and off the phone with Lajani and every PMOI contact he knows."

"Okay, keep me posted. I have some good news for you, though."

"I'll take all I can get."

"Farhad made contact with Simin. You know, Kirk's fiancé? She's not on the executive board at Facebook, but she's a whiz at social media.

She's agreed to put together all the videos and testimonials on social media for the PMOI to create a buzz about the regime change."

"I remember her. Just keep an eye on things for me, okay? She may be top notch, but the scale of this may be beyond her."

"Will do."

As Jenkins wrapped up her call, Farhad and Donya gingerly walked in.

"I gotta run."

Jenkins put down the phone.

"Hey guys, how are you feeling?"

"Not good," said Donya. "I wanted to stay in Tehran with Lajani, but he could tell I needed a break, so I asked Farhad to come get me. I can do what's needed from here."

Jenkins noticed Farhad's new haircut.

"Nice buzz cut. What brought that on?"

"One of the guys did it for me. I needed to feel cleansed in every way possible. It feels like a good way to make a fresh start."

"I can understand that. Besides, it goes well with the *Star Wars* t-shirt. It gives you that 'Rebel Alliance' look."

Farhad grinned.

"At this point, isn't that what we are?"

Jenkins noticed Farhad's broken tooth when he smiled.

"How's your tooth?"

"It looks worse than it feels."

Donya stumbled and Farhad caught her.

"I'm going to take her to lie down for a while."

"Of course. Do what you need."

Thrasher didn't acknowledge Farhad or Donya as he entered, and rudely blew the smoke from his cigarette in their direction.

"I may have something. I just got off the phone with some of the guys who set up one of our roadblocks. A Revolutionary Guard Humvee barreled past them and killed several PMOI in their way, but one of them got a good look at the driver. She swears it was Nassiri."

"Where were they headed?" Donya said, coughing.

"Toward Khorramabad. A few more of the PMOI guys called family and friends around the area. They say the IRGC has fortified the city."

"Why Khorramabad?" Jenkins asked.

"The Supreme Leader used to do a lot of preaching there," said Farhad.

Thrasher's eyes popped open.

"This is our best lead. We have to run with it. If Shir-Del is there, so is Nassiri. If we get Nassiri, Shir-Del won't have a good leg to stand on."

Jenkins bobbed her head back and forth as she considered the information. While standard intelligence reporting relied on word from the street, it wasn't generally considered to be a deciding factor.

"Jay, hunt that motherfucker down and kill him."

Thrasher grinned.

Now you're talking my language.

As Thrasher turned to leave, he noticed Farhad at his side.

"Where do you think you're going?"

"You're not doing this without me."

"Uh, guys?" Donya said.

She was looking out the window.

"I don't think you'll have to go far."

Chapter Forty-Six

Thrasher stubbed out his cigarette, grabbed binoculars from the table, and went to see what Donya was talking about. Under the midnight sky, he saw approaching headlights. He looked back at Jenkins.

"We've got a problem. Farhad, check the back."

Farhad hobbled as fast as he could to the other side of the building.

"How bad?" Jenkins said.

"I count five Humvees approaching from the east. It's gotta be Revolutionary Guard."

Farhad came back.

"Four more coming from the other side."

"Shit! How the hell did they find us?" Donya said.

"It doesn't matter," Jenkins said. "We've got to pack up whatever we can and find a way out of here. How are we set for weapons?"

"We've got some rifles and grenades, but they won't do us much good if they have high-caliber machine guns."

Jenkins looked to Thrasher.

"Got any ideas?"

"How many people do we have in the building?"

"Somewhere between fifty and a hundred."

Thrasher turned to Donya.

"What vehicles do we have?"

"Just our personal cars that we used to get here, and a couple of old trucks loaded with drums of chemicals that were never delivered. We still use them from time to time, but they're useless against their Humvees. The security gates are down so they can't get in, but we can't get out."

Thrasher slammed his fist against the table. There was no way he could get everyone out before the Revolutionary Guard arrived.

"Guys, they're almost here. We need a plan, fast," Donya said.

All eyes turned to Thrasher as he searched the room.

"Are there any tunnels under the building for moving freight?"

Donya shook her head.

Thrasher looked Farhad up and down.

"What?" Farhad said.

"Nice haircut."

"Uh, thanks."

"How many of those *Star Wars* t-shirts do you have here?"

"Ten or so, I think. Maybe less. Why?"

"Come with me," he said.

Thrasher turned to Jenkins.

"Tell everyone to kill all the lights and say a prayer. We're going to need it."

***

Outside, Nassiri and his team of Humvees and Jeeps armed with fifty-caliber machine guns turned their headlights off as they approached the chemical factory. They spread out across the width of the building, parking behind a barricade of barrels to keep a safe distance away in case the PMOI was armed with RPG's. Nassiri gestured for Vaziri to hand him the radio.

"Rear team, report."

"Rear team in place, and awaiting your orders, sir."

"Stand fast. Do not fire without my authorization. We must take Farhad alive. He'll likely be wearing another stupid *Star Wars* t-shirt.

Repeat, we must capture Farhad alive. Anyone else is fair game. Acknowledge."

"Affirmative, sir."

Through his binoculars, Nassiri studied each floor of the building. The PMOI had covered most of them with rags for curtains, but he could see lights on the second and third floors.

"What do we do if Farhad's not in there?" Vaziri asked.

"Then we take the building anyway and make someone in there talk. Got it?"

"Yes, sir."

Vaziri rolled his eyes. Nassiri saw a curtain move and someone peeked out. He only got a quick look, but he recognized the face immediately.

"He's there."

"How do you know?"

"I just saw that bitch, Donya. Farhad wouldn't let her out of his sight after what happened."

The lights in all the windows were suddenly turned off.

"They saw us. Tell the rear team to stand by."

Nassiri grabbed the megaphone.

"This is General Nassiri. We have the building surrounded. Come out and you will not be harmed. You can walk out peacefully or be carried out dead. The choice is yours. You have three minutes to decide!"

The only sounds outside were crickets and the hissing of Persian horned viper snakes in the sandy vegetation behind them. When the three-minute deadline passed without any movement from inside the building, Nassiri nodded at Vaziri, who grabbed the radio.

"All teams begin firing on the building."

Twenty men under Nassiri's command began firing their assault weapons and the fifty-caliber machine guns mounted on their vehicles. The bullets pelted the building, chipping away the cement exterior.

"Ceasefire, ceasefire!"

All the soldiers, including Nassiri and Vaziri, began coughing profusely. The steady wind was blowing cement dust in their faces.

"Nassiri!"

A figure appeared at the third-floor window. The lights inside were still off, and the debris clouded his view, so Nassiri couldn't see the person's face, but he recognized Farhad's *Star Wars* shirt immediately.

"Hold your fire! We're coming out!" Farhad yelled.

Vaziri smiled at his cousin, but Nassiri was quick to grab the radio.

"Eyes up, men. They could try anything."

They waited, but no one appeared. Nassiri was about to order more shooting when he saw a rifle extended from the same window, which fired several shots at the barrels in front of them. When they exploded, the ground was rocked with a thunderous combustion. Nassiri and his men took cover but they couldn't avoid the blaze pummeling toward them. Some men escaped the flames and assisted their colleagues by patting out the fire on their backs and arms. Others were not so fortunate. They were engulfed by the fast-spreading fire and tried to roll on the ground, but it was no use. The flames burned them to death.

When Nassiri and Vaziri reappeared unharmed to survey the damage, they heard several other explosions rock the other side of the building. Vaziri seized the radio to check on those men, but no one answered. All they could hear were shrieks and cries of pain.

Enraged, Nassiri exited his Humvee and made his way to an adjacent Jeep so he could fire the fifty-caliber weapon until there were no more bullets. Before he could get behind the gun, a string of Jeep Wranglers, Mini-Coopers, and Volkswagen Beetles charged through the building's gates, each heading in a different direction. In the passenger seat of each car was a man with a shaved head, wearing a *Star Wars* t-shirt, waving at IRGC soldiers.

The cars zipped by the Revolutionary Guard slow enough that they could see the t-shirts, but they couldn't get a good look at anyone's face. Under a pitch-black night sky, they all looked like Farhad.

"Which one do we go after?"

Nassiri cursed aloud.

"All of them! Go! Go!"

Vaziri told the rear team to follow all the escaping vehicles. Then, he turned to Nassiri.

"Which one are we going after?"

Nassiri was unsure what to do. Before he could decide, a beat-up truck tore out of the first-floor garage. This time, he got a good look at the driver. His blood pressure spiked when Farhad gave him a thumbs up sign as he drove by.

"You drive," he told Vaziri. "I'm going to shoot that little punk myself!"

Ten minutes later, when she was sure the coast was clear, Jenkins led another string of cars with the remaining PMOI members out of the building toward a safe destination. Thrasher was certainly rough around the edges, but the man was a genius.

Chapter Forty-Seven

Nassiri gripped the steering wheel with white knuckles, hell bent on catching Farhad. He had Vaziri radio the other vehicles so they would stop their pursuit and jump back onto Highway 2 in the eastbound lane heading westbound toward Tabriz.

"We'll drive Farhad to them and box him in!"

"Copy that," Vaziri said.

Nassiri slammed the pedal to the floor and glanced at the speedometer. The Humvee was approaching one hundred miles per hour. Even though the road had no lampposts and Farhad had turned his lights off, he knew they were closing the distance between them.

"How far out are the men?"

"The closest vehicle is about six miles away."

"Tell them to get their thumbs out of their asses and move it!"

Nassiri's excitement grew as they continued to get closer. Two-hundred-fifty meters, two hundred, one-fifty. At one hundred meters, Vaziri leaned out the window with his gun, preparing to shoot out the tires, but Nassiri saw the truck's tailgate drop. He grabbed Vaziri by his belt and jerked him back in. As the truck swerved left and right, the barrels loaded in the back came tumbling out one by one.

"Watch out!"

Vaziri seemed alarmed, but Nassiri smiled. Farhad was desperate. Putting obstacles in their path would only slow down the pursuit. He would eventually run out of barrels, and with his reinforcements approaching from the east, it was only a matter of time before he was caught.

Nassiri veered right and left to dodge the barrels rolling his way. The lid to the third to last barrel came flying off before it fell out of the truck, spilling all its contents onto the highway. With the wind blowing in their face, it took only seconds for the toxic fumes to reach them. Nassiri and Vaziri used their undershirts to cover their noses.

"He's only got two more!"

Suddenly, the liquid from the barrel lit on fire and a blaze of flames scorched its way toward them, lighting up the highway. As the second to last barrel tumbled onto the road, Nassiri closed in fast on the truck. Too fast. He looked down at the speedometer and grimaced: eight-five miles per hour. At the rate he was going, he shouldn't have been able to close the distance as fast as he was.

The truck is slowing down.

Just then, Nassiri saw a gun appear from behind the last barrel in the truck.

"Bail out!"

Chapter Forty-Eight

After Thrasher pushed the third to last barrel out of the truck, he sparked the Zippo lighter he'd pulled from his pocket and tossed it into the road. As the trail of fire made its way down the highway toward the oncoming Humvee, he knocked on the back of the window, signaling to Farhad that it was time to slow down. Once Thrasher pushed the second to last barrel out, Farhad took his foot off the gas and kept the wheel straight. Thrasher peeked over the last barrel. The timing needed to be perfect.

When the Humvee came within thirty yards of the rolling barrel, Thrasher took aim and fired. After the bullet hit, the truck lurched forward from the shockwave of the explosion. Thrasher saw two passengers from the Humvee jump out of the vehicle, which was vaulted into the air. Since the soldier in the passenger seat was late to move, the combustion from the blast propelled him outward and into a mound of adjacent dirt. The driver, however, sprang out in time, and smacked violently onto the pavement. His body rolled until the centripetal force brought him to a stop.

Thrasher banged his fist on the rear window.

"Stop the truck!"

Farhad hit the brakes so hard it sent Thrasher flying against the rear window. He thought he cracked it and had to check his head to make sure he wasn't bleeding. Once he realized he was okay, he jumped over the side and ran toward the soldier, who he hoped was Nassiri.

Time for round three.

Glock 19 in hand, Thrasher carefully approached the man, who wasn't moving. Thrasher nudged him with his foot. No movement. He leaned down to check the man's pulse. When he turned him over, Nassiri delivered a backhanded elbow to Thrasher's cheek and went for his gun. The Iranian had been playing possum.

Thrasher grabbed Nassiri's hands. He couldn't let him get his gun or the fight would be over before it began, so he repeatedly kneed him in the chest. When Nassiri's grip loosened, Thrasher spotted the HP Browning 9mm on his belt and reached for it.

Two guns are always better than one.

Nassiri anticipated this move. While maintaining his grip on Thrasher's gun with one hand, he caught Thrasher's wrist with the other. He spread their arms as far apart as possible. Thrasher was now face to face with Nassiri. The impact from hitting the pavement so hard had wrecked his face. He had deep lacerations in multiple places on his cheeks and forehead. Blood was dripping into his eyes.

Distracted by the extent of his horrific injuries, Nassiri took advantage of Thrasher's lack of focus by head-butting him, which cut his lip, knocked a tooth loose, and made him see stars.

Thrasher stumbled backward, which allowed Nassiri to pull his gun. Thrasher instinctively dove out of the way and took cover behind the wrecked Humvee. Nassiri fired off several wayward shots in Thrasher's direction, but because of the blood in his eyes, none came close to hitting him. When he heard the empty click from the gun, Nassiri went for the extra magazines on his belt, a move he could do blindfolded, but just as he did, he was struck with two bullets to the chest. He managed to climb to his knees and rip his uniform open. His hands inspected the wounds, but it was no use. All he could see was blood on his hands. Nassiri looked up to see his killer and was met with a kick to the face. He stared up at the man he had encountered twice before.

"American?"

Blood leaked from his mouth. Thrasher said nothing as he stood over him. He heard Farhad's approach from behind. Seeing Nassiri made

Farhad anxious, even though he was near the point of death. The mere sight of him was still terribly unsettling.

Thrasher turned to hand him his weapon, but to his surprise, Farhad refused.

"He'll die here on the road, right?" he asked.

Thrasher glanced down at the wounds on Nassiri's chest to be sure that the vital organs had been hit. Nassiri was alive, but there was no way he'd survive. Satisfied, he nodded to Farhad.

"He's gotten what he deserved. Let's go."

As Farhad walked back to the truck, Thrasher noticed how gingerly his invaluable Iranian source was walking, due to the effects of his rape. Despite the bullets in him, Nassiri had managed to roll onto his stomach and was attempting to get up.

Thrasher motioned to Farhad. Nassiri had managed to push himself into a fetal position, so his butt was sticking up in the air. He was barely breathing. Thrasher leaned down and whispered into his ear.

"You and the Supreme Leader have fucked the people of this country for far too long, which is bad enough, but then you made the mistake of fucking with people I care about. Now, it's time to return the favor."

Nassiri's eyes bulged as Thrasher placed the muzzle of his gun directly over Nassiri's asshole. When he fired, a slight grunt was heard as the bullet tore through Nassiri's insides. The whites of his eyes filled with blood from the internal bleeding, and his body released one last fateful breath as he slowly expired.

Thrasher turned to Farhad, who had a ghostly look on his face.

"You may not believe in retribution, but I do."

Thrasher removed Nassiri's uniform before it could get any bloodier than it already was and grabbed his hat and radio. As they walked back to the truck, he put the hat on Farhad's head and hugged him around the neck.

"Thanks, Jay."

"You're welcome, kid. But, when we're alone, you can call me Ben. You've earned it, my friend."

Chapter Forty-Nine

Vaziri blinked his eyes awake and groaned to the sound of men hollering his name. Seconds later, four men with flashlights approached him. He was laying on his stomach. The back of his uniform was charred, and his skin was badly burned, but he was alive.

"Colonel, are you okay?"

Vaziri tried to shake himself out of his daze as two soldiers helped him sit up.

"Colonel, what happened?"

"We were chasing Farhad, but he had help. Barrels came flying out of a truck. One of them exploded."

Vaziri's eyes popped open.

"Where's General Nassiri?"

Unsure of what to say or how to break the news, the soldiers looked at each other.

"Sir, the General is dead. It looks like he may have survived the explosion, but someone shot him. What do we do now?"

Vaziri gave the soldier his arm, a signal to help him to his feet. As he stood, he looked at the damage to the Humvee and the flames burning on the highway.

"Put his body in one of the cars. There's nothing we can do here. We need to get back to Khorramabad. With Nassiri gone, the Supreme Leader needs us to protect him. Let's move out."

Chapter Fifty

KHORRAMABAD, IRAN
FALAK-OL-AFLAK CASTLE

An hour after he had injected his most recent dose, Shir-Del noticed that the brown splotches on his skin had not dissipated as normal, and his muscles were cramping. This could only mean the dose he took was either too small or it wasn't working. If he'd taken too little, it was an easy fix, though he needed to be careful about over medicating himself. Carbamazepine wasn't known for being forgiving when taken in large quantities. If the medicine wasn't working, he had a major problem on his hands. While he waited for Nassiri to return with good news, Shir-Del began rummaging through his inventory inside the chamber room.

With his personal doctor now dead, Shir-Del couldn't be sure if his condition had been leaked. If so, anyone with this information could have made a deliberate effort to purchase every available vial of Carbamazepine on the globe to prevent him from acquiring it. Shir-Del decided to beat them to the punch, and he ordered as much of his medication as possible. He thought it had been a smart bet, until now.

He recalled a member of his staff being elated when he got a good deal by buying the medicine in bulk. At the time, Shir-Del viewed this as good news because the lower cost kept the purchase from raising a flag for any foreign intelligence agency that knew about his condition and were nosing about on the web. When the medicine arrived, Shir-Del never thought twice about inspecting it. Unfortunately, it appeared that his staff hadn't paid attention to the fine print on the orders. At the time it was received, more than half of the Carbamazepine was only three months away from its expiration date. Now, it was expired. Frustrated,

Shir-Del threw vial after expired vial against the stone wall, leaving a pile of shattered glass and liquid on the floor. Once he had finished going through all of it, only two boxes of medication remained that were *not* expired. If he was lucky, and he rationed it appropriately, it would last two months.

It was possible that Nassiri had just grabbed the first boxes of medicine that he saw when they were at his private residence in Qom. If this was true, Shir-Del had the unfortunate luck that those were mostly expired, which meant that non-expired meds might be sitting in his hidden room. He wanted to dispatch a soldier outside his door to pick up whatever was left, but he knew his home had probably been vandalized. It would be a miracle if any medicine was left. For anyone who found it, all it would take was an internet search to find out what it was used for. It didn't matter that Carbamazepine was used to treat a variety of conditions. The world would know that he wasn't one hundred percent healthy. Considering his current status, weakness was not a label he could afford.

Shir-Del went to throw another vial against the wall, but he stopped himself. It was no use. As he sat down to collect his thoughts, his door opened. Because of the burns Vaziri sustained, four IRGC soldiers helped him into the Supreme Leader's room. Alarmed by the stench of burned flesh, Shir-Del rose to his feet and shuffled across the room with his cane.

"What happened?"

Vaziri gingerly sat down on the nearest stool. His men stood at his side.

"We couldn't get him."

Shir-Del slapped him across the face.

Vaziri had half a mind to slap the old man back, but he resisted. Instead, he rubbed his jaw. The soldiers at his side took a step back.

"Supreme Leader, the PMOI had a plan in case we found them. There was an explosion on the highway. Nassiri is dead!"

Shir-Del nodded as he absorbed the information. Noting that Vaziri was in considerable pain, he looked at the extent of his injuries and then gently patted him on the shoulder.

"Don't worry, Supreme Leader, our team will protect you. But what do we do now?"

"You're Nassiri's cousin, aren't you?"

"Yes, Supreme Leader. Lieutenant Colonel Vaziri."

"First things, first. Vaziri, you are now in charge of the Revolutionary Guard."

The pain in Vaziri's back momentarily went away as he looked at his fellow soldiers, dumbfounded.

"Supreme Leader, I greatly appreciate your confidence, and I will gladly continue to serve you, but there are other men better qualified."

Shir-Del leered at Vaziri.

"Do you doubt my ability to lead this country, Vaziri?"

"Of course not, Supreme Leader."

"Then trust my judgement. Any man who endured what you have will quickly gain the respect of his men. Leaders are made by what they overcome."

"Yes, Supreme Leader."

"Now, tell me what happened. How did Farhad escape?"

Vaziri recapped the scene outside the factory and the explosion on the highway.

"How did Nassiri die?"

"He was shot, Supreme Leader."

"I thought you said that an explosion killed him."

"No, Supreme Leader. He jumped from the vehicle before the explosion occurred. Although badly injured, he survived the fall, but not the three bullets that hit him."

"So, either Farhad killed him or he had help."

"Yes, Supreme Leader."

"Did you bring Nassiri's body back?"

"Yes, Supreme Leader."

"Take me to it."

Vaziri escorted the Supreme Leader to Nassiri's body, which had been carried onto a table in an empty room on the lower level. One of the soldiers had covered the former Revolutionary Guardsman's face with one of their jackets, but Shir-Del removed it and stared at the lifeless face of the man he'd relied on to serve him. The eyes were open and mouth was agape. Shir-Del closed Nassiri's eyes, and spit on his face before covering him with the camouflage jacket. He turned to see an astonished look on Vaziri's face.

Shir-Del approached his new chief commander of the Revolutionary Guard and stuck his bony finger into his chest.

"I don't tolerate failure. You need to remember that."

A tight lump formed in Vaziri's throat.

"Yes, Supreme Leader."

"Check your phone. How are the videos of me trending?"

Vaziri pulled out his phone and scrolled through the feed.

"It looks good, Supreme Leader. Judging by the comments, people are arguing about the validity of the first video versus the one that Nassiri posted. Six million views."

Shir-Del nodded.

"Good, but not good enough. Tell me your ideas."

"I only have one. In order to win the war of public opinion, we need to show you as a sympathetic figure. But I don't know how."

Shir-Del combed his fingers through his long, grey beard. The idea of sympathy had merit.

"Do you think Farhad was alone? Or do you think he had help?"

"Supreme Leader, I don't know much about Farhad, but judging by the files Nassiri showed me before he was tortured, I would say he didn't have it in him to kill anyone. Afterward, it's hard to say. But I would bet he had help."

"Very well. Turn on the camera on your phone. I need you to record something for me."

Vaziri stood back to get the Supreme Leader in focus. The room was not well lit and there was an echo in the gothic room as they spoke, but it would have to do. He nodded when the video began.

"My dear people of Iran. By now, you have seen the video of me standing at Azadi Square. By the grace of Allah, I am alive and well, unharmed, and unaffected by the events that transpired. I come to you today to reveal a great injustice. I have evidence that the media campaign against me continues and is being pushed by the little pigs of Israel and their puppet, the Great Satan, the United States. Do not believe their lies."

Vaziri squinted his eyes, confused.

"Allah personally selected me to lead you, and I continue to fulfill His destiny. Iran's fate resides with me, not the influence of the West. Continue your fight, stand by my side and we will be victorious! We will never fail! And we will not stop until the last drop of blood from the Western infidels has been shed!"

Shir-Del used his finger to make his last point, then signaled to Vaziri to end the video.

"What evidence do you have, Supreme Leader?"

"They are behind this. There is no doubt in my mind."

Vaziri acknowledged what the Supreme Leader said but he had doubts.

Nassiri never said anything to me about it.

Shir-Del took another look at Vaziri's burns. The scorched skin was becoming dried and crispy. Other parts were oozing oil as the body tried to heal itself.

"Find a doctor and get checked out. Then, come back to my chambers. There's more work to be done, and I need to brief you on my condition."

Condition?

"Yes, Supreme Leader. What do you want me to do with this?"

Vaziri held up his phone, referencing the video.

"Post it immediately. I want the world to know of America and Israel's involvement."

Chapter Fifty-One

QOM, IRAN

Only minutes away from meeting Jenkins and the rest of the PMOI team in Shahin Shahr, Thrasher received a text from Jenkins. The Supreme Leader had sent out a Tweet. After he watched it, Thrasher got an idea. From the posted video, he couldn't tell where Shir-Del was, but he had a good idea where he wasn't.

"You know where the Supreme Leader's private residence is, right? The one he lived in when he was a member of the Guardian Council?"

"Yes, it's in Qom."

"Then, turn around."

"Huh?"

"Because that's where we're going."

"Why?"

"I've got a gut feeling."

Farhad gave him a sideways look as Thrasher lit a cigarette.

Three months ago, during an intense interrogation session with his personal doctor, Shahid Aslam, Thrasher and Farhad were fortunate to learn about the Supreme Leader's Chromosome Six Deficiency Syndrome. Later, Thrasher would end up having to shoot the doctor at the Pakistani border when the man shot Farhad and tried to turn on him, but he knew that the information about the Supreme Leader's condition was solid because he had overheard the doctor speaking to him about his medicine. With his doctor dead, the Supreme Leader was probably concerned that news of his condition may have leaked. While it was a hunch on Thrasher's part, he was willing to bet that the Supreme Leader kept an extra stash at his beloved private residence.

As nervous as Farhad was in his cell at Evin Prison, his body tensed up even more as he and Thrasher got closer to Qom. The highway was eerily empty. There was a mysterious but unmistakable tension in the air. It felt as if some heinous force was lurking inside the city, waiting for them to arrive.

The Supreme Leader's private residence was on the northern edge of Qom, so they didn't have to go into the heart of the city, but it didn't mean they couldn't run into any trouble. A mile before their exit, they saw cars parked on the side of the highway as clerics and protestors gathered. Thrasher gripped his Glock. Knowing the numbers weren't in their favor, he didn't want to shoot his way out, but would if he had to. Being captured was not an option.

"You're sure you know where you're going?"

"Yes. I've been there before."

"Then, take the next exit. Let's avoid the crowd up ahead."

The scene on the exit ramp was only marginally better. People were gathered on the side of the road. Farhad slowed his pace, careful not to make a scene, but it didn't matter. A quarter mile later, they were stopped by a roadblock led by a young cleric with a wispy beard and black kufi prayer hat, no doubt a university student only a few years younger than Farhad. A pair of goons armed with AK-47's positioned themselves in front of the truck.

Thrasher slyly slid his gun over to Farhad, then loosely attached himself to the door handle with the cuffs from Nassiri's uniform.

"Give them the look, and play it like Nassiri would," Thrasher said.

Farhad glared at the young cleric as he stepped up to the window.

"What's your destination?"

"We're on a special assignment for the Supreme Leader. Move out of the way."

Since Farhad was wearing Nassiri's IRGC uniform and hat, the young cleric had no reason to doubt that he was part of the Revolutionary Guard, but his guts told him otherwise.

"Who's he?"

The young cleric pointed to Thrasher, who was not dressed in an IRGC uniform, only jeans and a black t-shirt.

"He's my prisoner. That's all you need to know. Let us through."

"Sir, I'm sorry, but I've been ordered to stop anyone I don't know. And I don't know you."

"Son, look at the name on my uniform."

Farhad pointed to his name patch.

The cleric looked and saw the name NASSIRI, which he clearly recognized. Luckily for Farhad and Thrasher, the youngster had never seen or met Nassiri in person, so he didn't know what he looked like. It was a roll of the dice on Farhad's part. The rising sun to his back created a shadow across his face from the brim of his cap.

"Now, look at this."

Farhad pointed Thrasher's gun at him. The other clerics quickly raised their AK-47's and began shouting.

"I'm on assignment for the Supreme Leader. He doesn't stand for any type of failure. You can either move out of the way, or I can radio the Supreme Leader myself."

Farhad held up Nassiri's radio.

"But he will *not* be happy you are obstructing me from his orders."

The cleric's eyes narrowed as he pointed to Farhad's chest.

"Are you sure you're okay?"

Farhad looked down. Nassiri's uniform had bullet holes in it and was stained with blood. He needed to think quickly.

"I'm fine. The blood isn't mine. Do you want to be next?"

Farhad glared at the young cleric again, who took a step back. He didn't want to upset the Supreme Leader, so he waved the armed guards away.

"Let them through!"

A half-mile past the roadblock, the crowd thinned, and Thrasher looked back.

"We're clear. Good job talking your way through that."

After slipping his hands out of the cuffs, Thrasher slapped Farhad on the leg.

Farhad let out a long breath of nervous energy.

"Thanks."

"How far to the house?"

"A few more miles."

"How'd you find out about this place?"

"I'm a smuggler, remember? I don't just smuggle booze. I can get anything. Before he became Supreme Leader, Shir-Del was just another member of the Guardian Council with extravagant taste. It was rumored that he siphoned off some of the country's money to have a fancy library built in his house. What do you put in a library?"

"Books."

"Right. And in the Supreme Leader's case, rare books, and black-market paintings."

"And you smuggled them in for him."

"His people reached out through the grapevine. He never knew my name, and at the time, I never knew who the jobs were for. One of the first pieces I ever got for him was a missing Rembrandt painting."

"Which painting?"

"*The Storm on the Sea of Galilee*. It was his only seascape."

"Holy shit! That was stolen from a museum in Boston back in 1990. How did you end up with it?"

Farhad grinned and shrugged his shoulders.

"You've got your secrets, and I've got mine."

"That should've been one hell of a payday for you."

"It should've been, but the dealer stiffed me on half my fee because I was two weeks late getting it to him. I followed him because I wanted to see where it was being delivered. I figured I could steal it back from whoever he was giving it to so I could get the rest of the money owed to me. But when I saw it was Shir-Del standing at the door, I let it go."

As they made the turnoff to Shir-Del's house, Thrasher checked his weapon to make sure he had enough bullets. There was no telling what was awaiting them inside. When they pulled up, no one was there, but it was obvious that some type of skirmish had occurred. The beige columns were riddled with bullet holes, and the front door was kicked open.

Thrasher turned to Farhad.

"Stay behind me."

Thrasher walked through the two-story home, looking for anyone who might be there.

"What are we looking for?" Farhad said.

"Remember when we interrogated the Supreme Leader's doctor?"

"How could I forget?"

"Then you should remember he told us about his medical condition and the type of medicine he was on. I'm betting he has a hidden stash here, which he's going to need."

Satisfied that the coast was clear, Thrasher and Farhad scoured every closet, drawer and cabinet in the kitchen, bedrooms and bathrooms, looking for any place Shir-Del would have hidden his Carbamazepine. Thrasher came up empty. He hollered for Farhad, who came running.

"Find anything?"

"No. You?"

Thrasher kicked a broken vase across the floor.

273

"If he wanted to keep his condition a secret, there's only one place he'd hide it."

The heavy double doors to the library looked like they had been locked, but whatever mob came into the house eventually knocked them down. Thrasher and Farhad were overwhelmed when they walked in. The room had been modeled after the Abbey Library of Saint Gall in St. Gallen, Switzerland. It had once been filled with wall-to-ceiling books, supported by mahogany shelves that were only broken up by a walkway on the second floor, but all the books had either been stolen or thrown across the floor. The gilded frames once filled with lavish, black-market paintings were broken and scattered around the room. All that remained was the painted ceiling with replicas of famous Persian artwork, surrounded by lush borders.

"Looks like the Rembrandt I got for him is missing again."

Thrasher didn't acknowledge the statement. He was too busy staring at one of the bookshelves against the wall.

"What is it?"

Thrasher held up his finger. The corner of one of the middle mahogany bookshelves stood a few centimeters higher and wasn't flush with the one to its right. Thrasher pushed on it, but it wouldn't move. When he knocked on the back panel, he heard an echo.

There's something behind it.

He ran his fingers along the sides, looking for a button, but he didn't find one. He pressed on the decorative corners. Nothing there. Thrasher studied the bookcase up and down.

It's gotta be here.

He noticed all of the individual shelves on this particular bookcase were still in place and not knocked down or pulled out like the others. Starting at the bottom, Thrasher tried to pull each of the shelves out, but they wouldn't budge. When he pulled on one at chest level, it released toward him, and he heard a distinct unlocking sound. When the bookcase pushed forward, he hit the jackpot: a hidden closet filled with a dozen boxes of leftover Carbamazepine.

Bingo.

Thrasher smiled at Farhad, who couldn't believe what he was seeing.

"Take one of them back to the truck. I'll be there in a minute."

"Just one?"

"Trust me."

After Farhad left the room, Thrasher took the pad of matches from his pocket and began to ignite the rest of the boxes and every leftover book he could find. It was time to leave the Supreme Leader a message. When he got back to the truck, he pulled out his phone.

"Do I smell smoke?" Farhad asked.

Thrasher grinned.

"Let's hit the road."

On the other end of the phone, Jenkins picked up on the second ring. "Hello?"

"Did everyone else make it out of the factory okay?"

"We're all good. What happened with you and Farhad?"

Thrasher quickly filled her in on Nassiri's death and the looting of Shir-Del's house.

"That's great! I'll let Lajani know."

"What's the next move?"

"Meet us in Kermanshah."

Chapter Fifty-Two

KERMANSHAH, IRAN
OUTSIDE KHORRAMABAD

Kermanshah was two hours northwest of Khorramabad. Though its history dates back to the Paleolithic era, Kermanshah has steadily emerged as a modern city over the last fifty years. It is now considered one of the country's agricultural cores and is simultaneously becoming an industrial city with is sugar refineries, textile plants and carpet making centers.

The family home of Salim Ghiasi was a stereotypical Middle Eastern house. It was small by any standard, only eight hundred square feet, had only one bathroom, and guests had to sleep on the floor. With such humble beginnings, Jenkins was amazed that Ghiasi found a way to become a medical student. Despite the lack of comfort by western standards, Jenkins was honored that the family agreed to take them in so they could conduct their business. She assured them they would be compensated with some of Walsh's money once the ordeal was over.

Thrasher and Farhad arrived by early afternoon. Based on information from the locals, Jenkins informed them that the Supreme Leader was holed up in the Falak-ol-Aflak castle. He was either trying to make a dramatic last stand or using it as a home base to get the country back under his control.

"Probably a little of both," Farhad said.

When she gave Lajani the news, he agreed to transfer some Revolutionary Guard soldiers loyal to him to the area. But there were many more locals loyal to Shir-Del than there were soldiers Lajani could spare. With the assistance of Revolutionary Guardsmen still loyal to the

Supreme Leader, the locals had essentially barricaded the city. No one was getting inside that the locals didn't know.

"That's probably better. We don't want this to turn into a blood bath," Thrasher said.

"Lajani was thinking the same thing," said Jenkins. "I say we wait Shir-Del out. Lajani knows about his health condition. Assuming he took some meds with him before he holed up in the castle, the only way for him to get more is to have them delivered. Between us, the PMOI, and Lajani's forces, we can stop deliveries from being made. And since you have the only box of his meds, we can use it as a bargaining chip. Eventually, he'll either die or get so desperate he'll make whatever deal he can to live."

Thrasher swayed his head from side to side.

"That's only part of the equation. Even if he dies, his supporters will appoint someone else. And as they debate who the true leader should be, the country will tear itself apart."

Farhad nodded, impressed. Thrasher was finally understanding Iran.

"Plus, I don't want his body getting so out of whack that he starts making rash decisions. I don't want to test this psycho any more than we have to. If we want that son-of-a-bitch gone, we need to add some ingredients to the recipe."

"Such as?" Jenkins said.

Thrasher bit his lip for a moment.

"How are the videos from Azadi Square trending?"

"Millions of views, but I think we're losing ground. The Ayatollah's supporters, inside the country and out, are making a full court press. It's like the liberal Democrats and conservative Republicans back home. Everyone is insulting and threatening each other. In a way, it feels like we never left the States."

Thrasher huffed out a laugh.

"If we want to give Lajani a chance to succeed, we've got to publicly discredit this guy and show everyone how dangerous he is. It's time to fight fire with fire."

"Meaning?"

"We use the best weapon we have."

Thrasher pointed to Farhad.

"Me?"

"Farhad, whether you like it or not, you're the spokesman for a free Iran now. The people like you. You've got to keep making videos, calling out the Supreme Leader's regime. Make as many speeches and testimonials as you can."

"That's it?"

"No. Didn't you tell me you called an old girlfriend to make a web-site detailing all the horrors people have endured at the hands of the Ayatollah?"

"Simin's not my girlfriend, but, yes, I called her. She's working on it."

Thrasher looked at Jenkins.

"Tom knows about it. He says it's getting a ton of attention."

"Good. Call Lajani. Tell him we need enough soldiers to build a bar-ricade, a media truck, and enough construction equipment to erect a billboard outside the city limits."

"A billboard? For what?"

"We're gonna beat this bastard at his own game."

Chapter Fifty-Three

ASHEVILLE, NORTH CAROLINA
TWO MONTHS LATER

In addition to her job as a paramedic, Simin was working eighteen-hour days to collect videos from Farhad and other Iranians. The videos weren't limited to details of torture they endured under the Ayatollah. Users, especially women, posted testimonials about human rights in their marriages. According to the Iranian constitution, a husband has exclusive rights as the head of the family and can withhold financial mainte-nance if he determines his wife is not fulfilling her duties, which could mean anything from cooking and taking care of the children to their so-called sexual responsibilities. In short, the Ayatollah promoted the idea that women were the property of men who were legally allowed to beat them even if it resulted in severe injury or death. Since her mother had been raped, which resulted in her birth, Simin would be damned if she would allow women's rights to slip below the new Iranian radar.

Her efforts were paying off. Media outlets all over the globe were starting to reference the website she had built. After news agencies tracked her down, she received dozens of calls requesting interviews but didn't return them. The website wasn't about her. It was about Iran.

Her strategy was simple. She shared every testimonial she found online on each of her social media accounts, and always posted it with a link to the website. This way, she covered the individual stories and directed her followers to the main website, which acted as a repository for *all* the videos from each individual platform.

When she wasn't posting, she was scrolling through the videos to make impactful comments on individual posts. Even if the person in question or their followers hadn't heard about her other social media pages or website, when they clicked on her name they were sent to her main page, which let them see what she had built. Curiosity took over. It was effective but exhausting, non-stop work.

Kirk noticed Simin constantly rubbing her neck and her legs. He encouraged her to take some breaks away from the computer, but that resulted in a fiery comeback.

"If they don't rest," she said, pointing at her screen, "I don't rest."

All Kirk could do was nod. Simin was defensive about her social media domain. Once she got an idea, she didn't stop until the job was done. This time, though, the task was much closer to her heart, so he backed off.

He was about to take Gypsy for a walk when his phone rang.

"Hello?"

"K-2. What's the good word?" Dub said.

When Director Wallace found out about Dub's involvement in the embassy bombing in Pakistan, he was one call away from throwing him in jail or having him killed. But because he had been manipulated by former Senator Walsh, Jenkins and Delang talked him out of it. After all, he wasn't the first fly to fall into Walsh's web. Dub was forced out of the agency anyway, but thanks to Delang's connections with Kirk, he managed to get a job with Kirk's employer, the Gregory Group, a private security firm in Charlotte.

From their first meeting, Kirk and Dub hit it off immediately. Kirk took to Dub's new nickname for him, K-2, which was a play on the first letters of his first and last name.

"Well, the whole Iran situation has Simin quite busy, so I'm playing a supporting role. Who's rubbin' you wrong today, Dub?"

Dub laughed.

"No one yet, but Worm wanted me to give you a call. He wants you to get to Green Bay and work out details with their head of security."

"Worm" was the nickname for the Gregory Group's owner, Jason Gregory. He had earned the nickname due to his ability to wiggle out of precarious situations during his time as a Virginia Beach police officer. He tried to bury the nickname when he started his own company, but it always managed to find its way back to him. He allowed his employees to call him by the name in private, but never in public, and never in the presence of a client.

"Again? We were just there three weeks ago."

"He's trying to schmooze an elite, prospective client. Could mean big bucks for the outfit. But this client is incredibly meticulous about the details of his security. He wants all our movements to be pristine."

Kirk groaned.

"Okay, I'll take care of it."

Chapter Fifty-Four

KERMANSHAH, IRAN
OUTSIDE KHORRAMABAD

Jenkins was feeling optimistic. Thrasher's plan was working. Farhad was making multiple videos each day and posting them online. He continued to gain followers by the hour, and only stopped to eat or sleep. Across all social media feeds, the pirate symbol was circulating, along with the *#FarhadForIran* tag. Whether it was Farhad's videos or those posted by Simin to the new *fightforiran.com* website, Thrasher made sure the media van played them on the billboard he had constructed, along with gigantic, concert quality speakers Lajani had repositioned from the Milad Concert Hall. The people of Khorramabad needed to know their hometown hero was a monster, and the videos wouldn't stop playing until the point got across. They played day and night, only stopping for prayers, which Lajani insisted not be interrupted.

On the other side of the barricade, Shir-Del loyalists did the same thing. While they didn't have the benefit of concert quality speakers and advanced video equipment, the local clerics were using any available home audio equipment they had, alternating between preaching about Lajani's evil plot to overthrow the Supreme Leader and their desire to behead Farhad.

For all his talk about the evils of the western world, the Supreme Leader posted daily Tweets to counteract those from Farhad. The videos were turning into a sparring match, and Shir-Del became more emotional with each Tweet.

However, one mistake the Supreme Leader made was only reaching out on Twitter. Even before Lajani removed internet restrictions, Instagram was the only mainstream platform allowed in Iran. By ignoring it and omitting hashtags, Shir Del was neglecting an audience. Farhad doubled his efforts on Instagram, where he already had tens of thousands of followers. Using Facebook also allowed Farhad's videos to be shared with users around the globe.

Slowly but surely, Farhad was winning the online media war.

Iranians on both sides continued to bicker about which version of Iran they wanted, but Jenkins felt the energy becoming more positive with each passing day as Lajani toured the country making speeches while trying to keep the country in order. She had no idea when the man was sleeping.

Lajani continued to remind Thrasher and Jenkins that Shir-Del *had* to be running out of his medicine. Thrasher agreed. In each of the last three videos he posted, Jenkins and Thrasher noticed more brown and purple splotches on Shir-Del's skin, which they took as a good sign, but given his tolerance for pain, there was no telling how long he would hold out. However, Lajani was feeling international pressure. Anxious world leaders were calling for him to use brute force to overtake the city and arrest the Supreme Leader. He couldn't play the waiting game much longer. He needed to know what Shir-Del was up to inside the castle.

Back at the Ghiasi house, Thrasher and Jenkins discussed going behind enemy lines to plant a bug inside the castle. Since it was built on top of Golestan Spring, it had a well leading inside. Once they eluded the barricades and got into Khorramabad, all Thrasher and Jenkins would have to do is find their way to the well, discreetly climb up into the castle, and find the right room to plant the bug. There would be guards all over and killing them wouldn't be a problem for two experienced agents, but it wasn't an option. Thrasher and Jenkins needed to slip in and out of the castle undetected else they risked alarming the rest of the soldiers, which would prevent them from reaching their side of the barricade.

Farhad hated the idea from the beginning and begged his two friends not to go.

"You may be able to get to the Spring, but I can't guarantee getting you behind the barricade. Have you seen what's going on out there? Khorramabad is basically the Supreme Leader's hometown. Close to a million people live here, and *everyone* is loyal to him. I have no doubt that a hundred thousand people have surrounded the castle to protect him. He has home field advantage. It'll be impossible to get you two in there."

Pumped with the idea of bringing the standoff to a close, Thrasher was in no mood to be told he couldn't do something.

"Bullshit! Get me back there, and we'll end this fucking thing, once and for all."

"Jay," Jenkins interjected, "Farhad has a point. The numbers aren't on our side. This is no time for a pissing contest."

Thrasher turned his head.

Now, that's an idea.

"Actually, that's exactly what we need."

"Excuse me?"

"It's time to play the ace up our sleeve."

He went to the other side of the room, grabbed a vial of Carbamazepine, and tossed it to Farhad.

"What am I supposed to do with this?"

"Time to challenge that bastard. Make a video and show him you have some of his meds. Tell him you'll give him one vial if he meets you face to face with the guarantee you won't be harmed."

"You're crazy! Those people will kill me as soon as they see me!"

Farhad gave Jenkins a desperate look.

"This is where the rubber meets the road, Farhad."

He bit his lip.

"You think they'll really let me see him?"

"Only one way to find out."

Farhad handed his phone to Donya.

"Ready?"

Farhad nodded and held up the vial.

"Supreme Leader, I have something you want."

Minutes later, Shir-Del responded. The meeting was set for sunrise the next day.

"Okay, now what?" Farhad said.

Thrasher took an authoritative stance in front of Farhad. Jenkins winced. She knew exactly what Thrasher was thinking and positioned herself behind Farhad.

"What are you doing?"

"I'm sorry about this Farhad, but you'll thank me later."

"Huh?"

Before Farhad could respond, Thrasher reared back and delivered a brutal punch. Farhad was knocked out by the blow and keeled right over. Jenkins caught him before he hit the floor.

"Jay, what the hell are you doing?!"

Donya screamed and ran to Farhad's aid. His lip began to swell, and a large bruise was already forming on his face.

"You're gonna have to trust me."

"You want me to trust you after that? Fuck you!"

Donya charged at Thrasher. She tried to smack him in the face, but he blocked both attempts. He turned her around in a bear hug, keeping hold of her wrists.

"Donya, I've never let you down before and I'm not gonna start now. So, calm down! We need your help for the next part."

When she stopped fighting his grip, Thrasher released her.

"What do you need me to do?" she said, reluctantly.

Just before sunrise the next morning, Lajani showed up at the house to go over the plans for Farhad's confrontation with Shir-Del. As the sun peeked over the horizon, Lajani, Thrasher, Jenkins, and Donya drove Farhad to the entrance of Khorramabad. Farhad was visibly nervous. Despite the crisp morning air, sweat was beading on his brow. His knees bounced up and down in the back seat.

A half-mile before the border, the team encountered the first crowd of protestors. Lajani threw Donya's van into park. He, Thrasher, and Jenkins hopped out of the car with guns in hand and stood in front of the passenger side door where Farhad was sitting. They didn't want to raise their guns, but Farhad was the key to their plans. There was no way they were going to let anything happen to him.

"Back up!" Thrasher said.

Donya got out of the vehicle from the other side and stepped between the team and the crowd. She placed her hand on Thrasher's chest.

"It's okay," she said.

"Is he in there?" a boy said.

He wore a small version of the *Star Wars* t-shirt that Farhad was known for, and had burn marks on his face, probably from acid thrown by the Revolutionary Guard.

Donya nodded and opened the door. As Farhad got out, the crowd backed up and stared.

"What's all this?" he said.

Without warning, the boy let go of his father's hand and stepped forward. Confused, Farhad's eyes darted back and forth between Donya and Jenkins.

"What's your name?"

"My name is Farhad. Just like you," said the boy.

Unsure of what to do, Farhad leaned down and hugged the boy. The crowd erupted in applause and cheers. Shouts of "The Pirate of Iran" circulated as people fired their guns in the air.

Donya grinned at Thrasher, who nodded back. He finally understood.

"What's going on?" Lajani asked.

"He's the superstar, and this is his fan club," said Thrasher.

A slight wind blew as Lajani led the way. Thrasher and Jenkins escorted Farhad to the Khorramabad barricade. They tried to be gentle, but they had to push away some of the people who wanted to touch Farhad for being the person brave enough to stand up against the Supreme Leader. The energy from the cheering crowd bolstered Farhad's confidence.

This is what I'm fighting for.

When they arrived at the barricade, the scene was ominous. The cheers died down, but the crowd bravely stood behind their hero. If anything were to happen to Farhad, each of them was prepared to charge the blockade and fight until no one was left standing.

On the other side, they could see an intimidating crowd.

"Oh my God. Farhad was right," Jenkins whispered.

"About what?" Lajani said.

"I've never seen such a big crowd. How many, do you think?"

"If I had to guess? Half a million, easy."

The phenomenon of what she was witnessing made Jenkins wince. Most of them were probably armed, which meant the crowd behind her was heavily outgunned. If Farhad's supporters wanted a fight to the death, they might well get their wish.

Thrasher put both hands on Farhad's shoulders and looked him in the eyes.

"Remember what we talked about. When you get in there, you've gotta channel your inner Charles Bronson," he said.

"No problem. I'll just play it like you would."

Thrasher grinned.

"Take this."

He placed two pills in Farhad's hand.

Thrasher pointed to a cameraman standing in front of the media van and then turned away. He wanted to be sure they recorded Farhad walking toward the castle, but he couldn't risk his face being shown. By the time Farhad swallowed the decongestant, Thrasher was gone.

Donya ran up and put her arms around him. Farhad embraced her tightly. They both knew he might not come back. Farhad cursed himself for not rehearsing what to say to her before he left. He tried to speak but no words came. It didn't matter. Before he could say anything, Donya, with tears rolling down her face, planted a firm, passionate kiss on his lips. She didn't say a word before running after Thrasher.

Lajani stepped up to escort Farhad the rest of the way.

"It's time. You can do this. I *know* it."

"I got this, General."

Instructions from the Supreme Leader had been received by the guards at the barricade. Farhad was to be allowed through untouched on his walk to the castle. A sea of enraged people, all of whom had to restrain themselves from killing him, parted so that their enemy could make the mile walk past them to meet with their Supreme Leader.

Farhad glanced back once more at Lajani and Jenkins. Whether he liked it or not, the future of Iran was all on his shoulders. The wind from the west steadily picked up as he made his way toward the castle.

Chapter Fifty-Five

Standing post on one of the castle's watchtowers, Vaziri gazed through his binoculars at the barricade and watched Farhad approach. Once he neared the main staircase, Vaziri made his way down to the Supreme Leader's chamber on the northeast side and spoke on his radio.

"Supreme Leader, he's on his way."

"Good, I'm leaving it to you and your men that he is not touched."

"He won't be, Supreme Leader. You have my guarantee."

"Once he gives me the vial and I take my medication, he's all yours. We will hold him hostage for the rest of my medicine, which I'm sure he has. The crowd on the other side will burn Lajani at the stake if they don't get their so-called pirate back."

"Understood, Supreme Leader."

"And one more thing. When you torture him, make sure you do it slowly. We may be forced to give him back, but I want him in dreadful condition."

"Yes, Supreme Leader."

Ten minutes later, Farhad arrived at the castle's main entrance and was escorted up the steps by Revolutionary Guardsmen. When he arrived at the Supreme Leader's chambers, Shir-Del was sitting on the arm of a leather chair and leaning on his cane. His breathing was labored. His face was glistening with sweat.

Vaziri whispered to one of the guards.

"No one else gets in."

"Yes, sir."

Vaziri closed the door behind Farhad and took his place at the Supreme Leader's side. Shir-Del inventoried Farhad up and down. The purple bruise on his jaw and fat lip couldn't be ignored.

"What happened to your face?"

"I've been on the run. One of your goons almost had me last night, but I managed to slip away, again. Your men are incompetent."

Having not heard of such an encounter, Shir-Del glanced over at Vaziri.

"Search him."

Farhad raised his arms so Vaziri could pat him down. Knowing Farhad had been raped, he gave his rear an extra squeeze as payback for his incompetence comment. Farhad flinched but kept his pain to himself. Finding nothing but the vial of Carbamazepine and a cell phone, Vaziri handed the vial to Shir-Del, who snatched it from his hand. Having run out of his own stock, he began shooting up immediately. Farhad watched as the old man's eyes glazed over in relief.

With the medication now safely running through his veins, Shir-Del put the cap back on the syringe and nodded at Vaziri.

"Take him."

Vaziri stepped forward, but Farhad held up his hand.

"I wouldn't do that if I were you. Check the phone."

Vaziri stopped mid-stride and stared curiously at Farhad.

What does this little shit have up his sleeve?

When he looked at the phone, he saw a live stream video. Not knowing what he was looking at, he handed the phone to the Supreme Leader. He recognized it immediately and glared at Farhad with disdain.

Farhad took a deep breath and let him have it.

"That's my insurance, you fucking psycho. If I don't get back to my people, the person holding the sledgehammer on the other end of that phone is going to destroy what's left of your precious medication. Since we control the roads in and out of this town, you'll be dead within a week. So, you've got two choices. Surrender now, and you can live. Lajani will see to it that you do. Or you can know the same feeling that so many of your people have experienced because of the torture from this regime. You will die a slow and excruciating death."

Shir-Del felt his blood pressure rising.

"How dare you talk to me like that. I am your Supreme Leader!"

"Not anymore, you're not. You're nothing. You're a mad man with a serious health condition and the deranged notion that Allah selected you to lead the people of Iran. The incident at Azadi Square proved that. You're nothing but a fraud and a narcissist!"

Shir-Del approached Farhad until they were face to face. Being several inches taller, the Supreme Leader loomed over him. He hoped he could intimidate the booze smuggler, but Farhad stood firm. As he did, he saw more patches of discolored skin forming around the man's neck.

"Listen to me, you son of a dog. I know *my people*. I am responsible for *my people*. I do what is best for *my people*, so don't *ever* talk to me like that again. I am the Supreme Leader of Iran!"

"You're no leader; just another unhinged dictator. If you're such a great leader, how come you have to torture people and make them submit to your will? That's not doing what's best for *your* people. That's doing what's best for *you*."

Shir-Del had heard enough. His blood pressure was through the roof. Sweat was rolling down his skin and seeping through his thobe.

"What's best for me is what's best for these people! Ayatollah Khomeini built this country into what it is today, and I will not have his memory trampled by a bunch of western-loving, Jew-loving idealists. I am the Supreme Leader. The people will do what I say, when I say, and how I say. Allah has directed me to carry out his rule of law, and when Lajani is gone, that's what I'm going to do. If the people don't like it, I'll send every single one of them to Evin, and have their western ideals raped and tortured out of them. Iran is mine. Mine! *Fuck these people!*"

Shir-Del raised his cane to hit Farhad across the face like he had done to so many others. But this time, a hand caught it.

Chapter Fifty-Six

KERMANSHAH-KHORRAMABAD BORDER, IRAN

A half hour after Farhad left for the castle, Thrasher, Jenkins, Lajani and Donya nervously waited for the signal to sync. It was the only way to know that Farhad had made it inside the castle alive.

"You didn't have to hit him, you know," Donya said.

"If it makes you feel better, I didn't enjoy it," said Thrasher.

"We've only got one shot at this, Donya. The bruise on his face helps hide the bug planted in the false tooth we gave him," Jenkins said.

Donya looked at Jenkins. The gap in her smile where her tooth had once been was obvious.

"You think this will work?" Donya asked.

"There's only one way to know for sure," Thrasher said.

Voices finally projected from the speakers next to the billboard.

"What happened to your face?"

"I've been on the run. One of your goons almost had me last night, but I managed to slip away, again. Your men are incompetent."

"He's in," Jenkins said.

From her laptop, Donya cranked up the volume connected to speakers brought in from the concert hall to the max. Everyone on the Kermanshah side of the border listened to the conversation. The voices of Shir-Del and Farhad came through clearly. It took another minute for the protestors on the other side of the barricade to settle down, but they soon became transfixed by the dialogue. All that could be heard was Farhad bravely standing up to Shir-Del, and the Supreme Leader barking back at him. Time in Iran had come to halt. It felt as if everyone on both sides stopped breathing long enough to hear the outcome of the exchange inside the castle. Without warning, the most unexpected words erupted from the Supreme Leader's lips.

"Fuck these people!"

Audible gasps could be heard from everyone in the crowd.

Jenkins, Lajani, and Thrasher all looked at one another.

"I can't believe he said that. Now what?" Lajani said.

"You tell me!" said Thrasher.

As minutes passed, the crowds on both sides became irritated and rowdy. Their outrage over the Supreme Leader's comments grew.

Thrasher turned to Lajani.

"You've got to get control over this or it's going to turn into a riot," he said.

Lajani ran over to the media van and grabbed a microphone from a reporter, but he was interrupted by Jenkins.

"Look!"

They noticed a bubble of people in the crowd steadily making its way from the castle toward the barricade. Thrasher squinted but couldn't make it out.

"What is that?" Donya asked.

The answer became clear as the bubble moved closer. Vaziri had Shir-Del by the arm and was pulling the Supreme Leader toward the city border. Behind them was Farhad, surrounded by the remaining Revolutionary Guardsmen. Once they cleared the crowd, Vaziri dragged Shir-del to the nearest billboard pole, punched him in the gut, and tied his arms and legs to the post. The crowd from the Khorramabad side flowed onto the Kermanshah side to join their fellow countrymen. There was no fighting or bickering. They were united as one Iranian people.

Farhad slowly made his way through the crowd. He and Donya embraced, but this was no time for a romantic reunion. They quickly turned their attention back to the billboard.

Shir-Del gazed out into the masses, shocked by their lack of action. "I demand you release me!"

No one responded. A strong gust of wind suddenly changed from west to east. Grains of sand and dirt pecked at everyone's skin, but no one moved. When the wind died down, little Farhad was the first to emerge from the crowd. He approached the Supreme Leader, picked up a rock and threw it at his head. The rock hit right above Shir-Del's eye, busting open his skin. Shir-Del laughed.

Before little Farhad could return to his father's side, a woman stepped forward, picked up another stone, and threw it at the Supreme Leader. This one hit him it at the top of his forehead. A welt immediately formed. Again, Shir-Del laughed.

Over the course of the next hour, hundreds of others stoned their former Supreme Leader. Those that did not stood in silence, recording the event with their phones. Thanks to Lajani removing internet restrictions, many live streamed the event for the rest of the world to see.

After a chubby woman in a purple hijab threw her stone at Shir-Del, there was a pause in the assault. A faint sound could be heard. The crowd slowly moved closer to investigate. Shir-Del looked grimmer as they approached. Skin from his cheeks hung off his face. The skull bone from his forehead was exposed. His eyes had exploded from the direct hits. Blood ran down his face. His limbs were peppered with welts, bruised and swollen, yet he remained standing.

The closer the crowd approached, the sound emitting from the Supreme Leader became clearer. He was still laughing. Despite repeated blows to his body, he managed to tuck his chin and keep his voice box intact.

"No one could have survived that," Jenkins said to Thrasher. "How can he be alive? Wasn't the vial you gave Farhad filled with something to make him feel pain?"

Thrasher shrugged.

"Salim said the antibiotic would counteract the Carbamazepine. It either wore off quicker than expected or he has the most extreme Chromosome Six Deficiency condition ever recorded. I don't know!"

Shir-Del's laughter slowly got louder.

"He has defied death!" someone shouted.

"Praise be to Allah for sparing him!" said another man.

"He is our rightful leader. The Supreme Leader lives!" said a man from Khorramabad.

Thrasher pulled his sidearm from his belt.

"The hell he does!"

Jenkins grabbed Thrasher's bicep and yanked him back. He gave her a stern look.

"What are you doing?"

"You can't. Look!"

Jenkins pointed at all the cell phones recording videos of the incident and the image on the billboard broadcasting to the rest of the world. If Thrasher walked over and killed Shir-Del, his image would be beamed across the globe, and questions about his identity would be inevitable. There was nothing he or Jenkins could do. Only an Iranian could end the situation.

The entire world was watching. They were witnessing Shir-Del's triumph over his stoning. His survival could be interpreted by many as preordained from Allah. If he didn't die, the mission failed, and Shir-Del would become more powerful and admired than ever. Thrasher turned to hand his gun to Farhad.

"Farhad, Donya, this is your chance. You *have* to kill him. The people will follow you!"

"I think someone beat us to it," Farhad said.

He pointed to the billboard. Thrasher turned to see Lajani walking toward Shir-Del. He stopped three feet away.

"Supreme Leader?"

Shir-Del stopped laughing.

"Laj...Lajani?"

"Yes, it's me."

"Though I cannot see you, I know the people can. I've beaten you. I've survived and shown that I am the true Supreme Leader of this land."

"You've only survived *for now*. You may not feel the pain, but your body cannot endure. If the assault continues, you will certainly die. Stop this madness. It's time for you to step down. Iran has spoken."

Shir-Del laughed at him again and spit blood at Lajani.

"That shows how little you know about Iran. These people don't know what's best for them. It's up to me to tell them and protect them from the West. You don't have the guts to rule this country."

With the crowd and the world watching, using his one remaining hand, Lajani pulled his gun from his holster, placed the barrel against Shir-Del's temple, and pulled the trigger. Gray matter exploded from the other side.

"And you don't have the brains."

Chapter Fifty-Seven

CIA HEADQUARTERS
MCLEAN, VA

One week later, at five-thirty in the morning, Wallace emerged from the elevator that led from the parking garage directly to his seventh-floor office. During a tenure filled with nothing but busy days, this one promised to be busier than most.

The Supreme Leader was dead and General Lajani was now in charge, but from Wallace's perspective, Iran was a hot mess. He had expected this when Jenkins first pitched him the idea of overthrowing the Ayatollah but expecting it and having to actually deal with it were two different tasks. The good news was, most Iranians liked Lajani and were uniting under him. As outsiders looking in, the international community felt positivity exuding from Iran in a way that hadn't been felt in more than forty years. Unfortunately, Shir-Del loyalists had done their fair share of damage with their edited videos of the Azadi Square incident and were using Shir-Del's stoning episode as propaganda.

Thanks to Shir-Del's "fuck these people" comment, his loyalists didn't have much of a leg to stand on. But winning the battle on the ground wasn't good enough anymore. Battling against the online world was a totally different type of war that was never won by anyone.

Nonetheless, the Shir-Del loyalists inside Iran formed a domestic terrorist group of their own, dedicated to wreaking havoc across the country with IEDs, especially around Qom. Lajani was doing what he could to apprehend the suspects, but it couldn't be accomplished overnight. Travel bans and increased border security helped prevent additional weapons from being smuggled into the country, but the bloodshed would continue with innocent civilians often paying the price until Lajani could gain more control of the situation.

Fortunately for Wallace, the overthrow had some positives. The chief provision in the Algiers Accords of 1981, which formally resolved the Iranian Hostage Crisis, stated that the United States would never again intervene politically or militarily in Iranian affairs. While there was no way Lajani could publicly overturn this agreement without massive backlash from supporters he needed within his own borders, he undoubtedly owed parts of his successful overthrow of Shir-Del to the United States, and the CIA in particular.

Thanks to Jenkins's negotiating skills, Lajani privately agreed to reopen the U.S. Embassy in Tehran within a year. This meant that CIA personnel could operate in the country, unofficially. The catch was that the agency would have to work hand in hand with Iran's Ministry of Foreign Affairs to keep them informed of potential terrorist plots. It wouldn't be an easy mountain to navigate. The CIA isn't exactly known for sharing intelligence, let alone with foreign agencies. But Lajani had earned Wallace's trust. Only time would tell how long it would last.

Separately, President Cannon had the arduous job of selecting the perfect candidate to be named the new U.S. Ambassador to Iran. The president had a wish list but was playing his cards close to the vest. Wallace had no idea who to expect.

From both sides of the aisle, Congress celebrated the regime change in Iran. In his meetings with members of the Senate Select Committee on Intelligence, Wallace noted that Lajani, true to his word, froze all funds to Hamas and Hezbollah. As a result, Wallace easily received additional funds of his own, which would help Lajani covertly quell the violence in Iran and fight any remaining Shir-Del loyalists overseas. This would help the entire international intelligence community hunt down members of both organizations once and for all, though he omitted telling them that the Mossad was well ahead of the curve in this endeavor.

Today, though, Wallace was turning off his ears to anything related to Iran. He needed to turn his attention to other areas of the world he'd neglected. His Deputy Director, Jeremy Molinar, had done a fine job filling in for him, but it was time for Wallace to give other divisions the focus they deserved. One incident in China was specifically concerning.

On his orders, though she wasn't provided any information about Jenkins's mission in Iran, Jessica Shannon was dispatched to China to help disguise Jenkins so that she could travel to Iran without raising any flags. Shannon had a habit of not always checking in with the local embassy on time but eventually, she always did. Only days after she met with Jenkins, all check-ins from Shannon unexpectedly ceased. Wallace later found out from Jenkins by way of Delang that she and Thrasher killed a Chinese MSS agent in Isfahan not long before the incident at Azadi Square. It was no coincidence that a Chinese agent was in Iran, shooting at his people.

Concerned about Shannon's lack of check-in, Molinar sent Shanghai station chief Katie Gonzales to investigate. Because MSS was monitoring Shannon's hotel room, Gonzales couldn't just walk in, so she booked a room on the same hall. Both times she walked by she reported a flowery smell, most likely from a candle inside the room. This was the first red flag because hotels do not allow guests to burn candles in their rooms and getting caught in China could result in jail time. Over the course of the week, she spotted the hotel's chief of security and night manager regularly eating together, and repeatedly flirted with them at the hotel bar with the illusion of taking them both back to her room.

Given Gonzales's hourglass figure in a low-cut dress and enticing voice, the Chinese men were eager to get into her pants. Gonzales slyly slipped gamma-hydroxybutyrate (GHB) into their drinks when they weren't looking and timed its effects perfectly. Once the two men were inside her hotel room and unconscious, she grabbed their keys and headed to the security office. Since she had baited the men in the early morning hours, the security office was vacant when she entered. While she wasn't able to find any video evidence of Shannon after she was seen getting off the elevator to enter her room for what would be the last time, Gonzales saw MSS cameras outside and inside Shannon's former room just in case the CIA came snooping. She turned off the cameras, grabbed the master key, and quickly made her way to the room.

Clothes were scattered on the floor, and the bathroom was a mess. The bedroom also had a "bleachy" smell to it that could still be detected over the burning candles. This was why Molinar intentionally sent a woman for this job. Their perceptions of color and smell are superior to those of men. Gonzales used UV glasses from her purse to detect any signs of blood and braced herself when she put them on. Hotels could be the worst places to perform such an inspection, due to the volume of visitors, drink spills, and human fluid, and this room was no exception.

Surprisingly, Gonzales saw very little. It was odd. Too odd. Further examination revealed that the hotel had replaced the portions of drywall in the room as well as the carpet. Using a box cutter, she pealed back the carpet and found blood residue. After taking a sample, she rushed out of the hotel. Once she arrived back at the embassy, she submitted the sample to the lab for DNA testing. It later confirmed that the blood belonged to Shannon.

Wallace was known for looking out for his people. It didn't matter if they were an analyst, field operator, secretary, or janitor. As a former spy, he had seen too many colleagues get burned by either the D.C. political machine or foreign agents.

What blew Shannon's cover?

Assuming that Shannon was dead, where was her body?

How can I get it back?

While Wallace was dealing with Iran, and playing messenger between the president and Delang, Molinar pulled Shannon's file and combed through it. Nothing of interest popped up. She had checked in that morning as scheduled but missed all her subsequent scheduled check-ins. Her movements were by the book, and her fellow colleagues didn't reveal anything suspicious before her meeting with Jenkins.

Wallace sat back in his chair and tapped his lip. His instincts gnawed at him.

Maybe Shannon wasn't the intended target.

Wallace decided to investigate Shannon's connection to Jenkins. Even though she was technically no longer with the agency, Jenkins' personnel file remained stored in the agency database. When he looked, Wallace was immediately alarmed. Not only had someone recently pulled Jenkins's file, but the person who pulled it was none other than the Inspector General himself, Tony Prashad. This triggered alarms for Wallace.

Wallace didn't bother calling the Inspector General's office. He took the elevator to the third floor and as he walked through the main door, he noticed Prashad's personal assistant, Julia Busteed, looking particularly chipper and humming a happy tune.

"You seem like you're in a good mood," Wallace said.

"Oh, yes, sir. I'm planning my next vacation."

"Nice. Where are you going?"

"Bora Bora."

"I'm impressed. How do you swing that on a government salary?"

"Well, if you must know, I just won the pool!"

Busteed raised her hands and danced in her seat.

The pool she was referring to was an under-the-table bet, which many CIA personnel had going to identify Prashad's latest Capitol Hill love interest. For someone who had never been a spy, Prashad carefully guarded his sources inside Congress, so much so that his personal assistant and the internal staff at the CIA didn't know about them. What was more impressive was how he always used his charm to convince his sources to remain quiet about him. Six months ago, Prashad's normally upbeat mood noticeably changed. He became uncharacteristically sullen and reserved.

While he never specifically said so, it was obvious to most unattached ladies in the Inspector General's office that their single boss, a man with a sarcastic sense of humor, sharp jaw line and movie star good looks, who conservatively but consistently flirted with all of them, was suffering from a broken heart. But over the last few weeks, Busteed had noticed a little more pep in Prashad's step, and her gut instincts told her that the same woman who had previously stomped on his heart was back in the picture. In order to make the gossip more interesting, Busteed and some other assistants at the agency decided to form a money pool to see who could determine the identity of his secret lover.

The water cooler gossip quickly spread and took on a life of its own. Within days, it reached Wallace, who kicked in $20 on the condition that none of the assistants used agency resources, technological or otherwise, to find the answer. They would need to do old school grunt work. Until this morning, the only thing that anyone knew about the mystery woman was that she once called him her "cabana boy" over the phone. Busteed only caught it because she recalled Prashad being insulted, and he loudly repeated it over the phone for her to hear.

Wallace hated engaging in such immature chitchat, and probably could have figured it out on his own, but it was good for agency morale for the Director to participate in trivial pursuits occasionally. What surprised him the most was how quickly the First Lady found out. She had met Prashad when the president's then chief of staff brought him to the White House for an introductory interview, but nearly collided with him as they had both gone to turn a hallway corner. The man's cute dimples and Dennis Quaid smile nearly caused her to melt. While Prashad's interview with the president went well, the chatter among Secret Service agents was that the First Lady was the one who gave her husband the final nudge to nominate him for the position.

"I don't care what his qualifications are. That man is *gorgeous!*"

That's what she was rumored to have said. Privately, the president confided to Wallace that Prashad passed his "smell test" regardless of his wife's comment. What Wallace didn't know was if it was gossip about Prashad or the fact that the pool had nearly a whopping $5,000 in it that made the First Lady throw in $20 on the day he met with the president and Jenkins about the operation in Iran, but his bet was on the former.

"Oh really? How'd you find out?" Wallace said.

"My husband, Mike, and I went to that new Brazilian steakhouse just outside of Baltimore last night. You know, the one in Rockville?"

"Oh, yeah. What's it called? Chima?"

"That's the one. After we parked in the garage, we turned the corner and saw them kissing in front of his car. I couldn't quite tell who it was at first, but then I got a good look at her. You won't believe who it is. Mike had to practically pick my jaw up off the floor."

"Well don't keep me in suspense. Who is it?"

Busteed smiled.

"Wow, I know a piece of intel that even the Director of the CIA doesn't know. Let me sit here and soak in this moment for a second."

Wallace snorted out a laugh as Busteed closed her eyes and took a deep breath.

"Okay, okay. That's enough. Spill the beans."

"Hang on. One more minute."

"Jules..."

Busteed pulled out her phone and flipped to her photos.

"Here, I snapped a picture in case no one believed me."

The image of the unknown mysterious lady in Prashad's life was crystal clear and sent a cold shiver down the Director's spine. While he didn't respond, he didn't have to. When he slowly looked up at Busteed, the expression on his face said it all.

"That was pretty much my reaction, too. Latrina Pearl. It was a total guess on my part. I think I wanted it to be true more than I actually thought it would be."

All the questions about how Jenkins's file got pulled from the agency database were immediately answered.

Walsh.

Chapter Fifty-Eight

PHILADELPHIA, PENNSYLVANIA

Sudan Ambassador to the United States Nazir Agab swirled the glass of High West bourbon in his hand as he eagerly waited for Walsh at their usual rear table near the window of Jean-Georges restaurant on the fifty-ninth floor of the Comcast Center. Sixteen floors below, Walsh was in her office, and had been alerted by the hostess that Agab had arrived ten minutes ago. While she demanded punctuality by those who visited her, Walsh rarely exhibited the same courtesy in return. She viewed every angle in life as a weapon to use to her advantage, even time. In this case, she needed Agab to be anxious about receiving the money she intended to give him for his services.

When she finally decided to grace Agab with her presence, the Sudanese ambassador hopped up to greet her and politely pulled out her chair. She also noticed that Agab had taken the liberty of ordering her a glass of Maker's Mark, which was waiting for her as she took her seat.

This'll be a piece of cake.

"Thanks for making the trip to meet me, Nazir," Walsh said.

"It was no trouble at all. I was already in New York for a meeting, so it was a short drive. How is your development of the port going?"

"It's going well. The city council has agreed to make the additional space available for expansion, and with the regime change in Iran, it won't be long before the Office of Foreign Assets Control removes the trade restrictions. The CEOs of the shipping lines are eager to have more of their vessels call on Iranian ports with exports from the United States."

Agab grinned below his thin mustache.

"Which part of the United States?"

Walsh also grinned.

"Well, I have been able to make some phone calls to ensure that Philadelphia will be a major stop on the east coast vessel rotations."

"Sounds like you'll be swimming in money."

"I'm already swimming in money. The extra will be nice, but I'm in this for bigger game. Within two years, Mediterranean vessels pumping cargo into Iran by way of the northeast will run exclusively through Philadelphia."

"That's why I've always liked you, Vivian. You're a woman of vision. Cheers."

The two clinked glasses and tipped back their drinks.

"You said you had an offer for me. What can I do for you?"

"Are you interested in a million dollars?"

"Who wouldn't be?"

"Good."

Walsh pulled a thumb drive from her purse and slid it across the table.

"There's a local drug lord in your country who has a bounty out for a certain CIA operative responsible for the death of his client's son. I got a call from one of my contacts at Homeland Security two days ago. She'll be deplaning from American Airlines flight 177 in Norfolk on Thursday at 2 p.m. All you have to do is slip her picture to one of your contacts at Sudanese intelligence and have them follow her. After that, I'm sure the Sudanese drug cartels can make their own arrangements."

Walsh smiled.

"I'm sure that can be arranged. But I want two million. Director Wallace is known to have a keen nose for sniffing out arrangements like this. I'm putting my own neck on the line, and this could also jeopardize U.S. construction contracts for a bridge in southwest Sudan."

Walsh swayed her head back and forth, pretending to debate the counteroffer.

"Okay, but I have one condition. I want photographic evidence that the job was completed. I'm not taking any chances."

"That's all? Consider it done."

Walsh pulled out her phone, went into her Swiss banking app and wired the money to a new account she'd just created. Then, she slipped Agab a scrap of paper.

"Half now. Half on completion. There's the account information."

"Nice doing business with you, Vivian."

***

An hour later, Walsh was beaming ear to ear with a bourbon-induced smile that she didn't bother to hide. Walking still required a cane, but in her current mood, she felt like spinning it around and dancing like a Broadway star down the hall to her office. Once Jenkins was taken care of, she could once again set her sights on Delang. And this time, she would make sure the job got done right.

She was humming an unusually happy tune when her assistant, Dawn, saw her open the main door to her office.

"You're in a good mood. I trust the meeting went well," Dawn said.

"Better than good."

"Well, get ready to be even happier. There are some investors in your office. They didn't have an appointment, but they have a suitcase full of cash. I figured you wouldn't want me to turn them away."

"You figured right. What type of investors?"

"They said it's a unique opportunity for the port, but they would only talk to you."

"Okay, I'll head in. Please hold my calls."

"Sure thing."

When Walsh entered her office, one of the investors was sitting in the chair across from her desk. The woman had dark hair with touches of red. From behind, Walsh felt sure she had never spoken to her before. She approached with her hand extended.

"Hi, I'm Vivian. Thanks for. . ."

The door suddenly closed behind her. Walsh froze in her tracks when she felt the barrel of a gun pressed against the back of her head. She saw a familiar face when the person in the chair turned around.

"We told you what would happen if you fucked with us, Senator," Jenkins said.

"Us?"

The person behind her whistled for her to turn around.

"Right here, sweetheart."

Delang.

"You know, you're not the only one who is friendly with the Sudanese ambassador," he said. "Nazir and I know each other quite well. My friend, Tariq Al-Masari, introduced us years ago when Sudan was having trouble with Al-Qaeda insurgents. Imagine my surprise when he called to tell me he had a meeting scheduled with you."

Oh no.

"I thought you might want to see this."

Delang pulled out his phone and showed the screen to Walsh.

Tell her thanks for the money.

I'll give the thumb drive to you later today.

She's all yours.

Dammit! Does this guy know everybody?

Jenkins rose from her seat and approached Walsh.

"We gave you the opportunity of a lifetime, Senator. And you just couldn't let go of the past, could you?"

Jenkins kicked Walsh's cane out from under her and pushed her to the ground. Delang handed Jenkins his gun and took a seat behind Walsh's desk, propping his feet up to watch Jenkins operate. With her knee planted into Walsh's back, she firmly pressed the gun to the back of her head.

"Time for you to pay the piper, Senator."

"Stop, we can work something out!"

"Too late. It's one thing for you to come after me and Tom, but you have to answer for what happened to Jessica."

"What? Who? I have no idea what you're talking about!"

Jenkins twisted the barrel of the gun against her head.

"Don't lie to me!"

"I'm not. I swear. I don't know any Jessica. Please!"

"I'm sick of your lies. Get up! We're going for a ride."

"Wait," Delang interjected.

He snatched a silver picture frame from Walsh's desk and kneeled to show it to her.

"Who's the person with you in the picture?"

Walsh looked up.

"That's Philip. My driver."

"How long has he been working for you?"

"Seventeen years. Why?"

"Dammit," said Delang.

"What?" Jenkins said.

Her eyes bulged when Delang turned the picture around so she could see it. Walsh's driver, Philip Lee, was Chinese.

"You don't think. . .?"

Jenkins pursed her lips in anger.

When she asked him to inebriate Walsh's driver, Dub didn't hesitate to say yes. He had betrayed her on a prior occasion, but Jenkins had let him off the hook because he had been stupid and became yet another victim of the manipulative web that Walsh was known to spin.

Did Dub know Philip's true identity? Had he allied himself to Walsh yet again?

Chapter Fifty-Nine

LAMBEAU FIELD
GREEN BAY, WISCONSIN

November temperatures could be brutal in Wisconsin, and tonight was no exception. Dub was freezing his ass off in twenty-nine-degree weather while he stood guard at the top of the steps on the lower level, watching his boss interact with his prospective clients. The Gregory Group owned box seats in one of the luxury suites on the forty-yard-line behind the Packers bench, but Gregory enjoyed taking his clients to field level. Feeling the sting of the cold air, smelling the fresh cut grass and hearing the collisions on the field were part of the raw enjoyment of the game, and he wanted his prospective clients to share the experience.

The odd thing was, the Packers weren't even his favorite team. Gregory was a diehard Dolphins fan and made the trip to Miami whenever they were home during the season. But there was something about the allure of Lambeau Field that always seemed to dazzle his clients when he needed to close a deal. He had closed many deals in Miami, but he had also lost some. Lambeau Field, though, was undefeated in that regard. Any time he needed to complete a deal he deemed essential, if his client was a football fan and the Packers were in town, Gregory had his team suit up and escort the client to Green Bay.

A gust of Wisconsin wind sliced across the field and sent a polar chill cutting through Dub's body.

Why did it have to be a night game?

Dub was in the middle of wiping chilly snot from his nose when his earpiece buzzed.

"*Sandpiper*, this is *Cardinal*. Come back."

Sandpiper was Dub's callsign while Cardinal was Kirk's. Dub raised the microphone from his wrist.

"Go ahead, Cardinal."

"I'm sending *Oriole* to replace you. Come to the box. Some mutual friends need a word."

Mutual friends?

"Roger that, Cardinal."

Once Dub's replacement arrived, he headed upstairs. The elevator was full, so he double-timed it on an escalator. He was nearly out of breath when he arrived, but the running got his blood pumping and warmed him up. Kirk was snacking on popcorn when he arrived.

"What's up?" Dub said.

"Here."

Kirk handed him his phone.

"Hello?"

Before the caller on the other end of the phone could reply, Kirk pulled his gun and pointed it at Dub.

"If you screwed her again, I'm gonna kill you for sure."

Dub raised his arms.

"Whoa. Settle down. I didn't screw anyone. What the hell are you talking about?"

"Walsh's driver."

"Philip? What about him?"

"Did you know he's a sleeper agent for the Chinese?"

"What? Hell no. I knew he was Walsh's driver for several years and made small talk with him when she met with my dad from time to time, but that's it. A little while ago, Jenkins called and asked me to slip something in his drink so he would be out of commission the next morning. I watched over him to make sure nothing happened to him, but

I had no idea who he was. She asked me for a favor, and I did it. End of story."

Kirk jerked back the slide on his Glock 19 and pointed it at Dub once again.

"You sure?"

Dub stepped forward until his forehead was inches from the barrel of the gun.

"Damn right, I am. Now, you better put down that fucking gun or we're gonna have an incident here that'll make the Shootout at the O.K. Corral look like a Sunday school lesson."

Kirk lowered his weapon.

"You get all that? We good?"

"Yeah, we're good," a voice said from the phone.

Dub saw it was on speaker. He immediately recognized Jenkins' voice.

"Are you kidding me, Beth? Was that really necessary?" Dub said.

"You bet it was. Walsh told us her car was bugged. Her driver had a recording of the conversation Tom and I originally had with her in the limo. We're pretty sure he passed it on to his bosses at MSS. It got Jessica killed."

"Jessica's dead?"

Dub slumped into a chair. He knew Shannon well. Her skills with a makeup kit were legendary, and she once helped get him one of his sources out of a sticky situation in Oman.

"Dub? You still there?"

"Yeah. Just do me a favor. Let me kill him. I can be in Philly by to-morrow."

"Sorry, but that position has already been filled."

Chapter Sixty

PHILADEPHIA, PENNSYLVANIA

Philip Lee sat on a bench outside the Philadelphia Museum of Art, drawing the Rocky Balboa statue on his sketchpad. Philip loved to draw. It was his way to unwind. The forty-six-year-old Chinese operative often sat on the ledge of his apartment window, looking out over the city, drawing cityscapes or an old woman on a bench. If he liked his drawing, and the mood hit him right, he would go to a local art supply store and buy a canvas so he could spend the next few days painting. He hadn't done that in a while, though. Not since Walsh scolded him for showing up to work with dried paint on his fingers.

"I can't believe you showed up with that shit on your hands. Totally unprofessional. Don't let it happen again!"

Philip nodded and made a note to curb his artistic impulses for a while. This wasn't the first time he had sketched the Rocky Balboa statue, though. He found the Rocky character inspiring, and he had sketched it several times in different light or times of day. As he smudged lines with his fingertips to add shadow to the statue's abs, Philip remembered the first time he'd seen *Rocky IV.* One of his friends in Qingdao managed to smuggle it on his return trip from Tokyo. Having been raised in Communist China, Philip had been mentally engineered to hate Rocky, just like the Soviet crowd in the film. But as the bloody battle between Rocky and Ivan Drago raged on, like the Soviets, Philip found himself cheering for the American boxer in ways he never thought possible.

When *Rocky IV* was released in 1985, the Soviet Union was on the cusp of falling apart. The empire was financially strapped, and Gorbachev's new ideas were a godsend to the western world. China, however, was a different story. Though the protest in Tiananmen Square in 1989 made it appear that China could suffer the same fate as the Soviet Union, the Chinese Communist Party made sure it didn't.

Lee's parents were among the protestors arrested that day. When the Ministry of State Security raided their home, they found the VHS tape in his bedroom. As a result of their anti-communist behavior, his parents were imprisoned for five years, and Lee was sent to a child labor and re-education camp. After six long years, on what turned out to be his eighteenth birthday, the MSS approached him with an offer: if he joined the agency in their crusade against capitalism, his parents would be released. While it was feasible for him to refuse, Lee knew that doing so would make things worse for his parents, so he agreed.

Two months later, he was sent to America on assignment. Upon arrival, the MSS changed the spelling of his last name on his customs paperwork from Lei to Lee in order to make him appear more American. His first name in China had been Ping, but he requested it be updated to Philip because he was a fan of American basketball coach Phil Jackson.

He enrolled at Temple University and found American freedoms captivating. Lee managed to make the college team as a walk-on, but it didn't take long for him to become noticed on the national stage. He loved going on road trips with his team without the requirement of government papers to travel from state to state.

Unfortunately, the MSS was always paying attention. As his star began to rise in the basketball community, their long-term plan for him was to infiltrate the NBA and provide more leverage for Chinese influence in the league with its worldwide reach. Every few months, they would check on him and show him pictures of his family to let him know that they were doing well, but their presence always felt threatening. The government had the power to put his parents back in jail if he was non-compliant.

After the motorcycle accident derailed the MSS's plans for his basketball career, the agency's management debated assassinating him, but his handler talked them out of it. Though he had not formally graduated, they decided to utilize what he had learned from his finance major to see how they could infiltrate American financial markets. Unfortunately, the job didn't pan out. It proved too much for Lee thanks to the depression that ensued after losing his basketball career.

In one last effort to utilize their asset, the MSS moved him to Washington, D.C., where he got a job working as a chauffeur at a local limo company with many political clients. Since the company's owner was also a deep cover MSS operative, he had all the limos bugged. The gamble paid off. Within days of the installation, the MSS was receiving droves of information from seasoned politicians to be used for national gain or blackmail.

The best part for Philip was that he didn't have to say or do much. He reported to work, drove clients around town, and stopped on his breaks at his handler's workshop so the recordings could be changed out for fresh tape. In the meantime, he watched television and enjoyed the fruits of American life as long as he kept checking in. His life changed when fate intervened and allowed him to give a ride to a former acquaintance, then-Congresswoman Vivian Walsh.

After finally becoming Walsh's full-time driver, he thought he had earned the Senator's trust, but he quickly learned that trust was hard to come by in Washington, and even harder in Walsh's inner circle. The Senator and her chief of staff meticulously combed through Philip's background to ensure that he wasn't a mole or a foreign agent, but the MSS analysts sufficiently covered his tracks, and they didn't discover his true roots. Despite their extensive experience reviewing intelligence files, Walsh and Pearl were Capitol Hill politicians and not seasoned intelligence officers who would've seen red flags in Philip's manufactured backstory.

Since the Office of the Sergeant at Arms and Doorkeeper was responsible for security for all members of Congress, Walsh also called one of her friends there to have her limo checked for any surveillance equipment. What Walsh didn't know was that the MSS also had a separate, paid informant inside the Sergeant at Arms and Doorkeeper's office who gave them advance warning whenever the Office was planning to perform a random security check to ensure that the limos didn't have any devices installed to use for blackmailing a member of Congress. Whenever Philip received a heads-up, he called his handler, who quickly had the cars switched out for a back-up duplicate of the same year, make, model, and forged VIN number that was off the books and didn't have any surveillance equipment installed.

When several valiant efforts to catch Philip in a lie failed, Walsh finally accepted, falsely, that Philip was on the level. Upon becoming her full-time driver, she requested that he install a digital taping system inside her limo for personal use. Since the equipment was already installed, the MSS secretly rejoiced. She would later go on to give Philip tips on how to avoid being caught with the taping system by the Sergeant at Arms and Doorkeeper's office, which served the MSS well in learning how to further navigate their way through the American legal system.

Slowly, Philip's attitude as a sleeper agent for the MSS changed. He watched with awe how Walsh meticulously navigated the world of politics and disposed of her enemies. Based on her conversations with her rivals or allies, he began to understand China's necessity to stay involved in the politics of the western world. Moment by moment, as he passed along recordings of Walsh to his handler, he developed a genuine taste for being an undercover agent. Knowing he was secretly operating under the noses of some of Washington's most elite politicians was a delicious thought. The more he did it, the more he liked it. He rapidly became one of the MSS's most valued assets in America.

Two and a half months ago, after a long night at the bar with an acquaintance, Lee awoke with a massive hangover and called in sick to Walsh. She would later tell him that he had been set up, so that two CIA agents could corner her in the limo. Little did the agents know that the limo's recording system automatically kicked in when the car started, so he had a recording of what the agents were planning to do in Iran.

When he gave a second copy of the recording to his handler, he immediately sent it up the MSS food chain. Knowing that Iran no longer required visas for Chinese entering their country, Minister Zhou had a hunch that the American agent would travel through China in order to slip into Iran undetected. Given General Secretary Xu's recent agreement with the Supreme Leader, he couldn't allow the Americans to ruin it.

Lee wasn't aware of anything that had transpired in Iran and hadn't heard from his handler since he dropped off the recording. Yesterday, though, his handler finally reached out with a new assignment, and told him that a package would be waiting for him at the usual spot at 11 a.m. After he finished his drawing, Lee removed the package taped to the underside of the bench, stuffed both into his messenger's bag, and left.

After returning to his ninth-floor apartment a quarter mile away, he put his bag on the counter and microwaved a mini pizza while his computer finished booting up. Just as the microwave beeped, Lee heard a loud crash outside. Curious, he went to the window, where his view was partially blocked, but it looked like a city bus had t-boned an SUV in the middle of an intersection. He opened the window to get a better look, but before he could, he felt a stranger grab hold of his collar and belt, and threw him out the window. Lee screamed all the way down to the pavement.

Thrasher didn't bother to look at the mess splattered on the street. He grabbed the messenger bag and laptop, and calmly walked out.

"Too bad Walsh wasn't here to join you."

Chapter Sixty-One

Brenda Gabriele was in her second week as chief of security at the Isabella Stewart Gardner Museum. Tired of the bureaucracy, the one-time counter-terrorism agent had recently left the FBI to join some of her former colleagues in the private contracting business. However, a week before she was set to start her new job, she received a call about the position in Boston, which she found intriguing.

When the museum's longtime curator retired, the board of directors named Colleen Dixon to the position. Dixon had previously been the assistant curator of the Judy Garland Museum in Grand Rapids, Minnesota, where the famed ruby slippers from *The Wizard of Oz* were stolen. She worked hand in hand with the local FBI office and the insurance company to track them down. Eight years after Dixon was named the museum's government liaison, the FBI recovered the slippers, and the agent in charge of the case credited Dixon for her assistance.

Dixon's one condition to accepting the curator position in Boston was that she could bring in a new security team. The museum's internal security required a much-needed upgrade, and she wanted to double down on all efforts to find the art stolen in the 1990 museum heist. Chief among them was Rembrandt's only seascape, *The Storm on the Sea of Galilee.*

This is where Gabriele came in. In the early 2000s, the counter-terrorism division was where an FBI agent went if they wanted to gain accolades and move up the food chain with the hope of one day becoming an agent in charge of their own office. Gabriele did what many of her colleagues did, and transferred. She eventually gained a solid reputation for following the evidence. Her greatest success came in the Washington D.C. office, when she coordinated with another agent in New York to prevent Iran's assassination of then Saudi Ambassador to the United States, Tariq Al-Masari.

Before she transferred to the counter-terrorism division, she had been assigned to work in the white-collar crimes division in the Boston field office, with a focus on art theft. Thanks to films such as *The Thomas Crown Affair*, art theft had been glamorized. The public erroneously had the preconceived notion that art thieves were billionaires with bottomless accounts who spent their days flying from country to country, finding ways to steal priceless art so they could admire it in their living rooms. Nothing could be further from the truth. High-end art theft was often synonymous with dark elements of society, including drugs and human trafficking. While they didn't know each other, when Dixon got word from a mutual friend that Gabriele had once worked art crimes and had recently left the FBI, she scheduled a meeting. Gabriele then revealed that she had worked as a junior agent on the 1990 heist at the Isabella Stewart Gardner Museum. Having reviewed the evidence first-hand, Dixon hired her on the spot.

For Gabriele, the job was a perfect fit. Her experience and contacts at the FBI gave her access that Dixon needed, and Gabriele could work a less stressful job with better hours that allowed her to focus on one case at a time. The fact that no one would be shooting at her was a bonus.

On her first day, she asked for and received funds that allowed her to convert one of the museums smaller, less used wings into a security office, where incoming and outgoing packages could be better examined with new, cutting-edge equipment. With construction under way, Gabriele was responsible for ensuring that all workers had proper background checks, and that they never wandered from their designated area. Gabriele brought in former FBI colleagues now in the private sector to upgrade the museum's pressure sensors and install 4K high-definition cameras. Both carried hefty price tags, but Dixon was able to convince the board of directors to fork over the dough. The catch, though, was that Gabriele had to make serious headway in tracking down the stolen art.

By early afternoon, Gabriele was observing her colleagues' demonstration of the wall sensors when she received word on her radio that a package was waiting for her at the security desk in the main lobby.

"I'm in the middle of something. Go ahead and sign for it. I'll be there in a few minutes."

"Sorry, ma'am, but the delivery man says the package is for you, and only you can sign for it."

Gabriele groaned.

"Okay, I'll be right there."

She turned to her colleague who she'd once worked with in the St. Louis office.

"I'm sorry, Tyrone. I'll be right back."

"Take your time."

When she arrived in the lobby, Gabriele pulled her blonde hair into a ponytail and scrutinized the delivery man.

What an odd duck.

The sleeves to his UPS uniform had been cut off, which exposed tattoos of evil clowns and gargoyles, running the lengths of both arms. His rugged hat was pushed low on his forehead, and he had sunglasses on, despite the low light in the lobby.

"You're not the usual guy," Gabriele said.

"I'm filling in today. Sign here."

After signing her name on the electronic clipboard, the delivery man shoved the long cylinder box into her hands and abruptly left.

"Adios," he said.

Gabriele turned to the guard on duty, who shrugged.

An eerie feeling came over Gabriele as she walked back to the new security wing. Though she knew she should screen the package in accordance with the process she put in place, Gabriele stopped by her office and hastily opened it. Inside was an envelope and a scroll.

A gift from the people of Iran.

When she saw the word "Iran," Gabriele's counter-terrorism instincts kicked in immediately, and she stepped back.

It could be a bomb!

She pulled the radio from her belt and was about to order an evacuation of the building when she stopped to debate her decision.

"Screw it," she said aloud.

If they wanted to send a bomb, I would've been dead as soon as I opened the box.

She pulled the scroll from the cylinder, and slowly unwrapped it from the Glassine paper and bubble wrap it was packed in. After unrolling the canvas on her desk, she gasped and covered her mouth when she saw the image: Rembrandt's *The Storm on the Sea of Galilee* had returned home. After a moment of shock, she screamed so loud that others, including Dixon, came charging into her office. They, too, were astonished.

Before driving away, Thrasher smiled at the cries of joy he heard coming from inside the museum.

Chapter Sixty-Two

TEHRAN, IRAN
ONE MONTH LATER

It was a gorgeous day at Azadi Square. Security was airtight, but the masses showed up to hear Lajani's first official address. The scent of fresh cut grass from the honeycomb shaped landscape filled the air. Azadi Tower's marble structure glowed in the sunlight through a cloudless sky. The jewels set into the monument's ribs sparkled, but none more brightly than the faces of those who had gathered. It was the dawn of a new day for Iran.

Though Lajani hadn't been democratically elected to the position he now held, he wasn't like the Shah, who the CIA had put into place for their own benefit to keep the Communists at bay. And he wasn't like Khomeini, who claimed to be a conquering hero returning to his homeland but actually thought he was the Twelfth Imam whose destiny was to rule the country with an iron fist.

Lajani was a true man of the people. Like so many others in the crowd, he had survived the Iran-Iraq War, grown up in Tehran, witnessed the horrors of the Ayatollah regime, and as his missing right hand showed, he had experienced it himself. He knew Iran's system of government inside in and out. He knew what changes needed to be made but he was savvy enough to know which political levers to pull, and when.

The Shi'a faith, so beloved to him and the rest of his fellow Iranians, would always be a dominant factor in their culture, but Lajani recognized that while Iranians would always be connected to their faith and their past, they had to embrace new ideas for the future. Under his watch, unless provoked, that meant a guarded peace with the West. For the first time since Mohammad Mossadegh was Prime Minister, Iran had a leader with the people's best interests at heart.

At Lajani's invitation, Farhad and Donya had a front row seat. While neither of them had totally recovered from their injuries at the hands of the Basij, they felt less pain on that day. They were too excited about their personal futures and the prospects for their country.

Donya hooked her arm around Farhad's elbow. Today was one of the rare times she had seen Farhad wear something other than jeans and a t-shirt, and certainly the first time she'd seen him in a suit and tie. She'd picked out the black pinstripe with a powder blue, button-down shirt and a matching tie, but she didn't know he was still wearing a *Star Wars* t-shirt underneath.

Under the Ayatollahs, female beauty parlors were as much a part of Iranian society as they were in any other part of the world, but because there were so many restrictions on the female form and how they could be advertised, Iranian women had to depend on word of mouth to know where to go. Since the parlor owners were so concerned about Basij soldiers entering their establishments to shut them down or negotiate for sex to keep them open, they always required appointments. As the chaos from Lajani's coup simmered down, so did the restrictions. Parlor owners made sure not to advertise using outlandish images, but a picture of a woman's face with make-up became acceptable, as long as the woman was wearing a hijab.

When Donya walked into the beauty parlor that had been recommended to her, she was treated like the Queen of the Coup, a nickname that soon became as synonymous with her as "Pirate of Iran" was with Farhad. Her entire appointment was on the house, and at one point, she had three stylists working on her hair, makeup and fingernails. When she arrived home in Isfahan, the stunned look on Farhad's face and his speechless reply was all she needed to know about how pretty she looked. She practically had to pry his hands off her.

Farhad couldn't remember the last time he had worn a tie, but he was too preoccupied with how Donya looked and smelled to care about how uncomfortable it was. Even under her hijab, he could tell her thick hair had been slightly curled and lightened a shade. Her makeup was perfectly applied with a dash of shadow on her eyelids, and her thin lips were freshened with a scarlet lipstick. But it was the smell of her jasmine perfume that captivated him. It permeated his senses and sent a surge of excitement below his belt. He slyly tried to adjust himself, but Donya caught him. She playfully slapped him on the chest and smiled.

"Problems?"

"I can't help it. Between your perfume and looking at the phallic-like entry to the Tower, I feel nature engineering me for liftoff."

She smacked him again.

"You look beautiful."

"Thanks, handsome. When both our bodies have fully recovered, I promise we'll make up for lost time."

Farhad smiled at the idea of being able to be physical with her once again.

"What do you think he'll say? Have you seen his speech?"

"Why would I?"

"I don't know. You two have gotten close. He's hiring you for jobs from time to time. At the very least, I thought you might have sneaked a look."

"Not this time. I need to experience the authenticity of this moment."

Affixed with a new crown tooth of his own, Farhad smiled and leaned down to give her a kiss, but they were interrupted by a roar from the crowd, followed by thunderous applause. Lajani took the stage with his four military subordinates. His uniform was fresh and pressed. He was no longer toting a sling, but everyone could see that the right sleeve of his military jacket was missing a hand. The general stood at the podium and tried to calm the crowd, but they wouldn't have it. They continued their cheers until Lajani took a bow.

"Thank you. Thank you, my fellow Iranians. Thank you."

Lajani held up his one good hand to quiet the crowd.

"My fellow Iranians, thank you for gathering here today. As I gaze into this crowd of millions, I see people with so much in common. Look at the person to your right and left. Each of you chose to be here. I can't stress the word 'chose' enough. No one has forced you to be here. I take this as proof that our current path is what you desire for Iran."

The crowd applauded.

"You will notice I am still wearing my military uniform. To be clear, I am not your president or prime minister. I am, and will continue to be, the chief commander of the Iranian Revolutionary Guard. But while the mere mention of that branch of our armed forces used to carry a feeling of dread and force, it has a new meaning for Iran today. Yes, the Revolutionary Guard will always protect the Iranian way of life from any force with ambitions to destroy it, either internal or external, but under my command, it will no longer utilize brutal force to restrict the aspirations of the people it has been appointed to protect."

The audience cheered again.

"Under the guidance of our new government, Iran's future is bright. I am a leader, but I am not a politician. I am a soldier. I am *your* soldier. It is not my desire to hold my current position for any longer than is required. Our country needs formal structure, but not run by the military. It needs to make better friends of our current international partners, and allies of countries deemed enemies for far too long. A soldier cannot do that; only a government with elected leaders can. But rest assured, long after I have vacated my position, I will always be watching. And I will always fight for Iran."

The crowd once again gave Lajani a standing ovation, and this time, the leaders of his armed forces stood onstage and joined him.

"You will see that I am a modest man of few words, but many actions. My coup to remove the former Supreme Leader should speak volumes to both the people of Iran and the rest of the world. In 1953, the American CIA led a coup that deposed our democratically elected leader, Mohammad Mossadegh."

The crowd booed and hissed at the memory. Lajani held up his hand.

"My people, please. We know the results of that event, and the domino effect it had on our country. I didn't come here today to dwell on the past. We have done that long enough. It's time to do what is hardest for Persians to do. We must move on. Behind me is Azadi Tower. It will continue to stand as a shining example of Iranian resilience. We have endured the horrors of our past, yet we continue to stand tall. However, we must commemorate the past and give thanks to the man who was brave enough to stand up to the western world in the name of the Iranian people before he was unceremoniously deposed. As of today, this Square will be renamed Mohammad Mossadegh Plaza."

The crowd exploded into cheers and whistles.

"MOSSADEGH! MOSSADEGH! MOSSADEGH!"

Donya turned to Farhad.

"Did you ever think this was possible?"

Farhad looked around at his fellow Iranians. For the first time in his life, he wondered what would happen next. Not only for his fellow Iranians, but for himself. Would he still need to be the smuggler he had learned to become or was his future yet to be determined? Rather than fear such a question, it was one to welcome, and he was excited about finding answers.

"Kirk once told me that leadership doesn't mean convincing people to follow you. Leadership is getting people to believe in something so strongly that they lead *with* you."

Farhad looked up at Lajani, who gave him a wink.

"I can't say for sure I knew this was possible. But Lajani is the right man for right now."

Donya smiled.

"Then let's show him the way."

Chapter Sixty-Three

THE WHITE HOUSE

President Cannon was surrounded in the Oval Office by his White House Press Secretary, Luis Santos, and his entire senior communications staff. After several weeks of negotiating, General Lajani agreed to allow formal relations with the United States to resume. This meant the U.S. Embassy in Tehran would be converted from its current status as a Museum of Espionage back to its original form, though modern improvements certainly needed to be made. It also meant Cannon got to appoint a U.S. Ambassador to Iran. His list of choices was limited because he needed someone who Iranians could trust, someone who they could depend on to deliver accurate information to the Secretary of State, and most important, someone who could be confirmed by the Senate.

While it was by no means a traditional western democracy, Iran was now a country with an abundance of opportunities for the West. His administration had to tread carefully, though. After decades of turbulence with Iran, new relations with Iran were going to be tricky waters to navigate, so the United States had to handle the situation with kid gloves. Cannon didn't want anything coming back to bite him in the ass. It was important to avoid appearing greedy when making any deals. He needed an ambassador who knew when to feed the sharks and had the skill to dodge them when necessary.

Cannon turned to Santos.

"Ready?"

"Yes, sir."

Cannon led his entourage down the hall to the James S. Brady Press Briefing Room. He made a brief stop in the Roosevelt Room to check on his nominee.

"Are you up for this? They're not going to take it easy on you in there."

"Absolutely, sir."

Cannon nodded.

"You better be. We'll be watching closely."

The nominee gave the president a curious look.

We?

Cannon went directly to the briefing room, which was packed with reporters anxious to hear the president's announcement, which had thankfully been kept secret.

"Good afternoon, everyone. Please take your seats. The world has witnessed a tremendous and needed change in Iran over the last few months. I'd like to take this opportunity to formally apologize to the Iranian people for the 1953 coup that deposed Prime Minister Mossadegh. At the time, there was a legitimate fear that Communism would spread around the globe, which America had a duty to contain. Then-Prime Minister Mossadegh stood up for his country's rights, but he did so in a way that made some of the most powerful leaders in the world nervous at the wrong time. At the time, the coup was viewed as a success for the West, but in retrospect, it's obvious that short-term success can lead to long-term conflict. The Iranian people now have a leader in place who will allow them to determine their own future without internal or external influence. As they do, new international bonds can be formed with Iran in ways that haven't been possible in more than four decades."

A young reporter stood up and interrupted Cannon.

"Mr. President, aren't you concerned about a terrorist attack from radical elements connected to the previous Iranian government?"

"A terrorist attack is always possible, but our intelligence community will continue their diligent work in keeping us safe. Sit down."

Knowing that Cannon hated being interrupted, the veteran reporters gave the young reporter a harsh look. Now was not the time for peacocking.

"Following a series of conversations with General Lajani, I'm pleased to announce that formal diplomatic relations between the United States and Iran will resume. It is now my responsibility to appoint the first U.S. Ambassador to Iran in forty-four years. After a long internal debate and discussions with my staff, I have made my decision. It may not be popular, but in the end, the ambassadorship is about best serving United States' interests while also ensuring that we continue an open dialogue with the Islamic Republic of Iran."

To his right, one of Cannon's staff members signaled the nominee to come inside the press room.

"While my nominee has made mistakes in the past, I'm a man who believes in second chances. I have no doubt she is the best person for the job. Ladies and gentlemen, your new U.S. Ambassador to Iran."

The room gasped as former Senator Vivian Walsh walked through the doorway in an olive-green Neiman Marcus pantsuit. As she made her way to the podium, a staff member handed her a leather portfolio with her speech inside. The press corps exploded into a frenzy of questions.

Cannon extended his hand to Walsh.

"Congratulations."

"Thank you, Mr. President."

Flashes from press corps cameras filled the room like strobe lights.

"It's all yours," he said.

Cannon exited the room without taking questions from the press.

Once the room settled, Walsh opened her portfolio to begin her speech, but found a surprise inside. The first page wasn't her speech. It was a side-by-side picture of Robert DeNiro in his role from *Meet the Parents*. The image on the left showed the actor pointing two fingers at his own eyes. The one on the right had him pointing the same two fingers outward. Walsh looked up and saw a shadowy figure standing in the back of the room. It was the same person who ruined her Congressional career two years ago. She stared at Delang. The message was clear.

We'll be watching you.

She turned the page to start her speech but was interrupted by senior NBC News White House correspondent, Josh Lanier.

"Senator Walsh, why do you think the president chose you to be the new ambassador to Iran? You left Washington with a tarnished reputation under circumstances worthy of treason."

"First, I'd like to thank President Cannon for this opportunity, and for giving me a second chance to prove my value to this country and to the world. I'm going to start with your question, Josh. While those events have been well-reported, the past is the past. I've put it behind me, and so has President Cannon. It should also in no way change the fact that I performed good deeds as a former member of Congress. My record there is indisputable. For years, I portrayed myself to be of mixed heritage from my white father and black mother. You now know this isn't true. Throughout his entire life, my father was unaware of the mistake my mother made with an Iranian diplomat when she served as the U.S. ambassador to the Soviet Union. For many years, so was I. As his daughter, my heart belonged to the man who raised me as his own. Now, as a diplomat, my heart will always belong to America. Once I am confirmed by the Senate, I believe that my half Iranian heritage will create a level of trust among the Iranian people. This trust will be the foundation of a new relationship between the United States and Iran."

"Why should America trust you?" Lanier said. "Why should the people of Iran?"

Every member of the press corps stood with their hands raised, shouting questions. It was going to be the first of many stressful days for Walsh. When she looked to the rear of the room, Delang was gone.

Epilogue

Tucked behind tall hedges on the South Lawn, Thrasher, Jenkins, Kirk and Simin awaited the president's arrival in the White House Children's Garden. They were wearing their finest suits and dresses. Simin beamed with enthusiasm. Two years ago, she'd been smuggling contraband into Tehran with Farhad, and now she was a guest at the White House with her American fiancé. She didn't like surrendering her phone to security staff when she entered the West Wing, but they told her she would get it back after her meeting with the president. Nonetheless, she and Kirk tried to contain their excitement. While the two lovebirds talked, Thrasher and Jenkins had plenty to discuss as they sat in white chairs around a small pond.

"Any news about getting Jessica's body back?"

Jenkins shrugged.

"I thought for sure that when our PMOI pals delivered the MSS agent's body to the Chinese Embassy in Tehran, Wallace would be able to negotiate her return with Minister Zhou, but I don't think the Chinese were happy about what happened to their man. Besides losing half his face, his body was badly decomposed and riddled with bites from vermin. I'll bet General Secretary Xu is holding onto that card and will play it during his next round of negotiations with the president. We'll be able to get her back, but I'm not sure how soon."

Thrasher didn't like the answer, but he nodded. He and Jenkins rose to their feet when President Cannon turned the corner with Delang and a security detail close behind.

"Good afternoon, everyone."

"Good afternoon, Mr. President."

Cannon spotted Simin smiling from ear to ear. He stepped forward to shake her hand.

"You must be Simin. Tom tells me what a tremendous job you did creating the website that allowed the world to witness firsthand accounts of everything the Ayatollahs subjected the Iranian people to. I can't tell you how instrumental that was in allowing Lajani to complete the regime change. You did a fantastic job."

"Thank you, Mr. President. It was my pleasure."

"How did you know your little media campaign would work?"

"Well, sir, I can't take total credit. It was agent Jacoby's idea, but I bought into it. Since the Ayatollahs ruled with an iron fist, exposure is a far more valuable weapon than violence. As someone who used to live there and experienced hardships firsthand, I felt that I owed the people of Iran at least that much."

"Yes, Tom told me about your troubled background, and what happened to your mother. I'm very sorry."

Cannon looked at Kirk.

"We can't change the past, but it looks to me like you have a bright future. I'm told that you two are engaged, and you're looking to become an American citizen."

"Yes, sir. True on both counts."

"Well, as it turns out, I've got a little bit of pull around here. I'm sure we can find a way to fast track your application."

"Oh, my goodness. Thank you, sir!"

"My pleasure."

Cannon turned to Kirk and extended his hand.

"And you, Mr. Kurruthers. Tom has spoken nothing but good words about you, but I've never had the pleasure of meeting you."

"The pleasure is all mine, Mr. President."

"You know, in a way, the whole regime change started with your trip to Iran. How does it feel to know that?"

"A bit surreal, sir. I just wish my grandfather was alive to see Iran's rebirth."

"I'm sure he's proud of you, son. And judging by the smile on Simin's face, I think he'd love her, too."

"Yes, sir. He sure would."

Simin giggled when Kirk hugged her.

"Mr. President?" Simin asked. "Would it be too much trouble for us to get a picture with you? Security took my phone."

"I'll tell you what. My Secret Service agent will escort the two of you to the Rose Garden. After I'm done speaking with the rest of the team, I'll take you on a tour of the White House myself, and you can take all the pictures you want. Call it an early wedding present."

Cannon winked at her.

"That would be terrific. Thank you, Mr. President!"

"And Kirk, try not to stray too far. You've proven yourself quite the asset to our country, and you know how to handle yourself in tough situations. I may need to call on you again."

Kirk smiled.

"I serve at your pleasure, sir."

Cannon turned to his brawny Secret Service Agent, Craig Halasz.

"Take them over, please."

"Sir, I'm not supposed to leave you unattended."

"Craig, I'm with three CIA agents. I'll be fine in the five minutes you're gone."

"Yes, sir."

As Kirk and Simin turned the corner, Cannon looked at Thrasher and Jenkins.

"You two have been busy."

Jenkins let out a mild laugh. Even Thrasher's usually grouchy demeanor cracked a grin.

"Do we get any hazard pay?" he said.

This time, it was the president's turn to laugh.

"Director Wallace spoke quite highly of you, agent Jacoby. I must say I'm impressed with your field work, but I have a few questions."

"Fire away, sir."

"The cloud seeding. How did you know that would work?"

Thrasher smirked.

"Mr. President, in a land where everything is forbidden, anything is possible."

"That's a good line, but I'm afraid I'm going to need a little more than that."

"In short, I didn't know, but Lajani told me that the key to Iran's future was its past. At one of the stash houses, I saw a copy of the King James Bible and the Koran sitting next to each other. While the two books differ greatly, their stories about Genesis, Noah's Ark and The Exodus are in both. In the Koran, Moses is called Musa, and both religions preach about the plagues of Egypt. I remembered one of those plagues of Egypt was as an infestation of frogs. During my time in Iran, I recalled seeing a news broadcast about the UAE using cloud seeding to make it rain. It generated one hell of a thunderstorm, but it worked. I put two and two together. It was a bit of a reach on my part, and my theory depended heavily on the people of Iran believing that what they were seeing was an act of God and He was interfering in their affairs. Considering how the people of the Middle East, and especially Iran cling to their religion, I thought it was worth rolling the dice. But I had no idea the sky would turn those colors and create such vicious lightning. Those little pods pack quite a fucking punch."

Thrasher covered his mouth after unintentionally cursing in front of the president.

"You'll have to forgive him, sir," Jenkins said. "He wasn't exactly born with a filter."

Cannon laughed.

"It's quite alright. According to Director Wallace, you told him the Supreme Leader began experiencing physical issues and became extremely emotional when he confronted your Iranian source in the castle. What was Buckaroo's real name?"

"Farhad, sir," said Delang.

"Right, Farhad. We owe that young man a great deal of gratitude. But what made Shir-Del get so crazy when he talked to him?"

"Thanks to what happened last year," Thrasher continued, "we knew about Shir-Del's rare medical condition, and how he became volatile when he didn't get his prescribed dosage. Once we knew we had the only meds available, we had him cornered. But that wasn't good enough. We had to make him emotional enough that he would say unforgivable things he wouldn't normally say, *and* we had to catch him on tape. One of our PMOI colleagues is a medical student, and he provided us with a vial of an antibiotic that removes Carbamazepine from the body, which given his condition, would quickly take its toll. After he ran out of his own supply, we became his only lifeline to his meds. Thankfully, the vial of antibiotics that we gave him looked just like Carbamazepine. He was so desperate he didn't look at the label. All Farhad had to do was keep poking the bear."

"The strategy wasn't guaranteed, but it was our best play," Jenkins said.

Cannon shook his head in disbelief.

"You two have guts of iron. I'll give you that. You were lucky, but I'll take luck any day. What's next for you, agent Jacoby?"

"I was hoping you would tell me, sir."

"Ready for another assignment?"

"Affirmative, sir."

"Good. I think Director Wallace has something for you."

Cannon turned to Jenkins.

"And you, Miss Jennings? How's your eye?"

"Fully recovered, sir. I think it's safe for you to call me by my real name, sir, Beth Jenkins."

"Excellent. What's over the horizon for you? Back to the agency?"

"I'm afraid not, sir. I think the sun has set on my career with the agency. It's probably best that I go out on top. Tom and I have been speaking about starting a private contracting business together."

"I wish you the best. I hope you'll both keep your relationship with the agency intact. The country can certainly benefit from people with your skill sets."

"Of course, sir."

"Would you and agent Jacoby join the others in the Rose Garden? I'd like to speak to Tom alone."

"Certainly, sir."

When Thrasher and Jenkins left, Delang approached the president.

"Sir, do you mind if I ask why you chose former Senator Walsh to be your new ambassador? With her family blood ties, she'll get instant respect from the Iranians, but she's still a loose cannon."

"First rule of nepotism in politics, Tom. Always appoint someone you can control. Plus, as problematic and corrupt as she was in Congress, she's proven to be even more so in the private sector. Money buys a lot of friends and leverage in politics and business. I'll see to it that she's stationed in Tehran to limit her influence here, and you can bet I'll be watching her diplomatic activities like a hawk. She's got a lot of work cut out for her, but hopefully it'll keep her corrupt side at bay for a while. But, thanks to you and the team, I've got enough dirt on her to keep her in line. If she decides to ever step over it, I know who to call and what cards to play against her."

Cannon patted Delang on the shoulder.

"So, what's next for Iran, sir?"

Cannon moaned.

"Short answer? Growing pains. Lajani's got a lot on his plate. We'll keep an eye on the situation and help where we can, but this time, Iran's got to do things their way. There is one thing I know for sure, though."

"What's that, sir?"

"Freedom always finds a way to prevail."

Delang smiled.

"I'm more curious about your take on this, Tom."

"Sir?"

"You've been around. You know the Middle East better than any of the characters on my staff. What do *you* think about the new Iran?"

"I think . . . it's a start."

THE END

"Every new beginning comes from some other beginning's end."

—*Lucius Annaeus Seneca*

Author's Note

While I am aware that some authors have chosen to include the COVID-19 pandemic in their storylines, I have chosen to avoid it. I believe that fiction should be an escape from reality.

From the perspective of those who were involved in the 1953 coup, *Project Ajax* was viewed as a tremendous success. It deposed a leader, Mossadegh, who had started to cozy up to the Soviets and prevented the further spread of Communism. It was the first time the CIA had ever overthrown a government and served as a blueprint for how it should be done in the future. But the long-term effects of the coup have been nearly cataclysmic in terms of geopolitics and international relations with the Middle East. The Shah was not the strong leader he was believed to be, and he fled his own country when he couldn't hold it together. This led to Khomeini's return. We have all witnessed its effects. I believe that regime change in Iran will eventually happen. The Supreme Leader's government cannot sustain the economic sanctions. In the end, though, it will be up to the Iranian people to take action. Whenever this happens, let us all hope that Iran can choose its own destiny, and that it will bring peace to its people and the rest of the world.

Acknowledgments

Before I began writing this book, I was watching TV one night, wondering how I could bring the series to a successful close. As luck would have it, *Scream 3* was showing on a streaming services. To this day, I can't tell you what made me watch it. Compared to its two predecessors, the third installment was by no means the best. I knew this, and it scared me a bit because I didn't want my third novel to fall into the same category. But one scene stuck a cord with me when Patrick Dempsey's character said, "In the third one, all bets are off." I decided to go for broke and imagine what a regime change would look like in Iran. This isn't easy to accomplish in a single novel. I realize that some parts ask for a leap of faith or for you to suspend a bit of disbelief, but I hope you have enjoyed it.

These three books have been a long but worthwhile journey for me. Having my dream as a published author has been an experience like no other. There is no drug that can replicate it. It couldn't have been possible without the support of many along the way. I would like to thank the following people who have helped me during this process.

To **my wife, a.k.a. "Fireball,"** for your unyielding support and heartfelt belief in me. You have been my rock to lean on when I doubted myself. I couldn't have done this without you by my side on this risky journey into the literary world.

To **my parents and Jackie Leonard**, for their belief in my talents, for being my silent investors behind the scenes, and for spreading the word about my novels. Your support and encouragement has meant the world me. It is a debt I will never be able to repay.

To **Josh Lanier, Alan Scott, and Martha Scott**, for being my number one team of beta readers. I've depended on you for three books, and you've always been there for me. Thank you!

To **Jason Gregory, Jake Webb, Josh "Krutch" Kinnison and Dan McAdams**, for being the best friends a guy could ask for.

To the real **Brenda Gabriele**, for making such a great character and for being such a good friend to the family over the years. Thank you!

To **Pam Gregory and Kelly Melton**, who are diehard Green Bay Packers fans. Thanks for all your support!

To my agent, **Nancy Rosenfeld**, who took me on as a client when many other agents rejected me. My dream of becoming a published author could never have been possible without you. Thank you!

To my editor, **David Tabatsky**, for your patience fielding all my questions and your dedication to sharpening my novels. Thank you!

To **Hannah Linder**, for always creating the perfect book covers that I envisioned. Your skills always amaze me!

To **Chetan Batra**, for your amazing work on all of the book trailers for my novels!

I would also like to thank the following people in the podcast community for supporting my work and giving me the exposure to a wider audience every author needs: **David Temple** and *The Thriller Zone* podcast, **Chris Albanese** and *The Crew Reviews* podcast, **Dr. Jason Piccolo** and *The Protectors Podcast*, **Mike Martini** and the *No Limits Thriller* podcast, **Jeff Clark** and the *Course of Action* podcast, **John Stamp** and the *That's Criminal* podcast, and **DJ Kelly** and the *DTD Podcast*.

To **Kurt and Erica Mueller, and the rest of the incredible team at Speaking Volumes**, for your hard work on all three novels, and for taking a chance on a debut author with no prior writing credentials. I'll never forget the day I held my first novel in my hands and realized that my dream had come true. That couldn't have been possible without you. Thank you!

To **all of my readers, fans, and supporters.** When I began writing *Surviving the Lion's Den*, I did it for myself because I wanted to prove that I could. However, once published, I quickly learned that the novel no longer belonged to me. It belongs to you. For every time you buy one of my books, recommend it to a friend, leave a glowing review or contact me to tell me how much you loved it, you warm my heart. I'm honored that you chose to spend your time reading my novels. I love you all!

About the Author

Matt Scott has a bachelor's degree in political science and history from Hampden-Sydney College, a liberal arts institution in Virginia. He lives in Charlotte, North Carolina with his wife and dogs while also continuing his career as a Senior Financial Analyst for the Sealed Air Corporation.

Now Available!

MATT SCOTT
SURVIVING THE LION'S DEN SERIES
BOOKS 1 – BOOK 2

**For more information
visit: <u>www.SpeakingVolumes.us</u>**

Now Available!

MATTHEW J. FLYNN
BERNIE WEBER: MATH GENIUS SERIES
BOOKS 1 - 2

**For more information
visit:**

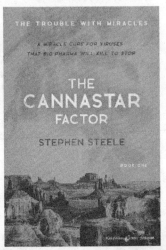
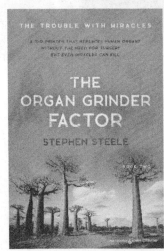
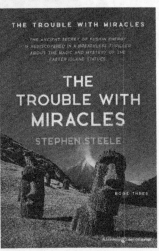

Made in the USA
Coppell, TX
02 April 2023

15126465R00215